Feather, Jane
   The widow's kiss

01-18

The
Widow's
Kiss

The Widow's Kiss

Jane Feather

BANTAM BOOKS

New York Toronto London Sydney Auckland

THE WIDOW'S KISS
A Bantam Book / January 2001

Book design by Virginia Norey.

Library of Congress Cataloging-in-Publication Data
Feather, Jane.
    The widow's kiss / Jane Feather.
        p.   cm.
    ISBN 0-553-80181-3
    1. Great Britain—History—Henry VIII, 1509–1547—
    Fiction. I. Title.

PS3556.E22 W53 2001
813'.54—dc21   00-060823

Published simultaneously in the United States and Canada

Bantam Books are published by Bantam Books, a division of Random
House, Inc. Its trademark, consisting of the words "Bantam Books"
and the portrayal of a rooster, is Registered in U.S. Patent and
Trademark Office and in other countries. Marca Registrada. Bantam
Books, 1540 Broadway, New York, New York 10036.

Prologue

Derbyshire, England—September, 1536

The woman stood by the open window, the soft breeze stirring the folds of her blue silk hood as it hung down her back. She stood very still and straight, her dark gown shadowy against the dense velvet of the opened window curtains.

She heard him in the corridor outside, his heavy lumbering step. She could picture his large frame lurching from side to side as he approached. Now he was outside the great oak door. She could hear his labored breathing. She could picture his bloodshot eyes, his reddened countenance, his lips slack with exertion.

The door burst open. Her husband filled the doorway, his richly jeweled gown swirling about him.

"By God, madam! You would dare to speak to me in such wise at my own table! In the hearing of our guests, of the household, scullions even!" A shower of spittle accompanied the slurred words as he advanced into the chamber, kicking the door shut behind him. It shivered on its hinges.

The woman stood her ground beside the window, her hands clasped quietly against her skirts. "And I say to you, husband, that if you ever threaten one of my daughters again, you will rue the day." Her voice was barely above a whisper but the words came at him with the power of thunder.

For a second he seemed to hesitate, then he lunged for her with clenched fists upraised. Still she stood her ground, a slight derisive smile on her lips, her eyes, purple as sloes, fixed upon his face with such contempt he bellowed in drunken rage.

As he reached her—one fist aimed at her pale face beneath its jeweled headdress, his only thought to smash the smile from her lips, to close the hateful contempt in her eyes—she stepped aside. Her foot caught his ankle and the speed and weight of his charge carried him forward.

For a second he seemed to hover at the very brink of the dark space beyond the low-silled window, then he twisted and fell. A shriek of astounded terror accompanied his plunge to the flagstones below.

The woman twitched aside the curtain so that she could look down without being seen. At first in the dark depths below the window she could make out nothing, then came the sound of upraised voices, the tread of many feet; light flickered as torch men came running from the four corners of the courtyard. And now, in the light, she could see the dark crumpled shape of her husband.

How small he looked, she thought, clasping her elbows across her breast with a little tremor. So much malevolence, so much violence, reduced, deflated, to that inert heap.

And then she seemed to come to life. She moved back swiftly to the far side of the chamber where a small door gave onto the garderobe. She slipped into the small privy and stood for a second, listening. Running feet sounded in the corridor beyond her chamber. There was a loud knocking, then she heard the latch lift. As the door was flung wide she stepped out of the garderobe, hastily smoothing down her skirts.

An elderly woman stood in the doorway, her hair tucked beneath a white linen coif. "Ay! Ay! Ay!" she exclaimed, wringing her hands. "What is it, my chuck? What has happened here?" Behind her, curious faces pressed over her shoulder.

The woman spoke to those faces, her voice measured, calming. "I don't know, Tilly. Lord Stephen came in while I was in the garderobe. He called to me. I was occupied . . . I couldn't come to him immediately. He grew impatient . . . but . . ." She gave a little helpless shrug.

"In his agitation, he must have lost his balance . . . fallen from the window. I didn't see what happened."

"Ay . . . ay . . . ay," the other woman repeated, almost to herself. "And 'tis the fourth! Lord-a-mercy." She crossed herself, shaking her head.

"Lord Stephen was drunk," the younger woman said evenly. "Everyone knew it . . . in the hall, at table. He could barely see straight. I must go down." She hurried past the woman, past the crowd of gaping servants, gathering her skirts to facilitate her step.

Her steward came running across the great hall as she came down the stairs. "My lady . . . my lady . . . such a terrible thing."

"What happened, Master Crowder? Does anyone know?"

The black-clad steward shook his head and the loosened lappets of his bonnet flapped at his ears like crows' wings. "Did you not see it, my lady? We thought you must have known what happened. 'Twas from your chamber window that he fell."

"I was in the garderobe," she said shortly. "Lord Stephen was drunk, Master Crowder. He must have lost his footing . . . his balance. It was ever thus."

"Aye, 'tis true enough, madam. 'Twas ever thus with his lordship." The steward followed her out into the courtyard where a crowd stood around the fallen man.

They gave way before the lady of the house who knelt on the cobbles beside her husband. His neck was at an odd angle and blood pooled beneath his head. She placed a finger for form's sake against the pulse in his neck. Then with a sigh sat back on her heels, the dark folds of her gown spreading around her.

"Where is Master Grice?"

"Here, my lady." The priest came running from his little lodging behind the chapel, adjusting his gown as he came. "I heard the commotion, but I . . ." He stopped as he reached the body. His rosary beads clicked between his fingers as he gazed down and said with a heavy sigh, "May the Lord have mercy on his soul."

"Yes, indeed," agreed Lord Stephen's wife. She rose to her feet in a graceful movement. "Take my lord's body to the chapel to be washed and prepared. We will say a Mass at dawn. He will lie in state for the respects of the household and the tenants before his burial tomorrow evening."

She turned and made her way back through the crowd, back into the house, ducking her head as she stepped through the small door that was set into the larger one to keep the cold and the draughts from invading the hall.

Lady Guinevere was a widow once more.

I.

London, April, 1537

How many husbands did you say?" The king turned his heavy head towards Thomas Cromwell, his Lord Privy Seal. His eyes rested with almost languid indifference on his minister's grave countenance, but no one in the king's presence chamber at Hampton Court believed in that indifference.

"Four, Highness."

"And the lady is of what years?"

"Eight and twenty, Highness."

"She has been busy it would seem," Henry mused.

"It would seem a husband has little luck in the lady's bed," a voice remarked dryly from a dark paneled corner of the chamber.

The king's gaze swung towards a man of square and powerful build, dressed in black and gold. A man whose soldierly bearing seemed ill suited to his rich court dress, the tapestry-hung comforts of the chamber, the whispers, the spies, the gossipmongering of King Henry's court. He had an air of impatience, of a man who preferred to be doing rather than talking, but there was a gleam of humor in his eyes, a natural curve to his mouth, and his voice was as dry as sere leaves.

"It would seem you have the right of it, Hugh," the king responded. "And how is it exactly that these unlucky husbands have met their deaths?"

"Lord Hugh has more precise knowledge than I." Privy Seal waved a beringed hand towards the man in the corner.

"I have a certain interest, Highness." Hugh of Beaucaire stepped forward into the light that poured through the diamond-paned windows behind the king's head. "Lady Mallory, as she now is . . . the *widowed* Lady Mallory . . . was married at sixteen to a man whose first wife was a distant cousin of my father's. Roger Needham was Lady Mallory's first husband. There is some family land in dispute. I claim it for my own son. Lady Mallory will entertain no such claim. She has kept every penny, every hectare of land from each of her husbands."

"No mean feat," Privy Seal commented. "But of course there is a father . . . brother . . . uncle to advise and arrange matters for her."

"No, my lord. The lady manages her affairs herself."

"How could she do such a thing?" The king's eyes gleamed in the deep rolls of flesh in which they were embedded like two bright currants in dough.

"She has some considerable knowledge of the law of property, Highness," Lord Hugh said. "A knowledge the bereaved widow puts into practice before embarking on a new union."

"She draws up her own marriage contracts?" The king was incredulous. He pulled on his beard, the great carbuncle on his index finger glowing with crimson fire.

"Exactly so, Highness."

"Body of God!"

"In each of her marriages the lady has ensured that on the death of her husband she inherits lock, stock, and barrel."

"And the husbands have all died . . ." mused the king.

"Each and every one of them."

"Are there heirs?"

"Two young daughters. The progeny of her second husband, Lord Hadlow."

The king shook his head slowly. "Body of God," he muttered again. "These contracts cannot be overset?"

Privy Seal, himself once an attorney, lifted a sheaf of papers from the desk. "I have had lawyers examining each one with a fine-tooth comb,

Highness. They are drawn up as right and tight as if witnessed by the Star Chamber itself."

"Do we join Hugh of Beaucaire in his interest in these holdings?" Henry inquired.

"When one woman owns most of a county as extensive and as rich in resources as Derbyshire, the king and his exchequer have a certain interest," Privy Seal said. "At the very least, one might be interested in adequate tithing."

The king was silent for a minute. When he spoke it was again in a musing tone. "And if, of course, foul play were suspected with any of these . . . uh . . . untimely deaths, then one would not leave the perpetrator in possession of her ill-gotten gains."

"Or indeed her head," Privy Seal murmured.

"Mmm."

"As I understand it Lord Mallory adhered to the Church of Rome," Privy Seal continued, stroking his long upper lip. "We could perhaps make some connection between him and the Yorkshire rebellion last year. What think you, Lord Hugh?"

"You would have Mallory make common cause with Robert Aske and his Pilgrimage of Grace, Lord Cromwell?" Lord Hugh looked askance.

"There's more than one way to skin a cat," Privy Seal said with a shrug. " 'Tis but an option . . . to confiscate the woman's wealth on suspicion of her late husband's association with Aske's northern rebellion. 'Tis a treason to question His Highness's decision to dissolve the monasteries. There's many a man been hanged for less, and many an estate thus confiscated for the royal exchequer."

"Aye," the king rumbled. "And I'll see Aske hang for it too." He looked up once more at Lord Hugh. "But back to this widow. She intrigues me. Do you suspect her of foul play, my lord?"

"Let us just say that I find the coincidences a little difficult to believe. One husband dies falling off his horse in a stag hunt. Now that, I grant Your Highness, is a not uncommon occurrence. But then the second is slain by a huntsman's arrow . . . an arrow that no huntsman present would acknowledge. The third dies of a sudden and mysterious wasting disease . . . a man in his prime, vigorous, never known a day's illness in his life. And the fourth falls from a window . . . the lady's own chamber window . . . and breaks his neck."

Lord Hugh tapped off each death on his fingers, a faintly incredulous note in his quiet voice as he enumerated the catalogue.

"Aye, 'tis passing strange," the king agreed. "We should investigate these deaths, I believe, Lord Cromwell."

Privy Seal nodded. "Hugh of Beaucaire, if it pleases Your Highness, has agreed to undertake the task."

"I have no objection. He has an interest himself after all . . . but . . ." Here the king paused, frowning. "One thing I find most intriguing. How is it that the lady has managed to persuade four knights, gentlemen of family and property, to agree to her terms of marriage?"

"Witchcraft, Highness." The Bishop of Winchester in his scarlet robes spoke up for the first time. "There can be no other explanation. Her victims were known to be learned, in full possession of their faculties at the time they made the acquaintance of Lady Guinevere. Only a man bewitched would agree to the terms upon which she insisted. I request that the woman be brought here for examination, whatever findings Lord Hugh makes."

"Of what countenance is the woman? Do we know?"

"I have here a likeness, made some two years after her marriage to Roger Needham. She may have changed, of course." Hugh handed his sovereign a painted miniature set in a diamond-studded frame.

The king examined the miniature. "Here is beauty indeed," he murmured. "She would have had to have changed considerably to be less than pleasing now." He looked up, closing his large paw over the miniature. "I find myself most interested in making the acquaintance of this beautiful sorceress, who seems also to be an accomplished lawyer. Whether she be murderer or not, I will see her."

"It will be a journey of some two months, Highness. I will leave at once." Hugh of Beaucaire bowed, waited for a second to see if the sovereign's giant hand would disgorge the miniature, and when it became clear that it was lost forever, bowed again and left the chamber.

It was hot and quiet in the forest. A deep somnolence had settled over the broad green rides beneath the canopy of giant oaks and beeches.

Even the birds were still, their song silenced by the heat. The hunting party gathered in the grove, listening for the horn of a beater that would tell them their quarry had been started.

"Will there be a boar, Mama?" A little girl on a dappled pony spoke in a whisper, hushed and awed by the expectant silence around her. She held a small bow, an arrow already set to the string.

Guinevere looked down at her elder daughter and smiled. "There should be, Pen. I have spent enough money on stocking the forest to ensure a boar when we want one."

"My lady, 'tis a hot day. Boar go to ground in the heat," the chief huntsman apologized, his distress at the possibility of failing the child clear on his countenance.

"But it's my birthday, Greene. You promised me I should shoot a boar on my birthday," the child protested, still in a whisper.

"Not even Greene can produce miracles," her mother said. There was a hint of reproof in her voice and the child immediately nodded and smiled at the huntsman.

"Of course I understand, Greene. Only . . ." she added, rather spoiling the gracious effect, "only I had told my sister I would shoot a boar on my birthday and maybe I won't, and then she will be bound to shoot one on hers."

Knowing the Lady Philippa as he did, the chief huntsman had little doubt that she would indeed succeed where her sister might not and shoot her first boar on her tenth birthday. Fortunately he was spared a response by the sound of a horn, high and commanding, then a great crashing through the underbrush. The hounds leaped forward on their leashes with shrill barks. The horses shifted on the grass, sniffed the wind, tensed in expectation.

" 'Tis not one of our horns," the huntsman said, puzzled.

"But it's our boar," Lady Guinevere stated. "Come, Pen." She nudged her milk-white mare into action and galloped across the glade towards the trees where the crashing of the undergrowth continued. The child on her pony followed and Greene blew on his horn. The now unleashed dogs raced forward at the summons, the huntsmen chasing after them.

They broke through the trees onto a narrow path. The boar, his little red eyes glowing, stood at bay. He snorted and lowered his head with its wickedly sharp tusks.

Pen raised her bow, her fingers quivering with excitement. The boar charged straight for the child's pony.

Guinevere raised her own bow and loosed an arrow just as another flew from along the path ahead of them. The other caught the boar in the back of the neck. Pen in her mingled terror and excitement loosed her own arrow too late and it fell harmlessly to the ground. Her mother's caught the charging animal in the throat. Despite the two arrows sticking from its body, the boar kept coming under the momentum of his charge. Pen shrieked as the animal leaped, the vicious tusks threatening to drive into her pony's breast.

Then another arrow landed in the back of the boar's neck and it crashed to the ground beneath the pony's feet. The pony reared in terror and bolted, the child clinging to its mane.

A horseman broke out of the trees at the side of the ride and grabbed the pony's reins as it raced past. As the animal reared again, eyes rolling, snorting wildly, the man caught the child up from the saddle just as she was about to shoot backwards to the ground. The pony pawed and stamped. Other men rode out of the trees and gathered on the path facing Guinevere's party.

Pen looked up at the man who held her on his saddle. She didn't think she had ever seen such brilliant blue eyes before.

"All right?" he asked quietly.

She nodded, still too shaken and breathless to speak.

Guinevere rode up to them. "My thanks, sir." She regarded the man and his party with an air of friendly inquiry. "Who rides on Mallory land?"

The man leaned over and set Pen back on her now quiet pony. Instead of answering Guinevere's question, he said, "I assume you are the Lady Guinevere."

There was something challenging in his gaze. Guinevere thought as had her daughter that she had never seen such brilliant blue eyes, but she read antagonism in the steady look. Her friendly smile faded and her chin lifted in instinctive response. "Yes, although I don't know how you would know that. You are on my land, sir. And you are shooting my boar."

"It seemed you needed help shooting it yourself," he commented.

"My aim was true," she said with an angry glitter in her eye. "I needed no help. And if I did, I have my own huntsmen."

The man looked over at the group of men clustered behind her, at the dogs they held once again on tight leashes. He shrugged as if dismissing them as not worth consideration.

Guinevere felt her temper rise. "Who trespasses on Mallory land?" she demanded.

He turned his bright blue eyes upon her, regarding her thoughtfully. His gaze traveled over her as she sat tall in the saddle. He took in the elegance of her gown of emerald green silk with its raised pattern of gold vine leaves, the stiffened lace collar that rose at her nape to frame her small head, the dark green hood with its jeweled edge set back from her forehead to reveal hair the color of palest wheat. Her eyes were the astounding purple of ripe sloes. The miniature had not done her justice, he thought. Or perhaps it was maturity that accentuated the grace and beauty of the young girl in the portrait.

His gaze turned to the milk-white mare she rode, noticing its bloodlines in the sloping pasterns, the arched neck. A lady of wealth and discrimination, whatever else she might be.

"Hugh of Beaucaire," he said almost lazily.

So he had come in person. No longer satisfied with laying claim to her land by letter, he had come himself. It certainly explained his antagonism. Guinevere contented herself with an ironically raised eyebrow and returned his stare, seeing in her turn a man in his vigorous prime, square built, square jawed, his thick iron-gray hair cropped short beneath the flat velvet cap, his weathered complexion that of a man who didn't spend his time skulking with politics in the corners and corridors of palaces.

"This is my son, Robin." Hugh gestured and a boy rode out of the group of men behind him and came up beside his father. He had his father's blue eyes.

"I claim the lands between Great Longstone and Wardlow for my son," stated Hugh of Beaucaire.

"And I deny your claim," Guinevere replied. "My legal right to the land is indisputable."

"Forgive me, but I do dispute it," he said gently.

"You are trespassing, Hugh of Beaucaire. You have done my daughter a service and I would hate to drive you off with the dogs, but I will do so if you don't remove yourself from my lands." She beckoned the huntsmen to bring up the eager, straining hounds.

"So you throw down the glove," he said in a musing tone.

"I have no need to do so. You are trespassing. That is all there is to it."

Pen shifted in her saddle. She met the gaze of the boy, Robin. He was looking at least as uncomfortable as she was at this angry exchange between their parents.

"Greene, let loose the dogs," Guinevere said coldly.

Hugh raised an arresting hand. "We will discuss this at some other time, when we are a little more private." He gathered his reins to turn his horse.

"There is nothing to discuss." She gathered up her own reins. "I cannot help but wonder at the sense of a man who would ride this great distance on an idle errand."

She gestured back along the path with her whip. "If you ride due west you will leave Mallory land in under an hour. Until some months past, you would have found hospitality at the monastery of Arbor, but it was dissolved in February. The monks seek shelter themselves now." Her voice dripped contempt.

"You would question His Highness's wisdom in dissolving the monasteries, madam? I would question *your* sense, in such a case. Robert Aske is dangerous company to keep."

"I merely point out the inconvenience to benighted travelers," she said sweetly. "Farewell, Hugh of Beaucaire. Do not be found upon Mallory land two hours hence."

She turned her horse on the ride. "Come, Pen. Greene, have the boar prepared for the spit. It will serve to furnish Lady Pen's birthday feast."

"But I didn't shoot it myself, Mama," Pen said with the air of one steadfastly refusing to take credit that was not her due. Her eyes darted to Robin. The lad smiled.

"But you shot at it," he said. "I saw your arrow fly. The boar went for your pony's throat. You were very brave."

"My congratulations on your birthday, Lady Penelope." Hugh smiled at the child and Guinevere was brought up short. The smile transformed the man, sent all his antagonism scuttling, revealed only a warmth and humor that she would not have believed lay behind the harsh soldierly demeanor. His eyes, brilliant before with challenge and dislike, were now amused and curiously gentle. It was disconcerting.

"I bid you farewell," she repeated as coldly as before. "Pen, come." She reached over and took the child's reins, turning the pony on the path.

Pen looked over her shoulder at the boy on his chestnut gelding. She gave him a tentative smile and he half raised a hand in salute.

Hugh watched Guinevere and her daughter ride off with their escort. The huntsmen followed, the boar slung between two poles.

The miniature had not done her justice, he reflected again. Those great purple eyes were amazing, bewitching. And her hair, as silvery pale as ashes! What would it be like released from the coif and hood to tumble unrestrained down her back?

"Father?"

Hugh turned at Robin's hesitant voice. "You found the little maid appealing, Robin?" he teased.

The boy blushed to the roots of his nut-brown hair. "No . . . no, in-deed not, sir. I was wondering if we were leaving Mallory land now?"

Hugh shook his head, a smile in his eyes, a curve to his mouth. This was not a particularly pleasant smile. "Oh, no, my son. We have work to do. Lady Mallory has only just made my acquaintance. I foresee that before many hours are up, she will be heartily wishing she had never heard the name of Hugh of Beaucaire."

He touched spur to his horse.

"Did you shoot it . . . did you shoot the boar, Pen?" A girl with wildly flying plaits and disheveled gown came racing across the packhorse bridge over the River Wye as the hunting party entered the grounds of Mallory Hall through the great oak studded doors of the stone gate-house.

Pen glanced at her mother, who said swiftly, "We have a fine boar for the feast, Pippa. The men are bringing it."

"But did *you* shoot it, Pen?" the child insisted, standing squarely on the path, looking intently up at her sister.

"My arrow fell short," Pen said crossly. Her little sister was always able to root out the truth. It wasn't that she was spiteful, she just needed to know things, right down to the most minutely exact detail.

"Oh, well, never mind," Pippa said. "I shall shoot a boar though, on *my* birthday."

"Don't be so certain," her mother said, leaning down to give her her hand. "Come up."

Pippa seized the hand and scrambled up onto the saddle. "I wish you would have let me go."

"You're not old enough for boar hunts," Guinevere said. "And you are sadly untidy, child. Have you not been at your books with the magister?"

"Oh, yes, but he became tired and said I could go and play," the child said sunnily.

"Why, I wonder, would he become tired?" Guinevere mused rhetorically. Magister Howard, who had been her own tutor from her eighth birthday, found Pippa's endless stream of questions as exhausting as they were tedious for an elderly and devoted scholar.

They rode into the lower courtyard of the Hall and Guinevere dismounted, lifting Pippa down.

"I'm going to watch them skin the boar," the child announced. "Will you come, Pen?"

"No, it's disgusting," Pen said.

Guinevere laughed and went into the house. The steward greeted her with a bow. "My lady, the preparations are made for the feast, but the cooks wish to know whether they should use marchpane for Lady Pen's cake. After the last occasion . . ."

Guinevere considered. Pippa's passion for the sweet and sticky marchpane had had unfortunate results the last time it had appeared on the table. "Oh, I see no reason why other people should be deprived. It's Lady Pen's cake, after all. We must hope that Pippa has learned a little moderation, Master Crowder."

She hurried up the stairs to her apartments above the north entrance where Tilly was rearranging gowns in the linen press.

"A successful hunt, chuck?" the elderly woman asked in her customary informal fashion. She had served Lady Guinevere from her babyhood.

"That rather depends upon how you look at it," Guinevere said, easing her riding boots off on the bootjack. She sat on a wooden chest and raised her skirts to take off the thick woolen hose she had worn for riding. "We have a boar, but Pen's arrow didn't find its mark."

" 'Tis to be hoped Pippa don't rub it in too much," Tilly said.

Guinevere didn't answer. She trod barefoot to the window that looked out over the rolling dales of Derbyshire. It was a magnificent vista, a heat haze shimmering above the hills and valleys threaded with the wide ribbons of the River Wye and the Dove. In winter it was harsh and gray with driving rain and bitter winds, a very different landscape from this summer afternoon.

Her encounter with Hugh of Beaucaire was not over. A man didn't come on such a journey to be turned away by the threat of dogs.

Even as she thought this, the loud commanding note of a horn came from beyond the gatehouse. She stood still, her hands resting immobile on the low sill. She knew that note.

"Pass my silk hose, Tilly. The ivory ones. And the green kid shoes."

"Visitors? Are we expectin' visitors?"

"No, but we have them it would seem." She drew on her hose and tied the garters, slipped her feet into her shoes.

A knock at the door heralded Master Crowder. "Madam, Lord Hugh of Beaucaire requests entrance."

"Yes, so I gather." Guinevere frowned in thought. She could refuse him entrance. It was her land, her house. But she had the absolute conviction that he was not going to go away. She didn't want his armed troop besieging her gates.

"Bid him welcome, Master Crowder."

She crossed the chamber to the window that looked down on the lower courtyard, the window from which Stephen had fallen. She watched the troop of horsemen enter the courtyard.

Hugh of Beaucaire dismounted and stood for a moment looking around, hands resting lightly on his hips.

He was very square and solid, Guinevere thought. Not fat at all, but somehow an unshakable presence. Definitely to be reckoned with. Well, charm was probably her best weapon. She had used it to advantage many times before; there was no reason to think that Hugh of Beaucaire would be immune.

She went down to the courtyard. In the doorway of the Hall, she stood still and quiet and said pleasantly, "Lord Hugh. Have you come to claim a traveler's hospitality?"

Hugh crossed the flagstones towards her. He reached into his doublet and drew out a folded parchment. "I am here on the king's writ," he said, handing her the parchment. "I have orders from Privy Seal to investigate the manner of your husbands' deaths, Lady Guinevere. Those and divers other matters that have come to the king's attention."

2.

S o *it had happened.* It was said that there wasn't a corner of
Henry's kingdom unvisited by Privy Seal's spies. Guinevere had
hoped against hope that her situation, more to the point her wealth,
would not come to the attention of the money-starved royal exchequer.
It was common knowledge that lands, wardships, knighthoods, the
profits of justice, enriched the king's coffers. Guinevere Mallory, a lone
and wealthy widow, was a ripe peach for the plucking. Any excuse
would do. Hugh of Beaucaire's investigation would provide the excuse
and he would gain his own reward.

A wave of frustrated rage washed over her. Her fingers curled upwards to close over the hilt of the small silver dagger she carried in her
right sleeve.

She was powerless against the might and machinations of Privy Seal.
But she could vent her fury on Hugh of Beaucaire. There she was not
entirely helpless. The carved hilt was cool and familiar against her fingers. She could picture the dagger's trajectory. How easy it would be to
flick the wicked point into the throat of the loathsome man standing so
square and confident in *her* courtyard, looking as if he already owned
the very flagstones beneath his feet. It was he, with his importunate
claims, who had brought her to the attention of Privy Seal.

But a cooler temper followed swift on her hot anger. Rage would not help her here. Her fingers uncurled and her hand dropped to her side even as her mind raced. She had to buy herself some time. Time to think clearly.

"You are arresting me?" she asked, turning the parchment over in her hands without looking at it. Her voice was neutral, almost indifferent, no hint of anger or apprehension.

"Not as yet. I am here to investigate and then to escort you with my findings to London. There are people who wish to talk with you." His brilliant gaze flickered over her, watchful and sharp. He had seen the movement of her fingers, read in her eyes the flash of murderous rage. It had vanished almost as quickly as it had appeared, but he had been ready for her, every muscle tensed.

So there was to be only one result of this charade. They would take her away regardless of her supposed guilt or innocence.

Guinevere knew that if once she left Mallory Hall for London under Hugh of Beaucaire's escort, she would not return. Once they had their hooks in her, they would not let go. The battleground was here. The enemy was here. If she couldn't defeat Lord Hugh and his investigation while he was under her roof, she would be lost.

She looked beyond Lord Hugh to where his men still sat their horses. There were ten of them, and the boy, Robin. Could her own men-at-arms defeat these men of Beaucaire? The Beaucaire men had the same hard-bodied, military demeanor of their master. Guinevere guessed that they were men who'd been honed on some battlefield across the Channel during the last wars with France and Spain.

Her own men would have no chance against these in a pitched battle. But a night attack, perhaps, when the enemy were off guard? It would take months for the news of their disappearance to reach London. She could deny that they had ever arrived at Mallory Hall. Anything could have happened to them on such a long and hazardous journey.

"Not a good idea," he said softly, his narrowed eyes seeming to penetrate her skull.

"What is not?"

"What you were thinking," he returned with a flicker of a smile that was far from humorous. "My men are more than a match for domestic men-at-arms. And you will find me more than a match for that little dagger you have up your sleeve."

Clearly she must school her thoughts more strictly in this man's company, Guinevere thought, furious with herself for being so transparent.

"Mama . . . Mama . . ." Pippa's high voice broke the taut silence. The child came flying from the kitchen court. "Master Crowder says we have visitors." She arrived panting at her mother's side and regarded the group of strangers with interest.

The children must not be frightened, must not know what was happening. Not yet, at least. Guinevere put a hand on the child's shoulder and introduced her calmly. "My daughter Philippa, my lord. Make your curtsy to Lord Hugh of Beaucaire, Pippa."

Pippa obeyed even as the questions poured from her lips. "Have you come far? Where have you come from? Are those your men? Who's that boy? Is that a falcon on your coat of arms? I have my very own peregrine . . ." Before Hugh could respond to this flood, she had caught sight of her sister coming out of the house and called excitedly, "Oh, Pen . . . see here, we have visitors. I don't know where they've come from but . . ."

"Hush, Pippa," Guinevere chided, as laughter sprang to life in Lord Hugh's eyes. Once again his countenance was transformed. And once again she was disconcerted. It was well nigh impossible to imagine plunging a dagger into this man's throat. His mouth . . . she seemed to notice it for the first time. It was full, sensuous, humorous. She noticed the deep cleft in his chin, the laugh lines etched around his eyes. And it came to her with a shock that this man's habitual expression was not the one of harsh, sardonic hostility he had directed towards her. That was not the way he regarded the world and life in general . . . only, it seemed, herself.

"I only wanted to ask if they were to come to Pen's feast," Pippa said righteously. "Pen, ask them to come to your feast."

Pen was looking at Robin. He smiled at her and she smiled back, remembering how he'd complimented her on her bravery when the boar had charged. "Yes, please come," she said. "I would very much like you to come. The boar is big enough, isn't it, Mama?"

"Indeed, we wouldn't impose on your birthday, Lady Pen." Hugh spoke swiftly, his eyes warm. It took a minute for the warmth to die out as he turned to Guinevere. "My lady, we will leave you to your celebrations. We'll make camp outside your gates and continue our business tomorrow."

Hostility had taken her nowhere, Guinevere thought. It was time to try something else. And the man with the humorous mouth and the laugh lines around those vivid blue eyes was a man who surely could be charmed. *Seduced, even.* What in the world was she thinking? To make a bedfellow of the enemy? A shiver went down her spine, and her scalp prickled.

"My daughter would like you and your son to come to her feast, my lord. We grant birthday wishes in our family." She inclined her head and offered him a tiny smile.

Hugh was suddenly confused as if his mind and his physical senses had somehow gone off in different directions. It was the most damnable smile. And her eyes! They were glowing like dark purple lanterns. A minute ago they had been filled with a savage rage, now he could read only invitation. *What the devil was she playing at?*

He glanced at Robin who in his eagerness had already dismounted. He looked at the two girls and told himself that it was reasonable for their mother to wish to keep unpleasantness from them for as long as possible. He was not brute enough to ruin the child's birthday. But how in the name of grace was he to share a sociable, convivial evening with a woman he was investigating for murder?

"Oh, yes, you *have* to come," Pippa declared. "Pen wishes it and it's *very* unlucky to refuse someone's birthday wish. It will bring you months and months of ill luck, a whole year of it."

"Don't exaggerate, Pippa," Pen said, flushing slightly. "And why have you got blood on your gown?"

"Oh, it's from the boar. I was standing too close when they were skinning it and it spurted. Greene was very cross," Pippa said blithely, brushing at the dark red spots on her muslin gown. "He called me something that I think was very rude, only it was under his breath so I couldn't quite catch it and he wouldn't say it again. He told me to go away . . . so you will come, won't you, sir?" she went on in the same breath. "You and that boy." She pointed at Robin.

Hugh knew when he'd met an unmovable object. He was aware that Guinevere was regarding him with an ironically comprehending smile, reading his thoughts as clearly as he'd read hers earlier. He threw in the towel. It would be an uncomfortable evening, but once it was over nothing would stand in the way of his investigation.

"We should be very happy to celebrate your sister's birthday," he said. "Robin, come and be introduced." He drew his son forward.

"How old are you?" Pippa asked instantly. "I'm eight and Pen's ten."

"Twelve," Robin replied with a slightly haughty air. "I am on campaign with my father."

"Oh, how grand," Pippa said, quite unabashed by the loftiness. "I wish I was a boy, then I could go campaigning too. But why are you campaigning here? Where are the enemies?" She looked around with an air of inquiry, as if expecting to see an army pop out of the ground.

"Pippa, that's enough," Guinevere said. "Go inside and ask Nell to help you change your gown. You can't attend the feast covered in boar's blood. Oh, and ask Master Crowder to come out, please."

Pippa was easily distracted and went off with a merry skip. Pen said feelingly, "I wish she'd swallow her tongue sometimes."

"Does she always talk that much?" Robin asked.

"She never stops." Pen gave an elder sisterly sigh.

"You sent for me, madam." The steward approached, his black gown wafting around him. He regarded the newcomers with an air of sharp curiosity.

"Lord Hugh is here upon the king's business. He and his son will be my guests for a few days," Guinevere said. "Have them shown to the apartments in the west wing. Lord Hugh's men may be housed above the stables."

"My men will bivouac beyond the gates," Hugh said firmly, a slightly mocking gleam in his eye. "They will not thus be a charge upon your . . . your kindness, madam."

"As you wish, sir," she said with a slight shrug.

The steward bowed low. "If you would follow me, my lord."

Hugh nodded and called to his men. "Jack, have my trunk brought into the house." He offered Guinevere a formal bow. "My thanks for your hospitality, madam. We must change our dress to do honor to your daughter's feast."

There was something unreal about this formal exchange of pleasantries, but Guinevere merely smiled agreeably and said, "I trust you will find our guest apartments comfortable, sir. We attend chapel for vespers at five."

Hugh bowed again and putting a hand on his son's shoulder, eased him towards the house in the wake of the steward.

"Who are they, Mama?" Pen asked, putting her hand in her mother's with a sudden little flutter of anxiety.

"They come from the king. Lord Hugh has some estate business to transact with me." Guinevere smiled reassuringly at her daughter. "It would please me if you would entertain Master Robin, Pen. Since I must entertain his father."

"I will try to keep Pippa from plaguing him," Pen declared.

"Then I wish you luck, love. You should change your gown too. You wish to look your best for the feast."

Guinevere stood in the court, watching her daughter run into the house. The Beaucaire men were withdrawing from the courtyard. Safely away from a surprise attack in the night. Damn the man's mockery! He seemed to be able to read her thoughts as clearly as if they were written down for him.

But what was she to do?

It was her life at stake. If he found her guilty of murder, she would lose her head. Or even worse, she would die at the stake. Murder of a husband was a petty treason and burning was the punishment for such a crime. Her children would be made wards of the court to be disposed of at the will of the king. Her estates would be confiscated, the revenues poured into the royal exchequer, after those like Hugh of Beaucaire had taken their share.

And there was nothing she could do to stop the process, if they were determined. Her guilt or innocence was irrelevant. They would take what they wanted from her as they had done from so many others.

For a moment she felt utter despair at the futility of pitting her puny wits against the might of the state. But the weakness vanished under a cold wash of anger. She could not give in without a fight. It was not only her own future at stake, but her daughters'. For their sakes, she could not assume the inevitable and yield without a defense.

Guinevere turned and walked slowly into the house and up to her own apartments. Her jaw was set, her eyes bright with purpose. She would fight them with whatever weapons were at her disposal. They would have to make some gesture towards the law, towards finding proof of her supposed crimes. They would have to try her on whatever charges they brought. They would manufacture evidence, scare up witnesses, but she knew the law. Better than most lawyers. She could defend herself even to the lords in the Star Chamber. There was no factual evidence linking her to her husbands' deaths. How could there be? Her ankle twitched of its own volition. Her foot had had a life of its own on the night of Stephen Mallory's death, but that was something only she knew.

She could not fight them with physical means, but she could use her head, her learning.

She stood frowning in the middle of her bedchamber, listening to the rooks cawing in the poplar trees alongside the river. She thought of Lord Hugh. Of what she had detected beneath the harsh exterior. She might loathe and despise a man who would trump up charges against a person for his own greedy ends, but that needn't prevent her using the other weapons at a woman's disposal.

Thoughtfully she opened the linen press and drew out an Italian gown of a rich amber velvet embroidered with black knots of a most intricate design. The square neck was studded with jet and the gown opened over an underskirt of gold-embroidered black silk. She examined it with pursed lips. Then nodded slowly. It would serve her purpose very nicely.

"Lord, chuck, such a to-do." Tilly bustled in. "Oh, is that the gown you'll be wearing, eh? Well, it's a right grand one. So who are these visitors then, that you'd wear such a gown to honor them?"

"They're from the king," Guinevere said, laying the gown on the bed.

"From the king!" Tilly exclaimed. "What's the king got to do with us then?"

"You may well ask," Guinevere said grimly. "Help me unlace, Tilly." She turned her back for Tilly's deft fingers at the laces of her stomacher.

Hugh looked around the large well-appointed apartments in the west wing. The window shutters were fastened back and the scent of roses wafted up from the garden below.

Robin was kneeling upon the window seat. "There's a wonderful topiary garden, sir. Peacocks and serpents and stags. I have never seen its like."

Hugh came to stand behind his son, his hand resting on the boy's shoulder. Beyond the topiary garden could be seen the river, flowing gently through a meadow dotted with grazing sheep. Everything about Mallory Hall was prosperous and orderly.

"Why do we lay claim to Lady Mallory's land, sir?" Robin looked up at his father, his blue eyes perfect mirrors of Hugh's. "If she has the deeds, I mean."

"She has the deeds, but she has no right to them, my son. The land was not Roger Needham's to will away. It belonged to his first wife, a distant cousin of ours. Lady Mallory contrived with some legal juggling to persuade Needham to cede the land to her at his death. But it was not his to will away. It belonged to his first wife's family and should by rights have been returned to them."

He moved away from Robin back into the chamber. "The land in dispute is particularly rich in lead. Lady Mallory understandably is loath to give it up, since she has been mining it very lucratively for years. It will form the foundation of a considerable fortune for you, Robin."

Robin got off the window seat. "Will it be easy to get it back?"

Hugh gave a short laugh, remembering the expression Privy Seal had used. "From what I've seen of Lady Mallory, very difficult, I should imagine. But there's more than one way to skin a cat." He opened the wooden, iron-bound chest that had been brought up for him. "Now, what finery shall we choose to honor Pen's feast?"

"She's very pretty," Robin said. "Don't you think she is?"

"Who, Pen?" Hugh looked up with a smile.

"Yes . . . yes, she is, but I was thinking of Lady Mallory."

"Ah." Hugh nodded and returned to the contents of the chest. "*Pretty* is not the word I would have chosen for her ladyship. Will you wear the blue doublet with the silver gown? Or the yellow and red?"

"The blue." Robin took the garments his father passed to him and shrugged out of the serviceable short woolen gown and linen doublet he'd worn for riding. "What will you wear?"

"I haven't decided as yet." Hugh stripped off his doublet, shirt, and hose. He strode to the washstand and splashed water over his face. "You will need to change your shirt and hose, too."

Robin examined his shirt doubtfully. " 'Tis not overly soiled. I changed it but a week ago."

"And you have been riding hard every day since," Hugh pointed out. "You reek, my son, and if you wish to make an impression on young ladies, 'tis best to make a sweet-smelling one. A good wash won't hurt you." He tossed a wet towel to the boy.

Blushing, Robin caught it.

Hugh laughed and sat down on the bed to put on clean hose. Whenever he was not on some military mission for the king he had been deeply involved in his son's care since the boy was five. Robin's mother had died giving birth to a stillborn baby and Hugh had buried his grief in caring for their son. Robin was so like his mother; sometimes an expression, a gesture, reminded Hugh so vividly of Sarah that it would take his breath away and the grief at her loss would be as sharp and poignant as it had ever been.

Now that the lad had almost reached maturity, he could accompany his father on his campaigns. This long journey into Derbyshire had been the first they had taken together and it had brought them even closer.

He fastened jeweled garters at the knee, covertly watching his son's own preparations. He had sensed that Guinevere felt for her daughters the same passionate love he had for Robin. Did they too remind her of the dead partner? Had she perhaps loved Lord Hadlow as he had loved Sarah?

Hadlow had fallen victim to a huntsman's arrow. A mysterious arrow that no one would own. It had carried nothing to identify it as belonging to one of the huntsmen present at the chase. Most arrows carried their owner's mark, so that there would be no dispute over who had brought down the prey. An unmarked arrow had killed Lord Hadlow and left his wife in possession of all the land between Matlock and Chesterfield. Land rich in coal and iron. Forested land, well stocked with game, surrounded Hadlow's manor house at Matlock. The woman now owned so many manors and hunting forests in the county, she could progress from one to the other without repeating a visit in a six month.

Hugh went to the window, lacing his shirt as he looked out again across the lush gardens to the water meadows beyond. Looking upon the softness of the mellow stone of the Hall and its flower-rich terraces, Hugh could understand how she might prefer Mallory Hall over all the others. Had she married Stephen Mallory just to get her hands on the Hall?

What manner of men had these husbands been? He knew very little about any of them, not even the first who had had some kinship through marriage to Hugh's own father. Roger Needham had been a lot older than his sixteen-year-old bride. Maybe twice her age. Not a particularly pleasant prospect for a young woman. The marriage would have been arranged for her and she could not have expected any real say in the matter. But no one would have obliged her to marry any of the other three men. She had entered into those alliances entirely of her own volition. And she had drawn up her own marriage contracts. Learned noblewomen were not unheard-of. The king's bastard daughter the Lady Mary was a distinguished Latinist and scholar and it was said that her four-year-old sister the Lady Elizabeth was rigorously taught. But a legally trained mind was a rather different matter, Hugh reflected.

There must be servants, old retainers, who had known the lady well over the years, who, with luck, had been with her through her marriages. The steward, for instance. The chief huntsman. A tutor, perhaps. A tiring woman, perhaps. In the morning he would throw his net wide and see what he caught.

He put on a doublet of crimson velvet and fastened a tooled leather belt at his waist just as the chapel bell rang for vespers.

"Come, Robin. 'Tis five already. We mustn't keep our hostess waiting." Hugh slipped his arms into a wide, loose gown of richly embroidered crimson silk lined with dark blue silk and slid his dagger into the sheath at his waist. He ran an appraising eye over his son's appearance, flicked a piece of lint from his shoulder, and ushered him out of the apartment.

Robin sniffed hungrily of the rich aromas of roasting meat drifting from the kitchens as they crossed to the chapel where the bell was still ringing.

All the senior members of the household were gathered for vespers on the long oak pews in the chapel in the upper courtyard. They glanced up as Hugh and Robin entered the dim vaulted space.

"That boy must sit with us," Pippa announced in her high clear voice from a box pew in the chancel. "Boy, come over here," she called imperiously.

"Pippa, don't shout!" Pen said in a scandalized whisper. "You're in the chapel! And his name is Robin."

"Oh, I forgot." Pippa clapped one hand over her mouth even as she beckoned frantically with the other one.

Hugh could see no sign of Lady Guinevere in the box pews as they walked up the aisle to the chancel. Perhaps a guilty conscience kept her from her prayers, he thought grimly.

"Come and sit by me," Pippa hissed, scrunching up on the pew, heedless of the creasing of her green silk gown as she made room for Robin.

Hugh restrained a smile. It was clear to him that Robin would infinitely prefer to sit beside the elder sister, who was smiling her own much shyer invitation. He gestured that Robin should enter the pew with the girls and then turned to take the one across the aisle. There was a stir at the chapel door and he looked back.

What he saw took his breath away for a minute. Lady Guinevere in a gown of amber velvet studded with blackest jet came up the aisle towards him. At her waist she wore a gold chain from which hung an enameled and gold pomander and a tiny watch studded with sable diamonds. She wore a diamond pendant on her breast and diamonds studded the high arc of her headdress that was set back so that her smoothly parted hair was visible on her forehead. Her pale hair in the candlelight seemed to shimmer beneath the bright glitter of the diamonds.

"Lord Hugh, forgive me for keeping you waiting. There were some matters to discuss with the musicians for this evening. Pen has certain favorite dances. I wanted to be sure they were included in their repertoire." Her voice was soft and musical, her smile *damnable*. It was full of warm promise, bewitching!

He remembered the Bishop of Winchester's declaration that the woman must have used sorcery to bring so many men to their knees. Ordinarily Hugh had no time for such nonsense, but at this moment he came close to believing.

Guinevere glanced over at the children. Robin jumped to his feet in the narrow box and bowed. She smiled at him. "I give you good even, Robin. Pippa, come and sit beside me, otherwise you'll chatter throughout the service." Smoothly she extricated her younger child, ignoring her protestations, and propelled her firmly into the far corner of the opposite pew, following her in.

"Lord Hugh . . . there is more than enough room for three."

He took his seat, still searching for composure. The scent of her surrounded him. A scent of verbena and lemon and rose water. He disliked the heavy perfumes women used at court to mask the riper odors of their heavily clad bodies. But this was a delicate fragrance that sent his senses reeling. He found himself glad that he had bothered to wash away his own travel dirt and put on fresh linen. And the reflection infuriated him. He was not here to be entranced by Guinevere Mallory.

The priest began the evening service, a form that everyone present knew by heart. Guinevere made the ritual responses while her mind was elsewhere. The effect of her appearance on Lord Hugh had been all that she had intended. However swiftly he had tried to disguise it, she had seen the pure masculine response in his eyes as she'd come up the aisle. And she could feel that same response in the taut upright figure on the pew beside her. He was utterly and totally immersed in her presence.

A little smile of satisfaction touched her lips as she bowed her head for the benediction.

The bells pealed jubilantly in the Lady Pen's honor as the family and guests left the chapel. Members of the household congratulated Pen and gave her flowers and little trinkets they had made for her. She smiled and skipped a little with pleasure and Pippa kept up a running commentary for Robin's benefit on every gift her sister received and on the identity of the giver.

"That's such a pretty pomander, did you see it? It was given to her by the stillroom keeper. I expect she's put all sorts of sweet-smelling herbs in there. . . . Can I smell it, Pen? D'you think it'll ward off the plague, Boy?"

"There is no plague in these parts," Robin said. "And my name is Robin."

"Oh, I'll try to remember," Pippa said blithely. "I forget because we don't see many boys here . . . not *your* kind of boy. Servants and grooms and people, but not *real* ones. So I just seem to think of you as Boy."

"How does anyone put up with you?" Robin said in an undertone. "D'you never stop talking?" He was wishing he had something to give Pen, searching his memory for the contents of the trunk he shared with his father, wondering if he had anything that would serve as a gift.

Then he realized that Pippa had fallen most uncharacteristically silent. He looked down at her and saw that she was looking dejected. "Oh, I didn't mean to be unkind," he said. "I was trying to think and you kept interrupting me."

Pippa immediately beamed up at him. "I know I talk too much, everyone says so. But there's always so much to say. Don't you find?"

Robin shook his head. "Not really."

Guinevere walking just behind the children overheard this exchange. She glanced involuntarily at her companion whose expression was once again warm and amused, the laugh lines deeply etched around his eyes.

"Was that little maid born talking?" he inquired, laughter lurking in the deep melodious voice.

"She was certainly born smiling," Guinevere responded, unable to help a flicker of answering amusement. "She has the sunniest temper."

An elderly man dressed in the furred gown that denoted his scholar's status, the lappets of his black cap tied firmly beneath his pointed chin, hurried up behind them. "Oh, dear, oh, dear, I so much wanted to be among the first to congratulate Pen, but Master Grice detained me in the chapel over the construction of some devotional text and now I find I'm almost the last," he muttered. "I wouldn't have the dear child think I was neglectful."

"I'm sure she doesn't, Magister Howard," Guinevere said. "Lord Hugh, allow me to present Magister Howard. He is the girls' tutor. But he was also my own." Her eyes flashed as she met his gaze. "I imagine you will wish to talk with him in the course of your . . ." She hesitated, frowning, as if searching for the right word. "Your . . ."

"My investigations," Hugh supplied blandly. "I think that's the word you're looking for, Lady Guinevere." He gave a friendly nod to the elderly man.

"Oh, my goodness!" the magister said. "What could you be investigating, sir?"

" 'Tis not a matter to be discussed during a celebration," Hugh said as blandly as before, standing aside to allow Guinevere to precede him into the house. He followed her into the banqueting hall through the opening in the carved screen that separated the hall from the passageway.

The long table on the dais in the hall was spread with a shimmering white damask cloth in honor of the occasion. Above in the minstrels' gallery musicians were playing a cheerful air and pages stood behind the chairs of family and guests with white napkins and flagons of wine to fill the goblets that this evening graced the table instead of the usual horn cups.

Servers ran from the kitchens with steaming platters of roasted meats and a cook stood at the carving table to one side of the hall. As he sliced the boar onto a platter held by a server, the rich juices were captured in the grooved runnel around the table and tipped into a bowl.

A large silver saltcellar stood in the center of the table that ran the length of the hall below the dais and members of the household took their accustomed places at the board, those of lower status sitting below the salt.

Guinevere moved to the center of the high table and invited Lord Hugh to the seat at her right.

Pen, as the older child of the house, was about to take her place on her mother's left when she realized that she could then have only one person to sit on her other side.

Pippa would expect to sit there. She always did, and on a birthday it was a particularly important place. Pen looked at her sister. Then she looked at Robin. She knew she could not choose Robin over her sister, even though it was her birthday. Pippa would be utterly miserable, and she wouldn't understand either.

"Robin, pray sit on my left," Guinevere said with instant comprehension. "Pen, you won't mind giving up your place to our honored guest, I know. You may sit beside Robin, and Pippa will sit on your other side."

It was an arrangement that solved Pen's dilemma and would not incidentally serve to separate both Hugh and Robin from the proximity of Pippa's chatter. Pippa looked momentarily disconsolate at being separated from the novelty of the boy's company but it was her sister's celebration and she didn't argue.

They took their places and the rest of the company sat down. The clatter of knives, the hum and buzz of voices rose above the music from the gallery. Guinevere found herself noticing her companion's hands. Noticing how square and workmanlike they were. Nothing of the effete aristocrat in the thick knuckles, the strong wrists, the large fingers. He wore a gold signet ring with a great winking sapphire; that and a ruby in the brim of his dark velvet hat were his only adornments. His richly decorated garments needed no jewels to set them off, however. She had the feeling that he wore these clothes uncomfortably, or at least with less ease than he would wear the more serviceable riding garments of a soldier.

"Does something interest you?" he inquired, one eyebrow lifted. "I should count myself flattered." There was no mistaking the mockery in his voice. Once more she was in the company of Hugh of Beaucaire who regarded her with undisguised hostility.

"Don't be," she said, reaching for her goblet. It held a deep red wine from Aquitaine. She glanced at her companion, waiting for him to sample his own goblet.

Instead, Hugh took hers as she set it on the table and drank from it very deliberately. As the page behind him leaned forward to place sliced boar on the gilded platter before him, he waved the boy aside.

Guinevere stared at him in momentary confusion.

He smiled his cold unpleasant smile and drank again. "We drink from one goblet, madam, and we eat from one platter."

"Whatever do you mean?"

"Men die in your company," he said, his eyes never leaving her face as he pushed the goblet towards her.

3.

Guinevere's fingers curled around the slender stem of the goblet. For a second she was afraid the fine Venetian crystal would snap between her fingers as she fought for composure. She must appear indifferent, show no hint of vulnerability to his insults and taunts.

She ignored his statement, inquiring coolly, "How do you find the wine, my lord?" She carried the goblet once more to her lips.

"As fine as any from the region," he returned. "I was forgetting, of course, that you inherited some vineyards in Aquitaine from your . . ." He frowned as if considering. "Your third husband, wasn't it?" Casually he leaned over and forked a piece of roast boar from her platter. His eyes resting on her pale countenance were as sardonic as his tone.

"Yes, he bequeathed me the vineyards among other estates," Guinevere agreed calmly, meeting his eye.

"And what exactly was it that sent this particular husband to his eternal rest? I forget." He chewed his meat, swallowed, reached again for the goblet to wash down the mouthful.

"The sweating sickness that killed so many in London, my lord, took its toll in the north some months later," she replied. She had been hungry after the day's hunting but now all appetite had deserted her. The meat on her plate looked gray and greasy instead of rich and succulent and the wine seemed to have acquired a metallic tang.

Hugh said nothing for a minute, leaning back as the page behind his chair refilled the shared goblet and placed a spoonful of parsnip fritters on the platter together with a heap of small sausages.

It was true, he reflected, that the sweating sickness had swept the country in the year that Lord Kirk had supposedly died of a wasting disease. He cast a sidelong look at Lord Kirk's widow.

Guinevere turned her head and met his eyes. A cold smile touched her mouth as she inquired with a delicately raised eyebrow, "You are wondering, my lord, if I might have done away with my third husband under the guise of the epidemic?"

He shrugged, crimson and dark blue silk rippling across his square shoulders. "I am here to look for answers, madam." He speared a sausage and ate it off the point of his knife.

"Answers, not evidence?" she inquired, her smile taut, but her sloe eyes clear and seemingly untroubled.

"Is there a difference?"

"I think so." Suddenly despite her underlying desperation Guinevere found that she was enjoying this battle of wits and tongues. She had always reveled in sharpening her wits in discussion or verbal sparring. Magister Howard would engage in legal and logistical arguments as a purely mental exercise, but only her second husband, the girls' father, had enjoyed the thrust and parry of a two-edged discussion. Timothy Hadlow had been a most unusual man: he had not considered it beneath him to lose an argument to a woman.

She said, "*Evidence* tends to imply a belief in some wrongdoing. *Answers* merely looks for explanations to a puzzle. There are no puzzles to be unraveled in the deaths of my husbands. Each and every one has a simple explanation." Her appetite had come back and she gestured to a page to serve her from a brace of woodcocks he held on a charger.

She pulled the bird apart with her fingers and nibbled one of the small crisp legs, watching her opponent as he considered his answer.

Hugh said in measured tones, "Then it is true that I look for evidence of suspicious circumstances in those so-convenient four deaths."

Guinevere drank wine before she said sharply, "Tell me, Lord Hugh, are you here to look for such evidence or to ensure that you find it?"

He made no answer for a moment, then said with a flash of anger, "You impugn my honor, madam."

Finally she had stung him. She could see it in the slight flush beneath the weathered bronze of his complexion, in the rigidity of his mouth, the set of his jaw.

"Do I?" she said sweetly, setting down the now clean bone before delicately licking her fingers one at a time.

Hugh found his gaze abruptly riveted to the tip of her tongue between her warm red lips, the contrasting glimpse of white teeth. He didn't think he had ever seen such a sensual gesture and for a moment his anger at her insult faded.

"Mama . . . Mama . . ." Pippa's piping voice suddenly ruptured the closed tense circle that contained them. Unconsciously they both relaxed as their intense privacy was invaded.

"What is it?" Guinevere smiled at her daughter, whose small face was brightly flushed with excitement beneath the plaited golden crown of her hair.

"Can I ask the boy to dance with me? They're playing a galliard and I practiced the steps just this morning."

Guinevere caught Pen's dismayed countenance, Robin's sudden blush as he realized that he'd been so busy satisfying his ravenous appetite that he'd neglected a social duty to his hostess, not to mention missing a perfect opportunity.

"It's Pen's birthday, Pippa, she must lead the dancing," Guinevere said gently.

Robin coughed, scrubbed at his mouth with his napkin, and said in a throaty rush as he jumped to his feet, "Lady Pen, will you permit me . . ." Hastily he wiped his hand on his thigh in case there was any residue of boar grease before extending it to Pen in invitation.

Pen blushed delicately and rose from her stool, giving Robin her hand. He led her down from the dais to a smattering of applause from the diners who rose in couples to join them in the stately moves of the dance.

Pippa bit her lip and made a valiant attempt at a smile as she joined the applause.

Hugh tossed his napkin aside and stood up. "Come, little maid, let us see how well you've mastered the galliard." He offered his hand with his warm and humorous smile and Pippa jumped eagerly to her feet, sending her stool spinning.

"Oh, I'm very good, my dance master told me so. Actually, I'm better than Pen," she confided in an unsuccessful whisper. "I have more rhythm and I'm lighter on my feet. I wonder if that boy will notice."

"Your sister is a very graceful dancer," Hugh said repressively. "You will have to be more than ordinarily good to give a more elegant demonstration."

"Oh, I am," Pippa assured him, totally unaware of any snub as she skipped beside him down to the floor.

Guinevere rested her head against the carved back of her chair, closing her eyes briefly. She felt for a minute utterly exhausted, wrung out as if she'd been in some kind of wrestling match. Then she sat up again, took a sip of wine, and watched the dancing. Pen and Robin were very earnest, Robin watching his steps. Pen's bottom lip was caught between her teeth, evidence of her own concentration. Conversation was obviously beyond them, Guinevere thought with an inner smile, some of her desperation and fatigue lifting as she watched.

Pippa was bounding around looking like a tiny green butterfly flitting around her tall partner. For all his square bulk and soldierly bearing Hugh of Beaucaire moved with smooth grace, Guinevere noted, and he didn't appear to find anything incongruous in his exuberant and minute partner. Pippa, unlike her sister, was talking nineteen to the dozen, and Guinevere saw how Hugh seemed to select only certain parts of the stream for a response. A man who didn't believe in wasting energy in futilities, Guinevere reflected. He was still smiling, his eyes were warm and filled with amusement as he bent now and again to respond to Pippa, and once more Guinevere wondered how two such separate personalities could exist in the same body.

She became aware of a strange tingle on her skin and a sudden wash of heat bringing the color to her cheeks. The last time she had felt like this was when she had first seen Timothy Hadlow. It had been on a Twelfth Night when the Lord of Misrule reigned and nothing was forbidden. She had laid eyes on Timothy Hadlow and he had laid eyes upon her. She could feel his hand now gripping hers as he led her wordlessly to that little room, barely more than a cupboard, where they had fallen to the floor, tugging and thrusting clothing aside in a glorious explosion of passion. She could see his bright hazel eyes in her mind's eye now, laughing down at her as he held himself above her, moving slowly within her, gauging her mounting excitement until the moment when he . . .

God's bones! She could feel the warm liquid arousal in her loins, the deep pulse in her belly, the heat of her skin, the jolt of excitement. No man before or since Timothy had given her this wondrous lusty desire.

Until now . . .

No, it was absurd, lunacy! Hugh of Beaucaire was her enemy, dedicated to bringing about her death, to robbing her and her daughters. This was not a man to lust after.

The stately measures of the galliard came to an end and Pippa darted away from Hugh and ran up to Robin, her voice rising above the minstrels' strings and the buzz of voices in the hall. "Did you see me dance with your father, Boy? I mean Robin. Don't I dance well? Will you dance with me now? It's a country dance. We can all dance together . . . you, me, and Pen." She tugged at their hands, pulling them back to the floor.

Hugh came back to the table; he was laughing, his stride light as he took the steps to the dais two at a time. "What a jaybird she is!" He sat down as the page pulled out his chair. He reached for the goblet and drank deeply. "Just listening to her gives me a thirst."

Guinevere smiled faintly. His proximity was setting her senses swirling. She could detect a hint of lavender, a trace of rosemary from his hair as he leaned sideways to help himself to a manchet of bread from the basket on the table. A man concerned with personal hygiene was an unusual one indeed, particularly when he'd been so many weeks upon the road.

To distract herself, she leaned back in her chair and told the page to tell the kitchen staff to bring in the birthday cake.

"I think, my lady, that if I may be so bold I'll beg Pen for the honor of a dance," Magister Howard called up from his place well above the salt at the long table in the main body of the hall. "If she won't despise an old man's creaking steps." He smiled a somewhat toothless smile and nodded, his black-hatted head bobbing like a jackdaw, his thin gray beard wagging.

"She will be delighted, Magister," Guinevere said, knowing that Pen, whatever her true feelings, would show her tutor only a smiling respect and apparent pleasure.

"And young Pippa will be even more so," murmured Hugh. "To have *That Boy* to herself."

Guinevere laughed. It was impossible not to respond to his amused tone. "It won't be for long. The magister's not as spry on his feet as he used to be although his brain is as sharp as ever. Anyway, the cake will soon attract Pippa's attention."

"Does the mother dance as well as her daughters?" Hugh inquired. "Or does she consider herself still to be in mourning?"

"I did not mourn Stephen Mallory," she said in a low voice. "And I'll not pretend otherwise."

Hugh regarded her closely, an arrested expression in his eye. One of the tall tapers that marched down the center of the table flickered in a sudden draught and her purple eyes seemed to catch the flame and throw it back at him.

Hugh said slowly and deliberately, "In that case, madam, will you dance?" He offered her his hand and there was challenge in his bright blue gaze.

Almost without volition, Guinevere laid her hand in his and rose to her feet in a graceful sweep of amber velvet. The diamonds at her breast and in the high arc of her headdress shimmered in the light of the torches sconced high on the wall. Her long black silk hood reached almost to her heels and as she turned in the stately movements of the dance it swirled against her velvet skirts.

She smiled at him as she had smiled at him in the chapel and Hugh felt again the bewildering sensation of losing his balance. He believed so strongly in her guilt, in his mission, in his determination to get back from her what was his by right, and yet in this moment beneath that smile all conviction, all determination melted like butter in the sun. Was this truly witchcraft? Was she trying to bewitch him as she had bewitched four husbands? He couldn't help but respond to her even as he struggled with himself to keep his distance, to keep his clear-sighted detachment.

"Mama's dancing . . . look, Pen, Mama's dancing," Pippa squealed from the other end of the set where she was bounding around Robin, who had had to yield his place with Pen to the magister. "She's dancing with your father, Boy Robin."

"So I see," Robin said. "I don't see why it should be a matter for such excitement. I'm going back to the table now. Are you coming or are you going to dance by yourself?"

Pippa looked momentarily crestfallen but she followed him off the floor and back to the table. "I haven't seen Mama dance for ages," she confided. "She never danced with Lord Mallory. Not even at Christmas and Twelfth Night." A little frown drew the faint lines of her brows together. "He was a very nasty man. He shouted and threw things. Everybody hated him. Once I heard Crowder telling Greene that Lord Mallory was a drunken brute."

Robin, who knew only that his father had come to lay claim to disputed property, was somewhat shocked by this confidence. "You shouldn't eavesdrop," he said. "One of these days you'll hear something you'll wish you hadn't."

"Oh, I don't do it deliberately," Pippa reassured earnestly. "It's just that sometimes people don't know I'm there."

"How could that be?" Robin wondered, opening his eyes very wide. "Are you telling me that sometimes you actually stop talking?"

"I think you're being horrid!" Pippa stated. "I'm going to talk to Greene." She slid off her stool and ran to where the chief huntsman was cradling a full drinking horn and engaging in an intense conversation with the sergeant-at-arms. Greene regarded the child's precipitate arrival with an air of mock dismay, but moved up on the long bench to make room for her beside him.

She propped her elbow on the table and, resting her chin on her palm, regarded him solemnly. "What were you talking about?"

"Nothing for your ears, little maid," Greene said.

"But it looked very important," she insisted.

"Aye, that it was," he agreed placidly, taking a long draught from his drinking horn. He winked at the sergeant-at-arms who grinned broadly. Pippa was a universal favorite. However, she couldn't be a party to their earlier discussion. Their talk had been all of Lord Hugh of Beaucaire and his men. The sergeant-at-arms had been in the court when Hugh of Beaucaire had announced his mission, and Greene had been witness to the initial encounter in the forest during the hunt. While no one knew exactly what was in the wind, it was clear to the senior members of Lady Mallory's household that there was trouble abrewing. And no one liked the idea of an armed bivouac beyond the gates.

"Were you talking about the hunt?" Pippa persisted.

"Aye," Greene agreed. "That we were."

"Did the boar really charge Pen's pony? Did she scream? I expect she did. Was that why her arrow missed?"

Robin, alone on the dais, was beginning to feel self-conscious and rather wishing that he hadn't driven Pippa away when a bustle from the hallway beyond the door in the wooden screen and the accompanying blast of a ceremonial trumpet interrupted the dancing. A procession of torchbearers entered the hall; in their midst walked the cook bearing a great square cake, its surface lavishly decorated with a complete replica of Mallory Hall, its gardens and gatehouse, even the topiary gardens. A miniature pony with a tiny figure representing Pen was riding over the packhorse bridge with the river flowing green and brown beneath.

Pen, flushed with pleasure, abandoned her partner and ran up to the table, Magister Howard wheezing in her wake. "Oh, Master Gilbert, how beautiful!" she breathed as the cook carefully placed the cake in front of her place. "Oh, I can't possibly cut it. We can't *eat* it."

"Of course we can, Pen!" Pippa declared, bobbing up beside her. "What a waste it would be if we didn't. Is it marchpane, Master Gilbert? I do so love marchpane."

"As we all know to our cost," Guinevere said with a half smile. "Master Gilbert, you are a true artist."

The cook beamed his pleasure and handed a knife to Pen. "Just cut it straight down the middle, Lady Pen, and I'll do the rest."

"You have to make a wish . . . make a wish!" Pippa cried, bouncing on her tiptoes to watch the magic moment. "You must wish for something wonderful . . . oh, why don't you wish for a new pony, or . . . or that your hair will go curly . . . or that next hunt you'll shoot a boar . . . or . . ."

"I can make my own wish, thank you," Pen said.

"You have to close your eyes and wish really really hard," Pippa advised, not in the least put out. She fixed her sister with an anxiously critical stare to make sure that she followed instructions to the letter.

A deep rumble of laughter came from Hugh, and Guinevere could feel his shoulders shake as he stood beside her. Pen glanced quickly at Robin who said, pointing, "If you cut straight from here, you won't spoil any of the decorations."

Pen nodded and took up the knife. She placed it carefully on the cake. Closing her eyes tightly she cut down.

"What did you wish . . . what did you wish, Pen?"

"I can't tell you that, it won't come true," Pen told her little sister. She shot Robin a sideways glance and he smiled at her.

"Well, I hope it was something really splendid," Pippa declared. "Such a cake deserves a really special wish, doesn't it, Mama?"

"Indeed it does," Guinevere said. "But you, my child, will have one very small piece. You may have one of these marchpane trees, but that's all for today."

She nodded at Master Gilbert who grinned and said, "I'll see to it, my lady." He took up the cake and carried it away for serving.

"Should the butler bring the fine rhenish, my lady?" Master Crowder in a waft of black gown appeared on the dais.

"Yes, indeed. I for one prefer it with a sweet dish." She glanced pointedly at Lord Hugh as she said in an undertone, "Perhaps you would care to open the flagon and pour it yourself, my lord. That way you could be certain you were in no danger."

Hugh, whose original barb had been intended only to make a sardonic point, said, low voiced and smooth, "I enjoyed the intimacy of our sharing, madam. It added greatly to my pleasure in the feast. I'd be loathe to drink alone now."

Guinevere felt her color rise as indignation warred with a resurgence of tormenting and unruly sensations. He had picked up her glove and, indeed, she had not expected him to do otherwise. But the lightly mocking taunt spoke so readily to her present confusion she was suddenly rendered mute. Did he feel any of this himself? she caught herself wondering.

She had sensed how he had responded to her when he first saw her in the chapel, and womanlike she knew what effect her smile and her soft melodious tones could have. They were the only weapons in her arsenal, and it was a pathetic enough arsenal compared with Hugh of Beaucaire's. But when she used them on this man she seemed to forget what she was using them for. Then just when they both slipped into a moment of ease, as they had while dancing, when her guard was down and she was powerfully aware of the humorous, warm, vibrantly attractive man, the fierce hostility and distrust between them would rise up like a tidal bore, sweeping away anything approaching accord.

She merely inclined her head and returned to her seat, supervising Pippa's consumption of marchpane and cake with a sharp eye. The butler with great reverence withdrew the stopper from the flagon of rhenish and poured it with appropriate solemnity into fresh goblets.

This time Hugh did not cover his goblet. He leaned back in his chair, watching the stream of golden wine glowing in the candlelight as it arced into the delicate crystal. There was enough worth in Venetian crystal on this table to build and fortify a small castle, he reflected. His eye roamed around the hall. The tapestries on the paneled walls were lush, their hues of varied blues and greens, gold, crimson, and silver thick and rich under the torchlight. The tapers on the dais table were wax not tallow and the air was perfumed with the scents of dried woodruff, watermint, and sweet herbs sprinkled lavishly upon the wooden floor.

King Henry's court was renowned for its show; nobles vied with each other to prove their wealth and standing, bankrupting themselves to dress their households in the finest garments. They displayed their possessions with an apparent disregard for their value that they believed only added to their consequence. Hugh had seen many a noble try to hide his wince as a priceless flagon of Venetian crystal was carelessly thrown to the floor on his own orders.

Guinevere Mallory was probably as wealthy as Privy Seal but the display of luxury around Hugh was not done for show. It was part of the woman. Something she accepted as natural. She was not trying to impress him.

He glanced at Robin who was eating cake and marchpane with the dedicated concentration of the perpetually growing, perpetually hungry youngster. Robin would inherit a small estate in Kent, his mother's dowry. Hugh himself, the youngest son of a family of sons, had little of his own. For his service to the king he had been given the lands of Beaucaire in Brittany. They were fertile but not extensive. He had money, the king was generous when he remembered to be, but he hadn't had the time to improve either the estate in Kent or his French lands, and he certainly didn't have the money to acquire the trappings of wealth he saw around him tonight. Compared with the Lady Guinevere, Hugh of Beaucaire was a pauper.

He sipped the rhenish, noting its quality. Which of the husbands had furnished this for the cellars?

"It meets with your approval, Lord Hugh?"

"It's very fine. I was wondering which of your husbands was responsible for this acquisition." His eyes, heavy lidded now, were slits of blue in his tanned face.

Guinevere hesitated, then said, "Lord Hadlow had agents in Burgundy, Bordeaux, and in the wine-growing districts of the Rhine. He taught me much and I buy through the same agents who served him."

"They make wise choices for you," he commented.

"No, my lord, they advise me. *I* make the choices."

"I see." He wasn't sure that he believed her. Women knew little about such things. But then women did not ordinarily write their own marriage contracts and inherit lock, stock, and barrel from their deceased husbands. He touched his lips with his fingertips, considering.

"Did none of your husbands have families who would lay claim to some part of their estates?"

"My lord, I am willing to answer your questions . . . to cooperate in your 'investigation' if you choose to use that term. But not at my daughter's birthday feast." Her tone was clipped.

"Later then?"

"When the children are in bed, if you will come to my apartments I will do what I can to put your mind at rest."

"Madam, I doubt that is within your capability."

"Not if you have already closed your mind to the truth," she said softly.

"My mind is always open to the truth."

She looked at him then, full in the eye, and her gaze mocked such a pathetic defense for his presence under her roof. "Is it, Lord Hugh?"

He was saved from the need to respond by a renewed tucket of trumpets. Pippa jumped to her feet the instant before her sister. "Pen, 'tis your procession! It's beginning. Boy Robin, you have to walk beside

Pen because you're an honored guest and Pen likes you . . . you do, don't you, Pen?" There was a momentary hesitation and then gallantly she continued the exuberant flood. "And I'll come behind you two. Mama will come behind us with . . ." She hesitated, looking at Hugh.

"*I* will walk behind your mother," he said firmly.

"And everyone else will come where they're supposed to," Pippa said happily.

The procession, preceded by trumpets and torch men, wound its way out of the hall, across the lower court, and out of the house. They went over the packhorse bridge, across the meadow under the starlit sky, and back up through the topiary garden that skirted the outside walls of the house.

Once more back in the lower court, Guinevere kissed her daughters good night and dismissed her household with smiling thanks and a generous purse to Master Crowder to be distributed as he thought fit.

Guinevere looked up to where a yellow half moon hung like a cut lemon in the brilliant night sky. She could smell wood smoke and pitch from the bivouac beyond the gatehouse. Slowly she turned to the man standing as still as she behind her.

"It's a beautiful night."

"Aye," he agreed.

" 'Tis a pity to spoil it." She sighed, the long fingers of her right hand twisting the rings on her left. "But that's as it must be. I am going to look in on the girls, then I will await you in my apartment. You will find it above the north entrance."

She turned without another word and Hugh watched the tall slender figure, her rich skirts swaying gracefully around her, cross the lower court and go back into the house. He could scent her perfume lingering in the soft air, but then he wondered if perhaps it was just the fragrance of the rose garden.

He was unaware that he echoed her sigh as he went to check on his men in their bivouac beyond the gates.

4.

The clock in the chapel tower chimed ten as Hugh crossed the lower court. He looked up above the north entrance to the window that overlooked the court. The wooden shutters were fastened back and the soft glow of candlelight filled the window space. A shadow passed across the light, a tall, graceful shadow.

He entered the house through the small door set into the larger one. Sounds came from the kitchens to the left of the passage; presumably the servants were cleaning up after the feast. He turned aside through the opening in the wooden screen into the banqueting hall. There was no residue here of the evening's festivities; the cloth had been removed from the table on the dais, the long trestle tables folded and put away with the benches. The floor had been swept clean of debris and the torches in the sconces extinguished except for two to light the stairs that rose from the far end of the hall.

Hugh mounted the stairs and took the long galleried corridor that led to Lady Guinevere's apartment. He paused outside the heavy oak door listening for the sound of voices. She would have her tiring woman with her. But there was only silence from within. He raised a hand and knocked.

"Pray enter, Lord Hugh."

He raised the latch and opened the door. Guinevere was seated at a table above which hung a small Italian mirror of silvered glass in an elaborately carved and painted wooden frame. Tall candles burned on the table to either side of the mirror. The wicks were scented, filling the air with the delicate perfume of verbena.

Guinevere rose from her chair, turned, and smiled at him as he stood in the doorway. "Pray close the door, sir."

Hugh put his hand behind him and pulled the door softly closed. She was smiling that *damnable* smile again and her eyes were luminous, her skin creamy and glowing in the candlelight, her mouth so warm and full and sensuous.

It was very still in the large chamber, the only light coming from the candles on the table. The walls were paneled in a pale oak, the ceiling ornate with gilded moldings. His eye went involuntarily to the great bed where the pillars were carved in sinuous lines, the bed hangings and coverlet of a rich turquoise tapestry embroidered with great yellow suns. The pillows and the edge of the sheet where it was turned over the coverlet were of whitest lawn. There was no fire in the stone hearth but a copper jug of tumbled golden marigolds brought the scents and sense of summer into the chamber.

"Be seated if you wish." Guinevere gestured to a wooden settle beside the hearth.

Hugh, instead, perched upon the deep stone seat at the window that looked out over the countryside. His voice was harsh, masking his inner turmoil, as he stated, "So Stephen Mallory fell from a window."

"Yes. From that one." Guinevere gestured to the window overlooking the court. "He was drunk at the time as anyone will tell you." She sat down before the mirror again and began to take off her rings, hanging them over the branches of a silver filigree orange tree that sat on the table. Her hands were perfectly steady.

Hugh rose and crossed to the opposite window. He stood looking down at the cobbles below. "I can't imagine how a man could have unintentionally tripped over this sill. It's too deep."

He glanced over his shoulder to the woman sitting before the mirror. Guinevere shrugged slender shoulders. "He was a big and heavy man. Clumsy with drink." Her tone was indifferent as if she cared neither one way nor the other whether he believed her.

She opened a silver box on the table and reached behind her to unclasp the chain of the diamond pendant that nestled between her
breasts. She placed the jewel on the black velvet shelf within the box. It
winked in the candlelight.

Hugh watched, mesmerized in the soft shadowy light of the chamber, his questions stilled upon his tongue. She unfastened the diamond-
studded arc set atop her black silk hood and placed it on the table. All
her movements were languorous and deliberate as if part of an elaborate ritual where each step was sacred.

She unclipped the pomander and the tiny watch from the chain
at her waist and placed them in the box with the pendant. She rose to
her feet and very slowly unclasped the gold chain itself, drawing it
away from her body, curling the delicate links into the open palm of
her hand.

Hugh felt he was losing touch with reality, as if his purpose for being
in this fragrant chamber of soft light and shadow was suddenly irrelevant. He pushed his way through the sensual tendrils she was weaving,
thrusting aside the dreamlike quality of the moment.

"What do you think you're doing?" His voice rasped in the quiet.
He was not asking for the literal answer she gave him.

" 'Tis late, my lord, and I wish to uncoif," she said, sitting at the table again. "Don't let me distract you from your investigation." Her
eyes darted up to the glass, catching his still-riveted gaze as he stood
behind her. For a moment there she had had him; for a moment she
had succeeded in deflecting his questions about Stephen's fall. Would
he ask them again?

She bent her head and slid off the black silk hood, then reached up
to remove the long golden pins of her white coif beneath.

It was too much for Hugh. "God's blood! Where's your tiring
woman?"

"In the inner chamber," she said, gesturing to a door in the far wall.
"I had thought you would prefer it if your questions to me were asked
and answered in private. I'm sure you'll wish to talk with Tilly yourself. You wouldn't like her *evidence* to be affected by what she'd heard
me say. Would you, my lord?" She smoothed the folds of the coif and
stretched sideways to lay it over a stool.

He found he couldn't answer her. Her hair was parted and braided, drawn back over her ears and coiled at her nape. Little tendrils escaping from the braids wisped tenderly over her ears and curled on her forehead.

With the same unhurried movements she drew out the long pins that held the plaits in place, her eyes still fixed on his in the glass. "You have seen a woman uncoif before, my lord?" She raised a chiseled golden eyebrow in faint mockery.

He found his tongue. "There are times when such bedchamber intimacy is appropriate and times when it is not, madam. This I deem to be an inappropriate time," he declared harshly.

Guinevere's soft laugh chimed. "Be that as it may, Lord Hugh, ask your questions of me now. You'll wish to question my household at your leisure, and they will be obliged to answer you as they can, but I will give you this one opportunity to hear me."

Her braids fell unloosened to below her shoulders and she began to unplait them, her long white fingers twisting deftly in the shining white-gold mane. She shook her head and the shimmering mass swung out around her. She reached for an ivory-backed hairbrush and began to pull it through her hair.

Hugh didn't know what he was doing. He moved a hand and clasped her wrist, his brown fingers dark in the mirror against her white blue-veined skin. She released her hold on the brush and he took it from her, beginning to brush her hair with long smooth rhythmic sweeps. Their eyes held in the mirror and for long minutes they were contained in a silence broken only by the soft swish of the brush and the occasional electric crackle from the pale river of her hair.

"You have some skill as a tiring woman, my lord." Guinevere broke the silence, her voice low and husky as she bent her head beneath the rhythmic strokes.

"It's been many years since I've done this for a woman," he replied, his voice as low as hers.

"Robin's mother?"

He nodded.

"She must have been very dear to you."

His hand stilled. He stared at the woman's face in the mirror and as he stared Sarah's face came back to him. A round freckled face with a snub nose and merry brown eyes. So different from Lady Guinevere's sculptured beauty. He had never heard Sarah mock, or taunt, or say an unkind thing. She had not been learned except in the ways of kindness and motherhood, schooled only in the management of a household, but he had loved her.

He dropped the hairbrush and it clattered to the table. The chamber came back into focus and he remembered why he was here, who this woman was. He spun away from her, away from that bewitchingly beautiful face, the brilliant, intelligent eyes.

"So Stephen Mallory fell from that window. Where were you when he did so?"

She turned slowly in her chair to look at him as he stepped away from her. What had happened to break that connection between them? It had been so strong, so real. But now he was regarding her with all the old antagonism and a very real and personal hostility.

"In the garderobe," she said slowly, aware that her palms were clammy, her cool composure reduced now to a facade.

"You didn't see him fall?"

"No." She had almost come to believe it herself, but as she told the lie she felt her foot twitch the way it had as he'd lunged for her. Her ankle tingled as it had after Stephen had caught his foot against it. She resisted the urge to bend and rub it.

"Did anyone see him fall?"

She shook her head. "Not as far as I know. The torch men came running when he cried out, but he was on the cobbles before they reached him."

"He was drunk?"

"He was always drunk. Viciously drunk." She said it simply but there was no disguising the bitterness of her tone.

"Was that why you don't mourn him?"

"Among other reasons." She turned back to the mirror, her hands falling into her lap as she watched his reflection. It was easier somehow than watching him in person.

"And what of your other deceased husbands? Did you mourn them? Or were they also unworthy of such respect?"

"You consider my feelings towards my husbands to be relevant to your inquiry, my lord?"

"I am inquiring into the circumstances of their deaths. Your feelings could provide a motive for those deaths," he observed dispassionately, his shoulders propped against the wall behind her, hands thrust into the deep pockets of his gown. He was master of himself once more, his expression cold and hard.

"A motive for what you intend to prove," she threw at him. "If you discover that indeed I had little love for any of my husbands that will give you a motive and you need look no further. Is that how you and your masters reason, sir?"

"I doubt your motives were as simple as dislike, madam. I believe them to be more venal," he stated.

"You talk as if my guilt is already an established fact. We have not as yet discussed the deaths of two of my husbands." Her tone was sweet as the marchpane on Pen's birthday cake, but her eyes were shrewd and cold. "Don't you wish to question me about those, or is it not worth going through the motions since you've already made up your mind?" She kept her back to him, her hands still lightly clasped in her lap.

"You will have a fair hearing," he said tightly.

Guinevere shook her head. "I know the facts of life, my lord. If Privy Seal intends to find me guilty for his own gain he will find me so. I assume you're merely his instrument . . . the cat's-paw you might say." Now she had really hit home. His vivid eyes burned and he pushed himself off the wall. For a minute she thought he was about to lay hands on her, then he strode instead to the open window over the courtyard. He put one foot on the low sill, resting a hand on his upraised knee.

He said with icy calm, "Be careful, madam. You talk treason. Such statements about Privy Seal impugn his master, the king. Were they to come to Lord Cromwell's ears, he will have your head."

Guinevere shrugged. "If he intends to have it, sir, he will have it on one pretext or another." She turned sideways on her chair to look at him fully. "However, I can see only one way in which they might come to Privy Seal's ears. Only one person heard me. Will you tell tales, Hugh of Beaucaire?"

Somehow she had forgotten in the crisp satisfaction of besting him that she had intended during this encounter to distract him with charm, to try to confuse his responses to her. At the beginning she had begun to do that, but once again the bright knife of antagonism cut the frail accord. And now she didn't care. Anger would distract him as well as sensual temptation.

But Hugh was not to be provoked again. He observed with a mocking amusement, "You have an asp's tongue, my lady. Poisonous enough, I dare swear, to do away with any number of self-respecting husbands. However, if you will accept a piece of advice, when you are questioned in London, you would do well to leave such venom behind. It will not find favor, I assure you."

"On what subjects am I to be questioned?" Guinevere inquired, striving to maintain her own air of mocking indifference despite the fear crawling down her spine at this reminder of the journey that lay ahead if she couldn't hit upon some desperate means to avoid it. It was all very well to play word games and rejoice in a well-placed dart, but it was an empty puerile triumph in the face of the real danger in which she stood.

"That is for them to say."

"And who is it who wishes to question me?"

"The king, for one. The Bishop of Winchester for another. Privy Seal for another."

Guinevere's laugh was low and humorless. "God's grace! Such marked and august attention for a mere widow from the northern wilds!"

"A very *rich* widow," he emphasized softly. "A lady four times widowed. Most conveniently widowed."

"And you are here as Privy Seal's cat's-paw," she reiterated with a bitter scorn fueled now by desperation and fear. "You are here to find what evidence will support the facts that suit you? You think you will gain the deeds to my estate by such means? Good God, my lord! Is your greed such that you would trump up charges against me and bring about my death to get your hands on land that does not belong to you?"

The mocking amusement died. Hugh's expression darkened, his mouth hardened. "My son has legitimate title to that land. If you are innocent of your husbands' deaths, then I will find you so. But if you are guilty, believe me, I will find you so."

"You will find me so because it will suit you to do so," she repeated in the same low and furious voice. "You think I do not know your kind, Hugh of Beaucaire?"

A cool breeze springing up from the Derbyshire hills set a candle on the table flickering. Guinevere leaned forward, cupping her hand around the flame to steady it. Her fingers shook slightly.

"There was an unmarked arrow that killed Lord Hadlow," Hugh said after a pause. "Do you have an explanation for that, my lady?"

She remained with her hand cupping the candle flame. "There were peasants hunting the woods that day. On the first Wednesday of every month, Tim . . ." Her voice caught for a second, then she continued, "Lord Hadlow made his tenants free of the forest to catch what they would for their own larders. He and I and Greene, our huntsman, believed that one of them let loose an arrow by mistake. No one would have deliberately killed Lord Hadlow. He was universally beloved by his tenants. But no one would come forward after he died two days later. Justice is rough, Lord Hugh, as I'm sure you'd agree."

It was true that the penalty for killing a lord and master, regardless of intent, was vicious and absolute. But the explanation struck Hugh as too easy, too pat to be believed without corroboration. He would need to visit the Hadlow lands and question the tenants himself.

"My first husband fell from his horse during a stag hunt," Guinevere said tonelessly. "I doubt he was sober at the time either. I was confined in childbed on that day. A stillborn babe," she added without inflection. "I doubt even Privy Seal could lay that death at my door, unless, of course, I am to be accused of witchcraft."

Hugh said nothing and after a second Guinevere swung round on her chair and her eyes now were frightened. "Am I to be so accused, my lord?"

"The Bishop of Winchester has some interest in discussing such issues with you." He saw the fear in her eyes and despite his hostility he felt compassion for her. There were few accusations harder to refute and few crimes more grimly punished.

"I see," she said in a low voice, turning away from him. "Murder is not sufficient it seems." Her hands lifted from her lap and then she let them fall again. "I bid you good night, Hugh of Beaucaire. I have nothing more to say."

"If you are innocent I will find you so," he repeated. She made no answer, merely sat still on her chair facing the mirror, and after a minute he turned and softly left her.

Guinevere let her head drop into her hands. She gazed into the mirror, her eyes fixed upon her reflection as if she could lose herself in it. *How was she to fight them?*

Then she raised her head and stood up slowly. She would fight them. She would find a way.

The door to the inner chamber opened and Tilly came in. She was in her night robe. "Lord, chuck, I thought you'd never be finished. Such talking at this time of night. Here, let me unlace you."

Guinevere gave herself up to Tilly's deft ministrations and climbed into bed. "Bring me a cup of hippocras, Tilly. I'll not sleep else."

"What is it that they want?" Tilly's eyes were sharp, belying her age. "Those armed men at the gate. This Hugh of Beaucaire. What's 'e after, chuck?"

"He would prove that my husbands met untimely deaths at my hands," Guinevere said with a little shrug.

Tilly seemed to hesitate, then she said robustly, "What nonsense! I'll fetch that 'ippocras now."

She hurried away on her errand but there was a worried frown on her brow. By any lights, it was an awkward business to lose four husbands to such accidents. It was ridiculous to imagine Lady Guinevere could have had a hand in any of those deaths, but it was an awkward business nevertheless. And few men had met a more deserved end than Lord Stephen. There was hardly a member of Lady Guinevere's household who hadn't secretly rejoiced at the end to his drunken, violent tyranny. And no one who had served Lady Guinevere since her childhood would ask too many questions about what had happened that evening in her chamber.

Hugh made his way thoughtfully to the guest apartments in the west wing. The house was quiet now but when he paused at a window in the gallery to look down into the lower court he saw the lights of the torch men stationed at the two far corners of the courtyard. There would have been torch men so positioned on the night Stephen

Mallory fell to his death. They were the first to reach Mallory's body according to Guinevere. Her chamber windows were unshuttered that night and would have been well lit by candlelight.

On impulse, Hugh retraced his steps and went back through the banqueting hall and once more outside. He crossed the court to where the torch man on the southwest corner stood holding his pitch flare. The man looked startled. He straightened from his slouch and stood to attention.

"Can I 'elp, sir?"

Hugh shook his head. "No, I thank you. Be at ease." He stood with his back to the wall and looked up at the window of the chamber above the entrance. The shutters were still drawn back, the glow of candlelight still within. Anyone standing at the window would have been visible to the torch man in this corner.

He made his way to the northwest corner by the arched entrance to the lower court from the driveway beyond. The torch man here regarded him in open puzzlement. Hugh looked up at Guinevere's window immediately above the man's station. The view was obstructed but if he stepped out a few paces from the wall he could see the window clearly. The torch man would have run to the body lying on the cobbles. If he'd looked up from there, the window would have been in full view. As Hugh looked up in frowning thought, the light in Guinevere's chamber was extinguished.

With a word of good night he returned to the house and the west wing.

A candle burned low on the mantel in the guest chamber. Robin was sleeping on the truckle bed at the foot of the big bed but as his father came in he stirred and turned over.

"Is that you, sir?"

"Aye." Hugh bent over him and ruffled his hair. "Go back to sleep, lad."

"Where were you?" Robin linked his hands behind his head. "I waited for you but then I fell asleep."

"I had some talk with Jack, and then some talk with Lady Mallory."

"Oh. I was trying to find something I could give to Pen for her birthday. I thought perhaps this would do." He sat up and reached under his pillow to bring out a green and gold silk kerchief. " 'Tis the one you brought me from Spain, but I thought if you wouldn't mind . . ." He looked anxiously at his father.

Hugh laughed. "No, I think it's a fine use for it. It will suit Pen to perfection."

"Yes, the colors will go with her eyes," Robin said somewhat dreamily.

First love, thought Hugh. Never easy, in present circumstances it was bound to be the very devil. "You enjoyed the feast then?" He shrugged out of his gown and hung it in the linen press.

"Oh, yes, but that Pippa . . ." Robin raised his eyes heavenward.

Hugh laughed again. "Yes, a regular jaybird. But a sweet little maid."

"She chatters so *much*. And she doesn't mind *what* she says. She told me her stepfather was a drunken brute . . . she said she overheard some of the servants saying so. She should know better than to say such ill-considered things, particularly to a near stranger," Robin declared from the superiority of his twelve years.

"I doubt Pippa considers anyone to be a stranger," Hugh observed as he unlaced his doublet. "Which of her two stepfathers was the drunkard, did she say?"

"Oh, yes, Lord Mallory. He used to throw things and shout. She said everyone hated him." Robin yawned and slid back under the covers. "How long will we stay here?"

"A few days."

"Just a few days?" Robin couldn't conceal his disappointment.

Hugh made no answer. He wasn't ready to tell Robin that Lady Mallory and her daughters would be accompanying them to London. It was for Guinevere to explain that to her daughters and her household in her own time. How long the true circumstances of the journey could be kept from the children remained to be seen. But Hugh would not hasten the revelation.

He peeled off his hose, discarded his shirt, and climbed naked into bed. The cool clean linen was soft on his skin. It had been many weeks since he'd slept in a bed. He closed his eyes and the image of Guinevere swam unbidden into his internal vision. Such a mobile countenance, such a graceful figure, such a razor-sharp wit. He could feel her hair rippling beneath his hand as he'd brushed it, each shining strand gleaming white-gold under the candles. He saw the deep cleft of her breasts, the soft white of her skin against her chemise that showed in a delicate mass of lace above the low neck of her gown.

And his body stirred as it had not stirred in many months. It seemed the sheets were imbued with her scent, warmed by her skin. He could almost feel her lying long beside him, the fluid curves of her body alive to his touch.

Had she thus bewitched four husbands? But he remembered the fear in her eyes at the mention of witchcraft, the shadow that had fallen across her face, leaching it of all color. It was the first time he had seen fear, seen through the cool courage to the desperation beneath her apparent composure, beneath the swift antagonism that had met his every dart with one of her own.

Of course she understood her danger.

He threw himself onto his side and pulled the covers up over his ears. Guinevere Mallory had made her own bed. She must lie in it.

5.

'TIS a bad business and no mistake, Master Crowder," Tilly confided, sieving a pan of barley water into an earthenware jug. "What's them folks from London got t' do wi' the likes of us? Askin' questions, pokin' around. That there Jack from the lord's men is askin' in the kitchens all about Lord Mallory, what manner of man 'e was."

Crowder was counting the silverware that had been used for Pen's feast back into the big chest where it remained between ceremonial occasions. "And I daresay he's getting an earful," he remarked. "Good riddance to bad rubbish, that's what I say."

"Aye, but ye'd best not say it too loudly," Greene declared from the far end of the long table in the pantry where he was eviscerating rabbits for the delectation of the hawks in the mews.

"What's that supposed t' mean?" Tilly visibly bristled, her white-coiffed head bobbing vigorously.

"You know what he means, Mistress Tilly," Crowder said, holding up a ladle to the light as he looked for smears. "Four husbands is a lot t' go through in twelve years. It doesn't look good."

"Ye'd best not be suggestin' . . ."

"No, no, of course I'm not. You know full well that I was with Lady

Guinevere's father and her uncle after that . . . just like you, and Greene here. I've known my lady since she was no more than a babe in arms. She wouldn't hurt a fly."

"Unless the fly was about to 'urt one of 'er babbies," Greene muttered. "There was times when I saw murder in 'er eye when Lord Mallory tried to raise an 'and to the little lasses."

"If 'e'd 'ave laid a finger on 'em I'd 'ave taken a skillet to 'is 'ead meself," Tilly stated, setting the jug of barley water on a slate shelf with something of a thump. " 'Twas bad enough what 'e did to my poor lady when 'e was in the drink. There was times when I saw 'er in the mornin', I'd 'ave put rat poison in 'is ale if I'd had 'alf a chance."

"Who's this ye'd 'ave poisoned, Mistress Tilly?" a seemingly jovial voice inquired from the doorway between the pantry and the buttery. Jack Stedman, Lord Hugh's lieutenant, regarded the pantry's occupants with a deceptively benign air.

"None o' your business, my fine sir," Tilly said, her worn cheeks rather flushed. "You an' your lot would do best to get back where you come from and leave respectable folks to themselves."

"Ah, but we're 'ere on the king's writ," Jack said, bringing his large frame fully into the pantry. He stood before the range, one foot on the andiron, surveying his companions genially. "Doin' the king's biddin' like."

"What's the king t' do wi' our lady?" Greene demanded.

Jack shrugged. "That I dunno. I jest does what my lord tells me. An' he's mighty interested in talk of poison an' such."

"Oh, take no notice of a foolish old woman," Master Crowder said. "Mistress Tilly doesn't know what she's saying most of the time. Isn't that so, Greene?"

"Aye," Greene agreed, filling a bowl with the bleeding fruits of his labors. "Poor old soul, daft in the 'ead she is sometimes." He winked at Tilly and shouldered his way past Jack and out of the pantry.

"I'll wager that's not so, Mistress Tilly." Jack grinned at her.

"Oh, I'm daft as a brush most o' the time," Tilly said, picking up the jug of barley water. "Outta my way, now. My mistress is waitin' on this."

Jack stood aside as she went out, then he came over to the table where Crowder was still at work with the silver. "That's a king's ransom," he remarked appreciatively. "I've seen less fine silver on the tables at Hampton Court Palace."

Crowder's gaze flicked upwards. "Y'are telling me ye've sat at the king's table?" he demanded scornfully.

"My master 'as. I seen what I seen."

Crowder made no response and after a minute Jack said casually, "An' what 'ave *you* seen, Master Crowder? From what I 'ear, that Lord Mallory was a right brute. What was all this about rat poison then?"

"Rats in the kitchen court, that's what," Crowder said. "Overrun we are with them. More than the dogs and cats can handle."

"An' ye think poisoning their ale will do the trick." Jack laughed uproariously. "Never 'eard of an ale-drinkin' rat before. But strange things go on in these parts from what folks say." He regarded the steward with a malicious gleam in his pale eyes.

"Oh, is that so, Master Stedman?" Crowder closed the great chest and locked it with the key that hung around his neck. He looked at Jack with undisguised dislike. "A word to the wise. We don't like snoops around here. Even if they are on the king's writ." He brushed at the fox fur edging his black gown with a fastidious air as if removing something distasteful then stalked from the pantry.

Jack looked after him thoughtfully. If they had nothing to hide why did they behave as if they had?

Tilly, carrying the jug of barley water that Guinevere used as a tonic for her complexion, stalked muttering out of the pantry and ran straight into the tall, square figure of Lord Hugh. He was standing, hands thrust deep in the pockets of his short gown of plain gray velvet trimmed with marten, looking idly around the small open court that connected the main kitchens with the pantry and buttery. No one would guess from his casual posture that he had his own reasons for being there. One could pick up a lot of interesting facts by strolling around areas where servants talked freely among themselves. The conversation he had just overheard in the pantry was a case in point. Their reaction to Jack's appearance had been particularly revealing.

"Good morning, Mistress Tilly." He greeted the tiring woman with a smile. "Could you spare me a minute?"

Tilly looked flustered. She propped the jug on her hip and wiped her brow with her free hand. Lady Guinevere had told her household to cooperate with Lord Hugh and his men if they asked questions but Tilly found herself unaccountably anxious under this lord's seemingly friendly brilliant blue gaze.

Hugh continued to smile. "I was wondering if anyone saw Lord Mallory fall from the window. You were not in the chamber with Lady Guinevere at the time, I believe."

Tilly tried to see around the question. What was he implying? "Who said I wasn't?" she asked with a touch of belligerence.

Hugh shrugged. "No one," he said calmly. "I was assuming that Lady Guinevere was alone with her husband at the time."

"I don't know why ye'd think that, sir. I'm 'er tiring woman. I always attends my lady after she's retired fer the night." Her faded eyes shifted away from Lord Hugh's intense scrutiny.

"I see," he said slowly. "Were you there when Lord Mallory fell, then? I understand Lady Guinevere was in the garderobe at the time."

"Aye, that's right," Tilly said, relieved to be able to verify this. She had seen her mistress come out of the privy just after the lord fell. "My lady was in the garderobe." She nodded in vigorous emphasis.

"And you were in the chamber . . . putting away your lady's clothes perhaps?" He raised an inquiring eyebrow. "Maybe you were busy at the linen press . . . you had your back to the window . . ."

"Aye," Tilly agreed. It wasn't a lie to let him believe something that was untrue. She hadn't actually stated that she had been in the chamber at the time, but it certainly looked better if her inquisitor believed that Lady Guinevere had not been alone with her husband.

" 'Tis strange," Lord Hugh mused, "that when I talked with Lady Guinevere about that evening she didn't mention that you were there at the time." He watched Tilly closely.

"Mayhap she forgot," Tilly said. "She was in the garderobe herself."

"Yes, that seems to be agreed," Hugh murmured. "Well, my thanks, Mistress Tilly. Don't let me keep you from your work."

Tilly bobbed a curtsy and hurried off, her heart pounding. She could almost feel his eyes on her back, boring into her as if they would ferret out the truth. She hadn't done anything wrong, she told herself. But it was best for everyone to think that her lady had not been alone.

Hugh turned at the sound of a booted step on the cobbles behind him. Jack Stedman, emerging from the pantry, slapped his hands together as if at a job successfully completed. "Well, that Lord Mallory sounds like a fine piece o' work," he confided. "Used to mistreat his lady summat chronic, so the servants say. No one shed tears when 'e died."

"So I gathered."

"But there's summat else, summat they're not sayin', sir, I'd swear to it."

"Some say too little, others say too much," Hugh commented thoughtfully. "I'd like you to talk to the torch men who were on duty in the lower court the night Mallory died. Ask them what they were doing before their lord fell from the window. Were they looking around, or dozing against the wall? Could they have looked up at Lady Mallory's chamber window? Were the lamps lit? See if you can get them to recall exactly what they saw. And then talk to their fellow torch men and the grooms. They all share living quarters and there may have been some talk, some gossip . . . speculation. See what you can pick up."

"Right y'are, sir." Jack offered a salute and hastened from the court.

Hugh walked across the upper courtyard and through the door in the south wing that led out into the gardens that surrounded the high crenellated walls of the Hall. They were beautifully tended, gravel walks meandering between flower beds and under rose-covered trellises. At the very edge of the gardens the land fell away to the banks of the River Wye and the lush water meadows.

Hugh stood and looked out over the verdant countryside. Mallory land for as far as the eye could see, and farther up the valley would be found the lead-rich lands between Great Longstone and Wardlow. Lands that were Robin's birthright.

Hugh was no lawyer but the lawyers he had consulted in London all agreed that the marriage contract between Guinevere and Roger Needham and its later addendum where he ceded her title to the disputed land were foolproof, as long as the lands had actually been in the

gift of Roger Needham. If it could be proved that they had not been his
to dispose of, then Hugh had a legitimate claim.

But this was proving hard to make. There appeared to be no
documents to bolster Hugh's claim that those estates were the rightful
property of his father's side of the family. But by the same token no
documents had been produced to prove they belonged to Needham. It
came down to two competing and apparently unprovable claims. But if
possession was nine tenths of the law, then the Lady Guinevere had the
advantage. *As she knew damn well!* The woman had left not the tiniest
loophole in her impeccably legalistic documentation.

If he was to wrest this land from Lady Guinevere he was going to
have to find a route that didn't lead through the courts.

He grimaced, hearing again her ringing, bitter scorn as she accused
him of intending to manufacture evidence against her for his own ends.
As if he would ever contemplate such a dishonorable act! But through
his anger at such an insult lurked the uncomfortable knowledge that he
had no need now to do anything more than bring her to London. Privy
Seal would do the rest. Hugh had set the process in motion by bringing
Guinevere's wealth to the notice of the king and his servant. The wheel
would turn without his further assistance and he would gain his reward when the spoils were distributed.

He pulled at his chin as he stared down at the green-brown curves of
the river below. He had not considered there to be anything amiss with
his original action. He had believed in his right to take back his property however he could from a greedy thieving woman who had arrived
at her vast wealth through suspicious means. But he hadn't met Guinevere then. Hadn't seen her with her daughters. Hadn't considered the
human consequences of his actions for the three of them. Names on a
page were so much easier to dispose of than warm living flesh.

But if he could find incontrovertible proof that she had murdered
one at least of her husbands his conscience would lie easy. And whatever she might say she had good motive for widowhood. If she had
done away with Stephen Mallory, it seemed no one of her household
would blame her. But he had detected something in her tone when
she'd talked of Timothy Hadlow that seemed to indicate she had very
different feelings for him. She had spoken of him with regret and admi-
ration. Even love. Hugh had wondered before if she had loved the

father of her children; her bond with the girls was so powerful and deep, it would make sense that she had had similar feelings for the man who had sired them. But there was no denying that Hadlow's death was shrouded in mystery. An unmarked, unacknowledged arrow.

Her household certainly behaved as if there was something to hide. Mistress Tilly had not been in the chamber when Mallory had plunged to his death. Guinevere would have mentioned it. So what had the woman been trying to cover up by pretending otherwise?

On sudden impulse, Hugh swung away from the lush view and strode off along the path that skirted the outer walls of the house and led to the stable block. He could think better when he was active. Robin's company would be pleasant but he had given the boy some tasks to perform in the bivouac that morning. Presumably he had given Pen her belated birthday gift before he set to work. A slight smile touched Hugh's mouth as he entered the stables and called to a groom for his horse.

He was waiting by the water butt, idly tapping his whip against his boot, when an explosion of snarling, growling, snapping brindle and white erupted from a corner of the block. Amid the jagged-toothed, loud, and vicious swirl of fighting dogs rose Pippa's high frantic tones. Hugh caught a glimpse of a red skirt plunging into the fray and his heart leaped into his throat.

He grabbed the full pail beside the water butt and raced forward, hurling the water at the colorful melee. The three lurchers fell back, shivering, jaws slavering. He slashed at them with his whip and they slunk away yelping, tails between their legs.

Pippa scrambled to her feet. Her golden hair was coming loose from her braid and the sleeve of her gown was torn, the hem caked in the dirt of the yard. She was drenched and looked very close to tears.

"They were going to kill him. They always pick on him," she said, sniffing and wiping her nose with the back of her hand, leaving a smear of dirt across her cheek. "He was the runt of the litter and the others always pick on him. Greene won't let me bring him in the house because he's a hunting dog but I'm going to tell Mama he has to."

Hugh was not interested in explanations. Fear fueled anger at her impulsive foolishness. "Have you no sense, child!" He bent over the soaked and tearful Pippa. "Has no one told you *never* to get between fighting dogs . . . or cats for that matter. You could have been torn to pieces." He picked up her arm and examined the skin beneath the ripped sleeve.

"Rolly wouldn't have hurt me," she said, but she looked down at her arm, sufficiently discomfited for Hugh to guess that the lesson had been given before.

"He wouldn't have known what he was doing," he said as severely as before. "I would have expected you to have more sense, Pippa!" He pushed the torn sleeve away from her arm to expose the wound. He could see no puncture marks and his fear receded.

"It's just a scratch," he said. "But it needs tending. It would serve you right if it had to be cauterized."

Pippa put her hand over the scratch, gazing at him with fearful eyes. "It doesn't, does it?"

"That's for your mother to say," he said. "You need to get out of those wet clothes. Come." He took her hand, calling over his shoulder to the groom who led out his horse, "Unsaddle him again. I won't need him after all."

Pippa lifted her scratched arm, peering at it closely. "It won't need cauterizing, will it, sir?"

Relenting, Hugh said as they entered the lower court, "No, I don't believe so."

Her dirty little face lit up. "Oh, I'm so glad! I once had to have a bite cauterized when I was playing with a squirrel. It hurt so much, and my skin was all burned. I cried and cried." She gave a little skip and her shoes squelched.

Hugh stopped on the cobbles. It seemed that the child was about to dismiss her recent experience as casually as she had dismissed others. He had seen men die a most dreadful death from dog bites and he felt a sudden terror at the girl's insouciance. As terrified as if she had been Robin. He bent and lifted her, holding her at eye level. "Pippa, do you understand that an animal's bite can kill you? Do you understand that?" He gave her a little shake in emphasis.

"But if it's cauterized?" she asked hesitantly.

"That doesn't always stop the poison." He held her steadily and her wide hazel eyes didn't avoid his gaze.

"Why?" she asked. "Why is it poison? And why doesn't it work to burn it?"

Trust this little maid to ask questions for which he had no answers. He set her on her feet again. "I don't know. I know only that it's true."

Pippa's nose wrinkled. "I like to know why things happen."

It occurred to him somewhat irrelevantly that Guinevere had probably been just such a perpetually curious child. "We all do," he said shortly, reaching into his pocket for a handkerchief. "Now do you understand what I've been saying?" He wiped her grubby nose with some vigor. "An animal's bite will kill you. Is that clear?"

Pippa nodded disconsolately, rubbing the reddened tip of her nose with the heel of her palm. "But I don't know what to do about poor Rolly."

"Pippa, sweeting, why are you so wet?"

"Mama . . . Mama . . ." Pippa twitched free of Hugh's grasp and ran to her mother who had just emerged from the house. "Rolly was in a fight and I wanted to save him."

"In God's name, Pippa, how many times have you been told not to get between fighting dogs. Let me look at your arm." Guinevere picked up the scratched arm. "Will you *never* learn?" Her anger, unusual and very real, had brought Pippa's tears flowing anew.

"We covered this ground quite thoroughly already," Hugh said quietly. "I hope I've frightened her sufficiently. But I think this time she escaped with a scratch."

Guinevere looked up at him, her expression startled. He smiled reassuringly as if there was nothing in the least out of place in his admonishing *her* child. Of course he didn't know how jealously Guinevere had always guarded her parental role. Neither of her daughters' stepfathers had ever been permitted to interfere in their upbringing.

To her surprise, she found that she didn't object to Hugh's intervention. And that struck her as very strange. He was her enemy and yet she trusted him with the most precious thing in the world—her children. She said only, "I see. Well, it's rarely helpful to go over well-traveled ground. Why are you so wet, Pippa?"

"Lord Hugh threw water over me," the child said, her voice still subdued.

"Over the dogs," he corrected. "You were in the line of fire."

Laughter sprang to Guinevere's eyes. She straightened. "Go straight to Tilly and show her your arm. She will decide what's best to be done with it. And ask Nell to change your gown before you catch an ague. By the way, why aren't you at your lessons with Pen and Magister Howard?"

"Pen's miserable because she quarreled with the Boy Robin about something and the magister tried to cheer her up by reading some of the *Odyssey* to us but I can't understand the Greek . . . neither can Pen or at least only a little but she pretends to . . . so he said I should go out and pick four different kinds of wildflowers and find their Latin names and I was looking for the flowers when Rolly got in the fight." This precisely accurate explanation was delivered in an unpunctuated stream.

"What did Pen and Robin quarrel about?"

"I don't know, I wasn't there and Pen wouldn't tell me." Pippa sounded indignant.

"Go and get dry." Guinevere waved her away and Pippa went off without her customary exuberant step, cradling her arm to her chest. Guinevere watched her go, a soft smile curving her mouth.

"Does she remind you of her father?" Hugh asked abruptly.

Guinevere seemed to consider. "A little, in the sweetness of her nature, perhaps. But Pen is more like Timothy, I believe. She has her feet very firmly planted on the ground."

She shook her head, her smile broadening. "In truth, Pippa is more as I remember myself as a child. Always flitting from one thing to another as new things drew my attention. I was not as indulged, though, so was obliged to learn self-discipline rather more readily than Pippa."

"She's very young yet."

"Yes." Guinevere shrugged. "But I have to admit that even at her age I was translating the *Odyssey* for Magister Howard with some competence. My daughters are not overly interested in scholarship." She sounded to Hugh as if she found this very puzzling. Then she shrugged again. "Pippa's always in some kind of utterly unintentional mischief. I must thank you for your timely intervention, Lord Hugh. I am in your debt."

There was a moment of silence, then he said, "That I doubt, Lady Guinevere." The smile still lingered in his eyes, in the curve of his mouth, but it seemed to have been arrested by something. She felt her own smile fading and swiftly changed the subject.

"What could the children have quarreled about?"

"I daresay we'll discover all in good time."

"Yes, I suppose so." She hesitated, then said rather distantly, "We take our midday meal in the dining room behind the banqueting hall. I trust you and Robin will be joining us."

He frowned. "Last night I accepted your invitation to Pen's birthday feast, but I'll not intrude upon your hospitality any further. During the course of my investigation, Robin and I will bivouac with my men."

And that would deprive her of any opportunity to influence him in her favor just as it would make it hard for her to learn how and where his investigation was progressing.

Guinevere abandoned her distant air and said quickly, lightly, "Oh, come, my lord. You wouldn't deprive Pen and Robin of the chance to make up their quarrel, surely? Besides, don't you think you owe me the opportunity to get to know me? How can you judge my character correctly if you spend no time with me? You must surely convince yourself that I'm capable of murder before you so accuse me."

She smiled, her eyes glowing with that damnable invitation again, and Hugh felt the now familiar confusion when his mind and his physical senses went off on divergent courses.

"Are you afraid getting to know me might compromise your investigation in some way?" she inquired softly when he hesitated. "Do you fear some sorcery, my lord?"

There was no disguising the mocking challenge behind the sweetly voiced question. Hugh felt the sun's heat on the back of his neck; the scent of rosemary and lavender perfumed the air; blue fire sparked from the sapphire broach she wore at the square neckline of her gown where the soft white lawn of her chemise showed. Her hood was of the same ivory silk that lined the slashed and puffed sleeves of her rose velvet gown.

"Perhaps," he said slowly, almost without volition. "But I doubt I'll fall victim, madam."

"How will you know if you hide beyond my gates?" She laughed, softly and melodiously, and her eyes still challenged him even as they invited him. "I find it faintly ridiculous that when men fear a woman they call her sorceress."

It was not a challenge Hugh of Beaucaire could resist. It stung him even as it enticed him. "I will accept your hospitality, madam, if only to prove to you that I conduct my investigations without prejudice," he declared.

Guinevere laughed again and there was no disguising her disbelief. "My lord, you come here with extreme prejudice; you owe me the opportunity to change your mind."

His eyes narrowed. "You are welcome to try, my lady." He bowed.

"Then we have a bargain." She held out her hand, the rings on her long slim fingers sparkling in the sun. He remembered how she'd removed the rings the previous night, one by one, hanging each one upon the branches of the little silver orange tree on her table. She had taken them off with all the languid sensuality of a woman removing her garments.

His scalp tightened. If the Lady Guinevere wanted to play this game, she would find she had drawn a worthy opponent. He took her hand and raised it to his lips, his eyes holding hers as he kissed her fingers with slow deliberation.

And Guinevere, who had felt so much in control of the exchange, suddenly realized that the reins were slipping from her grasp.

She said with a light laugh, "There is something quite deliciously *piquant*, I think one would call it, about offering hospitality to the enemy. Don't you agree, Lord Hugh?"

"And something equally piquant about accepting it, my lady," he returned blandly. "If you'll excuse me, I must search out Robin before we dine. He had some tasks to perform this morning, I would make sure they are done."

"Of course. We'll meet at noon." Guinevere swept him a curtsy, her rose velvet skirts fanning around her, then she turned back to the house.

Hugh remained where he was for a minute. Of course he didn't fear her. Fear was no rational response to a woman who was quite simply unlike any woman he'd ever known . . . a woman who ran her own life in the way that men did; a woman who took what was hers and, if he was right, what was not hers, with the same ruthless skill as Privy Seal. He didn't fear her.

But she excited him.

It was an acknowledgment he would rather not have made. With a brusque shake of his head Hugh went off to the bivouac in search of his son.

Robin was sitting on the ground in front of Hugh's tent assiduously polishing a breastplate. He looked up and gave his father a rather tense smile as Hugh strode into the small encampment.

"What's amiss, Robin?" Hugh said cheerfully. "You look as if you lost a crown and found a groat."

"Oh, 'tis nothing, sir." Robin rubbed vigorously at the dull metal.

"Did Pen not care for her birthday gift?" Hugh asked, bringing up the subject in a roundabout fashion. He wouldn't want his son to know that his quarrel with Pen was common knowledge. He sat on a canvas stool beside the boy.

"She liked it . . . or she said she did," Robin mumbled. He laid aside the breastplate and took up Hugh's massive sword belt with its great silver buckle. "Should I wax the leather, sir?"

Hugh stretched his legs and rested his hands on his thighs. "If you think it needs it. But why the long face, my son?"

Robin shrugged. "Pen says that the land we're claiming doesn't belong to us. She says it's her mother's."

Ah, so that was it. It had to come sometime, Hugh supposed. He said matter-of-factly, "Well, that's hardly surprising. She would agree with her mother. But my quarrel with Lady Guinevere is not reason enough for you and Pen to fall out."

"But we did," Robin said flatly, dipping a cloth in a container of beeswax. "I would be loyal to you, sir, as Pen would be loyal to Lady Guinevere. How could it be otherwise?"

"Oh." Hugh pulled at his earlobe thoughtfully. "That is very commendable of you both, and certainly understandable. You should discuss it over dinner. See if you can't come to some agreement about the annoying vagaries of parents."

Robin grinned even as he looked up from his work in surprise. "Are we to stay in the Hall then? Even though you and Lady Guinevere are at odds?"

"Lady Guinevere has invited us to do so." Hugh reached over and ruffled Robin's nut-brown curls. "Even when one is at odds, one can behave in a civilized manner as you and Pen will no doubt work out for yourselves. I see no reason to sleep upon the hard ground when there's a soft bed on offer. We'll have enough of tents on the journey back to London."

He rose to his feet. "Finish the belt and then wash yourself for dinner. If we're to sit with the ladies we must make an effort to be presentable."

6.

M agister Howard, would you mind giving the girls leave this afternoon? I have need of your counsel." Guinevere spoke softly from the door of the small chamber that served as schoolroom.

The magister looked up from his book. "Indeed, my lady. My wits are as always at your disposal."

Guinevere nodded. "Aye, Magister. Your wits and your learning. I have need of both at present." She smiled at Pen, who was sitting across from the magister. "That's a pretty kerchief, Pen. I don't recall seeing it before."

Hot color flamed in the girl's cheeks. She touched the kerchief that she wore pinned to her sleeve. " 'Twas a present, Mama. A birthday present from Robin."

"And a very handsome one," Guinevere said warmly. "The lad has an eye for color it would seem."

Pen's blush deepened but she avoided her mother's smiling look.

"Pippa tells me you and Robin have quarreled," Guinevere said. "It's close on noon and perhaps we should talk about it before Robin and his father sit at table with us."

"You would receive them *again*, Mama!" Pen exclaimed, jumping to her feet. "Last night it was my fault, I know. I invited them because I didn't understand properly why they'd come. But I *never* want to talk to him again."

Magister Howard rose somewhat stiffly from the table and left the chamber, a book beneath his arm.

Absently Guinevere picked up the small knife the magister used for mending pens and began to sharpen the quill that lay beside the inkwell. "It's uncomfortable, my love. But we must be courteous. It serves our purpose better to be so."

Pen said hotly, "Why would they lay claim to *our* land?"

"Because they believe it is theirs," her mother answered simply.

"But it's not."

Guinevere heard the sudden hesitancy, the questioning note behind the declaration. She said carefully, "At present it's debatable, Pen. At the time my first husband ceded it to me, he believed as did I that it was in his gift. But as yet I haven't been able to produce absolute proof that it was. I see no reason to hand it over without a fight just because Lord Hugh comes out of nowhere to claim it."

"But is it *ours?*"

Guinevere repeated gently, "Sweeting, at this point I can't discover a legal way of proving to whom it belongs. But I *am* trying."

Pen stood up, her hazel eyes intense. Both her daughters had their father's eyes, Guinevere thought, the shadow of the old grief touching her anew.

"But why won't you just give it to them, Mama? You have lots of land," Pen demanded.

"Why should I, Pen? Just because they come with great trumpets blaring and a show of arms, should I meekly yield something that legally could as well be mine as theirs?"

Pen chewed her lower lip and Guinevere saw by the ragged condition of her lip that the child had been chewing and nibbling for several hours.

"Magister Howard is good with the law," Pen said finally.

"Yes. He taught me what I know."

"I wish he hadn't!" Pen said suddenly. She pushed a stool aside and ran from the room, brushing past her mother who still stood at the table, the knife and quill in her hand.

Guinevere laid down the knife and quill. She couldn't blame Pen. The child was ten and yet older than her years in many ways. She had known, as Pippa had not, what hell her mother had endured with Stephen Mallory. Pen had been Stephen's preferred victim. Pippa had always eluded him. Guinevere had protected her daughter at her own expense, and she knew that Pen had understood that, however hard her mother had tried to insulate her from that knowledge.

Maybe Pen believed that if her mother had submitted herself to Lord Mallory, if she'd behaved as women were supposed to behave, then the bad things wouldn't have happened.

Guinevere sighed. She and she alone had picked Stephen Mallory for her fourth husband. The responsibility for that choice was only hers. If she'd known what kind of man he was, she would never have entertained his suit.

But she had Mallory Hall. In the end she had Mallory Hall. Pen would eventually understand that a woman could take care of her own.

And then she wondered how, even for a minute, she had forgotten that she was about to lose everything she had striven for. That if she didn't do something her daughters would lose their mother, be disinherited, thrown upon the mercy of the king's council. What price learning, determination, a willingness to fight for one's own, now? Hugh of Beaucaire would get the land one way or another. And yet she would not, *could* not, give it up without a fight. She would find a way to assert a legal claim so that if he took the land he would know he had stolen it. The knowledge of ill-gotten gains should diminish his triumph.

"That Lord Hugh and 'is men 'ave been snoopin' around askin' questions, my lady," Tilly announced when Guinevere entered her bedchamber a few minutes later.

"I warned you they would be." Guinevere poured barley water from the jug into a shallow bowl. "You have only to tell the truth, Tilly." She dampened a soft cloth in the barley water and held it to her cheeks. It was cool and refreshing and slightly astringent.

"Aye," muttered Tilly, bending her head over her mending.

"Is something wrong?" Guinevere, patting under her eyes with the cloth, turned towards her tiring woman. Tilly didn't seem as composed as she usually was.

Tilly shook her head and muttered, "I don't know what's to be done about that Pippa."

"Oh, Pippa!" Guinevere shook her head in agreement. "Did you dress her arm?"

"Aye, I put a poultice of mallows on it and bound it up. If I thought it would do any good I'd have cauterized it just to teach her to keep away from the dogs."

"No, you wouldn't have done," Guinevere said with a smile. She dropped the cloth into the bowl and went to her mirror, leaning forward to peer at her reflection. She thought she looked heavy-eyed, her complexion somehow dulled. Hardly surprising in the circumstances, she reflected.

She straightened with an almost unconscious sigh. She could think of one possible way of saving herself and the girls, but it was desperate enough to be considered only as a last resort.

The chapel clock struck noon and Guinevere hastened to the door. "I'll be working with Magister Howard this afternoon, Tilly. Would you watch Pippa for me. She can practice her embroidery. I don't want her running around with that arm in case it becomes inflamed."

"Aye, not that she'll take kindly to sittin' still," Tilly returned.

"You'll manage to persuade her." Guinevere laughed and left the chamber, but her expression became somber as she closed the door. Tilly had not seemed herself. It wasn't just concern for Pippa; Tilly always took the children's misadventures in her stride. Was it something to do with Hugh and his questions? It was understandable that the household would be disturbed by the newcomers and their undeniably menacing presence. Such an investigation would be bound to cause dismay and trepidation.

Occupied with these thoughts, Guinevere had to force a smile of greeting when she met Hugh and Robin downstairs, just entering the house. Robin bowed punctiliously, Hugh stepped aside so that she could precede him through the screen into the banqueting hall.

"That's a very pretty kerchief you gave Pen for her birthday, Robin," Guinevere said. "Such lovely colors."

Robin blushed. "I hope she likes it, madam."

"She was wearing it when I saw her just a few minutes ago." Guinevere opened the door to the more intimate family dining parlor at the back of the great hall. It was an oval chamber, paneled in warm mahogany with a big bay window opening onto the garden. Hugh glanced up at the beautifully molded ceiling, its panels painted with flowers in deep, vivid colors. Stephen Mallory may have been a brute, but it seemed he had some artistic leanings. Unless, of course, the decorations reflected his widow's taste, which seemed more likely.

His eyes rested on the straight slim back as she walked in front of him, her elegant velvet skirts swaying around her. He noticed for the first time the length of her neck, and he had a sudden image of that white neck stretched upon the block on Tower Hill . . . of the headsman's axe raised. Sweat suddenly beaded his forehead and he closed his eyes to dispel the image.

Pen and Pippa were already standing by their stools at the table with the magister; Master Grice, the household chaplain; and Master Crowder, who always ate with the family.

Pen didn't look at Robin but her cheeks were a little pink. She gave her mother an anxious glance, wanting to say something about what had happened earlier but unwilling to speak in front of everyone else. Guinevere smiled and gave her a little nod of reassurance and Pen visibly relaxed.

Pippa flourished her bandaged arm and announced importantly, "See what happened to me, Boy Robin. I got scratched by a dog and your father threw water all over me."

"There was good and sufficient reason for doing so," Hugh stated aridly. "However you seem none the worse for it. Does your arm pain you?"

Pippa frowningly examined the limb in question as if debating her answer. "Just a little but I think it's because Tilly bandaged it very tightly so it throbs."

"This afternoon you must sit quietly with Tilly," Guinevere said, standing at the carved chair at the head of the long table. She invited Hugh to take the chair beside her. "Robin, you will be next to Pen. Master Grice, we will hear the benediction."

It was an unnecessarily long grace to Hugh's way of thinking but it gave him time to reflect that Guinevere's fate was not in his hands. If she'd sent Stephen Mallory to his death, she must pay the price. The law which she manipulated for her own ends was a two-edged sword.

Pen cast Robin a sidelong glance as he took the stool beside her when the interminable grace had ended.

"Are you still quarreling?" Pippa inquired with interest. "What did you quarrel about?"

"It was nothing to do with you," Pen said.

"No," agreed Robin, presenting a united front to the inquisitive Pippa. He offered Pen a tentative smile and she returned it shyly, moving her sleeve so that the rich colors of the kerchief caught the sunlight slanting through the unshuttered window.

"And it's all finished with now anyway," Guinevere stated firmly as she saw Pippa's mouth open in protest. "Master Crowder, we'll broach a flagon of the burgundy, since we have guests."

"I'll drink no wine, my lady," Hugh demurred. "I have need of a clear head this afternoon."

Guinevere thought of Tilly's troubled air and turned to look at him, a cool smile flickering over her lips, her eyes blatantly mocking. "Of course one must keep one's wits about one when questioning kitchen maids and scullions . . . I, on the other hand, will take wine, Master Crowder. I too have need of my wits this afternoon and I find a little wine merely sharpens them."

The air seemed to crackle. Pen and Robin glanced at each other, and then Hugh smiled blandly. "We are all different, madam. A matter for gratitude rather than otherwise, don't you think?" He raised an eyebrow.

"It certainly makes life more interesting," returned Guinevere, taking up her napkin. Servants moved forward to fill the horn cups with ale and set the meat on the table, and the tension eased. It was a simpler meal than the previous night's feast but it was still lavish in the variety and number of the dishes.

"So, whom are you intending to interrogate this afternoon, my lord?" Guinevere inquired, her voice low, her conversational tone belying the inflammatory word. She sipped her wine and smiled at him.

"I intend to interrogate no one," he responded quietly in the same tone, laying several thick slices of mutton on a bread trencher. "But I do intend to *talk* with various people. I've already had some conversation with your tiring woman, although I would like to talk further with her later." He watched her, watched for some sign of wariness, of discomfort, but her expression gave nothing away.

So he had questioned Tilly. And something about the questions had upset the tiring woman. Guinevere continued to smile placidly through her racing thoughts. Tilly had been far away in some other part of the house when Stephen had fallen. She had had nothing to do with that evening. There was nothing she could tell Lord Hugh that would be relevant to his inquiry. She believed Guinevere had been in the garderobe, she had seen her come out. No one would suspect the moment when Guinevere's foot had caught her charging husband's ankle.

But had she done it on purpose? It was a question that had haunted her since that night. And it was one to which she could find no honest answer.

Hugh went on, "I would have some speech with Master Crowder, if that's possible?" He looked down the table at the steward who was noisily supping broth. Hugh raised his voice slightly and said, "Will you be able to spare me a few minutes, Master Crowder?"

Crowder set down his bowl. His expression was immediately guarded. "I can't think how I can be of help to you, my lord."

"No, but I can," Hugh said coolly. "And the magister too. You will be free, I trust, later this afternoon, Magister Howard?"

"I am working with my lady, sir," the magister said, his brown eyes sharply assessing in his thin intelligent face. "When she no longer needs me, I could be available."

"After vespers then," Hugh agreed with a pleasant smile. "If that will suit Lady Guinevere."

Guinevere's smile was tight. She was aware of Pen's anxious look. She said, "You have the king's writ, my lord, not I."

"How true," Hugh agreed.

"What's the king's writ?" Pippa asked, her eyes shining with curiosity. Her sister too looked intently at her mother.

Guinevere hesitated. How to answer the question without frightening the children? "The king's authority," she said. "Lord Hugh is here with the king's authority. You could say he has been commanded to come."

"Did the king tell him to take our land?" Pen demanded.

"No, Pen, the land in question is merely a matter of a legal dispute between your mother and myself," Hugh said. "Such disputes are not uncommon as your mother will tell you. It's certainly not something that should trouble either you or Robin or Pippa. Isn't that so, Lady Guinevere?"

"Yes, indeed," Guinevere agreed, wondering how he could be so seemingly sensitive to the children's anxieties while coldly contemplating taking their mother, their home, their future away from them. The man was an enigma, a confusing mélange of paradoxes. A ruthless, cold, calculating individual with a warm, merry smile, a wonderful sense of humor, and such an easy confidence with children . . . how could a man who so obviously loved children, who in turn trusted him without question, be the heartless arm of the terrible Lord Privy Seal?

How could such a man cause the tiny hairs on the nape of her neck to lift, the little pulse in her belly to beat, when his brilliant eyes met hers? How could such a man remind her of the glories she had shared with Timothy Hadlow?

She set down her wine cup with a hand that was not quite steady and said, "I must ask you to excuse me, Lord Hugh. I have much to do this afternoon." She rose from the table and everyone automatically rose with her. "Please don't let me interrupt your dinner. Magister, I'll be in my inner chamber when you're ready. Pippa, you must find Tilly as soon as you've finished eating."

She left the dining parlor with measured step, ignoring her small daughter's incipient protest, and went to her own apartments knowing that as always she would find peace and distraction in her books. Her step quickened with her mind as she anticipated the excitement of finding the legal answer she sought to her present problem.

The inner chamber was her workroom. A sparsely furnished room with a long table piled with books, some leather bound, some with wooden covers and silver or gilt binding at the corners. There were also pamphlets, printed for the most part in English. Of all Guinevere's possessions, her books were the most potent evidence of her wealth, and the source of her legal knowledge that furnished that wealth.

She bent over the books, looking for the tome containing the Statute of Uses.

There was a scratch at the door and without looking up, she called, "Pray enter, Magister."

The magister came in, rubbing his hands together so that the dry skin rasped like sandpaper. "How can I assist you, my lady?"

"I had a sudden thought," she explained somewhat distractedly. "If Roger Needham's ownership of the lands he ceded to me after our marriage appears in the public record then no man can cause it to be put aside. Isn't that so, Magister?"

"That is so." He came over to the table. "But it is not so registered, madam. If it were, Lord Hugh could not make his claim."

"Yes, I know that, but if I can argue from the Statute of Uses that intent was clear . . . Ah, here it is." She lifted the heavy book and carried it over to the high reading pulpit that stood beside the deep window embrasure. The magister followed her and together they pored over the tome.

"See . . . it says here: If circumstances prevented registration but intent to register can be proven, then the ceding may be considered under the Statute of Uses to have been legally binding on all parties. See." She pointed with a well-manicured fingernail at the Latin. "Have I read it aright?"

Magister Howard peered closely, his lips moving soundlessly as he read. After a minute he pronounced, "It would appear so, my lady."

"Good," Guinevere said. "Now, Roger Needham came into possession of the land through his first wife, who was a distant cousin of the same branch of the family as Lord Hugh's father. When she died the land fell to the survivor, her widower. Lord Hugh is claiming the land for himself because he maintains that the widower was only entitled to hold the land in his lifetime. He had no right to cede it to a second wife. But if the land Lord Hugh is claiming is actually mentioned by name in the premarriage contracts between Roger Needham and his first wife and there are no stipulating articles about its disposal, then that would indicate intent to make that land over in perpetuity to Roger Needham, and the Statute of Uses gives him the right to dispose of it how he wishes."

Magister Howard adjusted the laces that tied his black cap tight over his head. He pursed his lips and considered the argument, sucking at his cheeks in a manner that made him look like the giant carp in the fishpond and always made his pupils struggle with suppressed laughter. Guinevere was hard pressed even now to contain her amusement. But she had too much respect for his learning and intelligence to hasten his opinion despite her impatience.

Finally he spoke. "It could be so argued, my lady."

"Good. Now all we have to do is look up the premarriage contract and pray that the land is named."

She went over to an iron-bound chest that stood against the far wall and knelt on the floor to open it.

Hugh leaned casually against the stone mantel of the fireplace in the steward's small office behind the pantry. "Thank you for sparing me the time, Master Crowder."

"My lady said we were to assist you, my lord," the steward said stiffly. He shuffled his feet with every sign of impatience and looked up pointedly at the brass clock on the mantel.

"I won't keep you long," Hugh said. "I have but one question at this point. Where were you at the time Lord Mallory fell from the window?"

Crowder frowned. It seemed an innocuous enough question. "Why, I was in here with Mistress Tilly."

"Mistress Tilly was here with you?" Hugh asked quietly.

"Aye. We were talking about the evening. There'd been guests for dinner and much drinking. Lord Stephen had been . . ." His expression darkened and he shrugged. "Not to speak ill of the dead."

"Quite so. Although that doesn't seem to be the general attitude. It seems freely acknowledged that Lady Guinevere's husband didn't treat her with due respect and consideration."

"That he didn't." Two spots of color glowed on Crowder's angular cheekbones. "A saint she is. She bore it like a saint. I've known my lady since she was a baby. When Lord and Lady Ashbourne died and left her an orphan, her uncle, Lord Raglan, was appointed guardian and she moved under his roof. I went with her, with Greene and Mistress Tilly. We were her household in Lord Raglan's castle, and when Magister Howard was made her tutor he joined us. We occupied one wing of the castle and Lord Raglan, who was a widower, left us pretty much to ourselves. I doubt my lady saw her guardian more than twice a year, on her birthday and at Christmas. When Lady Guinevere was married to Sir Roger, we all accompanied her."

"I see." Hugh nodded and straightened from his relaxed posture. Crowder had painted a bleak picture of Guinevere's lonely childhood. It was no wonder she had sought solace in learning and company in her books. "So when Lord Mallory fell from the window, you and Mistress Tilly were in here. Did you hear anything?"

"Oh, aye. We heard the scream," Crowder stated. "Mistress Tilly shrieked, ' 'Tis my lady!' and ran to my lady's chamber. Lord Mallory was in foul temper that night and as drunk as we'd ever seen him. My lady had angered him at dinner and we were all afraid of what he might do."

"Did she often anger him?"

"She wasn't afraid of him. And she wouldn't let him touch the lassies. Wouldn't let him go anywhere near them," Crowder said with emphasis.

"With good reason, it would seem."

"Oh, aye." The steward nodded firmly.

Hugh nodded just as the chapel bell rang for vespers. "I thank you for your time, Master Crowder."

"You won't find any here who'll say a word against my lady," Crowder said, gathering his black gown around him. "Not even on the rack."

Hugh flung up his hands in disclaimer. "I trust you don't think I've come armed with such instruments."

Crowder looked at him with unmitigated suspicion. "We don't like snoops, my lord, and that man of yours has been asking questions all afternoon in the stables. I won't say he needs to watch out for himself on a dark night, but he's not making any friends." With that, he rustled out of the door.

Hugh exhaled softly. Threatening one of the king's lords on the king's writ was treasonable. Either these Derbyshire folk had little understanding of the power and reach of the king's authority or their love for their mistress gave them a foolhardy courage.

However, Crowder had confirmed Hugh's suspicions. Mistress Tilly had been lying about that night. But why, if Stephen Mallory's death had been a drunken accident, did the tiring woman think she needed to pretend that Guinevere was not alone with her husband at the time?

Hugh left the steward's office and made his leisurely way to the chapel as the bells continued to peal.

"My lord . . ." Jack Stedman called out as he came hurrying through the arched gateway into the lower court.

Hugh stopped. "What is it, Jack?"

Jack looked to be bursting with news. He ran to Hugh, panting breathlessly. "Some information, my lord. Important information."

Hugh glanced over his shoulder at the chapel. The bells had stopped ringing. The noon grace had been sufficient religion for Hugh for one day but the young could benefit from a second dose. Robin would have to stand in for him at the observance this evening.

Hugh nodded to himself. Age had its privileges. "Let's go to the camp. You may tell me in private."

He strode out of the Hall with Jack at his side. They walked too quickly for conversation as they crossed the packhorse bridge and left the grounds through the stone gatehouse. The smell of the cooking fires was pungent in the warm air of early evening.

A trestle table set for supper stood under a spreading beech tree and Hugh drank deeply from an ale jug before saying, "So, what is this information, Jack?"

"Well, I was talkin' to the torch men what were in the court the night the lord fell. One of 'em let slip that he seen someone at the window jest afore the lord fell, an' then 'e seen a shadow there right after."

"Did he say who it was?"

"No, 'e clammed up when I pressed 'im. Said as 'ow 'e could've been mistaken."

Hugh pursed his lips, frowning in thought. "Where was the man standing?"

"In the southwest corner of the court, sir."

That was the corner where Hugh had stood and looked across to Guinevere's open window. He had had a clear view of the lamplit window. "Go and fetch this man, Jack. I would have speech with him myself. He might be more persuadable if he finds himself summoned for questioning."

"I'll take a couple of men with me, make it look more official like," Jack said.

Hugh perched on a fallen log and stretched his legs out in front of him. The picture was beginning to draw itself. Guinevere had said she was in the garderobe when her husband came in. If it could be proved that she was lying, that in fact she'd been beside her husband at the window, then he would have sufficient justification for carrying her to London to answer a charge of murder.

Jack and his men reappeared in twenty minutes escorting a scared-looking youth in rough homespuns. "This 'ere's Arthur," Jack said. "Where d'you want 'im, m'lord?"

"Take him to my tent."

"I ain't done nothin' wrong," the youth protested.

"No one said you had," Hugh responded. "I just have a few questions for you. Answer them truthfully and you may go on your way. But I'll know if you're lying so don't try it," he added with a ferocious frown. "Deceiving the king's envoy is treason and if you're lucky you'll only hang for it."

The young man trembled, his face ashen; his eyes full of dread blinked rapidly as he gazed at Hugh like a cornered animal. The punishment for treason for any but a nobleman involved hideous mutilation at the hangman's hands.

Hugh gestured towards his tent and two men grabbed the youth's elbows and marched him off. Hugh disliked using intimidation to achieve his object but he didn't shrink from it when it was expedient. He followed his men and their prisoner.

"Now, tell me exactly what you saw the night of Lord Mallory's death. You were standing in the southwest corner of the lower court, is that correct?"

"Aye, sir." The young man nodded like a marionette in the hands of a demented puppeteer.

"You were looking up at Lady Guinevere's chamber?"

The nodding continued.

"And . . ." Hugh prompted, folding his arms and fixing the youth with an intent stare.

"Well, I see'd summat at the window," his quarry mumbled.

"Something or some*one*?"

" 'Twas a shadow."

"Of what?"

There was a long silence and Hugh found it in him to feel sorry for the youth. "Come now," he said brusquely. "Has someone told you not to tell what you saw?"

Arthur shook his head, then nodded, then shook it again.

"I am confused," Hugh said aridly. "Yes, or no?"

"I think I saw my lady at the window," Arthur said in a rush. "It was 'er shadow. I thought nothin' of it because she often stood there in the evenin' jest lookin' out. An' then after my lord fell I saw the curtain move an' jest a bit of 'er shadow again. I *think* it was, but I can't be certain like." He stared fearfully at his inquisitor. "Greene said I should forget it . . . 'e said I never saw any such thing."

Greene, the other member of Guinevere's household who had been with her from early childhood, had joined the closed ranks around their lady, Hugh reflected. And again the question arose, why, if it had been an accident, were they creating this web of lies?

"All right, Arthur," he said. "You may go."

Arthur scuttled off, shoulders hunched, head down.

Hugh walked to the tent opening and stood there gazing around his orderly encampment. His men were at the supper table and after a minute he decided to join them. It was time to confront Guinevere with his findings and he would not, Judaslike, break bread with her first.

7.

Robin wondered where his father was. He looked covertly over his shoulder at the back pews in the chapel in case Lord Hugh had slipped in after the service had started, but the familiar figure was not to be seen.

Robin felt a stab of anxiety. His father was always very careful to tell him if his plans had changed or if he was to be delayed, but he hadn't been seen since the noon meal.

Robin had spent the afternoon finishing off his tasks with the armor and then, finding that Pen had been freed from her tutor for the afternoon and Pippa was closeted under the guardianship of the tiring woman, he and Pen had walked dreamily and mostly tongue-tied along the riverbank among the water meadows. He'd picked her a bouquet of pale pink marshmallows. A bouquet, wilting a little now, that she still wore pinned to her gown.

"Where's your father?" Pippa's penetrating whisper under the cover of her hand chimed accurately into his thoughts.

He shrugged and Pen murmured, "I expect something delayed him."

"Perhaps he went hunting, I hope he didn't fall from his horse . . . or get lost in the woods," Pippa said in the same piercing whisper. "It happened to—"

"Hush!" Pen hissed as Master Grice paused in the litany to glare repressively at the youngest daughter of the house.

Guinevere, coming out of her intent reverie, added her own glare from the box pew across the aisle and Pippa subsided, nursing her bandaged arm.

Guinevere's mind was not on vespers. She was still riding a wave of what she admitted was unholy pleasure in the afternoon's legal gymnastics. The disputed land was clearly named in the premarriage contracts between Roger Needham and his first wife. Guinevere had triumphed in this battle and Hugh of Beaucaire would be forced to acknowledge it. The fact that her victory was probably moot since there was a lot more at stake than a legal wrangle was one that in her present exhilaration she chose to ignore.

She glanced around the lower court as they came out of the chapel at the end of the service and couldn't conceal from herself the flicker of disappointment that there was no sign of Lord Hugh's powerful frame. "Is your father not supping with us, Robin?"

"He didn't say anything to me, madam." Robin looked embarrassed at his father's unexplained absence. "Usually he tells me if his plans have changed. I expect he had some unexpected business to deal with."

Guinevere nodded. "Yes, I'm sure. Should we wait supper for him?"

Robin shook his head. "No, he wouldn't want that, my lady. He wouldn't wish to cause any trouble."

Oh, really? Guinevere kept the cynical comment to herself.

"I hope he didn't get lost and fall from his horse like Josh Barsett," Pippa said. "You remember, Mama, how no one could find him and he lay for hours and hours before the charcoal burner found him and his leg was all swollen up and blue? They thought they were going to have to cut it off only—"

"Yes, I remember," Guinevere interrupted dampeningly. "But Robin's father, unlike Josh Barsett, knows the back end of a horse from the front."

"Oh, I didn't mean to say anything bad about the Boy's father," Pippa assured hastily. She turned anxious eyes to Robin. "I didn't mean to worry you."

But Robin was so amused at the absurd picture of his father falling off a horse that he only grinned and tugged at her braid in brotherly fashion. "I didn't hear a word you said. I'm learning not to listen to you."

"That's very rude," Pippa said. "It's not my fault that the words just tumble out all by themselves."

"Well, maybe if you put food in your mouth it'll keep the words in," Guinevere said with a smile. "Let's go in to supper." She swept Pippa before her into the house.

As supper drew to a close, she cut off Pippa's minute and stomach-turning description of a lurcher raiding a vole's nest along the riverbank, swallowing squealing baby after squealing baby, "Just like little pink sweetmeats . . . all made of marchpane." Pippa held up a marchpane-covered plum as example.

"I think we've heard enough," Guinevere said firmly, turning to Robin. "When you see your father, Robin, could you tell him that I'll be walking in the garden in an hour if he's able to join me?"

Robin nodded vigorously. "Oh, yes, of course, madam. I'm sure he's in the encampment."

As soon as supper was over, Robin hurried to the bivouac.

Hugh was chewing reflectively at a chicken drumstick when his son raced into the circle of tents. He took in Robin's breathless haste, his flushed cheeks, and said sharply, "Is all well?"

Robin skidded to a halt in front of his father. "Yes, sir. I was worried, though. We missed you at supper."

"There was no need to worry." Hugh smiled at his son. "I'm quite capable of taking care of myself, you know."

"Yes, sir." Robin grinned.

"I'll make my apologies to Lady Guinevere later." Not that the lady would be interested in such mundane apologies when he'd confronted her with his evidence of her lies, Hugh reflected.

Robin pushed a flopping lock of hair off his damp forehead. It was a warm evening and he'd run fast. "She said I was to tell you that she'll be walking in the garden in an hour if you could join her."

Hugh glanced up at the sky. The sun was low on the horizon; in about an hour it would have set completely. He nodded, his expression grim. "As it happens I have certain matters to discuss with Lady

Guinevere myself. We'll move into camp tonight. Do you go back to the house and pack up our traps. Take one of the men to help you carry the trunk here."

Robin hesitated. "Are we . . . are we leaving, sir?"

"Yes," Hugh said shortly. "As soon as may be. Go about your business." He threw the clean drumstick onto the grass and brushed off his hands in a gesture of dismissal.

Robin hurriedly obeyed, leaving his father to pace the grassy circle around the campfire, hands thrust deep into the pockets of his gown, while he waited for the sun to go down.

He wasn't looking forward to the coming interview. To his surprise he took no satisfaction in having been proved right. Guinevere Mallory had done away with a drunken violent brute who probably deserved what he'd received. But Hugh of Beaucaire carried the king's writ, and his own sympathies, if such they were, were not relevant.

He watched Robin racing like a young colt back to Mallory Hall, one of Hugh's men following at a more sober pace. Now Robin would inherit rich land that would enable him to establish his own dynasty. Such wealth would give him access to court, to the favors that brought high place, influence, and yet more wealth. Robin would not have to be the soldier of fortune his father was.

And the land, God rot, did not belong to Guinevere Mallory. It had not been Needham's to cede away.

The outcome was just.

Guinevere strolled through the rose garden, a basket over her arm, scissors in her hand. She paused now and again to smell the fragrance of the flowers as she cut them, to gaze out over the sweet landscape lying now under dusk's shadows. The sound of cooing came from the dovecote; behind her rose the mellow stone walls of the Hall.

She couldn't lose this. She couldn't lose it at the whim of a greedy king and a rapacious Privy Seal. There had to be some justice in the world.

From the moment she had understood the joys of an analytical mind and could read and speak Latin as well as the common tongue, she had become fascinated by the law. Under Magister Howard's able tutoring she had learned the legal rules and rotes of justice. She *believed* in justice. It was the cornerstone of her world.

She could not in law lose what was hers simply because someone else desired it.

And yet she knew that she could. Justice was a movable feast in King Henry's England.

The scissors slipped on the tough stem of a white rose in bud and nicked the tip of her finger. She sucked at the bead of blood, tasting its saltiness. What was losing her land compared with losing her life?

She heard a step behind her. A familiar step, firm and yet light. A usurper's step.

The step of a man who could make her blood sing.

"Lord Hugh." She turned, a taut smile on her lips.

"Have you pricked yourself?"

"No. The scissors slipped. 'Tis nothing." She put the basket of roses on a stone bench beside the path.

He pulled a kerchief from his pocket and without asking permission deftly dabbed the blood from her finger, observing calmly, "For some reason, fingers bleed out of all proportion to the wound."

"Yes, I've noticed." She watched his own fingers, brown, thick, strong, yet so astonishingly neat in their movements. She could feel the warmth of his touch on her hand, a tactile, malleable warmth like melted candlewax.

Then abruptly he dropped her hand. "We have matters to discuss, madam."

She opened her mouth to speak but he swept on, his eyes never leaving her face.

"Ever since I arrived here, you have lied to me. I am surrounded by lies. Those I speak to twist and turn the facts in an effort to conceal the truth."

Guinevere was now very pale. "What truth, my lord?"

"The truth that you pushed your husband from the window."

"Who so accuses me?" Her lips were bloodless.

"I do. Your tiring woman says she was in the chamber with you and Stephen Mallory that night, but your steward tells me she was with him in his office. You tell me you were in the garderobe when Mallory fell, but one of the torch men saw you standing at the window both before and immediately after your husband's death. If you were not implicated in his death, why am I being lied to?"

Fury now made her complexion ashen. She understood now why Tilly had been so distressed. Her eyes were purple fires in her white face. "You have dared to bully my servants! I told them to cooperate with you, to tell you what they knew. There was nothing for them to hide. You must have terrified Tilly into lying to you! You go creeping around like some viper trying to trap *my* people, people who are loyal to me, who've been with me since childhood, you try to trap them into betraying me." Forgetting the scissors she still held, she jabbed at him in emphasis.

Hugh grabbed her wrist. "In the devil's name, what do you think you're doing?"

She looked down at her captive hand and slowly her fingers opened; the scissors dropped to the ground. "I didn't realize I was still holding them."

"I'm to believe that?" he demanded scornfully. "Four dead husbands and then you attempt to stab me!"

"Oh, don't be ridiculous!" Still livid, she glared at him, twitching her wrist free of his hold.

There was a moment's silence as Hugh acknowledged that he *was* being ridiculous. Guinevere had had no intention of stabbing him. He said more moderately, "Perhaps you could explain why you said you were in the garderobe when it seems that you weren't."

"What did the torch man see?"

"You."

Guinevere shook her head. "How could he be so certain? Or did you use some *persuasive* techniques to get him to say what you wanted him to say." Once again her voice dripped scorn. "We both know you weren't intending to leave here without the evidence you sought."

Hugh's lips thinned. "That tune grows wearisome. The man saw you at the window both before and after Mallory's fall."

"And he saw me push him, did he?"

"No. But the implication is clear."

"Do you have any idea how large Stephen was, my lord?" she asked in a tone of mild inquiry. "I'm not a small woman, I agree, but compared with my husband . . ." She gave him a rather pitying smile. "Anyone who knew Stephen will tell you that he was a very tall man, running to fat but still very strong. He was a drunkard and often unsteady on his feet. When he lost his balance after too good a dinner, which happened on several occasions, again as any member of my household will tell you, it was like trying to right a fallen oak. I would not have had the strength to push him out of the window."

But a well-placed foot to a flying ankle could do the job just as well. She pushed the thought aside and faced him with that same pitying smile.

Hugh's conviction wavered. "*Were* you at the window?" The light had faded now in the fragrant garden and he could barely see her face.

She turned away from him to look out over the shadowed countryside below. She was very still, her tall body erect. She said softly, "Yes."

"Then why did you lie?"

She turned back to face him, her face a pale glimmer, her eyes so dark as to be almost black. "It was a harmless enough untruth. I wanted to avoid any mutterings in the countryside. Folk around here are inclined to superstition and they love gossip. To lose four husbands could be considered careless, after all." Her voice took on a sardonic edge. "Didn't you and your masters come to that conclusion yourselves?"

It was not an unreasonable explanation, Hugh reflected. He stood looking at her, trying to read her mind. There was still something she was hiding, he would swear to it. Was she a greedy and acquisitive murderess, or simply a brilliant scholar who put her learning to work in protecting her financial interests? He had no conclusive evidence of her involvement in any of the deaths and yet she had had both motive and opportunity in at least one of them.

"So, Hugh of Beaucaire, are you going to arrest me?" The sarcastic edge to the challenge grated on him.

"It's not my place to do so. It is, however, my place to escort you to London where others may make that determination. We leave at sunup the day after tomorrow. You will be ready."

So soon. Would she have time to make her move before then? She thought of the document tucked in the rose basket that she had intended to flourish with such triumph. The document proving that

Roger Needham had had the right to cede the disputed land to his second wife. Much good would such an empty triumph do her now.

Guinevere's expression was calm, showing none of her panicked speculation. She would not give him that satisfaction. "I can't promise to be ready so soon."

"You will be ready, madam," he repeated. "It's already past midsummer and I'll not risk being still upon the road when the days grow short."

"I presume I may bring my own servants," she said distantly.

"You may. But they must be provisioned and prepared to take care of themselves. My camp cannot supply a domestic household. I can accommodate you and your daughters and a woman to assist you. Anyone else must make their own arrangements."

"I will discuss it with the senior members of my household," she stated, her mind racing as she examined and discarded possibilities.

Hugh nodded. "As you wish. I understand they've been with you since you were orphaned as a child. As long as you can pay their way, I have no objections."

"Until I'm rendered a pauper I can pay their way," Guinevere said, making no attempt now to disguise her bitterness. Hugh of Beaucaire would expect her to be distressed and bitter, and if he was not to suspect she had other plans, she must give him what he expected. "I shall need the magister in London to help me with my defense, always assuming I'll be permitted to make one."

Hugh had a sudden picture of what awaited her in London. *What was he doing? Conspiring in the downfall of this woman and her children?*

A cloud that had obscured the moon drifted away and the garden was bathed in silver moonlight. Her upturned face had a translucent beauty as she threw her challenge at him. And it happened to him again, that bewildering sensation of losing his balance, his focus, so that he was certain of nothing but a confused swirl of emotion. His arrested gaze was fixed upon her face and he saw that she had read his expression, that she had seen the abrupt unbidden surge of desire in his eyes. Her pale cheeks took on a touch of color, her lips parted on a tiny exhalation, and her eyes were luminous.

Without volition, he bent and took her mouth with his own. For a moment the world receded. His hands spanned her narrow back, pulling her against him, and her mouth opened beneath his. He tasted her warm richness as her tongue explored his mouth; he inhaled the fragrance of her hair and skin. His senses spun and as she leaned into him her body quivered with her own responding desire. Their tongues moved in a greedy dance of passion and she sucked on his lower lip as if it were a ripe plum.

Then she broke away from him. The passion died slowly from her eyes, a strange horror taking its place as she stood looking at him like a cornered fox; then she was gone, her swift step crunching on the gravel as she hurried back to the house, the graceful folds of her dark hood swaying behind her.

Hugh touched his mouth, then he swore beneath his breath. An oath of frustration and confusion. *How had that happened?*

Absently he plucked a rose from the bush beside him, heedless of its thorns as he stared back at the house, its windows aglow with lamplight. One by one he pulled off the petals of the rose and they dropped to the ground at his feet.

How had that happened?

Guinevere's hands shook as she gathered up her skirts and almost ran up the stairs to her own apartment. *How could it have happened?* It was as if they'd been bewitched; some wand-waving fairy had thrown a magic circle around them. A circle that excluded all bitterness, all enmity, all desperation.

She closed the door of her chamber with a slam and stood leaning against it as if barring the way to a horde of pursuing demons. She was breathing fast and her mouth still carried the memory of that kiss. She lifted her hands and watched them quiver. Her entire body was thrumming, arousal still pulsing in her loins, and she wanted to weep with terror and frustration.

Tilly jumped up from her sewing stool and threw up her hands, sending needle and thread to the four winds.

"Ay! Ay! Ay! What's happened! You look as if you've seen a ghost."

"No ghost, Tilly." Guinevere moved away from the door, taking a deep steadying breath. "The devil maybe." She went to the window looking down into the court. The torch man at his post in the southwest corner glanced up and then looked hastily away. She turned back to the room. "Why did you feel you had to lie to Lord Hugh?"

Tilly looked stricken. "I don't know, dearie. It seemed best to say that you weren't alone with Lord Mallory. I thought it best."

"It wasn't necessary." Guinevere put a hand on the elderly woman's shoulder. "But I know you meant well."

"Oh, mercy me! Did I cause you trouble, chuck?"

"I don't think it made any difference really," Guinevere replied with a little sigh. "The outcome was always going to be the same whatever anyone said."

She took up a candle from the table and when she next spoke her voice was strong and commanding. "We have a lot to do. Will you fetch the magister, Crowder, and Greene. I need to talk to you all in the inner chamber."

Tilly bustled away and Guinevere entered her inner chamber. She lit candles from the one she held in her hand and then sat in a folding leather chair at the table. Her hands fell limply to her velvet lap and she closed her eyes, composing herself.

Those she had summoned appeared in a very few minutes, their expressions grave and attentive. Hugh of Beaucaire's real reason for being at Mallory Hall was no longer a secret from them, although they kept their knowledge from the rest of the household.

"Lord Hugh expects us to leave for London at sunup the day after tomorrow," Guinevere said without preamble. "I don't need to tell you what will happen if we're forced to go to London." Heads nodded solemnly.

"So I must put myself and the girls out of reach. I intend to remove secretly to the house at Cauldon that was left me by my father. I don't see how Lord Hugh could possibly find us there, I'm sure he doesn't know it exists."

"Aye, my lady. I doubt anyone knows," Crowder said. "It's not been visited in years." He shook his head reflectively. "There's no knowing what state it's in."

"There's a caretaker, isn't there?"

Crowder looked a little embarrassed. "Aye, but I've not looked in on him for a while, Lady Guinevere. There's so much else, so many other estates to—"

"Yes, I understand," she interrupted briskly. "And that's all to the good. Cauldon is a forgotten and neglected house close to a day's ride from here. No one will think to look for us there."

She paused for a minute, then said, "I should like you all to go with me." She looked at each somber face in turn. "But I will understand if you feel unable to face such an exile. We'll not be able to live as we're accustomed." She gestured around the chamber, a gesture that encompassed more than the signs of wealth and comfort visible in their immediate surroundings.

"God's blood, chuck!" Tilly exclaimed. "You think we'd leave you and the lassies?"

Guinevere shook her head at the chorus of protestations from the others. "You must think carefully. Privy Seal has a long arm. I hope that by leaving him in possession of most of my land and fortune, he'll not look too hard for us. But I can't be certain of that."

"We'll not let you go alone," Crowder said simply.

Relief flooded her. Now she could manage. She smiled gratefully. "I can't tell you how much that means to me. Indeed, I don't see how I could manage without you."

"Well, my lady, 'ow's this to be done then? Wi' Lord Hugh an' his men at the gates, 'ow are we t' give 'em the slip?" asked Greene, getting down to business in his customary forthright fashion.

"I've been thinking, and I don't see how we can get away from this house without detection. So this is what we will do. The girls, Tilly, and I will start this journey with Lord Hugh. I'll tell him that the rest of you will need more time for preparations, provisioning, and such like, and will follow us as soon as possible. I'll try to persuade him to take the Derby road instead of the route through Chesterfield, which would take us far from Cauldon. On the Derby road we should be close to Kedleston by the end of the second day. That will put us within a night's ride from Cauldon."

She glanced around to see how her plan was being received. There were nods of agreement. She continued strongly, "As soon as we leave, Master Crowder and the magister will take all we need to establish

ourselves at Cauldon. Greene, I'll need you to follow us at a safe distance. When we camp on the second night, near Kedleston, we'll make
our escape. I don't know exactly how as yet, it'll depend on how Lord
Hugh sets up his camp. But I'm confident we can do it."

Guinevere was aware as she spoke that she was very far from confident of this last most vital link in her plan, but it was all she could
come up with.

"Aye, an' I'll be waitin' fer ye," Greene said, needing no further explanation of his role.

"Yes, we can't travel without armed escort, particularly at night. If
we escape undetected we should reach Cauldon before we're missed at
daybreak. If we muffle the horses' hooves they'll make no sound as we
pass through the villages on the way and with luck no one will be
aware of our passing."

"Aye, and I'll bring up the rear, sweeping our tracks as we go,"
Greene said. "A good thick branch'll do the trick."

"We'll have vanished like wraiths," Guinevere declared. "Gone in
the night without trace." She nodded. It was as good a plan as she was
going to come up with.

"And what of my part, Lady Guinevere?" inquired the magister,
leaning forward anxiously, scratching his beaky nose.

"You must take care of the books," Guinevere said simply. "You
will know how best to pack and transport them."

Magister Howard sucked in his cheeks in his carp imitation as he
considered the issue, then he nodded. "Aye, I can crate 'em, I believe."

"Then that's all." Guinevere smiled around at them. "I am truly
grateful to you all." She rose to her feet and went to a corner cupboard.
She took out a leather flagon and a two-handled goblet and came back
to the table with them. "Let us drink to the success of our enterprise."

The wine was plum-dark, strongly fortified, and saved for the most
important occasions. She filled the hanap, took a sip, then passed it to
the magister.

They all drank in silence, all aware of the risks they were about to
take. If the enterprise failed, they would all stand accused of treachery
for aiding and abetting the escape of one who traveled to London on
the king's orders to face the charges of Lord Privy Seal and the might of
the State.

8.

W e're going to London . . . we're going to London . . ." Pippa chanted as she danced down the long gallery. "Isn't it exciting, Pen?" She turned around and danced backwards as she called to her sister who was following rather more slowly.

Pen was not so sure. While the prospect intrigued her and she felt a peculiar little tingle when she thought of spending so much time in Robin's company, she had detected something troubling behind her mother's cheerful announcement of the coming adventure.

Her mother had sent for them to her inner chamber, a formality she reserved only for the most important matters. She had been smiling when they'd entered somewhat apprehensively, and she had certainly made it seem as if the journey would be one of great excitement as well as very educational. She had explained how she had to go to London to argue her claim over the disputed land in the courts. Lord Hugh and his men would provide the escort they needed for such a journey. She had said how much they would enjoy London. Although she had never been there herself, she had read so many descriptions of the great river Thames, the hustle and bustle of the streets, the grand mansions of the nobles, and King Henry's great palaces at Greenwich and Hampton Court and Whitehall. They would see them all, she had promised.

But Pen had seen the shadow behind her mother's smile. It was the same shadow she used to have when Stephen Mallory was rampaging through the house. And it had been absent since his death until Lord Hugh and his men had arrived. Pen still didn't understand why her mother chose to go to all this trouble just for some land that they didn't need. They had more than enough of their own.

"Well, say something, Pen!" Pippa demanded, interrupting her sister's reverie. "You haven't said how exciting it's going to be."

"You're such a child!" Pen snapped.

Pippa looked hurt. "So are you!"

"*I'm* not always babbling."

"But don't you want to be with the Boy? All those weeks riding together. Surely you want that." Pippa put a cajoling hand on her sister's arm. "I won't get in your way, really I won't."

Pen grinned reluctantly. "Yes, you will. You won't be able to help it. Come on, Mama wants us to help Nell pack up our clothes."

"We won't have to have lessons with the magister while we're journeying," Pippa said gleefully. "Surely you're pleased about that, Pen."

Pen was still too much of a child not to be pleased at the prospect of no lessons, but she knew her mother would miss the long sessions in her workroom reading with the magister. One couldn't really read on horseback, and the magister was such an indifferent horseman himself he wouldn't be able to think of anything but staying upright. Pen couldn't help a little chuckle. The magister on a horse looked just like a sack of wet flour. Her mother would have to rely on Lord Hugh for adult conversation.

The chuckle gave way to a tiny frown scrunching the girl's pale eyebrows. Sometimes it seemed as if Lord Hugh and her mother were quite friendly. They laughed at the same things sometimes, and there seemed to be a warmth between them. But at other times it seemed they hated each other. She knew Robin was as confused as she was, but it wasn't something they talked about. It had been bad enough when they'd quarreled over the land dispute. Of course she would take her mother's side, and of course he would take his father's. Since then they'd silently agreed never to mention the subject. But could they manage not to on such a long journey in such close company?

Such close company. Weeks and weeks of it . . . A shiver ran down her spine, but it wasn't caused by alarm, or anything else bad.

Pippa was prancing ahead again, unconcerned that Pen hadn't answered her question. There could be only one answer anyway.

"Wait for me!" Pen called and picked up speed to catch up with her exuberant sister.

Alone in the inner chamber, Guinevere paced between the windows, her hands unconsciously cupping her face. Had she managed to convince them there was nothing to worry about? Pippa, yes, but perhaps not Pen.

Well, there was little else she could do to reassure them for the moment.

She returned to her chamber and examined her reflection in the glass. Little lines crept around her eyes and her pallor seemed excessive. Excessive enough for some help. She opened the small pot of dried and powdered geranium leaves, dipped a finger into the water in the ewer and dabbed up some of the red powder. She brushed it lightly on her cheekbones, then smoothed it in with a dry fingertip. It gave her a slightly rosier glow. Her teeth, thanks to the twice daily vigorous application of dried sage leaves, gleamed white when she smiled.

She brushed a finger over her lips and they seemed to come alive with the physical memory of that kiss. She could taste his mouth on her tongue. The muscles of her sex tightened and her belly seemed to drop. *Lust.*

Timothy.

She spoke his name under her breath and it was a cry for help. How could she weave her way through this deadly skein when lust reared its head? Once before she had yielded to the glorious seduction of pure passion, and that had led to the deep wonders of loving fulfillment.

She missed it so much. Such an ache of longing for what had been. Not a day passed when she didn't think of Timothy . . . see him in some expression, some gesture of one of the girls, hear his voice, his laugh in her head. And at night she would feel him in her dreams.

Lust that led to the deep wondrous satisfactions of love.

Lust for Hugh of Beaucaire would lead only to the scaffold.

Guinevere smoothed down her skirt of dark red silk. She adjusted her coif, white beneath the charcoal-gray hood. She touched the pearl pendant at her throat. Then she went to do battle with Hugh of Beaucaire.

She found the steward in his office. He was making lists of provisions. "Master Crowder, I would have speech with Lord Hugh. Would you send a servant to summon him?"

Crowder knew his lady and knew she was putting her plan into action. It was in the set of her head, the martial gleam in her eye, the crisp well-modulated tones. He'd never seen her fail yet.

"Master Robin is hanging around outside the northwest entrance, madam. Should I suggest he request his father's presence?"

"Is Pen with Master Robin?"

"No, madam. But I think he's hoping she might be soon."

"We're going to have to pick up some pieces there, Crowder."

"Aye, m'lady." Crowder nodded. "But Lady Pen's as sensible as they come."

"True enough, but first love . . ." Guinevere shook her head ruefully. "Send Robin for his father, then. I'll receive him in the hall . . . No, wait." She put up a hand at a sudden thought.

Crowder paused expectantly. "I'll go to him myself," she said, her eyes narrowing. "It would be a good opportunity to take a look at his encampment, see how things are arranged. It might give me some ideas as to how we can arrange our escape."

"I was thinking, madam, it would be best to employ servants for the new house from the Cauldon area," Crowder said. "If we took people from here someone might let something slip."

"Yes, I'd thought of that myself. If Lord Hugh decides to search for us, he's bound to come back here first. No one must have any idea where we might have gone." She gave Crowder a smile designed to reassure herself as much as the steward and walked out into the bright sunny lower court. She left the house through the northwest door and saw Robin sitting on the stone wall of the packhorse bridge, looking disconsolately back at the house.

"I give you good day, Robin," she greeted him cheerfully. "The girls are busy packing for the journey tomorrow. There's much to do. But I'm sure Pen would be happy to talk with you for a few moments if you go into the house."

Robin looked yet more disconsolate. "My lord father, madam, says I mustn't disturb you today. I thought I'd wait and see if maybe Pen came out for a walk . . . or something."

"Well, why don't you take the path around the side of the house that goes through the gardens. You could stand under the girls' chamber window and look conspicuous," Guinevere suggested. "The window's bound to be unshuttered on such a lovely day. I'm sure Pen'll look out once in a while. And even if she doesn't, Pippa certainly will."

Robin grinned. "I wouldn't really be disturbing anyone, would I?"

Guinevere shook her head. "I don't think your father would consider a mere stroll in the garden to be disobedience. Is Lord Hugh in the camp?"

"Aye, madam. He's making preparations for the journey with Jack Stedman."

"I trust he's not too occupied to talk with me," she said easily, turning away towards the stone gatehouse.

Her heart was beating uncomfortably fast as she approached the circle of tents set about a hundred yards from the gatehouse. How would he behave after last night? She was determined to act as if she had no recollection of what had happened. She would be cool in her manner as befitted a prisoner with her jailer, and quietly determined in her demands.

She had the sense that so long as those demands were reasonable, Hugh would accede to them. He was far too confident, far too naturally commanding, to need to prove his present power over her by making her life on the journey any more difficult than it had to be, and she knew in her blood that he was not a cruel man. No one who treated children with such a natural warmth and humor could be all bad. But this reflection did nothing to still her heart's pounding. If she could decide that her anxiety was simply about the situation she was facing, then it would be a lot easier to deal with. But she couldn't blind herself to the truth.

There was an atmosphere of orderly bustle in the camp. Her eyes swept the scene, noticing how the horses were kept hobbled in a rudimentary stockade to one side. They were not guarded, but would they be on the journey? She must take belladonna in case there was a guard who must be put to sleep. Tilly would be useful there. She had a knack for striking up conversations. In her motherly fashion she would soon put a man at his ease and off his guard.

"Lady Guinevere?" Lord Hugh's pleasant tones sounded behind her and she spun round with a little gasp. She hadn't expected him to appear from that direction. "My camp is honored indeed."

His expression gave nothing away but she thought she could detect a lingering warmth in the brilliant blue gaze bent upon her, just the residue of a curve to his mouth, as if he'd surprised himself by being pleased to see her.

"There are some matters I would discuss with you, Lord Hugh."

"Why did you not send for me?"

"Prisoners do not in general send for their jailers," she returned.

The warmth sprang to full life and the curve became an amused smile. "Are you determined to be provoking?" he asked mildly. "I won't be provoked, madam. I am in far too good a humor."

"Oh? And what brought that on?" Immediately she regretted the question.

His eyes narrowed. Slowly he moved a hand and placed his fingers over her mouth, like a blind man reading sensation. "A memory I don't seem to be able to lose," he said softly. "Why did it happen, Guinevere?"

She would not, *could* not take this path. "I don't know," she said in an exasperation that was only part genuine, but was directed as much at herself as at him. She turned her head aside so that he dropped his hand. "And I would rather not talk about it again. It was moon madness."

He shrugged and the light faded from his eyes so that they took on the cool hue of pewter. "As you please. What are these matters we have to discuss?"

"The details of the journey. I find that Master Crowder, Magister Howard, and Greene cannot be ready to leave in the morning."

"So . . . you leave them behind." He spoke as if it were a foregone conclusion.

"No, I do not," she said steadily. "You have decreed a very abrupt departure, my lord. There are estate matters that must be addressed. I can't leave an entire household without money or orders." She regarded him with a mocking smile. "Of course, I realize that someone else is going to take over Mallory Hall, some absentee landlord. But it won't happen immediately and my people must not suffer from my absence."

Hugh pulled at his earlobe. "So what do you suggest, madam?"

"If you insist . . ." She paused, infinitesimally but significantly . . . "Then Tilly, my daughters, and I will be ready to leave with you at sunup tomorrow."

"I do so insist." With a gesture, he invited her to continue.

"My household will follow us as soon as the arrangements have been made. Provisions for the journey, for instance. They shouldn't have any difficulty catching up with us, we won't be able to ride too fast with the girls."

"Very well." He inclined his head in acknowledgment.

"I need to know the route you intend to take, my lord."

"We will go through Chesterfield."

"It makes better sense to take the route through Derby," she said. "You're not particularly familiar with the roads in this county?" She raised an eyebrow.

"We came through Chesterfield. It seemed a sensible route."

"The road through Derby is more traveled and the surface is better," she said firmly. "It will be easier for my people traveling with carts of provisions to catch up with us if we take the Derby road."

She turned aside for a minute, then said in a voice that sounded stifled, "Lord Hugh, I must have the magister at my side in London. It will take him at least a day to crate the books I'll need. Surely you'll not deny me the chance to defend myself."

"That was never in question." Hugh had the feeling that more lay beneath this conversation than was apparent, and yet he couldn't identify it. Everything she said made sense, and he had no brief to deny her right to defend herself. If she needed books and her mentor he wouldn't keep them from her. "You know the county better than I, madam . . . by the bye, Matlock is on the Derby road, is it not?"

"Yes, indeed."

"Mmm," he murmured. Passing through Matlock would enable him to make some inquiries into Timothy Hadlow's death. Even though he had sufficient cause to accuse her of Mallory's murder, and he only needed one murder to bring her to Privy Seal, the circumstances of Hadlow's accident, if such it was, intrigued him. As indeed did the circumstances of Guinevere's marriage to Hadlow. He would like to discover whether it had been considered happy, and there would be tenants in Matlock and the surrounding countryside who would know things, and who would certainly have opinions.

"Very well," he said with a brisk nod. "We will take the Derby road."

"Then I'll tell my people that they should try to catch up with us when we break the journey at Kedleston," Guinevere said, her voice calm. "I assume you'll permit us to rest for a day every so often? My children can't be expected to ride day after day without respite. Every second day, they'll need a break."

"I had assumed as much," Hugh said. "But when and where we break the journey will be for me to decide. It'll depend on weather conditions as much as anything else."

"My daughters are not campaigners," she said tartly. "You cannot expect from them what you expect from Robin."

"I understand that," he said quietly. "You need have no fear that I'll expect more from them than they can manage."

No, she thought. Whatever else she might fear it wasn't that. She offered him a neutral smile. "I thank you, Lord Hugh, for your understanding."

Hugh nodded, then said in a different tone, "What have you told Pen and Pippa?"

"What I imagine you've told Robin." Her voice was sharp.

"There's no need for them to be alarmed," he said in awkward agreement.

"Isn't there, my lord?" Her eyes defied him to deny it. "Have you thought for one minute what will happen to my children?"

She turned in a swirl of dark red silk and walked away.

Hugh swung away into camp. He would take her daughters. He would fight for them in the proxy courts and he would win them. But how could he say that to Guinevere? Telling her that he had made determination for her children was tantamount to agreeing that she was about to end her life on the scaffold.

Just before dawn the next morning Hugh rode into the lower court. He sat his black destrier, one hand resting on the hilt of the sword at his hip, as he looked around at the bustle of departure. Two men were strapping wooden trunks onto the back of a packhorse. Grooms held Guinevere's milk-white mare, two ponies, and a sturdy mule. The mule was presumably for the tiring woman. It looked strong enough but it would slow them down. The ponies were of good blood, but they too wouldn't have the speed of his own horses, or, indeed, of Guinevere's beautiful mare. And once the servants with their carts of provisions and books joined them the procession would slow even more.

He had close to two months to make the journey before the shortening days of autumn. He was going to need all that time, Hugh reflected grimly. Heading up a combination of nursery and traveling library was a far cry from commanding a brigade of hard-riding soldiers.

He glanced up at the lightening sky. His horse shifted beneath him, sensing his rider's impatience. Hugh wanted the business over and done with. He was wrenching a woman and her children from their home, and he had no wish to drag out the process.

Guinevere appeared from the house. She was with the magister and Crowder and did not immediately acknowledge Hugh's presence.

Guinevere knew he was there, though. It was impossible not to be aware of him in the early-morning gloom. He was such a . . . such a *substantial* figure, she thought, groping for the right word to describe him. Substantial, powerful . . . she could well imagine he inspired fear and awe in his men, and the mental image of him with drawn sword on a battlefield sent a shiver down her spine.

With that cropped iron-gray hair beneath a flat black cap, the piercing light of his brilliant blue eyes, his square shoulders accentuated by the leather doublet he wore beneath a short gown of gray worsted, he struck her as a veritable Genghis Khan, raiding and dispossessing innocent women and children. Even if she succeeded in escaping him, she was still going to be driven from her home, reduced to relative penury, condemned to lose everything she'd worked so hard for, to spend the rest of her life in some form of exile. It was a recognition bitter as wormwood.

"We'll be waiting for you at Cauldon, my lady," Crowder said in a whisper.

"God willing," she returned. "Where are the girls?"

"They wanted to say farewell to the dogs," the magister told her.

Guinevere glanced across at the man on his horse. She could feel his impatience from here. "You'd better send someone to fetch them, Crowder." She walked slowly towards the massive destrier. "Lord Hugh, you're anxious to complete this dispossession, I see. 'Tis not yet dawn."

He looked down at her, noting how pale and composed she was. But there were bruised shadows beneath her sloe eyes. She was wearing the gown of emerald green silk that she'd been wearing when he'd first seen her hunting in the woods; the same dark green hood with its jeweled edge set well back from her forehead revealing the pale shimmer of her hair.

"I see little point in delaying the inevitable, madam."

"No."

"Mama . . . Mama . . . is it time to go?" Pippa's voice preceded her flying appearance from the upper court. "We've been saying goodbye to the dogs and the stable cats. The big gray one, the one we call Wolf . . . her kittens are old enough to leave her now. Pen and me, we're going to take one each with us. Oh, good morning, Lord Hugh. See my kitten." She greeted him sunnily, holding up a tiny bundle of silver fur. "Pen's is ginger. It's a male and mine's female, so when we get to London they might have kittens together. We haven't thought up names for them yet."

God's bones! A nursery, a library, and now a farmyard!

He glanced at Guinevere and saw that she was regarding him with sly challenge, waiting to see how he was going to deal with this one.

"Your mother will explain to you why it's impossible for you to bring kittens on such a journey," he said, with a decisive nod at Guinevere.

"Oh, but Mama, they'll remind us of home," Pen said, coming up to them clutching her own soft parcel of ginger fur. She was looking distressed, as if the reality of leave-taking had suddenly hit her. "We have to leave everything behind, couldn't we just take these two? They won't be any trouble. They're so tiny."

"Yes, *please!*" Pippa chimed in. "They won't be any trouble, we'll look after them, and they'll remind us of home."

Guinevere regarded Hugh with an undeniably malicious glimmer in her eye. "Just a memento," she murmured. "It's so very hard for them to have to leave *everything* behind."

Hugh glared at her. He could feel two pairs of pleading hazel eyes fixed hopefully upon him. How could he possibly refuse them in the circumstances? As Guinevere damn well knew, he reflected savagely. She was watching his dilemma with undisguised enjoyment.

He turned away from the mockery in her gaze and said curtly to the girls, "Very well. But they're your responsibility and I don't want to lay eyes on them, *ever*. Is that understood?"

"Oh, yes," Pen said, her expression transformed. She tucked the kitten into her cloak. "Thank you." She gave him a smile that was so like her mother's it took Hugh's breath away. No wonder Robin was smitten.

The sun rose above the horizon and the soft pink light filled the lower court, setting the mellow stone of the house aglow. "Mount up!" he commanded curtly. "I wished to leave at sunup. We've a good many miles to cover today."

He turned his horse and rode through the arched doorway and out onto the gravel path. At the bridge he drew rein and waited for them. The small procession of women and children emerged within minutes from the house and Hugh again felt that inconvenient stab of remorse . . . of fear for what lay ahead for them.

Supposing he just abandoned his mission. Just turned and rode away.

But why should he? Guinevere Mallory was no innocent. She had seduced four men, and four men had gone to their deaths. He had evidence of conspiracy, of deceit, of motivation for murder. She should be given the opportunity to defend herself from the charges, but it was not his business to absolve her.

Guinevere rode onto the bridge, then she turned her horse and looked up at her home. So beautiful, so peaceful, under the soft light of early morning. She could smell the roses from the gardens beyond the bridge. She looked across at the river, at the silver flash of a jumping fish, the widening ripples of its disappearance beneath the water. A dragonfly, brilliant blue, whirred above the water meadow.

She looked up at Hugh of Beaucaire and said coldly, "Well, my lord, if this forms part of your reward for my persecution, I trust you'll cherish it." Then she nudged her horse into motion and rode past him towards the gatehouse.

Robin and the soldiers were mounted and ready for departure just beyond the gatehouse. Hugh, still stinging from her remark, was tight-lipped as he instructed the children and Tilly to ride between two lines of his men. Robin eagerly took up his place beside Pen.

"My lady, you will ride with me," Hugh said distantly.

Guinevere shrugged. "I am obedient to your orders, my lord."

"It will be easier for everyone if that remains true," he said, riding up to the head of the small cavalcade.

Guinevere followed him, contemplating a response, but one look at his expression convinced her to remain silent, at least for the moment. She refused to glance behind her, to take one last look at her home. Anger and bitterness helped to keep the sorrow and fear at bay.

"Don't expect any sympathetic help from me when one of those wretched kittens runs off and you have a wailing child on your hands," Hugh said, unable to hide his continuing irritation.

"Why would I expect such help from you?" She was genuinely surprised he could have such an idea. "I can manage my daughters myself, Lord Hugh. As I always have done."

"What of their father? Did he take no part in their upbringing?" Despite his annoyance, he waited with interest for her response.

"Pippa was a babe-in-arms when he died. Pen was barely three," she replied in a low voice.

Hugh kept his eyes on the road ahead as he asked, "Did you love him?" *Now, why had he asked such a question? What difference did it make to anything?* And yet he wanted to know.

"I thought I was supposed to have had him killed," she returned sarcastically. "Or did I shoot the arrow myself? I forget."

"Did you love him?" Hugh repeated, and this time he turned to look at her.

Instead of answering, she asked her own question. "Did you love Robin's mother?"

"Yes," he said simply. "I loved Sarah."

"I loved Timothy Hadlow."

The two statements lay between them in a silence that was somehow light, freed of resentment and irritation. It was almost as if they'd had a furious quarrel that had cleared the air, Guinevere thought, puzzled.

After a minute, she changed the subject. "Where do you intend to stop for the night?"

"Wherever we get to by late afternoon," he said. "Somewhere between Matlock and Ambergate, I would think."

"The convent at Wirksworth was once renowned for its hospitality to travelers," Guinevere observed. "It would have been the ideal rest stop if Privy Seal's men hadn't burned it to the ground. They raped the nuns too."

"Be careful what you say. 'Tis known that Stephen Mallory adhered to the Church of Rome," he warned her. " 'Tis known that he had dealings with Robert Aske. Pitch sticks and it won't help your cause."

"Stephen knew the man, yes. But I did not," she declared. "And as soon as Robert Aske's Pilgrimage of Grace ran into trouble, Stephen dropped Aske like a hot brick. Aske's in jail in York now, or so I heard."

Robert Aske had started the Pilgrimage of Grace in the north of England to protest the dissolution of the monasteries. The risings had succeeded for a while the previous year, but had been put down by the Catholic Duke of Norfolk with a savagery that was fueled by self-preservation, by his need to prove himself loyal to the king even if it meant persecuting those who were defending his own faith.

"He'll be executed," Hugh said grimly. "And it won't be an easy death. Take my advice and steer clear of the subject in London. It reeks of treason."

"Murder, witchcraft, and now treason!" Guinevere said in tones of mock amazement. She laughed mirthlessly. "What else will they accuse me of? But I can only lose one head, my lord, so maybe I'll choose my own crime."

Hugh had no answer.

9.

Just outside Matlock they stopped to water the horses and break their fast. Hugh, eating bread and cheese, was consulting a map with Jack Stedman and didn't notice the tiny ball of silver fur playing with a loosened lace of his riding boot. He stepped back and the ensuing yowl as he trod on the kitten's tail was straight from the Inferno.

"God's bones!" he bellowed, staring down at the hissing, spitting mite, its hair standing on end, its tail fluffed like a brush. *"Pippa!"* He bent and gingerly picked up the kitten by its scruff, holding it away from him between finger and thumb.

Pippa raced across the small glade, babbling as she ran. "Oh, there she is! I was so worried. I thought she was lost . . . and I hadn't even found a name for her! Pen's calling hers Nutmeg, which is such a good name, and I have to find one just as good. Oh, don't hold her like that, sir. It'll hurt her."

"It's the way their mothers carry them," Hugh told her with an expression of distaste as he dropped the creature into Pippa's outstretched hand. "And if I see the wretched animal again, I shall drown it!"

"You wouldn't!" Pippa stared at him as horrified as if he were a headless ghost. "You *wouldn't*, sir." She hugged the kitten to her breast.

"Don't put it to the test," he said, turning back to a grinning Jack Stedman.

Pippa, for once at a loss for words, trailed off, clutching the kitten, and Hugh continued his conversation with Jack. "So while we are in Matlock, Bill Waters will take charge of the party. We'll make an evening bivouac around Ambergate." He pointed with a crust of bread to the point on the oiled parchment. "We'll catch up with them there. Tell Bill to find a suitable spot; we'll need water, flat ground . . . well, he'll know what we'll need. Once they've found a campground tell him to post Robin on the road to direct us to it when we come up."

"Aye, sir. You want to leave at once?"

"As soon as you've given Bill his orders."

Jack nodded and hurried off. Hugh finished his bread and cheese and went for his grazing horse. Between them, he and Jack could interview quite a few folk in Matlock over an hour or so. He looked around for Guinevere and saw her walking along the bank of the stream where the horses had been watered. He rode over to her.

Guinevere had been for a stroll, glad to stretch her legs while she refined her escape plan. If Hugh set a guard over the camp, Tilly would have to take care of him with the belladonna. After that the trickiest part would be cutting the horses out from the rest without attracting attention. They could manage with just two mounts, she thought. Her own and one of the ponies. Greene would be close by and he could take up Tilly. Pen could ride alone and Pippa would ride with her mother.

Where was Greene now? she wondered. Was he close by? She knew he could be within a few feet of her and she'd see no sign of him unless she gave the signal they'd agreed upon. His father had been a huntsman and Greene had learned his trade from earliest childhood. He was a superb tracker and a past master at concealment.

"My lady?"

She looked up at the familiar voice. Lord Hugh rode up to her.

"Is it time to leave again?"

"You'll be mounting shortly," he said. "I'll not be riding with you this afternoon. One of my men will be in charge of the party."

"Oh?" She raised an eyebrow. "Why is that?"

"Jack and I have some business in Matlock."

"Oh?" she said again. "What business could you have in Matlock?"

"Just a few questions," he returned with a cool nod. "We'll catch up with you when you make camp around Ambergate this evening."

"I see," she said.

He nodded again and rode off.

Guinevere turned back to the stream, her eyes narrowed against the sun's glare. *Questions in Matlock?* Presumably he was making inquiries about Timothy's death. He'd hear nothing to his advantage, she thought. Whoever had been responsible for that arrow was not about to reveal himself. And if there were folk in the village who knew, they had closed ranks around one of their own.

But supposing he did hear something that could be interpreted in a certain way? Turned against her somehow? The whole business had been such a complicated tangle of fear, lies, and secrecy. They were uneducated folk and seven years had passed since the accident. Under questioning, terrified by the king's writ, one of the peasants could say something that could be twisted to suit Lord Hugh's purpose.

Dear God, it was impossible to go on like this! She pressed her hands to her head as if she could contain the despairing buzz in her brain. She had but one hope. Tomorrow night. Everything depended on tomorrow night.

A long blast of a horn signaled the end of the break and Guinevere walked across to where her mare waited, held by one of Hugh's men.

"Beautiful animal, m'lady," he observed, helping her to mount.

"Yes, she is." Guinevere leaned over to pat the animal's silky neck. "When we make camp tonight, I would prefer it if she and the ponies were kept away from the others. The mare's very highly strung and gets easily upset. She likes the company of the ponies because she knows them."

"Aye, madam. We'll find a tether for them some way apart from the others," the man said cheerfully.

Guinevere breathed again. That had been accomplished easily enough. And what was done tonight would be done tomorrow.

Just before Ambergate, they stopped in a pleasant clearing in the middle of a copse. A stream ran clear over big rocks.

"I'll lay odds there's trout in there," Bill Waters said from his horse beside Guinevere's. "Fresh fish for supper wouldn't come amiss, madam."

"No," Guinevere agreed. She looked around the clearing, assessing it.

Bill dismounted and began to give orders to the men about setting up the camp.

Guinevere dismounted beside him. "I would like my tent pitched over there," she said authoritatively, pointing to a flat spot on the outskirts of the clearing. "I like my privacy. There will do nicely."

Bill looked somewhat discomfited. "Lord Hugh won't feel comfortable with you that far away, madam. There are wild things in the woods. I 'ave me orders to pitch the tent for you and the lassies close to Lord Hugh's. An' he won't want to be that far from the center of the camp."

"Nevertheless I'd like the men to put up my tent over there for the moment and if Lord Hugh objects then I can discuss it with him when he arrives," she instructed calmly.

Bill hesitated, but there was something about Lady Guinevere that didn't permit argument. Or at least not from him. Lord Hugh would deal with it when he returned. "Right y'are, m'lady." He went off, calling orders.

Tilly, grumbling and rubbing her lower back, came over to Guinevere. "My Lord, chuck, I'll be glad when this is over," she muttered. " 'Tis a good thing fer me back that we'll not be goin' much farther."

Guinevere glanced around. She spoke swiftly in an undertone. "Tilly, now seems a good moment to become friendly with the men."

"Oh, aye," Tilly said easily. "I'll go an' sort out the cookin'. Don't you worry, m'lady. I'll 'ave their life stories out of 'em afore you know it. And anyone what needs a simple or a powder, I 'ave just the thing."

Guinevere nodded. Tilly knew her part. "We need to know if anyone will be guarding the camp at night. I think I've managed to ensure that our horses will be tethered separately, so it'll be easier to slip away with them. But if there's a camp guard we'll need to put him to sleep. You brought belladonna?"

"That an' a few other things that might be useful," Tilly said. "But fer now, I'll see if we can't get a decent meal off that fire. Looks like they're catchin' a good few fish, but they won't know what to do wi' 'em." She bustled off towards the newly kindled fire.

It was close to four o'clock when Hugh emerged from a small stone cottage hard by the village green in Matlock. Jack was sitting on the ale bench outside the tavern just across from the well and rose immediately, draining his ale pot. He raised a hand and Hugh gestured that he should stay where he was.

Hugh crossed the small green and straddled the ale bench. "I'm dry as a witch's tit," he declared. He leaned sideways to put his head around the open door and shouted for ale.

He said nothing while he waited for it and Jack offered no conversation. Hugh drained his ale pot in one gulp, and set it with a thump on the bench beside him. "So, what did you hear?"

Jack shrugged. "Nothin' much, sir. Seven years is a long time an' memories seem right short around 'ere." He looked shrewdly at Lord Hugh. "You do any better, sir?"

"Mayhap," Hugh said musingly. "Mayhap I did, Jack. Come, let's go. We need to ride hard if we're to reach the camp by sundown."

They rode hard and fast, the horses kicking up dust as they galloped down the narrow road towards Ambergate. Peasants hauled their carts to the side of the track out of their path and stared fearfully after the fast-disappearing riders. The pace of life in the Derbyshire countryside was in general slow and they were not accustomed to seeing men in armor riding hell-for-leather.

Neither man said anything as they rode. The pace was too fast, the dust too thick. Hugh was preoccupied, a deep frown drawing his thick eyebrows together, and Jack knew from experience that his master was mulling over something of considerable import. But even if their progress had been leisurely Jack would not have ventured a question. Lord Hugh spoke of his concerns only when he chose, and gave short shrift to probing.

Robin was sitting on a fallen log beside the path in the lengthening shadows of dusk when the two horsemen rounded a corner and came into view. The boy jumped to his feet and waved.

The horsemen drew rein and their sweating beasts panted and hung their heads.

"All well, Robin?"

"Aye, sir. The camp's just a few yards through the trees. There's a clearing," Robin said eagerly.

"Then lead on, my son."

Guinevere was sitting on a blanket on the grass outside her tent, her skirts spread around her, when Hugh, Jack, and Robin entered the clearing. The girls were playing beside her with the kittens.

Hugh took in the scene in one swift, comprehensive glance. He saw where Guinevere's tent had been pitched and a frown creased his brow. The rich smells of cooking came from the fire and he noticed that Tilly had put herself in charge of supper. Judging by the cheerful atmosphere it seemed that no one resented her taking control.

Hugh dismounted and crossed the grassy circle to where Guinevere and her children sat. Pippa grabbed up her kitten at his approach and held it tightly to her narrow chest.

"You seem to have made yourself comfortable," Hugh observed, surveying the round tent.

"Yes, I thank you. Your men have been most helpful in unloading our trunks. The tent is most commodious. Much more so than I imagined." She smiled at him. It was that damnable seductive smile again and once again confusion flooded his clear-cut intentions. It was as if north had become south.

He glanced down at the girls still sitting on the grass and held out his hand to Guinevere. "Would you join me in the tent?"

"Certainly, sir." She took the proffered hand and rose gracefully to her feet, still smiling. Her skirts swung and settled around her.

Hugh raised the flap of the tent and gestured that she should enter. He came in after her, having to turn sideways and duck his head to insert his powerful frame through the small opening.

It was surprisingly roomy inside. There was ample space for the four cots with their straw-filled mattresses.

"I'm sorry to have to disturb you but the tent will have to be pitched closer to mine," he said without preamble.

Guinevere regarded him in silence for a minute, then said, "I like my privacy."

"I assure you I won't be disturbing it," he returned blandly.

"How much closer?"

He went to the entrance and looked out. "Fifty feet."

Guinevere shrugged. There was no way to argue with him and even fifty feet closer in would still give her some space. Probably more than she'd have been granted if she'd made no stand at all.

"As you command," she said.

He turned back to her, a flicker of a smile touching his mouth, but he merely asked, "Did you bring your own bedding?"

"We have blankets," she responded.

"I can spare you a lantern. Candles are too dangerous around canvas. I would prefer that you didn't leave the tent at night, but if you must, make sure you carry the lantern and declare yourself to the guard."

"Where will the guard be stationed?" she inquired, going back to the entrance to look out again.

"He'll be walking the perimeter of the camp. He'll also be responsible for keeping the fire alight." He was standing close beside her and she could smell his earthy tang of horseflesh, leather, and fresh sweat. Out of nowhere a wave of desire swamped her.

Grimly she fought it down, seeking help in sarcasm. "Are you afraid of attack by a horde of savage Derbyshire shepherds?" she asked.

"Oh, you can do better than that, madam," he responded, regarding her with narrowed eyes and a glimmer of amusement as if he had guessed at her reaction. "That jab was very feeble, definitely not worthy of you."

Guinevere shrugged in an effort to mask her dismay at the thought that she might have given herself away. "You must be afraid of something?"

"I merely take precautions." He ducked back through the tent opening ahead of her. "Your tent will be moved immediately."

The children and kittens had disappeared and for a moment Guinevere and Hugh seemed isolated from the bustle of the camp. "Did your business in Matlock prosper?" Guinevere asked casually.

"That rather depends on what you mean by *prosper*," he replied.

"Did you discover what you *wished* to discover?" she pressed.

He looked at her, his eyes quite unreadable. "Again, madam, that rather depends upon what I *wished* to discover."

And what was that supposed to mean? Frustrated, she sought for some way of probing further but he didn't give her the chance.

Abruptly he gestured in the direction of a large square tent from which a pennant showing the falcon of Beaucaire fluttered in the freshening breeze. "We will sup in my tent. It's my turn to extend the hospitality of my table, my lady."

Just what had he discovered in Matlock?

Guinevere swallowed her frustration and swept him a mock curtsy. "You are too kind, sir."

He bowed, then took her hand as he straightened. His clasp was warm and dry, his voice low and melodious, his vivid eyes curiously soft and yet penetrating.

"It seems to me that we can pass what is bound to be a somewhat tedious time in pleasant conversation or you can hiss and spit like that damned kitten and we'll both be miserable."

Guinevere had heard from an indignant Pippa about the earlier incident with her kitten and Hugh's bootlace. She laughed slightly. "It must be galling for a man who's fought on so many battlefields to be attacked and routed by a kitten."

"I don't like cats," he stated. "Dogs, horses, yes. But cats, no! They make my flesh creep."

"How strange. You associate them with witchcraft perhaps?" she inquired sweetly. "It is after all one of the charges leveled against me."

He put his hands on her shoulders, pressing lightly but imperatively. "Let us call a truce for this evening at least, Guinevere. Sparring with you has its charms, I admit, but I'd appreciate a rest for a few hours. What d'you say?"

Guinevere moved her shoulders in wordless rejection of his hold and he let his hands drop to his sides. Deciding that she would never discover what he'd heard at Matlock if she kept him at arm's length, she said with an assumption of cheerfulness, "I too am awearied of sparring. And it's certainly bad for the digestion to quarrel at mealtimes, not to mention setting a bad example to the children."

"That was rather what I thought." He offered her his arm. "I have a rather fine burgundy. I'd be interested in your opinion."

Pippa was sufficiently cowed by her earlier experience with Lord Hugh and her kitten to agree meekly to confining the animal with its brother in one of the trunks in their tent during supper. "I still haven't found a name for her," she lamented. "I can't think of anything as good as Nutmeg."

"How about Quicksilver?" Hugh suggested, pouring wine into two goblets. He handed one to Guinevere. "Since the wretched creature's always underfoot, it seems a remarkably suitable name."

Pippa frowned. "Well, it is," she said thoughtfully. "But if you don't like her, sir, you can't name her. It'll bring her bad luck."

"You're so superstitious," Robin declared. "You're always talking about luck."

"Well, I believe in it," Pippa said stoutly. "So does Pen. Don't you?" She turned in appeal to her sister.

"Yes," Pen said with an apologetic glance at Robin.

"Yes, you see it's bad luck to walk on the lines of the flagstones, Pen always walks right in the middle of them, and it's good luck to hold a piece of silver when you look at the new moon and turn it in your hand, and it's bad—"

"You've made your point, Pippa," Guinevere interrupted. "This is a fine burgundy, Lord Hugh."

"I thought you might enjoy it. Pray be seated. Not exactly the height of luxury I'm afraid, but better than the cold ground." He gestured to a three-legged wooden stool.

"We don't usually carry such comforts around with us on campaigns," Robin said importantly to Pen. "Sometimes we have to travel very light. If we have to fight . . ." He hesitated, catching his father's eye, before saying, "Of course I haven't been in a battle yet."

"I hope you never will," Pen said vehemently.

Robin looked at her with clear disappointment. "But of course I will. I'm a soldier, like my father."

"I might be a soldier," Pippa announced. "I haven't decided yet what I want to do. I might be a lawyer like Mama. Or I might be a soldier. I don't know whether I want to get married," she added thoughtfully.

Amused, Hugh glanced at Guinevere, but his smile faded as he read the shadows in her eyes. She looked at him bleakly and sipped her wine.

What future did her daughters have? Guinevere thought that her children, grown under the guidance of their unconventional mother, would find no husbands of any kind. They would now have no dowries. What man would appreciate them for their unusual qualities? *Had Hugh of Beaucaire no sensitivity?* And yet she knew that he had. Was it greed or the soldier's unquestioning acceptance of his orders that led him to ruin her and her children? Or did he truly believe in her guilt?

Was she guilty? Would Stephen have fallen if she hadn't moved her foot at just that moment?

⤬

Guinevere slept poorly that night. Tilly's snores rumbled softly, drowning out the children's even breathing and the snuffling from the kittens in the trunk. In the early hours of the morning, Guinevere threw aside her blanket and slipped to the grassy floor. She wrapped the blanket around her shoulders and went to the tent's opening. She unlaced the flap and stepped outside into the moonlit night. The fire glowed orange in the center of the camp and the wavering light of a pitch torch moved around the perimeter as the guard made his rounds.

Her mare whickered from her tether to one side of the tent. Guinevere trod soundlessly across the damp grass, her eye on the flickering light of the sentry's torch. She stood in the deep shadow cast by the mare's body and stroked her velvety nose. She watched the torch and began to count softly under her breath.

She estimated that it took close to five minutes for the guard to complete one circuit of the camp. Not long enough for them to slip away. Tilly would definitely have to prepare him one of her special potions.

"What are you doing out here without a light?"

Guinevere jumped and the horse threw up her head with a whicker of alarm.

Hugh held up the lantern he carried so that it cast its light upon Guinevere's countenance and threw his own into harsh relief. He was looking very annoyed.

"I saw no need to bring a lantern this tiny distance from the tent. Isolde was restless and I couldn't sleep myself so I came out to soothe her."

He put a steadying hand on the mare's neck. "The guard has orders to shoot on sight. His aim with a longbow is invariably accurate."

"He couldn't see me here in the shadows."

"Nevertheless . . ." He held the lantern higher and his expression softened. "It's been a long and tiring day. Why couldn't you sleep?"

Guinevere shivered and drew the blanket tighter around her. "An unquiet mind, Lord Hugh. What about you?"

"I rarely sleep more than a few hours at a time when I'm on the road."

He looked down at her in the lamplight. He didn't know what had awoken him, but he knew it had had something to do with Guinevere. Now he wanted to hold her, to smooth the worry lines from her brow. He wanted to kiss that warm red mouth. His lips still carried the memory of that last kiss, his body could still feel her against him, the press of her breasts, the curve of her hip, the narrow back beneath his hands.

He spoke her name without volition, spoke it quietly, questioningly. "Guinevere . . ."

She shivered again, and it had little to do this time with the cool night air and the thinness of her chemise beneath the blanket.

"Don't," she said. "Hugh, *don't*!" She wanted to turn and run but she couldn't make her legs work. She just stood looking at him, burning in the brilliant blue fire in his eyes. She knew what he wanted just as she knew she wanted the same thing. And it was madness. But her body cried out for what he could give her and she couldn't tear her eyes from his.

It seemed as if the world itself held its breath. And then slowly Hugh exhaled and she found herself doing the same. She turned away and walked slowly back to her tent.

She lay on her cot, gazing into the pale darkness. Her body hurt with a frustration deeper than anything she could ever have imagined. Why had she bothered to deny herself? What difference would it have made to take what he offered? After tomorrow she would never see him again.

Please God, she would never see him again.

Greene straddled the lower branch of an oak tree at the edge of the copse as dawn lightened the eastern sky. He too watched the guard's torch that flickered palely in the growing light. The guard had been changed twice between sundown and sunup. The best moment for his lady to make her bid for freedom would be at the middle of the second watch, when the night was deepest and even the horses slept. While it would leave them still upon the road at dawn, it was the time when all but woodland predators were asleep. Even the horses in the stockade were dozy. And by dawn they would be within striking distance of Cauldon.

He hummed under his breath between bites of the thick mutton chop that served as his breakfast and continued his vigil.

Guinevere had dozed fitfully in the hours since she'd left Hugh but was now up and dressed while the children still slept.

She slipped out of the tent and watched the dawn, listening to the morning chatter of the birds. The air was soft and promised another hot day.

There was no need now for a lantern to declare herself to the guard, it was quite light enough. Casually she strolled towards the trees. If she was stopped she had the perfect excuse. A lady had needs that required the seclusion of the bushes. She wouldn't say anything of their flight to the children until that night, she decided. She would tell them when she put them to bed. It might keep them from sleeping but at least Pippa wouldn't flood her with questions in the middle of the night while they were trying to make their escape. She could just imagine her chatter bringing the entire camp down upon them.

In the seclusion of the trees, she whistled, the soft call of a blackbird. Almost immediately came the *rattatat* of a woodpecker. She breathed deeply in relief. Greene was there. Watching. Waiting. She had no need to see him now, but when they made camp this evening they would talk. Just knowing he was there brought immeasurable comfort.

She turned and walked back to the camp.

Hugh watched her from behind the broad trunk of an oak tree. He'd been about to leave his tent when he'd caught sight of her walking purposefully towards the copse in the soft dawn light. There was something about her posture that had convinced him she was not heading for privacy simply to answer a call of nature as he might have assumed. Instead of hailing her, he'd followed her. Stalked her, he corrected with a grim smile. He was no mean huntsman himself. He'd heard her blackbird's call, and the immediate answer.

Who the hell had she been signaling? And why?

He could have the copse searched. His men would soon find anyone lurking there. But maybe he would just let things unfold in their own time. Guinevere would reveal her hand at some point and it was going to be very interesting to see what she had in mind.

Hands thrust deep into the pockets of his gown, Hugh strolled, whistling casually, back into his camp.

IO.

A re you going to call your kitten Quicksilver, Pippa?"
Pippa was intent upon feeding her pet scraps of meat from
the breakfast table. "I don't know yet," she answered her sister.

Robin knelt on the ground beside her. "I think it's a really splendid
name."

"But your father chose it, and he doesn't like her," Pippa said, dipping her finger in a pot of milk and offering it for the kitten's rough
tongue. "It truly is bad luck."

"Oh, that's nonsense, Pippa." Pen set her own Nutmeg on the
ground.

"But you believe in luck!"

"Yes, but Robin says Lord Hugh doesn't like *any* cats. It's not just
yours," her sister explained. "The name suits her."

Pippa continued to offer the kitten milk, her mouth taking a stubborn turn. Pen wasn't being true. They'd always played the luck games
together. They didn't walk on flagstone cracks, they didn't walk under
ladders, they always turned around seven times and sat down if they
had to go back into the house for something they'd forgotten. They
laughed about it, but it was important. It was what they did together.
And now what Robin said was so much more important to Pen than
the things they'd done together.

"Oh, come on, Pippa!" Pen cajoled. "It's such a good name."

"I'm going to call her Moonshine," Pippa said, picking up the kitten. She walked off, scratching between the kitten's ears.

"Oh, dear," said Pen, looking dismayed.

"Doesn't she like my father?" Robin was bristling.

"Yes, of course she does. Pippa likes everybody." Pen sighed. "It's just that . . ."

"Just that what?" Robin put a hand over hers and Pen flushed a delicate rose. Hastily he snatched his hand back, blushing himself as if the touch had been an unfortunate accident.

"I think she thinks that I like you more than I like her," Pen said, still flushing, her voice very low.

"Oh," Robin said.

"But it's different," Pen went on, her eyes studiously fixed on the kitten in her lap. "I like you in a different way. But she's too young to understand that."

"Oh," said Robin again. He put his hand over hers and this time kept it there. "I like you in the same way," he said. An awkward silence fell between them as they continued to hold hands, both uncomfortably aware of how hot and sweaty their hands were yet neither able to make the first move to break the contact. They were both relieved when the blast of a horn told them it was time to mount up for the day's ride. They jumped to their feet and hastened to their horses.

Guinevere offered Hugh a bland good morning as he rode up beside her. He returned it with a cool smile that gave away nothing of his inner thoughts.

What the devil was she plotting?

Hugh hadn't known Guinevere Mallory more than a few days and yet it was as clear as day to him that her fertile brain was working overtime behind that mask. He could only think that she was planning some kind of flight. But how did she think she could get away from him? He couldn't imagine how she was intending to spirit herself, the girls, and presumably Tilly away from an armed camp. At night, obviously. And just as obviously she must have arranged for some help . . . whoever had been in the copse answering her signal. Did this plan have something to do with why she had been so insistent that they take the route through Derby and not Chesterfield? Where was she going that she was confident he wouldn't find? Whatever plan she had, it would be a sound one, carefully thought out. Guinevere was not one to embark upon the impossible.

He glanced sideways at her, noting the calm set of her profile, the erect carriage as she sat her beautiful white mare. She seemed utterly serene.

His mouth thinned. Lady Guinevere, for all her cleverness, wasn't going anywhere but to London under his escort.

He would let her make her move and then make his. It had some of the cruelty of a cat playing with a mouse, he was forced to admit, but he wanted to watch her plan unfold. And he had to acknowledge a certain satisfaction in contemplating the endgame. This was one battle of wits he was going to win.

"I believe you mentioned Kedleston as a suitable resting place for tonight," he said. "Is there anything special about it?" His smile was as smooth and bland as a saucer of cream.

"Not really. But you could reprovision if you needed to."

"It's a little early on the journey for that. But we'll stop there this evening if you so wish?"

"If *you* so wish, Lord Hugh," she returned with seeming indifference. The route from Kedleston to Cauldon was direct. If they went on a few more miles towards Derby they would have to double back when they made their escape. It would add an hour or two to their flight. Ordinarily it would be a minor annoyance, but minor annoyances were assuming major importance as the time grew close for her bid for freedom.

His suave smile flickered.

That was enough talk of Kedleston, Guinevere decided. It was too close to home. She changed the subject to one that would divert them both. "I own I'm curious as to what you discovered in Matlock, Lord Hugh." She turned her head to look at him, her gaze penetrating.

"What did you expect me to discover?"

"Nothing," she stated.

He shrugged. "My task is to take my findings to Privy Seal. It's not for me to interpret them."

"That is the most disingenuous statement I've ever heard," Guinevere declared. "How am I to defend myself if I don't know what so-called evidence you've drummed up?"

"You'll be informed in due time."

And you, my lord, will discover in due time that your claim to my land is invalid.

She couldn't decide whether to tell him this evening, before she made her escape, or to leave the premarriage document in her tent for him to find, together with an explanation of its legal meaning. He'd probably get the land anyway, unless the king and Privy Seal were angry that she had escaped them while under his escort. But even if he did get it, she knew enough of him now to know that the fact that it was not legally his would really rankle. It was all the revenge she could have, but it was better than nothing.

The temptation to tell him to his face was considerable, just for the satisfaction of seeing his chagrin. But Guinevere decided it was one she would have to forgo. She had too much on her mind to complicate her thoughts with vengeance, however sweet.

Just outside Kedleston, Hugh chose a campsite in a large field with a pond surrounded by woodland. It was far more exposed than the glade they'd found the previous night, Guinevere thought as she sat her horse and took covert stock. It had been but a short distance from the encampment to the seclusion of the trees last night. This spot was very different. But what could she do about it?

She prepared to dismount and found Lord Hugh on the ground at her side. "Allow me, my lady," he said with a smile that glimmered with wicked amusement. He raised his hands to her waist and she pushed them away with indignation. "I am quite capable of dismounting unaided," she said.

"Oh, don't deny me the opportunity for chivalry," he said, ignoring her flapping hands and lifting her easily to the ground. "I must set Robin a good example."

"I suppose showing excessive courtesy to a prisoner is one way of doing it," she observed, moving away so that his hands fell from her waist.

Hugh merely grinned and remarked, "You'll wish to have your tent pitched some way apart again." The cynical gleam in his eye was well concealed.

"I like my privacy," she replied, as she'd said the previous evening.

"Indeed," he murmured. He watched with the same cynical smile as once again she arranged to have her horse and the ponies tethered close to her tent. All set for a quick departure. But how was she going to deal with the guard? It would be interesting to see.

"I trust you'll join me for supper," he said.

Guinevere hesitated. She had intended to beg off sharing his meal, but now it occurred to her that maybe she could slip something in his wine. She'd been concerned when he said he only ever slept a couple of hours at a time on campaign. Supping with him could give her the opportunity to change that.

"The girls will eat with Tilly in my tent. They're tired after two days of riding," she responded with cool composure. "But I should be honored to join you and Robin, sir."

"The honor will be all mine, madam." He bowed over her hand. "Robin will take his supper with the men. At six then."

"I look forward to it." She smiled, her face a mask of serenity. "If you'll excuse me, sir, I'd like to stretch my legs a little while the tent is being erected." She walked off towards the line of trees that surrounded the field. The girls ran up to her and Hugh watched as she bent and said something to them. Immediately they turned and left her to her solitary walk, going instead to the pond.

Hugh nodded grimly and waited a few minutes before making his move.

Guinevere strolled into the trees. It was a sparsely planted woodland and there was little concealment. She went deeper and then whistled her blackbird's call softly. She waited, listening, and almost immediately came the *rattatat* of a woodpecker. The sound led her to a screen of holly bushes.

Greene stood up slowly, silently, barely disturbing the underbrush. "Is all in place, my lady?"

"I am so glad to see you," she said, unable to disguise her relief, although she had known he would be there. "We can do it, I think. But the field is very exposed."

He nodded. "I am aware, my lady."

"We will make the attempt just after midnight. It took the guard about five minutes last night to circle the perimeter of the camp. The camp won't be any more spread out today, but it's in a more exposed situation. It'll take us longer to get from the tent into concealment among the trees." She spoke in a rushed whisper. "Tilly will give the guard a sleeping draught to put him out just after midnight."

"I think it's surer if I take care of 'im myself, madam," Greene suggested. "I can smell rain so it'll be a cloudy night. I can come up be'ind 'im easy."

"You won't hurt him."

"Nah, jest a tap'll do it," Greene said confidently. "It'll put 'im t' sleep surer than anythin' Tilly can come up with. Don't you fret, m'lady."

A twig snapped somewhere behind Guinevere. Greene was suddenly gone and she was gazing at a holly bush. She turned slowly. "Is anyone there?"

No sound greeted her. Her hands were clammy as she walked back the way she'd come. Then a doe jumped past her in a flash of creamy beige and white, snapping twigs and rustling leaves as she ran from whatever had startled her. It took a few minutes for Guinevere's heart to settle to its normal rhythm.

She emerged into the field and saw that the tents were already up, the jaunty pennant flying from Hugh's. The fires were lit and men were talking and laughing in the atmosphere of orderly bustle that Guinevere now expected from Hugh of Beaucaire's troop. There was no sign of Hugh. She assumed he was in his tent.

Pen and Pippa were with Robin at the pond. He was showing them how to skim stones across the water. It was time now to talk to the girls although she still hadn't decided on the best, least alarming way to explain their flight.

Guinevere ducked into her tent where Tilly was arranging the bedding. "Will you fetch the girls, Tilly. They're down by the pond. It's time to break the news."

"Oh, aye," Tilly said matter-of-factly. "I'll tell 'em to come up fer their supper. I'll tell 'em they're goin' to eat in 'ere tonight."

She bustled off and Guinevere sat down on one of the trunks and composed herself. They mustn't see her anxiety, her desperation, her knowledge that this was the last chance to save them all.

Pippa's high tones heralded their arrival. She tumbled into the tent.

"Why are we eating in here, Mama? We want to stay outside and play with Boy Robin. I nearly threw a stone all the way over the lake." She demonstrated with a wide-flung arm.

"It's a pond not a lake," Pen corrected, following her sister into the tent with rather less exuberance. She surveyed her mother. "Is something wrong, Mama?"

"No," Guinevere denied, smiling. "Close the tent flap, Pen, and sit down." She gestured to one of the cots.

"Is it something exciting?" Pippa demanded, bouncing on the straw palliasse. Pen, her own expression grave, closed the flap and sat solemnly beside her sister.

"I think so." Quietly Guinevere explained that instead of going to London they were going to leave Lord Hugh's men that night and go to a new house.

"Can we take the kittens, Mama?" Pippa demanded as soon as her mother paused.

Guinevere got up from the chest and sat down on the cot between them. "Yes, you may." She put her arms around them and drew them close against her.

"But you said you wanted to go to London," Pen pointed out.

"I've changed my mind, sweeting."

"But why must we go in the night, Mama?" Pen pressed, her eyes wide with alarm.

Guinevere knew there was little she could say to reassure her daughter. Pen was far too intelligent to believe in tales of an amusing midnight adventure. "Lord Hugh has orders to escort us to London. I've decided I don't wish to go there after all, but Lord Hugh will feel it's his duty to take us whether I wish to go or not. So we must slip away without his knowing."

"I want to go home," Pippa said, turning her own now frightened eyes on her mother. "Why can't we just go home?"

"Maybe we will later," Guinevere said, hugging the child close. "But for the moment we are going to go to this other house. Greene will be waiting for us when we leave here."

"Greene!" squeaked Pippa. "Where is he?" She looked around as if expecting to see the huntsman materialize from the canvas walls around her.

"Don't interrupt Mama," Pen commanded.

"He's waiting for us in the woods. Now, listen carefully. You'll have supper with Tilly and then you must go to bed. Tilly and I will wake you up when it's time to leave. Greene and Crowder and the magister will be with us. And Tilly of course. So it'll be just like home really."

The girls looked a little reassured at the prospect of familiar faces.

Tilly came into the tent at that moment with a laden tray. " 'Ere's supper," she said cheerfully. She scrutinized the girls and tutted. "Dearie me, such long faces. What will Greene say when 'e sees you lookin' like a wet Monday, Pippa? He'll think y'are scared of summat. You know how y'are always tellin' 'im y'are scared of nowt."

"Well, I *am* scared of nowt," Pippa stated with bravado. "You're not scared, are you, Pen?"

"There's nothing to be scared of, is there, Mama?" Pen managed a tremulous smile.

"No," Guinevere said firmly. "Would I let anything bad happen? Now eat your supper and then tuck into bed in your clothes. That way when we wake you up you'll be all ready to go."

"I shan't sleep," Pippa said, taking a veal pasty from the tray. "I'm far too excited to sleep. Will you sleep, Pen?"

"I don't know," Pen said, examining the contents of the tray. She didn't like pasties when the filling spilled out and she couldn't see one that was whole. She took a chicken drumstick instead. The skin was crisp and the meat juicy. It comforted her.

" 'Ere's a nice drop o' murat," Tilly said, filling two cups with the drink of honey flavored with mulberries. She shot Guinevere a significant glance. The sweet drink, a treat on any day, would soothe them.

Guinevere nodded. Already their fear seemed to have subsided; Tilly would do the rest. She would put them to bed and stay with them until Guinevere returned from her supper with Hugh. Whatever the girls might say, their mother was fairly confident that they would sleep.

Supper with Lord Hugh. She would be at her most charming and entertaining. They could and did enjoy each other's company whenever they could hold their mutual antagonism at bay.

Or hold at bay that strange lustful connection that hit them between the eyes when least expected, and never invited.

She squashed the inconvenient reminder. Tonight she would show him only her friendliest face. She took the small traveling glass from her trunk and examined her appearance in the lamplight. Her hood was askew after the day's riding and her coif was dirty. She rubbed at her neck and regarded the grime on her fingertips with distaste.

"Tilly, could you fetch me some water? I'm all begrimed from the dust of the road!"

"Aye, chuck. There's hot water on the fire." Tilly picked up a jug and left the tent.

Guinevere unpinned her hood and coif and asked Pen to unlace her gown.

"My fingers are sticky," Pen said doubtfully.

"Mine aren't!" Pippa bounced up.

Pen glared at her. "Mama asked me." She licked her fingers vigorously and attacked the laces of her mother's stomacher.

Guinevere stepped out of the emerald silk. It lay in a crumpled heap at her feet. Because she had been riding she wasn't wearing the cone-shaped farthingale that ordinarily ensured that her skirts were perfectly creaseless. She said pacifically, "Pippa, sweeting, I need you to find the turquoise hood. The one with the silver edging."

"I know where it is!" Pippa bounded to the trunk, burrowed, and emerged triumphant, flourishing the deep blue hood. "But you always wear the gray gown with this."

"It's in the other trunk."

She had brought two gowns and a very little jewelry with her; all her other clothes and possessions would by now be laid in the cupboards and linen presses at Cauldon. Tonight she would sup with Lord Hugh in a gown of silver-gray silk with a raised pattern of black swans. She would wear sapphires . . . and she would send him to sleep with the sweetest of dreams.

II.

G uinevere entered Hugh's tent precisely at six o'clock. "I give
you good even, Lord Hugh."

Hugh bowed, an appreciative gleam in his eye as he took in her appearance. "Madam, you do me much honor." He looked down ruefully at his own dust-coated garments. "I fear I haven't had a chance to
change my own dress."

"You have so many responsibilities," she said smoothly. "So many
matters that require your attention. How could you have time for such
trivialities?"

Hugh bowed again. "You are most understanding, my lady." He
poured wine and handed her a cup, then gestured to the table where
appetizing steam rose from a covered pot. "One of the men shot a rabbit this afternoon. It seems we're the beneficiaries."

"One of the advantages of supping at the commander's table,"
Guinevere murmured, taking one of the stools at the table, her silvery
skirts falling in graceful folds around her. She sipped her wine as Hugh
ladled rabbit stew into two bowls before taking his place opposite her.

The valerian that would ensure Lord Hugh slept deeply that
night was concealed in her handkerchief, but for the moment she
couldn't see how to administer it. He set his wine cup on the table but
his hand remained loosely curled around it as he took a forkful of

stew. She slipped the handkerchief from her sleeve and dropped it in her lap.

Hugh watched her covertly. From what he'd overheard earlier she and Greene had all their plans for tonight in order. But even the best-laid plans could go awry and she must know that. But if she was apprehensive about the coming flight, she gave no indication of it. Her countenance was as composed as ever, her beautiful sloe eyes alert and yet seemingly tranquil. In her rich gown she could have been sitting at her own high table instead of in a campaign tent in the middle of a field, and he wondered why she had chosen to dress up for him on this of all nights. Despite his annoyance at the trouble she was causing him, he admired her courage, and he was stirred as always by her beauty, by that indefinable sensuality that awoke his own deep unwitting response.

God's bones! He wanted to make love to her; the longing to explore that long supple body made his hands quiver, his breathing quicken.

"Do you have a house in London, Lord Hugh?" she inquired pleasantly, breaking off a crust from the loaf of bread.

The question was a relief, hauling him back from the dizzying brink of desire. "A modest one," he responded. "In Holborn."

"Is that close to the river? I know very little of London."

"You are perhaps more familiar with the geography of ancient Rome or Athens," he observed.

She inclined her head in smiling acknowledgment and reached forward to dip her bread in the large saltcellar that stood in the middle of the table. Her hand slipped and with an awkward jerk her elbow caught the saltcellar, knocking it to the grass beneath the table.

"Oh, how clumsy!" she exclaimed, stooping to pick up a pinch of the spilled salt. "The girls will say it's such bad luck. I can't remember whether I have to throw it over my left or my right shoulder to cancel out the ill luck."

"You'd better do both," he said, bending to retrieve the saltcellar.

"It's such a waste of salt too. Can you manage to salvage some of it? Let me help you."

"There's no need." He scooped the precious commodity into the palm of his hand.

Her handkerchief was in her hand. Swiftly she leaned forward and dropped the fine powder it contained into his wine cup, praying it would dissolve before he raised his head.

He straightened, shaking the rescued salt from his palm into the salt-cellar again. *What had she done?* He knew the spilled salt was a ploy. She didn't give anything away in either voice or countenance but every one of his senses was alert, aware of some danger. She had done something.

Poison? Did she intend to dispatch him to whatever world now held her husbands?

She sipped her wine and repeated, "Is Holborn near the river, Lord Hugh?"

The wine, he thought. It had to be the wine. "No, it's some streets away. You'll see for yourself as you'll be residing under my roof until Privy Seal makes disposition for you."

Over my dead body. Guinevere smiled and dipped bread in her stew.

Hugh picked up his cup, cradling it in his hand, watching her. He thought her eyes had grown sharper although she didn't look at his cup. He raised it to his lips. She remained intent on her supper, but he thought he could detect just the slightest tremor in her fingers as she took a forkful of buttered greens.

He swirled the wine in the cup. It looked unadulterated but he was not about to take any chances. He pretended to sip and then set the cup down. Guinevere's smile didn't waver.

Treacherous, manipulative witch! He smiled back and helped himself to more stew.

Guinevere continued to question him about London life with all the appearance of one searching for relevant information. He continued to pretend to sip at his wine. After a while a trooper came in and removed the bowls and stewpot, placing a basket of wild strawberries on the table.

"Has Master Robin finished supper?" Hugh inquired. Guinevere in housewifely fashion was sweeping crumbs from the table into the palm of her hand, absorbed in her task.

"Aye. He went to water the 'orses, sir."

Hugh nodded. He raised his cup, holding it at waist level. Quickly he tilted it and a stream of wine fell soundlessly to the thick grass at his feet. "Tell him he should bed down with the men tonight." He raised the cup to his lips, confident that Guinevere had not seen its emptying. "I'll be sitting late and the lamp will keep him awake." He glanced at Guinevere as he said this. She appeared unperturbed.

"Aye, sir." The trooper went off.

Hugh leaned across for the flagon and refilled his cup.

"I was hoping you would consider taking a break tomorrow," Guinevere said, popping a strawberry into her mouth. "The girls are very tired."

"Are *you*?" He watched with a sort of mesmerized fascination as she took another strawberry. Her long slender fingers conveyed the fruit to her warm red mouth. Her teeth gleamed white for a second and she closed her eyes with pleasure as the sweet juice spurted on her tongue.

"No, not in the least. But I'm accustomed to riding all day. Hunting is one of my greatest pleasures."

"One you shared with two at least of your husbands."

"My first husband would not hunt with a woman," she said neutrally.

"Ah, yes. As I recall you were in childbed when he fell from his horse."

"Precisely so, my lord." *He'd refilled his cup.* He was not a man given to drink, and Guinevere had plenty of experience of those who were, but she'd noticed that he usually drank several cups of wine at supper. Tonight, thank God, was no different.

"My second husband, however, was a different matter. He and I hunted together frequently." Her gaze rested briefly on his face. "As I imagine you discovered on your sojourn in Matlock."

"There was some mention," he returned indifferently.

He wouldn't give an inch. She controlled the rising frustration, telling herself that whatever he'd discovered no longer mattered. Once she was safely away, hidden away, he could believe anything he wished.

It was growing dark outside the tent and lanterns were lit around the encampment. Hugh reached for flint and tinder and lit the lantern on the table. Its golden glow gave Guinevere's ivory complexion a soft pink tinge as she leaned forward to the strawberry basket.

"I seem to have eaten them all," she said in such surprise he was hard-pressed not to laugh. "Did you have any at all?"

"One or two maybe."

"How greedy of me," she said with a rueful headshake. "I confess I have a serious weakness for strawberries."

"It didn't escape my notice," he observed gravely.

Guinevere laughed and once again it was as if they were enclosed in a magic circle where there could be no antagonism, only this sense of an overpowering connection between them. As if somehow they were *meant* to be sitting here together in the lamplight, laughing about her greed for strawberries as if nothing else lay between them.

Abruptly she rose from the table and the circle shattered. "My lord, it grows late. I must leave you."

Yes, so I gathered. A cynical flicker darted across his brilliant blue gaze but he rose to his feet and said only, "We'll make a late start in the morning, and ride for half a day only. Will that rest the girls sufficiently?"

"That's very considerate of you, sir."

He bowed. "While you're under my charge, madam, I have only your best interests at heart."

Guinevere dipped a curtsy, mockery in every graceful line of her body. "You are too good, sir."

"Sometimes I think that's true," he remarked coolly. He took up the lantern. "Come, I'll light you to your tent."

He walked with her to her tent. "Good night, my lady."

"Good night, Lord Hugh." She gave him her hand in a brief clasp, then slipped into her tent.

"Until later," he said softly.

Tilly was dozing but jerked awake as soon as Guinevere entered. "Did he take the valerian?" she whispered.

"He drank the wine," Guinevere said, her voice low in deference to her sleeping daughters. "I couldn't use too much in case he would taste it. I just hope it'll be enough."

"Well, I gave the guard a jug of my special frumenty," Tilly said. "To ward off the cold while 'e's doin' 'is rounds. Right grateful, 'e was. Says 'is ma used to make it fer 'im."

"Well, Greene's going to take care of him as well," Guinevere said.

"So we'll have double insurance. One way or another he's going to be asleep at midnight."

"Aye, 'tis better to be safe than sorry." Tilly nodded at the platitude. She gestured towards the girls. "Lassies went out like lights too."

"That's good. You go back to sleep, Tilly. I'll wake you when it's time."

Guinevere sat on the edge of her cot and began to unpin her hood and coif. She didn't need long folds of material to encumber the ride that lay ahead. She pulled on the woolen riding hose she wore beneath her skirt, tucking her chemise into the waist, then shook down her skirts. There were no other preparations she could make.

It was only just past nine. She should sleep for a couple of hours but she was too keyed up.

She extinguished the lantern, lay back on the cot and reviewed her plan. The guard was not a problem. The horses were tethered close by. They had rope halters and saddle blankets thrown over them. Guinevere and Pen could ride well enough for a few hours with just those for saddle and bridle. They would carry nothing with them so would be able to move swiftly. Greene would be waiting. He'd take Tilly up with him so that Pen could ride alone and they'd make faster time. They'd have five hours until dawn. Six hours, with luck, before their absence was noticed. Maybe even longer since Hugh had said they would make a later start on the morrow.

She lay wide-eyed, her vision adjusting to the tent's gloom. She wouldn't be able to light the lantern again and she could now hear the faint patter of raindrops on the canvas. The night would be dark. All to the good, but the ride in the rain would be less than pleasant. But they had fur-lined, hooded cloaks.

She slipped off the cot and went to the trunks. Tilly had already laid the cloaks out on top of one of the trunks but restlessly Guinevere shook each one out and then replaced it, smoothing out the folds, finding some measure of reassurance in these small albeit unnecessary preparations.

The children slept. Pen murmured something in her sleep. Her voice sounded anxious, slightly breathless, and Guinevere bent over her. The child was frowning and muttering. Something was troubling her dreams but there was nothing her mother could do at this point to reassure her. Guinevere wondered if the girl's confused dreaming had anything to do with young Robin. Pen had not mentioned his name since she'd learned of their impending departure. Which, of course, was typical of the child. She would not voice her own concerns when she knew her mother was troubled.

Guinevere turned to Pippa, who was dreamlessly asleep, her arms flung above her head, fingers lightly curled.

Dear God, she had to get them to safety.

She walked to the tent opening and listened to the rain now drumming fiercely. She untied the flap and peered out. The night air smelled of wet grass. The campfire was still alight and hissing. When she stepped out into the rain she could see the guard's torch flaring on the perimeter of the camp. She looked at her watch, peering at the diamond-encircled face in the darkness. Eleven o'clock. Just one more hour.

Tilly woke just before midnight almost as if she had an internal alarm. She sat bolt upright on her cot and blinked sleep from her eyes. "Did you sleep, chuck?"

"No. Let's wake the children." Guinevere swung her cloak around her shoulders. "They'll need their cloaks. The rain's let up a little, but it's still wet out there."

Guinevere bent over Pen's cot and shook her gently, whispering her name. Pen's eyes shot open. She stared in momentary bewilderment, then she sat up. "Is it time?"

"Yes, sweeting. You'll need your cloak."

Tilly had awoken Pippa who opened her mouth on a stream of words only to have it firmly closed by the tiring woman's warning finger. The girls stood shivering in the aftermath of sleep while Tilly and Guinevere bent to wrap them warmly in their cloaks.

Lamplight suddenly shone, moving against the rain-wet canvas of the tent. A hand moved over the laces that fastened the tent flap.

Slowly, with a despairing sense of inevitability, Guinevere stood straight, one hand resting on Pen's shoulder. The lamp threw its light into the tent and Hugh of Beaucaire, his iron-gray hair flat and dark with rain, stepped inside.

In his anger at her plotting, his very real fear that she had tried to poison him, he had been ready with sarcasm, with triumph at outwitting her, but now as he saw the frightened faces of the children he knew he must save his triumph for when he was alone with Guinevere. He spoke quietly. "Madam, I would have speech with you."

He turned to the tiring woman. "Woman, I would have you put the children back to bed. 'Tis too foul a night for travel." He stepped backwards into the rain, holding the lantern high as he awaited Guinevere.

"Mama . . . ?" The children spoke in unison, scared and confused.

She knelt down on the grass and tried to smile. "Well, it seems we're going to London after all, my loves. You mustn't worry now. Go back to bed and I'll be back in a few minutes."

Hugh was getting wet. "Madam." His voice was now sharply imperative.

Guinevere stood up. She touched her children's faces, nodded at Tilly, and went out into the rain, drawing the hood of her cloak over her head.

"Something appears to be preventing my guard from making his appointed rounds," Hugh observed, taking her arm in a firm clasp as he marched her towards his tent. "I haven't seen his light for close to five minutes."

"Really," Guinevere said distantly. "Perhaps the rain put it out."

"Perhaps so," he agreed with every appearance of amiability. "I daresay we'll discover the truth soon enough." He held open the flap of his tent for her.

She entered, tossed back the hood of her cloak in a shower of raindrops. Her pale hair was parted in the middle and the silvery braids were coiled around her ears.

Hugh set the lantern on the table. She looked so much younger without the hood and coif, so damnably innocent and vulnerable. "What were you trying to poison me with?" he demanded harshly.

Guinevere shrugged. "No poison. Just valerian. You would have had a good night's sleep for once. You might even have been grateful. I take it you didn't drink it."

"You will have to get up very early in the morning to get the better of me, madam. I give you fair warning," he told her, feeling an overpowering relief that she hadn't intended his death. Or at least, that was what she said. He had no proof. It could as easily have been poison as valerian. *Jesus, Mary, and Joseph! How was he ever to know what she was?*

Guinevere shrugged in what could have been either denial or acceptance. She glanced down at the table where the lamp glowed, and saw that he'd been writing; the ink was dry now on the parchment.

He followed her glance. "A dispatch to Warwick Castle. My lord of Warwick will provide us with a few days of hospitality on the king's command. I'll send a messenger on ahead in the morning."

" 'Tis a long way to Warwick."

"Aye. By then we'll be glad of hot water, soft beds, efficient servants, and food from a kitchen."

Guinevere made no reply. She walked back to the tent entrance that he'd let fall as he came in after her. She stood with her back to him. "How did you know?"

"As I said, you'll have to get up very early in the morning to get the better of me."

"That's no answer." She remained with her back to him.

"You gave yourself away."

Surprised, she spun round to face him. "How?"

He hesitated, then said, "Maybe someone else wouldn't have noticed. But I did. There was something about your manner when you went off into the woods that alerted me. I followed you. I heard your signals, and then this evening, I heard you with Greene. I knew you intended to remove the perimeter guard so I waited until his rounds seemed to have stopped and then stepped in."

"I see. You let me think we were going to succeed when all along you knew you were going to stop me." She gave a short angry laugh and turned away from him again. "Did you enjoy humiliating me? Did you enjoy letting me hope while you were preparing to dash me down?"

He ran a hand over the back of his neck as if it itched. "I was angry with you, Guinevere. Angry that you would think you could outwit me. I needed to prove to you that you can't."

"*Why?*" she demanded in an undertone, still with her back to him.

"Why would you stop us? We would have gone into penniless exile. Isn't that enough for you? You would have had then the estates you claim. What more do you want, Hugh of Beaucaire? *Must* you see me destroyed, my children destroyed? No dowries, no husbands. You know the realities." She turned back to him, her eyes bitter as aloes. "You want to see us *all* destroyed?"

"No . . . no . . . I don't want that." He moved towards her, unable to bear the pain in her eyes, to bear his own guilt. "Not for anything would I see you and your children ruined."

"But you will do so," she said. "For whatever twisted reasons of your own, you'll destroy us."

"Damn you! I will not."

"Don't deceive yourself!" she taunted. "You don't deceive me with your prating, your gentleness to my children. You're a monster, Hugh of Beaucaire!"

"Not so!" He seized her elbows, she turned aside, his hand clasped the back of her head, cradling her skull. She leaned back into his palm, their eyes met.

"What *do* you want, my lord?" She threw it at him as a challenge even as she knew the answer and knew she had opened Pandora's box. She swallowed, moistened dry lips, seeing her face reflected in his eyes. "What *do* you want," she repeated softly.

"You," he responded. "As you know full well, my lady." With almost agonizing slowness he lowered his mouth to hers, almost as if he was giving her time to pull away.

But she didn't. *Why* didn't she?

His lips for a second were light, soft on her mouth, then he caught her face between his hands and he was kissing her with an almost savage ferocity. There was an instant when it seemed she would resist him, then with a shuddering little sigh her mouth opened beneath his insistent tongue and she was returning his kiss with the same wild need.

She put her arms around his neck, drinking him in, licking along the inside of his lips, exploring his taste as she drew deeply on his tongue, grazing it lightly with her teeth.

He moved his hands beneath her cloak, smoothing down her back, over the swell of her backside beneath the silk of her gown. She pressed herself against his length and her belly jumped as she felt his penis beneath his hose, hard, insistent, wanting, against her thighs.

Her head fell back and he kissed her throat, licked slowly along the line of her jaw, tenderly, leisurely almost, even as his hands gripped her bottom and his erection jutted against her.

There were too many clothes between them. Feverishly she reached up to unclasp her cloak, letting it slip to the ground. It was as if a great weight had fallen from her. In the same moment, impatiently he shrugged out of his gown.

His mouth moved down the column of her throat to the smooth white flesh of her bosom above the ruffled edge of her chemise where it showed above the neckline of her gown. His blind hands were now deftly unlacing the back of her gown. He raised his head for an instant as he slipped the loosened gown forward over her shoulders. It fell to her feet. They stood in a puddle of silk and velvet.

He bent to kiss her breast, pushing aside the ruffles of the chemise to devour the sweetly swelling flesh, drawing his tongue down the deep cleft.

He held her hips in the woolen hose as he kissed her breasts and with rough haste she unbuttoned his doublet, pushing it from him. She tore at the buttons of his shirt in her anxiety to feel his skin, pressed her own lips to the fast-beating pulse in his throat. She curled her fingers in the light scattering of graying hair on his chest, reveling in the feel of the muscles beneath, the clearly defined rib cage. She clasped his narrow waist and bent to kiss his nipples, flicking her tongue until they hardened into tight erect buds.

Neither of them spoke. There was a fierce intensity to their movements even when they were leisured, as if they were both afraid of interruption. Not from without, but from within. As if they were both afraid that the other would make this wild magic stop.

Hugh unfastened the tapes of her riding hose and thrust his hands deep inside, grasping her bottom with a sigh that made her shudder. He moved one hand to her belly, his nails scraping the soft skin, while his other remained on her backside. His fingers reached down inside the hose, threading through the dampening tangle of black hair, reaching deep between her thighs into the hot furrow of her body. He held her thus between his two hands. Her arms were again around his neck, her mouth on his, and she rose on her toes with a soft groan of hungry delight, opening herself for the probing intimacy of the twin caresses.

He lifted her slightly in this fashion, tumbling her backwards onto his narrow cot, dropping to his knees as she released his neck, flinging her arms above her head in a gesture of wanton abandon. He peeled her hose to her ankles where it became entangled with her boots, and pushed up the chemise so that it wrapped around her throat in a white froth of linen and lace.

Guinevere felt more naked than if she was completely so, and it sent her excitement to fever pitch. He was kissing her breasts as his hands continued to stroke between her thighs. The fur covering on the bed was hot and soft beneath her bare back. She lifted her hips to meet the jut of his penis, and thrust her hands into the waist of his hose, reaching down to grasp his backside, feeling how the skin was coarser than her own, slightly hairy. It made her want to laugh with delight. She moved a hand around to grasp his penis. It was hard, hot, rigid with corded veins.

She scrabbled at his hose, desperate to release this that she wanted so much, more it seemed at this moment than she had ever wanted anything before. He helped her with a judicious wriggle of his hips so that the hose like her own now tangled around his booted feet.

She wanted to coil her legs around his waist but couldn't because of the tangle of hose and boots. He raised her legs himself, running his hands down the backs of her thighs, then he lifted them high over her head and drove deep within her as he knelt upright, holding her ankles. She tried to hold on . . . hold back the wave of delirious unspeakable delight that grew and grew in her belly and loins. It had been so long, an eternity since she had felt this. And she had never expected to feel it again.

She bit her lip, tasting salt blood, as she fought back the ecstatic cries that would betray them. She looked up into his eyes. He gazed down at her, lost in his own approaching tempest. They had said not a word but now, very softly, he whispered her name, then he threw back his head with a bitten-back groan and his tempest became hers and hers became his.

He collapsed on his belly beside her, his head buried in the fur coverlet, his breathing fast and heavy. He cupped her left breast in the palm of his hand, feeling the racing of her heart beneath her damp skin. Then the sound of voices beyond the flimsy canvas of the tent brought him up to his knees.

"God's bones!" He scrambled off the cot, hauling up his hose, pulling his buttonless shirt across his chest as he reached for his doublet. How had he forgotten he'd sent Jack to search for the missing guard?

Guinevere was already on her feet, still dazed but not so much that she couldn't appreciate what was happening. How long had it lasted? It could have been five minutes, it could have been fifty. She pulled down her chemise, yanked up her hose, picked up her gown. She couldn't lace it herself but her cloak would hide the disarray.

Hugh grabbed up his gown and strode to the tent opening. He jerked his hand backwards in a sharp imperative gesture that she interpreted correctly as meaning she should stay where she was. Then he stepped out into the drizzling moonless night.

"My lord . . . my lord . . . we've found Red." Jack Stedman's voice reached Guinevere as she stood just inside the tent. "Looks like 'e took a blow to the 'ead. But there was a jug beside 'im. Smells like frumenty. Frumenty wi' a goodly portion o' spirit too."

"How badly is he hurt?" Hugh's voice was as calm and even as if that wild ecstasy had never happened.

"Not bad. Just a bump. I reckon 'e was 'alf asleep anyway wi' this stuff."

"We'll address that issue in the morning. One of Lady Mallory's servants is in the woods. You had better send men to find him."

"You won't find him." Guinevere spoke quietly as she came out of the tent, her hooded cloak wrapped tightly around her. In the dark, her expression was unreadable. "Not if he doesn't wish to be found. He'll know by now that something's gone wrong."

Jack Stedman stared at her in astonishment, searching for an explanation for her extraordinary appearance from his master's tent.

"I had some plan to leave Lord Hugh's escort," Guinevere explained distantly. "Lord Hugh discovered my intent. It was a matter that required some discussion." She gave Jack a faint but sardonic smile and turned to Hugh, glad of the darkness that obscured his returning gaze.

"If you give me leave, Lord Hugh, I will call Greene and send him for the rest of my household who are accompanying me to London. They should reach us here by noon with the necessary carts of provisions and my books. As I recall, you said you'd not object to a delayed departure on the morrow."

He gave her a short nod. "We will await your convenience, madam. Let us go and find your huntsman."

They walked side by side into the trees at the perimeter of the field. "I must ask you to lace my gown," Guinevere said in a tone that made it clear she would rather do anything other than have to ask him for such a service. "I would keep what happened tonight from even Tilly." She gave him her back.

"You cannot deny to yourself what happened," he returned softly as he felt beneath her cloak for the laces. "*Damn!* How can I do this when I can't see!"

"You managed well enough before."

"Unlacing is easier than lacing," he observed dryly, feeling for the eyes. "Even in the heat of passion . . . or should I say, *especially* in the heat of passion."

"I would rather you said nothing at all about passion," she declared in a fierce undertone. "Here, let me try, if you can't do it."

He almost slapped her hands aside and caught up the folds of her cloak, throwing it over her shoulder. "Now I can see what I'm doing." There was silence broken only by the dripping of the trees. Then he said, "There, I think that's all of them." His hands dropped from her back and only as she breathed again did she realize she'd been holding her breath.

"Guinevere, you cannot deny what happened," he repeated. "Not to yourself . . . not to me."

"Can't I, Lord Hugh?" She moved away from him into the trees. She glanced over her shoulder at him, but again her expression was veiled in the drizzling gloom. "Can't I?"

Pursing her lips she whistled her blackbird's call. Within seconds it was answered by the *rattatat* of a woodpecker.

12.

Ondon. Guinevere had had a mental image of the city but she had not been able to imagine this tempestuous and noisy place with its dark, squalid alleys and narrow lanes, its higgledy-piggledy houses tumbling together. And the smell. The stench of sea coal and the filth from the kennels was thick on the air. The air itself seemed tangible, so heavy and humid on this September afternoon. Hawkers' cries, voices raised in anger, screams of rage or pain mingled with excited yells from cockpits and bear-baiting yards produced a cacophony that gave her a pounding headache.

A tucket of trumpets rose above the racket and she saw coming towards them along the narrow alley a mounted procession led by scarlet-uniformed heralds. Outriders swept pedestrians aside and Hugh, riding at the head of his own cavalcade, gestured that his troop and Guinevere's little party should draw to the side of the narrow thoroughfare to let the oncoming party through.

Some arrogant nobleman, Guinevere thought with a degree of disdain, backing her mare against the waist-high hedge of one of the small white daub houses that lined the lane. Hugh presumably knew to whom he should give precedence. She regarded the procession as it swept past with the same disdain, although not unmixed with curiosity.

A round-faced man with a hard mouth rode in the center of the group. His gown of silk velvet edged with a rich dark fur was studded with jewels, and a great diamond winked in the turned-up brim of his velvet cap. He looked neither to right nor left, ignoring the people who were giving him way with a sneering insolence that set Guinevere's teeth on edge. She glanced sideways to where Hugh sat his destrier, his expression impassive.

The last outrider passed and Hugh turned his horse back into the center of the lane, his men following. After a minute, Hugh drew his horse to one side and waited for Guinevere's little troop to come up with him. He fell in beside Guinevere.

"So what did you think of our Lord Privy Seal, madam?" he inquired.

"That was Thomas Cromwell?"

"Aye." One of his unpleasant smiles flickered at the corners of his mouth. "The true ruler of the land, or so he'd have the people believe."

"He looked a hard man," she observed, aware of a fluttering coldness in her belly.

"An understatement," Hugh said. He gave her a curt nod and urged his horse forward to move up and rejoin his men.

Her first glimpse of Privy Seal, the man who would decide her fate.

The cold flutter in her belly deepened and the sense of despair that she fought so hard to keep at bay returned in full measure. She glanced at the girls who were riding on either side of her. They were gazing in open fascination at the tumultuous scenes around them. Pippa's mouth was a round O and for once she was bereft of speech.

"There are so many people, Mama," Pen murmured in awe. "More even than at the Michaelmas fair in Derby."

Robin, who was riding as usual at Pen's side, observed with unconscious superiority, "Oh, you couldn't compare a crowd at a country fair with London town, Pen!"

Pen flushed. "I *know* that. I was just saying."

"Derby's huge," Pippa said, flying to her sister's defense. "It's as big as London, isn't it, Mama?"

"I don't think so, sweeting," Guinevere said, managing a smile.

"And this is just an ordinary Wednesday," Robin pointed out. "It's not even a fair day." He glanced at Pen and said placatingly, "I could show you some of the sights if you'd like, Pen. If my father will permit me."

"You'll show me, too, won't you?" Pippa piped. "I want to see the sights too."

"If my lady will permit, I will take you both myself," the magister declared. "You must both have an educational tour. If Master Robin wishes to accompany us, then I'm sure that will be very well."

Robin looked so horrified at the prospect of being shepherded around the city by his beloved's dusty tutor that Pen went into a peal of laughter, quite forgetting her momentary irritation with her swain. "Magister Howard is very knowledgable," she said. "He'll tell us all sorts of things that I'm sure you don't know."

"I daresay," Robin muttered. "I think I should ride up with Jack Stedman in case my father has orders for me." He urged his chestnut into a trot and drew away from the little party that surrounded the Lady Guinevere and her daughters.

"Eh, but I'll be glad when this is over," the magister said with a sigh, sucking in his cheeks as he jogged and swayed in the saddle. " 'Tis a monstrous tiresome journey this."

"Close on eight weeks," Guinevere agreed. She looked back to where Tilly on her mule rode close beside the cart loaded with provisions and Guinevere's precious crate of books. Master Crowder managed the two cart horses with dour efficiency, but it was clear he considered driving a cart to be beneath his steward's rank. Greene rode at the rear of their little household procession, his bow at the ready, a quiverful of arrows at his back, a pike notched to his saddle.

Guinevere reflected that Hugh had shown uncommon gentleness to her retainers. Where he might have punished them for their part in her attempted escape, he had instead not spoken of it. He had not forbidden Greene to carry arms and had allowed them as a group to set up their own camp, to provision and cook for themselves. Greene hunted fresh game, Crowder and Tilly saw to its preparation. They were to all intents and purposes traveling separately except for the perimeter guards, now doubled around the camp at night, and Robin's presence at Pen's side whenever he had no duties to perform.

Since that night, Hugh and Guinevere had barely spoken to each other. Guinevere had dictated this state of affairs. She had withdrawn from Hugh, met his attempts at conversation with cool brief responses, answered his smiles with neutral courtesy. It had taken very few such exchanges before he had bowed to her wishes. If she would deny what had happened between them, then so would he.

And Guinevere was determined he would never guess at the effort it cost her to deny herself the pleasure he was so willing to share with her . . . how many times she asked herself what difference it would make if she yielded to the joys of his loving . . . how many times she asked herself what good it did her to be so stubbornly self-denying. Her situation would not change whether she enjoyed an illicit liaison with Hugh of Beaucaire or not. It was clear to her now that she could not affect his decisions, whether he did what he did out of duty or self-interest. He would not save her just because he had yielded to her charms and his own desire.

So why not enjoy it while she had the chance? She tried to ignore the niggling recognition that it could well be her *last* chance on earth to indulge in such physical pleasures.

But she had no answer except that she *could* not. And so their exchanges were marked by a distant formality and concerned only the details of the journey. Hugh informed her each evening of the route they would take the following day and courteously asked her if she had any difficulties or requests. He accommodated the girls' need to rest for a day every so often but Guinevere knew the delay irked him. He was as anxious as she to get this dreadful journey over with.

And here they were now, in London. Journey's end. *Life's end.*

No, she would not allow herself to think of defeat. While she had breath to fight, she would fight.

They were approaching the menacing walls of the prison at New Gate and a sea of people gathered at the gates blocked their way.

"Now what?" Guinevere mused aloud. Then an imperative blast of a horn came from the head of their procession and Jack Stedman came galloping back to Guinevere's little party.

"Madam, I'll take the lassies' reins. Put your horse to the gallop, we need to pull ahead of this crowd." He seized the reins of the girls' ponies and drew them up beside him. "Hold tight, little ladies." The ponies raced along beside him, the girls pink-cheeked in mingled excitement and apprehension.

Guinevere didn't question the instruction. Isolde leaped forward at a nudge of her heels and the magister, moaning loudly, lumbered behind, clinging on for dear life, swaying in his saddle like a drunkard as his horse, infected by the urgency, rushed after the white mare.

Guinevere glanced over her shoulder as the mare flew past the crowd. Greene was riding ahead of the cart now, cracking his whip to clear a path for the mule and the slower-moving vehicle.

And then they were clear and Hugh slowed his horse, the rest slowing around him. Guinevere rode up to him. "What was that about?"

"Take a look." He gestured with his whip.

Guinevere looked back. The crowd had parted. They were yelling invectives, waving their arms. A horse dragging a hurdle emerged from the gates. A man was tied to the hurdle.

"Some poor bastard on his way to Tyburn Tree," Hugh said. "If we got stuck behind that lot, it would take us until nightfall to get to Holborn."

"Mama . . . Mama . . . what's happening?" Pen and Pippa spoke in unison as they rode up, still accompanied by Jack Stedman.

" 'Tis a hanging," Robin told them eagerly. "They're going to hang a man at Tyburn and they drag him through the streets so many people can see him and the crowd gets bigger as they go along. It takes a long time to get there and Holborn's on the way to Tyburn so we'd be held up behind them."

"Will we see it?" Pippa asked, her eyes wide with curiosity. "I've never seen a hanging. I've seen people in the stocks, and being whipped at the cart's tail, but I've never seen anyone hanged before."

"Well, you're not about to now," Hugh said. "What a bloodthirsty jaybird you are. Come, let's get moving before they catch up with us. Greene seems to have brought the cart through all right. I think you'd all do best to ride up here with Jack and me for the rest of the way."

Guinevere acquiesced with a tiny shrug and turned Isolde alongside Hugh's destrier. The magister, grumbling, his mouth pursed with effort, tried to persuade his own mount to follow, but the horse, confused by the noise and the conflicting messages he was getting from his rider's squeezing knees and contradictory tugs on the reins, balked and turned his head, snapping at the magister's feet in the stirrups.

"Eh, sir, you 'ave to show 'im who's in charge," Jack said, hiding a grin as he leaned over and seized the reins from the magister's slack grip. He tugged the recalcitrant horse around.

"Thankee, thankee," the magister muttered, tightening his hold on the reins. "Eh, I'll be glad when this is over."

"You're not alone in that, Magister," Hugh said aridly. He cast a sidelong glance at Guinevere but she avoided his eye. Despite the lengthy tedium of the journey she still managed to appear fresh; her clothes showed remarkably few signs of wear and tear. Every night, Tilly carried hot water into Guinevere's tent and was frequently to be seen with her hussif, mending clothes.

Guinevere still held herself with the grace and elegance of the lady of Mallory Hall, and although her eyes were shadowed they were still a pure clear purple. Her mouth was as warm and red as ever, although her jawline was taut now, her expression often drawn. But her complexion was soft and glowing with the long days in the fresh air, her hair the same shimmering silver-gold. He could still feel its silky length rippling beneath his fingers . . .

God's bones! How he wanted her! Every waking minute he was tormented by his desire for her, and his sleep was invaded by restless passion. Did she feel any of this herself? If she did, she was an expert at concealing it, he reflected grimly. She had been as wild for that loving as he, so now, in the face of this cool withdrawal, he could only assume that her loathing for her escort, for the man who was intent on handing her over to the ruthless might of the State, was far more powerful than the inconvenient vagaries of lust. And in all honesty he couldn't blame her. As far as Guinevere was concerned, Hugh of Beaucaire was responsible for her present predicament.

Unless of course she had killed a husband. Then she and she alone was responsible for her present predicament. Even as Hugh reminded himself of this, he wished he could take more comfort in the reminder. With a silent oath, he encouraged his horse to pull a little way ahead of Guinevere's Isolde.

Guinevere was distracting herself from Hugh's proximity by mentally running through the various strands of her defense. She tried to banish the arrogant, contemptuous face of Privy Seal from her mind's eye, to refuse to allow herself to despair of having any impact on that harsh countenance. She and the magister had spent the long evenings of the journey discussing possible strategies, but they had had no access to the crated books. Once they were able to consult the texts, matters would become clearer.

They were now crossing the Holborn River that flowed into the mighty Thames. The bridge was thronged with iron-wheeled carts, women selling apples from wheelbarrows, boys carrying trays of hot pies over their heads. Mangy dogs ran between horses' hooves and the wheels of carts. Men cursed the dogs, slashed at them with whips. Pippa's pony started as a cur snapped at her heels. Expertly the child tightened her grip on the reins and curbed the pony. She was turning in triumph to her mother when the kitten leaped from its customary niche on the saddle, tucked into the folds of Pippa's cloak, and disappeared into the melee of wheels and hooves.

"*Moonshine!*" Pippa yelled, hauling her pony to a dead halt. She was about to fling herself from the saddle when Guinevere grabbed her.

"No . . . no, Pippa, you can't go after her. You'd never find her down there."

Pippa wept. "I can, Mama. I *can*!"

"My sweet, you can't." Guinevere tightened her encircling hold of the child's waist. "Sweeting, you can't."

"But where is she . . . what will she do . . . what will happen to her!" Pippa began to sob, her breath coming in great gasps.

"What's happened?" Hugh was there, his voice sharp with anxiety. "Is someone hurt?"

"No," Guinevere said, her arm still around her sobbing daughter as the pony shifted uneasily beneath Pippa. "Moonshine was frightened and jumped out of Pippa's arms."

Hugh looked at the throng on the bridge. He could see no sign of the silver kitten. Around them the crowd ebbed and surged. There were angry shouts. Their halted procession was taking up a large space on the bridge's narrow span. He looked at Pippa's drenched face.

"I don't know what we can do, Pippa."

"But what will happen to her?"

"Cats are survivors," he said. "She'll hunt rats and mice." He had an inspiration. "Didn't you say her mother was a barn cat?"

Pippa nodded miserably.

"Her mother will have taught Moonshine to hunt. She'll know what to do."

"Lord Hugh's right, Pippa," Guinevere said, leaning sideways to kiss the child's cheek. "Moonshine will become a London cat. She'll be able to look after herself."

"You could have Nutmeg, Pippa," Pen offered, her own face stricken at her sister's loss. "I don't mind." She unwrapped the ginger kitten from her cloak.

"Put him away!" Pippa said fiercely. "He might jump off, too." She added, "I don't want your kitten, Pen. He's lovely, but I want mine." Her eyes, wide with unhappiness, searched the melee. "Will she be all right, Mama?"

Guinevere looked at Hugh. He opened his hands in a little gesture of sympathy, of shared parental understanding.

"She'll do as well here as at home," she said. "There are foxes and wolves at home. There aren't any here. Moonshine will find a life for herself."

"I don't think so," Pippa said. She lifted her chin and sniffed bravely. "But we can't find her, can we?"

"I'll stay and look for her," Robin offered. "May I, sir?"

Hugh hesitated. Every instinct told him it was a futile exercise and it would be better not to give Pippa false hope, and yet he could not resist the child's pleading eyes in her tear-drenched face, or her pathetic attempt at brave acceptance.

"Take Luke with you and be back in the house before curfew," he said.

"Yes, sir." Robin smiled encouragingly at Pippa. "I'm sure we'll find her." He called for Luke, dismounted, handed the reins to the soldier and disappeared into the melee.

"Pippa, love, don't expect too much," Guinevere said, stroking the child's cheek. "One little kitten in this crowd. She could be anywhere."

"Robin will find her," Pen declared. "I know he will."

Hugh shook his head. "Your faith is commendable, Pen, but I agree with your mother. It's a very long shot." He urged his horse forward again. "Come, let's get off this bridge. We're but fifteen minutes from my house. Jack, do you follow closely with the girls."

Guinevere rode beside him, just a little ahead of the rest. She had not broached the subject of her lodging since he'd told her that she would be held beneath his roof. She had not argued the issue then because she'd assumed her flight would succeed and the issue become moot. Now, however, it was imperative. She *could* not, *would* not accept his hospitality, either as prisoner or guest.

"My lord, I prefer not to presume upon your hospitality," she stated formally. "If you will direct my steward to a decent inn we will make shift for ourselves. I shall understand that you might wish to put a guard upon the inn. You may have no fear we will escape your vigilance."

"Oh, I assure you, madam, I have no such fear. Until Privy Seal makes some disposition for you, you will be under my roof," he returned in flat tones. He began to whistle softly, looking straight ahead as they left the little river behind and entered the maze of lanes that formed the district of Holborn.

Guinevere set her teeth. That whistle irritated her beyond measure. "Nevertheless, sir, I would prefer to seek my own accommodation."

"You may bring up the subject with Privy Seal, or even the king," Hugh told her. "For the moment, you remain in my charge until I'm commanded to yield it up."

She glanced at him with a mockingly raised eyebrow. "I see. My arrest is made manifest, it seems."

He shrugged. "If you wish to put it that way."

"I have always preferred to call a spade a spade, my lord."

Hugh looked at her intently. "Strangely, I have difficulty believing that, Lady Guinevere. On the contrary, I've noticed that you're adept at denying realities if it suits you to do so."

Guinevere's hands quivered on the reins. "Some things are too trivial to warrant acknowledgment," she stated.

Hugh's intense gaze remained on her face. "You lie, my lady," he accused softly. Then he looked away from her and began to whistle again.

Guinevere fought the surge of emotion. She gazed around with every appearance of nonchalance, noting the half-timbered daub cottages behind neat hedges, the larger houses behind stone walls. It was much quieter here than in the warren of streets beyond the bridge. Some of the lanes were cobbled, providing some relief from the clouds of dust that rose from the summer-dry mud. The kennels were sluiced and the stench was much less pronounced than it had been before.

They turned onto a broader thoroughfare. A stone wall loomed at the end with high wooden gates set in its center. Above the wall, Guinevere could see the lofty tops of trees.

The herald broke from the ranks behind them and cantered up to the gate, raising his trumpet to his lips. He blew a single blast and the gates swung open. Two gatekeepers bowed low as Lord Hugh and his party passed through.

Hugh's house was neither modest nor grand. It was a half-timbered stone building, low-ceilinged, thatch-roofed. Some of the upper windows were glassed and caught the sinking sun. Smoke arose from two stone chimneys. The grounds were well maintained, but were not elaborately landscaped. They were more functional than ornamental.

Like their owner, Guinevere thought, surprised into a smile.

"Something amuses you?"

The smile was hastily quashed. "Hardly, my lord."

"Well, allow me to bid you welcome." Hugh drew rein before the oak front doors and dismounted. He turned to help Guinevere but she avoided his hands and slid to the ground unaided.

The magister tumbled off the back of his mount with a sigh of relief. "I'll not be sorry if I never see a horse again," he declared, rubbing his backside. "If man were made to ride, the Lord God wouldn't have given him legs."

"We couldn't possibly have walked all this way, Magister," Pippa said. "Miles and miles and miles. Your legs would have worn out." She was still looking subdued but her curiosity about her new surroundings was too strong to be extinguished by her unhappiness over Moonshine.

"Come inside." Hugh gestured to the now open front door where stood a man in the black gown of a steward. "Master Milton will have arranged the guest apartments for you. Your household should be here in a few minutes, they weren't far behind. Mistress Tilly will be brought to you. Master Milton will make arrangements for you, Magister, and for Crowder and Greene." He nodded interrogatively at the steward who bowed his agreement as he ushered them into the house.

A large square hall with fireplaces at either end formed the main living space. It was a handsomely paneled chamber with deep window seats to the low-silled windows and an oaken floor. A long oak table with benches on either side stood in the middle, wooden settles flanked the fireplaces. It was handsome but it lacked a woman's touch, Guinevere thought. Again, it was functional, neat, like its master.

"I've been home rarely these last two years," Hugh said, almost as if he was apologizing for the sparseness of his abode. "But Master Milton will do whatever is needful for your comfort."

The magister, with a sigh like air escaping from a cushion, collapsed onto one of the window seats and untied the lappets of his cap. He flapped his hand in front of his face to create a cooling draught.

"For as long as we're obliged to trespass upon your hospitality, Lord Hugh, Master Crowder will take care of our needs," Guinevere said. "I'm not yet reduced to penury and will not allow my household to be a charge upon your purse."

Two red spots appeared high on Hugh's cheekbones. "That will not be necessary," he clipped. "I realize I can't hope to offer the comforts of your own home, we are not all as rich as Croesus. But I will do what I can."

He had neatly turned the tables, making her sound arrogant and discourteous in her reluctance to accept his hospitality. But she would not play that game. She ignored the comment, instead looking around the apartment with apparent fascination.

Hugh strode to the staircase that rose from the corner of the hall. "Come, madam, I'll show you to my so-humble guest apartments. Pen . . . Pippa . . . come with us now."

Pen, clutching Nutmeg, came over immediately. Pippa, however, was engaged in describing Moonshine's disappearance to a clearly confused Master Milton. "You see, Boy Robin *might* find her," he was being earnestly assured. "I do so hope he will. And if he does, I'll need to give her some milk. I'm sure she'll be frightened. Don't you think she'll be frightened? Will you have some milk for me, Master Milton? Just a little saucer. I give it to her on the tip of my finger. She licks it off, but her tongue's so rough. Did you know a kitten's tongue was rough? I think . . ."

"Pippa!" Guinevere called, feeling Hugh's large frame aquiver with laughter beside her, his flash of anger vanquished by the child's artless prattle. "Master Milton has work to do."

"I was only explaining about Moonshine, in case Robin brings her back." Pippa trailed over to them, once more despondent.

"Don't expect too much," Hugh said quietly.

"I'm not really," Pippa replied, slipping her hand in her mother's.

Hugh led the way up the stairs. At their head a passageway ran to the left and another straight ahead. Hugh led the way down the second corridor. He opened a door at the end and stepped inside.

Guinevere and the girls followed him. He looked around with a critical frown and she thought he was looking anxious, as if something should be found wanting. It was a simple chamber, the floor scattered with sweet herbs. "You and the girls will share the bed," Hugh said. "There should be a truckle bed for Tilly." He bent to look beneath the big poster bed and pulled out a cot. "I trust this will suit you."

"Amply, I thank you." Guinevere drew off her gloves and went to the window. It looked out over a kitchen garden and an orchard beyond. There were outhouses, the brewery, bakery, and washhouse. Farther off, she could see the roofs of neighboring houses. She could hear the city noises drifting over the rooftops and the air lacked sweetness. It was all very orderly, but so alien. And she was very afraid.

Hugh touched her shoulder. He could feel her fear and he couldn't help himself. She jumped as if scalded.

He stepped away from her. "I'll leave you now. We sup at seven, when the city gates are closed for curfew." He closed the door behind him and went downstairs. The rest of Guinevere's party had arrived and Master Milton was busy making disposition. Tilly followed two stalwart manservants carrying Guinevere's trunks and crate of books abovestairs.

Hugh summoned Jack Stedman. "Discover where Privy Seal is at present. I imagine he's at his own house in Austin Friars since he was riding through the city just an hour ago. Present my compliments . . . I doubt you'll be permitted to see the man himself but one of his gentleman ushers will bear the message. Say that I am returned to London with the Lady Guinevere."

"Aye, my lord." Jack offered a half salute and hurried away. Hugh called for wine and sat beside the hearth where a servant was kindling a fire against the coolness of the September evening. Now they must wait.

13.

Guinevere came down to the hall with the girls just before supper. Servants were laying the long table with drinking horns, wooden trenchers, spoons, and knives. There were no elegancies here, Guinevere reflected as she cast a sweeping eye over the table, noticing that Hugh of Beaucaire had not taken to the use of forks at his table. But since he was rarely at home, he would see little need to spend money on such niceties. She noticed the single manacle in the wall by the front door. It was a common feature of dining halls; Mallory Hall had its own. It was a partly jesting forfeit for a guest who became offensive in drink. His arm would be manacled and the contents of his drinking cup poured down his sleeve. It was a humiliating rather than a painful penalty, although costly and irritating to have one's expensive garments soaked in wine.

It was never administered at Mallory Hall under her own dominion, although Stephen had delighted in mortifying his guests if they gave him half a chance. Guinevere preferred merely to absent herself from table if matters became too rowdy.

Pippa ran over to Hugh, who had risen from the settle at their appearance. "Is Robin back . . . is Robin back, sir?"

"Not as yet," Hugh said, bending to kiss her anxiously upturned face. "But he should be here any minute. The bells will sound for curfew in five minutes and he knows he must be within doors by then."

Guinevere was struck by how natural that kiss had seemed. Hugh thought nothing of it and neither, it was clear, had the child. Guinevere was aware that she was smiling. Hugh's response to Pippa pleased her on some deep level that she couldn't understand. Once again she felt the powerful sense of connection with him. The sense that it was right that they should be here together, sharing this moment. Once again there was no antagonism . . . it almost seemed no possibility of antagonism. And once again she was awash in confusion.

"May I offer you wine, my lady?"

"My thanks." She took the cup he handed her. Her smile didn't falter and she read the answering light in his eye. There was a question in his steady gaze as he raised his cup and made a tiny gesture of a toast. Guinevere raised her own cup, touched it to her lips. Her eyes seemed riveted to his and for a long moment it seemed she could not break the connection. She had forced the distance between them on the journey to avoid just this, but now there was no distance and it seemed impossible to retrieve it. There was only this sense of excitement, of promise, of possibility. And for as long as she was obliged to share his roof, it would always be there, weakening her resolve, invading her thoughts, muddling her senses.

At last she managed to turn her head aside, to address some calm remark to the girls.

Hugh sipped his wine, his hungry eyes resting on her profile, on the soft white skin of her throat, on the turn of her slender shoulder, on the swell of her breasts beneath the pleated lace of her chemise.

Then came the sound of voices outside and his gaze shifted to the door. "Robin," he said, adding, "and just in time," as a great peal of bells sounded from across the city, telling travelers that the city gates were now closed and all working fires must now be covered.

Pippa had already run to the door, jumping on tiptoe to lift the heavy latch. "Have you found her . . . did you find her?" she demanded almost before the door was opened.

Robin came in beaming. "I found her and then she ran away again. I had to chase her all over the bridge. I thought I'd lost her and then I heard her. She was clinging to the ledge under the bridge. I had to climb over the rail to get her." He handed the bedraggled little creature to Pippa.

"Oh, that's so wonderful!" Pen exclaimed, hurrying towards him. "You're so clever, Robin. I knew you'd be able to find her." She took his hand and squeezed it tightly.

Robin's beam widened so that it seemed it would split his face in two. "Did you? I was so afraid I wouldn't, and this gaggle of boys followed me the whole time. They kept asking me what I was looking for and when I finally picked up Moonshine I think they thought I was a bedlamite! Who else would chase all over for a *kitten*?"

"Well, anyone would!" Pippa exclaimed, her voice muffled by the kitten's fur as she nuzzled her neck. "You're a splendid *Boy*," she said vehemently. "I hope one day I meet one just like *you*."

Robin blushed to the tips of his ears and Hugh caught Guinevere's eye. He was trying not to laugh and she bit her own lip struggling for sobriety. The lad was looking embarrassed enough as it was. That strand of taut promise was snapped for the moment, in its place only this calm and amused friendship. And Guinevere didn't know which of the two was the most dangerous.

"Well, now that all's well that ends well, I suggest we sup," Hugh said, gesturing to a hovering manservant to sound the gong that would summon the household to table.

Hugh's household was not large, and Guinevere noted that only the kitchen servants responsible for serving did not sit at the master's table. There was room enough for maids and grooms, and by their grease-spattered aprons she could identify the potboys and spit turners who had their seats far below the salt.

There were no pages behind the diners at Hugh of Beaucaire's table. Servers placed heaped platters along the middle of the table and everyone helped themselves, spearing venison on knife points, spooning rich gravy from steaming bowls, dipping bread in broth. A minstrel plucked a lute in the small gallery high up on the end wall.

Hugh and Guinevere ate for the most part in silence. It was not an uncomfortable silence. For once there were no barbed undercurrents, and yet Guinevere felt as if the quiet of their present companionship,

their seeming serenity, had a limited time to run. As if she were standing on a sultry summer evening, the tightness in her head a warning of
an approaching thunderstorm.

When the meal drew to a close, Guinevere told the girls to take the
kittens to their chamber and feed them there. Tilly would then help
them to bed.

"I must ask you to excuse me," Hugh said, rising from the table. "I
have business in the stables. Robin, you will accompany me."

"Aye, sir. Should I fetch your heavy cloak? It grows chilly," Robin
asked, eager as always to do his father's bidding.

Hugh nodded with a smile and the lad ran off to his father's chamber, which lay above the hall.

"I must see how my household has fared in my absence," Hugh
explained.

"Of course. I do not expect to be entertained, sir. Besides, the magister and I have work to do."

"Make free of the fire," he offered, gesturing to the blazing hearth.
"You won't wish to disturb the girls in your chamber."

"No," Guinevere agreed. But she hesitated, wondering if it would be
wise to formulate strategies for her defense in the public hall of her
jailer's house.

"You need have no fear you'll be overheard," Hugh said with an
ironical glitter in his eye as he read her thoughts. "I will promise to
make a great clatter with my boots to give you fair warning of my
return."

Guinevere turned away from his gaze. She said to the magister, who
was bobbing at her side, "I'll fetch the books we'll need, Magister.
Make yourself comfortable at the fireside." She gave Hugh a cool nod
of farewell and glided to the stair, her back straight as a ruler, her dark
velvet gown over its cone-shaped farthingale swaying gracefully with
her smooth step.

She felt a surge of optimism as she sorted through the crate of books
in her chamber. At last she and the magister would be able to test their
theories against the legal facts. Her books had always provided answers. Surely they would help her now.

She hurried downstairs with her selection. The magister was seated
on the settle, his skinny shanks in their wrinkled black hose stretched

to the fire. "Oh, this is comfort indeed," he declared, rubbing his hands together. "Lord Hugh has ordered extra light for us. See, we have two extra lanterns and there are new candles in the sconces." He gestured to the greater illumination by the fireside. "So considerate of him, I thought."

"Indeed," Guinevere agreed dryly, depositing her books on the opposite settle. She got straight down to business. "As we've discussed, Magister, the issue is one of evidence. They have no evidence, no hard evidence, to link me to any of my husbands' deaths." She paused, staring into the fire, frowning fiercely.

What had he discovered at Matlock? If she didn't know the evidence against her, she couldn't formulate a defense.

She shook her head. She had to work with what she had. "We know Lord Hugh can bear witness to some contradictions in my statements and in Tilly's concerning Lord Mallory's fall. If they wish to make something of those contradictions, then we are in difficulties."

"I think it safe to assume that they will," the magister said, pursing his lips and sucking in his cheeks. He asked hesitantly, "You are convinced that Lord Hugh will tell of these contradictions?"

Guinevere continued to stand staring into the flames, her hands pressed against the folds of her gown. What *had* he discovered at Matlock?

"Yes," she said after a minute. "He will give his evidence as he sees it." She shrugged and sat down on the settle beside the books. "My task will be to convince the lords that those contradictions do not constitute hard evidence."

"We should examine the common law on circumstantial evidence," the magister said. "A conclusion drawn by inference from known facts that have no clear explanation is a weak one. We must find an alternative persuasive explanation for those facts."

"Aye," Guinevere agreed. "But what of charges of witchcraft? I see no way to refute those charges if they're leveled. Only my husbands could deny that they were bewitched, and my husbands no longer walk this earth." She pressed her steepled fingers to her lips.

"I beg you, madam, let us take one issue at a time," the magister said with a worried frown. "We have hard evidence supporting your claim to the land Lord Hugh lays claim to. That's one big issue in our favor. No one can dispute the legality of the premarriage contract with Roger Needham, and if you're on solid legal ground there, a reasonable man might assume that you are on the other issues."

"A reasonable man, yes. But is Lord Privy Seal a reasonable man?"

"Come now, madam, let's not prejudge the case," the magister begged. "The law will have an answer for us, it always does. Let us take a look at Fortescue's *De laudibus legum Angliae.*" He leaned over and selected the book in question.

An hour later, the magister yawned deeply and shifted on the settle, trying to ease his aching bones. "God's mercy, but I doubt I'll ever have ease again," he muttered. "Riding like that, day after day."

"We'll cease our discussion for tonight." Guinevere closed the book. "You need your rest, Magister."

"I'm an old man, madam. Not made for travel," he said.

"I should not have brought you," Guinevere said remorsefully. " 'Twas not kind in me to force such privations upon you."

"Bless you, madam, I'd not leave you to face this alone." Magister Howard threw up his hands in horrified disclaimer. "But we've made some progress I believe."

Guinevere was less sure of this but she agreed with a smile, unwilling to distress her old mentor. "Seek your bed, sir. We'll continue on the morrow."

The elderly man rose creakily to his feet. "I'll not be sorry to lie down among feathers again," he said. "I give you good night, my lady."

"Good night." She watched him go, leaning her head against the high carved back of the wooden settle. Legalistic arguments seemed so empty, so pointless, and yet they were all she had. That and her own eloquence. Would it be enough to sway a man of Privy Seal's complexion?

She heard the clatter of booted feet on the flagstones beyond a doorway at the rear of the hall that she assumed led to the kitchen quarters and the stables. Lord Hugh spoke from the doorway. "Did I make sufficient noise?"

"Your consideration, my lord, overwhelms me."

Hugh came into the hall. He strode to the fireplace and stood looking at her, one hand resting on the back of the opposite settle. "You have finished? Is the magister gone to his bed?"

"We've finished for this evening. The magister is tired after the journey." She remained with her head against the back of the settle, her hands clasped lightly in her lap, her eyes half shut. But she could feel his steady gaze upon her.

"You look exhausted yourself." He turned as the front door opened. Jack Stedman came in on a blast of autumnal night air.

"Eh, 'tis gettin' right parky out there," he commented, pulling off his cap. "Weather's turned around, I shouldn't wonder." He didn't see Guinevere who was hidden from the door by the high back of her seat. "Privy Seal's usher took the message an' kept me kickin' me 'eels for close on two hour afore 'e come back, m'lord." Jack sounded apologetic for the delay. " 'Twas such a crush in 'is antechamber a man couldn't 'ardly move."

"Is there a message?" Hugh inquired.

"Aye, m'lord. Y'are summoned with the Lady Guinevere to attend at 'ampton Court tomorrow at three in the afternoon."

Hugh nodded and glanced involuntarily to the settle where Guinevere sat unmoving, her eyes still half closed. "That will be all for tonight, Jack. At sunup I'll need a barge at Blackfriars Steps. Make sure it's one with some shelter from the elements. You'll accompany us, together with two of the men."

"Aye, sir. And Master Robin?"

"He may stay here. Tell him he may have a holiday . . . if keeping company with young Pippa can be so described," Hugh added dryly.

Jack grinned. "Aye, sir. Good night." He touched his forehead in a half salute and left, cramming his cap back on his head.

"So soon," Guinevere said. She rose slowly to her feet and faced him. "Could you not have granted me a few days of respite, my lord, before sending your message?"

He answered quietly, "A delay would have been no respite. 'Tis better to do what has to be done."

"But I am not ready yet."

"There will be no trial tomorrow," he said. "There will be questions, but no trial."

"I am afeard," she said in a low voice. "Do not tell me I have no cause to be."

"I would not tell you that."

She looked up at him, her face naked and vulnerable, her eyes haunted with fear.

The fire crackled behind her, the only sound in the now still house. She could hear her quickened breath, softly sibilant as it left her parted lips. She could hear the blood in her ears.

"Come to me," Hugh said. It was part plea, part command.

Guinevere stood still, feeling the warmth of the fire at her back. The glow of the lanterns, the bright light of the candles streaming upwards from their sconces cast a circle of light around them. Beyond the circle the hall was in shadow.

"Come to me," he said again. He placed his hands on her shoulders, feeling the delicacy of the bones beneath his fingers.

She didn't move, neither away from him nor towards him. This night she needed what he would offer her more than she had ever needed anything. The comfort of connection, the strength that came from knowing one was not alone. The power of loving that, for however short a time, would quiet her fears, soothe her fearful soul. But still there niggled the knowledge that if she took Hugh she would take that comfort from the man who had caused this agony of despair.

And so she made no move towards him, but when he drew her against him, cupping her chin to lift her face, she offered no resistance.

He kissed her, gently and then with increasing pressure as if he would wake her up, bring forth from her the passionate response that he knew waited for release.

"Come to me," he whispered against her mouth. "Guinevere, come to me." He held her strongly now so that she could feel his strength, feel it encompassing her, offering surcease, the chance for the first time since Timothy's death to lay down her own burdens for however brief a moment and nourish herself at the wellspring of a power and energy not her own.

Her mouth opened for his probing tongue and she leaned back into the strong hold, opening her throat, her breast, in an instinctive movement of surrender. He moved his mouth to the porcelain column of her throat, kissed the fast-beating pulse, trailed his lips to her breast, feeling the warmth of her skin through the fine lace of her chemise. He felt her passivity, not a negative passivity but one that came from an active decision to receive him, to draw from him.

A river of delight washed through him. She was more truly his at this moment than ever during the wild madness of that night in his tent.

"Come," he said softly, taking her hand. He picked up a lantern with his free hand and led her to the stairs. She gathered her skirts and stepped up beside him, her body slim and tall and straight as they ascended the stairs.

He turned to the dark passage that led to the left of the stairs, holding his lantern up high. Her hand in his was cool, the fingers curled around his own.

He lifted the latch on the door at the very end of the passage and pushed it wide. A candle burned on a small table and a banked fire glowed in the hearth. The light from his lantern threw back the shadows as they entered the chamber.

It was as neat and orderly as his tent had been. The poster bed was uncarved, the coverlet a simple quilt. An iron-bound chest and a plain armoire held his possessions.

" 'Tis plain, I know," he murmured.

Guinevere smiled and spoke for the first time. "I expected nothing else of its occupant."

"You have an understanding of me, it seems." He set the lantern on the mantelpiece and gazed at her as she stood in her dark velvet, one hand resting on the wooden bedpost.

"A little," she agreed.

"Come to me." He held out his hands and this time she stepped across the waxed floor towards him. She stood before him, making no other move, her eyes fixed upon his.

"I will try to give you what you wish," he said, his voice suddenly husky, coming from deep in his throat. He reached for the jeweled headdress and she bowed her head to make it easier for him.

He withdrew the pins slowly, one by one, laying each one on the small table, then lifted the silver fillet from her head. He took the pins from her hood and then her coif and then her hair, releasing the coiled braids. He had no brush but used his fingers to loosen the coils, playfully flipping the long strands out until they framed her face. Her earlier pallor had gone and her ivory skin glowed.

"You are so beautiful," he said, kissing her warm mouth. "You must tell me if there's anything you want of me. I would not fail you, Guinevere."

"You will not," she said with perfect truth. She caressed his cheek, ran the pad of her thumb over his mouth. He would not fail her . . . not in this at least. She turned her back.

He unlaced her gown, slowly this time, lifting it away from her, letting it fall to the chest at the foot of the bed. He unlaced the bodice of her chemise and slid his hands inside to cup her breasts, then her shoulders. Her skin was so warm and soft and fragrant.

"Show me something of yourself first," she said with a languid smile. "I would see you naked." She ran her flat palm over his cheek, tracing his mouth with her little finger. His hand came up to grasp her wrist as he sucked her probing finger into his mouth, delicately nibbling the tip. Her entire body seemed to come alive under the exquisite sensation.

He drew back, his brilliant eyes glittering with desire. He began to undress for her. Guinevere watched him with lustful greed as slowly he revealed himself to her. He slipped off his gown, his doublet, unlaced his shirt, removing each garment with deliberate care, laying them over a stool beneath the window.

Guinevere's gaze dwelled on the broad expanse of his chest, lightly dusted with gray curls, the tight little buds of his nipples, the span of his waist . . . so narrow when compared with the breadth of his chest and shoulders. She gazed with uninhibited lust as he unfastened his garters and peeled off his hose. He stood straight and looked at her with a quizzical little gleam in his eye. She gazed at the concave belly, the hard muscular thighs, the vigorous jut of his penis from the wiry tangle of graying hair.

"Do I please you, madam?"

She nodded, her tongue moistening her lips. "Oh, yes."

He turned to place his hose on the stool with his other garments, offering his taut buttocks to her gaze. She came up behind him, placing her hands on his backside, kneading the muscled flesh. He remained still for her caress, for the stroking finger that slid between his thighs, then he put his hands behind him and clasped her hips. She leaned into his back, nuzzling the sharp points of his shoulder blades. His hands slipped to her backside, stroking the flesh beneath her chemise.

"I think it's time for a little equity," he said with a soft laugh, turning to face her. "I would feast my eyes upon you now, my lady."

He pushed her chemise off her shoulders, down to her waist. The soft mounds of her breasts, the nipples hard and erect, disappeared into his warm palms. He held them, glorying in their weight and fullness. Her eyes closed on a deep shudder of pleasure as his fingertips teased the rosy crowns. He ran his hands down the narrow rib cage, feeling the shape of her as he had not done in the crazy haste of their last loving. He took a step back to look at her, bared to the waist, her silvery hair shimmering against her skin that glowed pink with her growing arousal. Her breasts rose and fell with her quickened breath.

Reaching forward, with slow deliberation he pushed the loosened chemise from her hips. It slithered to her ankles, leaving her naked but for her silken hose and garters.

He looked at her, drinking in the mature fullness of her graceful form. This was no girl. He could see the tiny silver stretch marks on her thighs and belly where she had carried her children, the rich blue-veined heaviness of her breasts that had fed her babies, the almost imperceptible thickening of her waist. But she was more beautiful, he thought, for these imperfections than she would have been in the unflawed youthfulness of her girlhood.

Putting his hands on her hips, he turned her, felt her shiver at his touch, at the warm imprint of his hands. He ran a flat finger down her spine. Her skin rippled. Holding her shoulders, he bent his head and his tongue followed the path of the finger. Guinevere bit back a moan at the burning sensuality of the hot moist stroke. Her feet shifted on the bare boards.

He caressed the curve of her hips, the firm rise of her backside, the supple length of her thighs. Then he turned her around again.

She reached her arms around his neck, pressing her nakedness against his. She kissed his mouth, her loins pressed hard against him in eloquent desire. Hugh took a step to the bed, holding her to him, her mouth still locked with his. She fell back as the edge of the bed caught her behind the knees and he came down with her.

He stretched himself beside her, and raised himself on one elbow. She lay on her back looking up at him, and with a curious little gesture of abandon, she stretched her arms above her head, crossing her wrists, yielding up her body to their mutual pleasure.

He smiled slowly, then bent to kiss the base of her throat as his hand smoothed over her belly. He tickled a fingertip in her navel, noting with a secret delight how deep it was. He touched the line of her body, from below her ear to her hip, feeling the tender curves, the deep indentations, and she moaned beneath his hand, whispering his name. His mouth moved to her breasts, his teeth lightly grazed her nipples.

She writhed on the bed, feeling her sex swell with pleasure, her loins filled with a liquid urgency. No longer able to control her responses, she brought her hands down. One slid to his buttocks, the other clasped the turgid flesh of his penis. The blood in the corded veins pulsed strongly against her palm. With a delicate fingertip she pushed back the little cap of skin at its tip, circled the smooth roundness, even as with the finger of her other hand she slid between the cleft of his buttocks, lightly tickling the hard, heavy globes.

Hugh groaned softly under the knowing caress. He moved down the bed and her hands slid away from him. She felt his flat palms inside her thighs, pressing them open. She spread them for him, once more giving her body over to him. He kissed the inside of her thighs, lifted her legs and kissed the hollow behind her knees, stroking down her calves, his fingers cleverly massaging. His tongue trailed along the backs of her thighs; his mouth pressed kisses into the soft creases where her thighs met her bottom. He spread her legs wide and buried his mouth in the hot sea-scented furrow of her body.

His tongue entered her, his mouth nuzzled the hooded bud of her sex. His breath was cool, a wickedly sensual breeze on the hot and swollen lips he caressed.

Guinevere's fingers curled in his hair; her thighs tightened; her hips lifted as he slid his hands beneath her bottom, pinching the soft flesh as he brought her closer and closer to the brink with his tongue. But before she was engulfed he took his mouth from her. She shuddered, aching with longing. Her legs curled around his hips as he moved up her body again. She pulled his head down to her face and kissed him, tasting herself on his tongue, inhaling the intoxicating scents of her own arousal.

He drove deep within her and she held him there, feeling him fill to the very core her exquisitely sensitized body. She felt the pulse of his flesh within her. Then he withdrew slowly, so very slowly, to the very edge of her body until only the tip of his sex touched her. Her opened body cried out for him; she pressed upwards trying to draw him within her again; their eyes held and they could see themselves reflected in the dark irises of the other. It was as if their souls touched, as if each was the mirror image of the other, and when he entered her with one long slow thrust, their bodies became one, their spirits dissolved. They were one.

After many minutes, Hugh disengaged and rolled to the side. He lay on his back, a hand resting on Guinevere's sweat-dampened belly, feeling the rapid pulse beneath his palm. It slowed as his own did, in synchrony it seemed. She sighed, a deep indrawing of breath, a slow exhalation. Then she turned her head to look at him.

He touched her cheek and she smiled, but he sensed the gathering shadows behind the smile.

"*Tristesse de l'amour?*" he inquired gently.

"Perhaps." She reached up and lightly touched his cheek. "I thank you, Hugh."

"You have nothing to thank me for," he responded, lightly grasping her wrist. "I gave to you only what you gave to me."

"I doubt that," she said softly. "But it must never happen again, Hugh. You understand that?"

He shook his head. "No, Guinevere, I do not."

She sat up and said with difficulty, "I wish that you could . . . could understand how frightening this is for me. How I must not, *cannot* yield up myself again in this fight. I have so much to lose, Hugh. So much more than you. Can you not understand that?"

"Yes . . . yes, of course I understand that." He sat up, touched her bare shoulder. "But must you make that lie between us?"

"Yes, I must," she said flatly. "I cannot see clearly if I do not."

There was a short silence, then she said, "I must go to my own chamber."

He watched as she gathered up her clothes. She stood naked, holding the pile of silk, lace, and velvet in her arms. "If you have a night robe I could borrow . . . ?"

"Yes, of course." The old constraint was between them again. Guinevere was forcing its return. That glorious moment of union had done nothing to alter the brutal facts that lay between them.

In his frustration he wanted to shake her, to force her to admit that such loving transcended anything that could thrust them apart. Instead, he swung off the bed and took a fur robe from the armoire. "This will serve." He placed it around her shoulders.

"My thanks," she said and moved to the door. At the door she turned, her hand on the latch. "I do thank you, Hugh."

He made a small helpless gesture of denial.

She seemed to hesitate, then raised the latch and slipped from his chamber.

14.

Guinevere awoke well before dawn from a curiously deep and dreamless sleep. She stirred and Moonshine, who had been sleeping in the small of her back, rose on stilt legs with a slightly indignant glare, stretched languidly, and jumped to the floor. Nutmeg, who'd been curled between the girls' soft bodies, joined his sister. They stalked to the door, stood there, regarding Guinevere in lofty demand.

Guinevere slid to the floor, careful not to wake the still-sleeping girls. She padded across to the door and let the pair of kittens out. Presumably they'd learned their way to the outside the previous evening.

Tilly sat up on the truckle bed and yawned. "You were late to bed, chuck," she observed. Her eye fell on Guinevere's discarded clothing. Guinevere had been too exhausted, too confused, to put them away. Hugh's furred robe lay over a stool.

Guinevere didn't immediately answer the tiring woman. She picked up the robe and slipped it over her naked sleep-warmed body. Her senses swirled as she inhaled the scent of him, felt the heavy warmth of his garment almost as if it was his body against hers. A great melancholy filled her. She could never take from him again what he had given her last night. He had given her what she had craved, had so desperately needed, but she dared not let him love her again. Not if she was ever to be free of him. Their souls had touched last night and while then it had been only joyful, in the cold light of morning the depths of that emotion terrified her. She had to fight Hugh if she was to defeat Privy Seal, and it would be like fighting herself.

"So that's the way the land lies," Tilly murmured with instant comprehension. "Can't say I'm surprised."

" 'Tis a bad thing to have happened, Tilly," Guinevere said slowly. "It should not have happened."

"Well, that's as may be," the other returned with the air of one who didn't believe it. She got off the truckle bed and stretched.

"It begins now, Tilly," Guinevere said slowly. "I must be ready by sunup to accompany Lord Hugh to the palace at Hampton Court."

Tilly's expression grew solemn. She glanced towards the big bed where the children were stirring, and raised an eyebrow in silent inquiry.

"I'll explain to them," Guinevere murmured.

"Where's Moonshine?" Pippa demanded, speaking even in the moment she came out of sleep. She sat up rubbing sleep from her eyes. "I dreamed I'd lost her again."

"She's gone out with Nutmeg," her mother reassured her.

"Oh, we have to find them." Pen scrambled out of bed. "They don't really know their way around yet."

"Hurry and get dressed then." Guinevere moved to the linen press, gesturing to Tilly that she should follow her. She spoke softly, so that the children would not hear. "I think I'll wear the black gown and hood," she said. "I believe the demure widow will be the best appearance to present. The silver fillet to the hood, and maybe no breast jewel, just the pomander on my girdle. I don't wish to thrust my wealth in their faces."

"Aye, chuck, 'tis a wise thought." Tilly took out the black silk gown. The material although rich was unadorned, with no raised pattern of embroidery or embedded jewels.

"I'll fetch you hot water." Tilly hurried away. Guinevere turned back to the girls who were struggling with their clothes. Guinevere went to help them, untangling Pippa's knotted laces, straightening Pen's collar.

"My loves, I have business to do today," she said casually.

"What kind of business?" asked Pippa, twisting her head to look up at her mother over her shoulder.

"Just some discussions about the estate with Lord Hugh and some other men," Guinevere said. "There, now. You're all straight." She bent to kiss them both then went to the dressing stand where Tilly was placing a steaming jug of hot water.

She dampened a cloth, holding it to her face before drawing it over her throat and neck, achingly reminded as the warm cloth passed over her skin of Hugh's moist caresses, of the way his tongue had painted a path over her body.

The skill of his lovemaking, his tenderness, his need to please her were all characteristic of the man so beloved of his son, so trusted by her daughters. But she knew that the man she was to face today and in succeeding days was a very different one. A man with a harsh sense of his duty. A man who had his own purpose in bringing her down. A man who, she was convinced, never shirked his purpose or evaded his duty.

"Where are you going?" asked Pen.

"To Hampton Court. I'll tell you all about it when I get back."

The girls gazed at her wide-eyed, so intrigued by this prospect that they forgot the urgent need to go in search of the kittens. Instead they plied their mother with questions that she was hard-pressed to answer as she dressed in her black widow's weeds and ate a little of the bread that Tilly had brought for her, dipping it in a cup of warm milk. She had no way of knowing when she would next eat.

There was no looking glass in the chamber. Such things were the kinds of luxuries that she guessed were beyond Hugh of Beaucaire's means. She had only her little traveling mirror with which to examine her image. Her face was pale beneath the white linen coif and the black hood. The pleated lace of her chemise decorously reached her throat. Ordinarily she would have pinned a jewel at the throat but not today. The square neckline of the gown was severe in its lack of adornment. She looked more like a nun than a witch, she decided, her lip curling in a cynical smile. Whether it would convince them remained to be seen.

"My thick cloak, Tilly. 'Twill be cold on the river at this hour." She opened a drawer in the armoire and took out a rolled parchment.

Tilly handed her a heavy woolen hooded cloak. She slipped it over her shoulders, slipped the parchment into the deep pocket of her cloak, and stood for a minute readying herself for the ordeal ahead. Then she bent and kissed the girls good-bye. "I won't be back until late tonight, my loves. Be good."

"We're always good, Mama," Pippa protested.

"Yes, I know you are." Guinevere smiled. She was reluctant to leave them. Terror swamped her anew. *She would come back to them. Of course she would.* But she couldn't swallow the lump of fear in her throat as she turned to the door.

Tilly hugged her. "Don't you fret, my chuck. It'll all turn out for the best. You just see if it don't."

Guinevere gave her a half smile and left the chamber, resisting the urge to clasp her children to her for one last time. They must catch nothing of her fear.

She descended the stairs to the hall, her step slow, her heart hammering against her ribs. Hugh stood beside the hearth, cloaked and ready for departure.

Her heart turned over as she read the light in his vivid blue eyes, saw the soft curve of his mouth. She forced herself to speak formally. "I give you good morning, my lord."

He came towards her, smiling, his hands outstretched in welcome. He would not allow her to distance herself from him again. She had done it last night, after their loving, but he was resolved to overcome it. There was no sense to her refusal to acknowledge what they had, what they were to each other.

He took her hands, bent and kissed her mouth. She turned her head aside with a murmured protest. "Don't turn from me, Guinevere," he said. "What good does it do either of us?"

"I cannot," she replied with low-voiced urgency. "Hugh, I cannot. You are determined to destroy me. You will gain the land you claim when I am brought down. Do you deny that?"

Hugh dropped her hands. "No, I do not deny that," he said. "But I do deny that I am determined to destroy you." His eyes glittered fiercely. "I am not so determined. How could you believe that when you know what we can be to each other? There are facts, and others will ask you about them. It is out of my hands. I can in no way influence matters. Regardless of my own feelings, I was instructed to bring you to London for examination. And I will do my duty."

"A cold, hard duty," she said flatly. "One that leaves no room for pity. You are my jailer. For a prisoner to make love with her jailer, to seek comfort from him, is perverse."

"Is that the only light in which you see me?" he demanded. "Is that what you would call what we had together last night—a perversion?"

She shrugged. "In light of the facts I can think of no better term, my lord."

Hugh struggled with his anger and disappointment. He was certain she didn't truly view their loving in this way, but she was obdurate and he could see no way to soften her.

"If I could change things, Guinevere, you must believe me that I would," he said. "But I cannot, so let us go." He shook his head as if to clear it of confusion. "We will walk to the steps at Blackfriars." He preceded her to the door.

Guinevere drew her cloak tightly around her. She was cold, but it had little to do with the briskness of the cloudy early morning. It was a cold that came from deep inside her. It was part fear and part sorrow for the hurt she had caused him. But she could see no other way to preserve her integrity. She had to fight for herself and her children and she could not do that by consorting with the enemy even when he came to her in the guise of friend and lover.

They walked in silence through the lanes of Holborn. The world was up and about despite the early hour, messengers running through the streets, hawkers crying their wares, women yelling, "Gardezleau" as they hurled night soil from the top windows into the kennels below.

A man in crimson livery rode by, spurring his horse. The hooves kicked up mud and filth and Guinevere jumped aside only just in time to avoid being trampled. "Didn't he see me?" she demanded furiously.

"A man on Privy Seal's business doesn't stop for pedestrians," Hugh said. "Are you all right?"

"Yes, thank you." She brushed at her cloak where dust and dried mud clung. She remembered the procession of the previous afternoon when the world had come to a halt to give precedence to Privy Seal and his outriders. "It seems our Lord Privy Seal's presence is everywhere."

"Visible and invisible," Hugh responded. Guinevere controlled a convulsive shiver.

A dull metallic gleam shone through a gap in the row of houses ahead of them. As they approached, the broad gray reaches of the Thames opened before them. The river if anything seemed busier than the lanes they had just left.

Ferrymen gathered at the base of the water steps at Blackfriars, touting for customers in their skiffs and wherries. A large barge, with a richly adorned canopy and flying the king's pennant, was tied at the steps. A group of musicians were stepping aboard, carrying their lutes and lyres.

"The musicians are being transported to the palace to play at the king's feast this evening," Hugh informed Guinevere. He stood looking around for Jack Stedman and the barge he had commissioned.

"Ah, there he is." He gestured to a barge anchored some way out in the river. Berths at the water steps themselves were hard to come by. He beckoned an urchin. "Whistle up that barge, lad. Three long and three short."

The boy blew the correct blasts on the tin whistle he carried around his neck. Hugh's falcon-embossed pennant immediately fluttered at the stern of the barge and the oarsmen began to pull to the steps. Hugh gave the urchin a coin, then ushered Guinevere down the steps.

Guinevere now became aware of the whistles and trumpet calls all around them as servants called barges for their masters, each with a different sequence of notes. It struck her as extraordinary that any one craft could distinguish its own call signal from the cacophony. But the system seemed to work.

Their own barge pulled into the steps and Hugh jumped aboard. He held out his hand for Guinevere. She took it to step aboard and he did not immediately release it. His fingers curled around her own and she could feel his strength, feel the dry warmth of his palm through her gloves. She slipped her hand free and walked to the stern where a cresset burned against the dim early light, sending a pale circle over the gray water.

"Good morning, m'lady."

"Good morning, Jack." She nodded at the man. "This is a fine barge you've found. It has housing too, I see."

Jack looked pleased at the compliment. "Reckon as 'ow we might need it, madam. There's a cold wind and 'twill be worse when we're movin'. An' fer comin' back like, we'll mebbe light the brazier." He gestured proudly to the somewhat perfunctory shelter provided by an awning over a long bench. A small charcoal brazier was in the corner.

Coming back! Would she come back? She turned to Hugh, asked with an effort at casualness, "How long will the journey take?"

"Five hours if the wind and tide are with us. Longer if not." If he was aware of her agitation he gave no sign.

The barge was out in midstream now, part of the flow of traffic. Despite her wretchedness, Guinevere was distracted by the scene. Within a very short while they were in the countryside, rowing past grand mansions with gardens sweeping to the river where they had their own water steps and landing stages, many of them with private barges tied alongside. Green fields stretched to either side, with placidly grazing sheep and cows. They passed the great expanse of Richmond forest, picked their way around the many small islets that the rivermen called eyots that dotted the center of the river. Moorhens gathered dabbling in the reeds, swans floated gracefully over the cold gray water. Around every broad reach were to be found small hamlets, ragged children fishing from the banks.

Hugh left her side and went to stand with Jack Stedman and his men in the bow of the barge. He found he could not bear to be beside her, feeling her fear and knowing that he had no comfort to offer, and, even if he had, that she would not today accept it. He was the enemy, the cause of her present distress.

The oarsmen were singing to themselves in rhythm with each mighty pull on the oars. Small fishing boats bobbed in their wake. As the hours passed, Guinevere wished that this interminable journey would be over and she would at last know exactly what she faced.

"We have bread, meat, and ale. You should eat something."

Hugh's voice startled her, so deep was she in her lonely reverie.

"Thank you, but I am not hungry."

"You need to eat," he repeated. "Swooning at the king's feet for lack of food will do little for your cause. His Highness has little patience with human weakness, particularly in a woman. It embarrasses him. You do not wish to embarrass him, I can assure you."

"I'm not in the habit of swooning," Guinevere pointed out tartly.

"These circumstances are a little unusual." He ushered her under the awning and opened a basket. He took out bread and meat and laid thick slices of the meat on a hunk of bread and handed it to her. Then he filled a horn with ale and set it beside her on the bench. "You will be better for it."

He helped himself and then left her in solitude, taking his own meal back outside. Guinevere wondered whether he was leaving her to her own reflections for her benefit or for his.

An hour after noon, they passed Hampton's great deer park that stretched along the banks of the Thames. In its midst could be seen the turrets and gabled roofs of the palace. The water steps were thronged with liveried ushers and boatmen. The musicians' barge had just docked and their own barge waited in midstream until the players had disembarked and the barge moved away to give them space to tie up.

Guinevere stepped onto the landing stage of Hampton Court. It had started to drizzle, a wet English mizzle that seemed more as if the clouds sniveled than real rain. She drew the hood of her cloak over her head.

A crenellated arch surmounted the head of the stairs. Hugh behind her was giving instruction to Jack Stedman and the bargemen, then he stepped beside Guinevere and took her elbow.

He escorted her up the stairs. From the arch a redbrick path wound its way through the grounds before the palace. Neat hedges lined the path, enclosing small gardens and trellised arbors. Niched statues nestled on plinths. Through the hedges she caught glimpses of flower gardens, ornamental lakes pitted with raindrops, and orchards whose trees bent low with September fruit. The path widened, opening onto a massive square, parkland on three sides where deer cropped the grass beneath great oak trees dripping with rain. On the fourth side lay the great towered entrance to the palace.

"Where do we go?" Guinevere whispered, looking in bewilderment at the thronged and noisy scene. Horsemen, carriages, crowded the square. Liveried servants ran hither and thither; importantly dressed gentlemen ushers moved in stately fashion after the elaborately suited nobles they were designated to escort and take care of. No one seemed to notice the drizzle.

"We go to Privy Seal's antechamber," Hugh told her. " 'Twill be crowded with petitioners but keep your hand in my arm and I will make way for you."

He pressed ahead through the throng and under the great arched gateway. A staircase rose to the left inside the gateway; ahead lay the base court; beyond that yet another arched gatehouse. Guinevere gazed around, fascinated despite herself.

Hugh bent his head to her ear and pointed to the staircase within the gatehouse. A wide set of shallow stairs disappeared into torchlit realms above. "That is the king's staircase," he murmured. "It leads to his private apartments and presence chamber."

Trumpets sounded from all four corners of the base court. Guinevere couldn't distinguish one call from another but they all seemed to have a purpose. Men, pages, ushers seemed to move according to the messages the trumpets sounded. No one in this increasingly damp melee seemed confused.

Hugh moved across the cobbles of the base court, heading for the gatehouse immediately opposite. Guinevere's arm was firmly tucked into his. He walked with the assured step of one who knew exactly where he was going and as such drew no attention. They stepped beneath the arch of the gatehouse and Guinevere saw that the court that lay ahead was suddenly more tranquil.

They crossed the court in the increasingly heavy rain. Guinevere, despite her apprehension, was astounded by the gilded magnificence of the building that rose sheer and buttressed to the north side of the court. She stopped in the center, ignoring Hugh's imperative tug on her arm, and looked around. An exquisitely decorated astronomical clock graced the heights of the gatehouse behind her.

"Such splendor," she murmured in awe.

"Aye," said Hugh shortly. " 'Tis said that Hampton is the king's favorite palace. Come, we must make haste." He hurried her across the court and within the deep archway opposite.

There, Hugh turned aside down a long corridor. It was thronged, men and women pressing themselves against the walls, looking as if they had been there for so long they were rooted to the spot. When a man whose garments and demeanor seemed to denote importance passed among them a great clamor rose from the petitioners, hands grabbed at his sleeve as he swept by.

"What is it that they want?" Guinevere was both fascinated and repelled by the scene.

"This is the chancellor's antechamber. They are petitioning him . . . to right some wrong in the courts . . . to settle a dispute . . . to grant some boon," replied Hugh.

"I wonder you didn't petition the chancellor yourself," Guinevere muttered, conscious of the parchment in the pocket of her cloak. The document that would deny Hugh's legal claim to her land. If they'd fought this battle in the chancellor's court, maybe she would not be here now, facing what she was facing.

Hugh glanced down at her. "Had I thought it would do any good, I would have done so. But since the death of Thomas More, the office of the chancellor has once more reverted to corruption."

"Is that not treasonous talk?"

"Quite possibly."

"You told me to be careful of such talk."

"And I still say so. I tread less slippery ground than you, Guinevere."

She said no more and walked beside him, clinging to his arm, as he carved a path for them through the press. Then he turned aside into a corridor, also lined with people. He marched past them right up to a set of closed double doors at the end of the corridor. Two ushers in red velvet gowns edged with dark fur stood at the door.

"Hugh of Beaucaire," Hugh said curtly. "With the Lady Guinevere Mallory. In answer to a summons from the king and the Lord Privy Seal."

For a minute it looked as if the usher would deny him. His air of lofty superciliousness did not falter. Then he caught Hugh's eye and thought better of it.

He bowed, tapping his ceremonial staff on the flagstones, and opened the doors at his back. He stepped backwards and the doors closed again.

Guinevere felt sick. She clasped Hugh's arm tightly and tried to control the deep shivers in her belly. He put his own hand over hers as it rested on his arm.

The usher returned. "Lord Privy Seal will be pleased to see you at three o'clock. 'Tis now but two."

"Then we will wait," Hugh said equably. "You will show us to a privy chamber where we may do so out of this mob."

The man sniffed, then gestured to a small door. "If you would wait in there, my lord, you will be sent for."

"I thank you." Hugh gave the man a polite nod and ushered Guinevere into a small quiet chamber. Envious eyes followed them.

They were left there for no more than fifteen minutes, however, before the usher reappeared from a door at the rear of the chamber. "If you will follow me, sir . . . madam."

They followed him into a narrow passage, lit by pitch torches in sconces along the high stone walls. At an oak door, the usher knocked with his staff, then flung it open.

Guinevere stepped in ahead of Hugh as he stood back for her. The man she had seen on horseback the previous day sat behind a massive oak table in the window. He surveyed her through cold eyes in a hard round face.

She was in the presence of Thomas Cromwell, Lord Privy Seal. The most feared man in the land.

15.

Guinevere held herself very still, determined that she would not show her fear of this man. "I give you good day, my Lord Cromwell," she said with composure. Her eye took in the other occupant of the chamber. A man in the scarlet robes of a prelate.

"Bishop Gardiner," Privy Seal said, gesturing to the man who stood in the window embrasure. "He has some interest in your case."

"I am a case, my lord?"

"A woman who has seduced four husbands with witchcraft," rasped the bishop. "You stand accused of such."

"Who so accuses me, my lord bishop? Are there witnesses?"

The bishop's complexion took on a hue to match his robes. "Witchcraft requires no witnesses and the Church has no truck with lawyerly tricks, madam."

Thomas Cromwell waved a hand at the bishop. "Come, my lord bishop, we run too far ahead of ourselves. Lady Mallory is here to answer some questions, that is all."

If the statement was intended to calm Guinevere's fears it didn't succeed. She felt like a fly in the spider's web, watching the measured approach of a predator who knew it could take its time. She shot an involuntary glance over her shoulder at Hugh, who stood a little behind her, his expression impassive.

Her glance served to direct Privy Seal's attention to Hugh. "Ah, Lord Hugh," he said with a terrifying impression of good humor. "You have accomplished your long journey without mishap, I trust."

"Without mishap, my lord," Hugh agreed calmly.

"Good . . . good." Privy Seal nodded with an absent air. He returned his gaze to Guinevere.

"So, my lady, let us discuss the will of your first husband, Roger Needham. Who was responsible for drawing up the marriage contracts?"

"My uncle." As was her habit Guinevere clasped her hands lightly against her skirt and regarded her questioner steadily.

"Oh, forgive me . . . how remiss!" Privy Seal steepled his fingers. "Pray take a seat, madam." He gestured to a low stool to one side of his table.

Guinevere knew that she would immediately be at a disadvantage sitting so low in front of Cromwell at his worktable and with the two other occupants of the room remaining on their feet.

"I am perfectly comfortable standing, my lord, although I thank you for the consideration," she replied.

Privy Seal looked displeased but he said only, "How did it come about that Roger Needham bequeathed to you the estates claimed by Lord Hugh of Beaucaire? It appears that they belonged to Needham's first wife and were not his to cede."

Guinevere drew the parchment from the pocket of her cloak. "I possess the premarriage contract between my late husband and his first wife," she said. "It specifies that the land in dispute formed part of the marriage settlement. It was therefore Roger Needham's to dispose of."

She heard Hugh's swift indrawn breath behind her but didn't turn her head.

"May I see it?" Cromwell stretched out a hand. Rings bedecked his thick fingers.

Guinevere handed him the document and he opened it carefully, smoothing the folds with all the fussiness of a woman with a flatiron.

He read it in silence. Guinevere was acutely aware of Hugh behind her . . . of his stillness that was as eloquent as a tirade.

At last, Cromwell looked up. "Were you aware of this clause in the premarriage contract, Lord Hugh?"

"No," Hugh said flatly. "Had I been, I would hardly have made my claim. This is the first time it's been mentioned. For some reason, Lady Guinevere chose to keep it to herself."

"I doubt much would have been gained by my revealing it earlier, sir," she said quietly, turning her head a fraction to see his face. It was tight and pale, his eyes bright with anger.

"I would have appreciated it, madam. If indeed this document *would* stand in a court of law?" he added.

"It would, sir," she stated, her purple eyes regarding him steadily.

She turned back to Privy Seal. "My claim is indisputable, I believe, Lord Cromwell. Just as I believe you will find that I have legal title to all the lands I presently hold."

"We will examine those titles anon, Lady Guinevere. I would ask you now a little about your husbands, their wills, and their untimely deaths."

Thomas Cromwell's eyes flickered to the arras decorating the inner wall of his chamber. Hugh followed the glance and knew what it meant.

In a narrow passage beyond the arras a great figure dressed in black and purple pressed his eyes to a pair of peepholes. They looked directly into Cromwell's privy chamber, cunningly concealed in the design of the arras. A round hole, as neatly concealed, enabled him to hear everything that went on even as he watched.

"Body o' God!" Henry murmured to his companion. "But she's more comely than the miniature. I'd not have thought it possible."

"Comely and devious, Highness," whispered Lord Dalgliesh, the king's personal attendant. A man not coincidentally in the pay of Privy Seal, charged with reporting every minute detail of the king's conversations, every event of his daily round.

"Mayhap . . . mayhap," the king muttered. "She has a lawyer's head on her shoulders, I'll grant you that. But 'tis hard to see witchcraft in such a countenance."

"But therein lies the essence of witchcraft, Highness," oozed Lord Dalgliesh.

Henry nodded and continued his observations.

Within the chamber Guinevere continued to answer the questions put to her with a calm steadfastness. She was careful not to make the mistake of offering a defense before it was called for. Privy Seal did not accuse her of anything, although the drift of his questions was clear. He expressed incredulity when she explained how she had drawn up her own marriage contracts, suggested that perhaps she was not being entirely truthful.

Guinevere merely repeated what she had said.

"But how could this be?" the bishop demanded. " 'Tis unheard-of for a woman to have such knowledge."

"I understand the Lady Mary is learned," Guinevere said. She felt Hugh stir behind her and realized she had made her first mistake.

"Indeed, and what know you of the Lady Mary, madam?" a great voice boomed from behind the arras. The tapestry was flung aside and the massive figure of King Henry barreled into the chamber. "What know you of the ingratitude of a baseborn daughter?"

Guinevere fell to her knees. It seemed the only possible salutation to this astounding mass of humanity all aglitter with gold, ashimmer with jewels. His curly reddish-brown hair was cropped close beneath his velvet cap and his bright eyes glared at her from his huge face.

Hugh had snatched off his cap and was bowing low. Privy Seal rose from his chair, the bishop bowed. Guinevere remained on her knees.

"Well, madam?" demanded the king, making no attempt to raise her up. "You would bandy the name of the most ungrateful bastard in Christendom, would you?"

"Forgive me, Highness," Guinevere said simply although she had no idea what she had done to cause this terrifying reaction.

The king paused, then with one of his startling changes of mood he threw back his head and gave a great shout of laughter. "Well, maybe I will. 'Tis a fair maid, y'are, I'll say that for you." He took her hand and drew her to her feet.

"No maid, Highness," Guinevere said, trying to control the violent trembling of her legs caused by this amazing presence.

Henry's laugh bellowed again. "A woman of wit," he declared. "Of course, were you a maid you would hardly be here to answer our charges, is that not so?" And suddenly there was something sinister in the malicious glimmer of his eye.

"I have as yet heard no charges, Highness," Guinevere said steadily.

Henry grunted. "You shall hear them soon enough, madam. And you will answer them before our council in the Star Chamber."

"As Your Highness decrees," she said softly.

"Until then you will lodge under Lord Hugh's roof," the king announced. "He will be responsible for you." He glanced at Hugh, acknowledging him with a nod.

Hugh had told her to bring the matter of her lodging up with the king, so now was the moment. Guinevere raised her head, and said quietly, courteously, "If Your Highness pleases, I would prefer not to remain under Lord Hugh's roof. I feel sure he finds it an imposition and I would make other arrangements. I have coin to pay my way."

Immediately she knew she'd made yet another mistake. She again felt the air stir in the chamber, and she sensed Hugh move behind her. The king stared at her as if she had taken leave of her senses.

"Pay your way!" he exclaimed. "What manner of woman is this? Body of God! Rejecting the kindness we offer her. By God, madam, you are too hot," he declared. "An intemperate wench indeed. You would dare to question my decree? You would dare to think your arrangements better than mine?"

Too late, Guinevere tried to rectify the damage. "I meant no disrespect, Highness, indeed not."

But Henry swept on on his own tide of indignation. "So you would prefer not to lodge under Lord Hugh's roof? Then, madam, you may lodge in the Tower."

Again she heard Hugh's quick intake of breath behind her. She searched desperately for words that would alter the king's decree, that would soften the ruthless expression, the eyes that glared at her with capricious rage. But before she could formulate any words, the king was striding heavily to the hidden door from which he'd entered. She glanced at Privy Seal and saw no mercy there in the cold eyes, the harsh mouth.

"So, madam, you have chosen your lodging," Privy Seal said. "It seems, Lord Hugh, that your guest is an ungrateful one. In addition to being somewhat secretive," he added maliciously. "What say you, Hugh?"

"The Tower is hardly suitable lodging for the lady," Hugh said. "As yet she stands accused of nothing."

"Your defense astonishes me," Cromwell said. "Lady Guinevere insults you, destroys your claim, outwits you, and you defend her." He gave an exaggerated shrug and glanced at the bishop. "Such charity, my lord bishop, can only be commended."

"Surely you would not also question the king's decree, Lord Hugh?" Bishop Gardiner demanded.

"Hardly," Hugh said with a tiny shrug of his powerful shoulders.

"Then pray escort the lady to the guardhouse." Cromwell drew a sheet of parchment towards him and took up a quill. "There she will find escort to her new lodging. We will notify her of the date of her trial when we have consulted with the other members of the king's council." He looked coldly at Guinevere as he sanded the sheet he had been writing upon. "Until we meet again, madam." He stamped his great seal on the parchment and handed it to Hugh.

Hugh glanced at it, his expression grim, then rolled it and tucked it into an inside pocket of his gown.

Guinevere, still numb with shock, turned to the door when Hugh touched her arm. She allowed herself to be escorted from the chamber.

"Whatever possessed you?" he demanded almost before they were outside. "What possessed you to anger the king? He's as ruthless as he's changeable. Do you not know the Lady Mary is out of favor? She refuses to yield to her father's demands that she admit her illegitimacy and it's almost treason to mention her name in his presence."

"I didn't know. How could I?" she said bitterly. "I am not familiar with the deviousness of this miserable court."

"I would have thought someone as devious as yourself would have little difficulty adapting," he said. "Why did you not tell me of that document?"

"I could see little point."

"No, you chose to keep it and reveal it when I would be caught off guard and at a disadvantage," he stated.

"I chose to reveal it when it could do me the most good," she returned.

Hugh shook his head. "In the scheme of things it matters little now. Once you put the king's back up . . . for God's sake, Guinevere, I told you many weeks ago that you would be wise to moderate your tongue!"

"I made a simple request," she said, her spirit returning under the sting of this attack. "You told me yourself to bring up the matter of my lodging with the king or Privy Seal. I followed your advice."

"It was not advice meant seriously," he said. "I never expected you to take me at my word. I would never seriously suggest you do something so foolish . . . so dangerous as to contradict the king."

He strode on in silence for a minute, then asked, making no attempt to conceal his hurt anger, "Why would you wish to lodge elsewhere? I realize my house is not as commodious or as comfortable as your own, but it's a damn sight better than the Tower."

"I cast no aspersions on your hospitality, my lord," she returned, her voice low. "But you know why I cannot remain beneath your roof. I must fight you, Lord Hugh, not love you, if I am to remain alive for my children."

"You have no need to fight *me*," he said quietly. "I do not seek your downfall, Guinevere."

She gave a little helpless shrug. "So you say. But in my eyes you are my enemy and I cannot grow close to the enemy. Therefore I will lodge in the Tower until such time as these matters are resolved."

With difficulty Hugh controlled himself. Such obstinacy was beyond mending. Abusing her would do no good. He marched beside her in grim silence, guiding her out of the palace and into the long, low, gray building that housed the king's guard.

"This lady is to be escorted to the Tower," he instructed the captain of the guard. He took the rolled parchment from his gown and handed it over. "Here are Privy Seal's orders."

The captain read them carefully, then he looked up at the still, black-clad figure standing behind Lord Hugh. He wondered what such a beautiful lady could have done to anger the king and Privy Seal. She was unquestionably a noblewoman. Only the nobility were lodged in the Tower at the king's pleasure. But the name Mallory was not familiar to him.

Of course, she could be guilty of nothing, he reflected. It might simply suit Privy Seal's purposes to persuade the king to have her put away. Either way it was not his business to speculate.

Hugh turned to Guinevere and said in an undertone, "I must leave you here. I'll do what I can to plead your case. The king's mood is mercurial and when he's no longer angry with you I may be able to persuade him to be merciful if I can catch him in a good humor."

Guinevere shook her head. "It's better thus. Alone I will have nothing to distract me from my defense. But there is one thing I must ask you to do for me." Her voice faltered, tears for the first time started in her eyes. She blinked them back.

"You would ask that I care for your children," he finished for her. "You have no need to ask me that, Guinevere. Whatever the outcome of this business you need have no fears for your daughters' safety. I will ensure that their care falls to my hand."

"You are very good," she said softly. "You will tell them now what will alarm them the least?"

"You know that I will." He took her hand and for a minute she let it lie in his clasp.

"Will I be permitted my books, do you think?"

"Nothing was said in Privy Seal's orders to forbid it. I'll have your books and other necessities sent to you in the morning."

She withdrew her hand from his. "I thank you, Hugh. For that and for your care of my children. I know they will be safe with you."

"You trust me with your children but you will not trust me with yourself!" he exclaimed in a vigorous undertone.

"I cannot," she said quietly but firmly.

He regarded her in unsmiling silence for a minute, then with an almost defeated shake of his head, turned on his heel and left her.

The captain of the guard regarded his prisoner with renewed interest. He hadn't heard more than a word or two of the murmured exchange but its intensity had been obvious. Tears glittered in the lady's eyes, although that was only to be expected in one facing the terrors of imprisonment in the Tower.

"We are ready to depart, madam," he said. "The barge awaits us."

Guinevere nodded and drew her cloak tightly about her. A troop of soldiers fell in around her and she was escorted back down the path to the water steps through the now pouring rain. The river was flecked with rain, the gray sky lowered, and it was hard to imagine the long hot days of summer in Derbyshire, with the sweet valleys and rolling hills basking in the sun's heat. Here was all dark and dirt and damp.

She stepped into the barge, grateful for the awning that would keep off some at least of the rain. She sat on the bench beneath the scant shelter and the rain dripped off her hooded cloak. She shivered in the chill dankness as the oarsmen took up their oars and pulled the barge into midstream.

Hugh would be on his way home to fires and supper, the chatter of children. She was on her way to prison. But she would be well away from the temptations of Hugh's bed, she told herself. It was what she had wanted, she told herself.

But it was hard to maintain her resolve as after long hours in the dark and the wet the barge approached the great gray edifice of the Tower. Instead of pulling up at the dock of the Lion Gate, it went on a few yards. Inset into the wharf at water level Guinevere saw a heavy gate, like a portcullis, that led into the Tower through a narrow tunnel. The gate was opened and the barge pulled under the wharf and into a small pool. Huge water gates opened as they crossed the pool and the barge drew alongside a shadowed dock. Green slime coated the steps and landing stage and dripped from the walls of the great bastion towering above the dock. Four yeoman warders of the king's guard stood on the landing stage waiting to receive the prisoner.

Traitors' Gate! she realized. *She had entered the Tower by the gate through which it was said no prisoner ever left.* The reputation of Traitors' Gate had reached even the farthest wilds of Derbyshire. Terror swamped her. She would never see her children again.

Her hands were icy cold in their gloves as she stepped out onto the slimy landing stage. The captain of the king's guard handed Privy Seal's rolled parchment to one of the yeomen then offered Guinevere a formal salute before stepping back into the barge.

"This way, madam." The king's yeomen fell in around Guinevere and she was escorted up a narrow flight of stone steps within the great wall of the bastion and out onto a rampart. She could hear ravens croaking somewhere below. She was escorted down another flight of stone stairs and into a large grassy inner courtyard. The high walls of the Tower rose on four sides, broken at several points by round turrets reached by stone staircases and ramparts.

Guinevere was ushered across the green to a low building that looked disconcertingly like an ordinary house. The ravens hopped across the green, croaking their melancholy tune in the rain. A yeoman knocked with his staff on the front door and it opened instantly.

"Prisoner, Lady Mallory, for the Lieutenant of the Tower," the guard intoned.

"Who is it? I wasn't told to expect anyone this evening." A stout man, a napkin tied around his neck, emerged from a door to the right of the hall. His rich dress denoted a man of some importance. He took the parchment and read it swiftly, then subjected Guinevere to a steady scrutiny.

"So, Lady Mallory, you are to be my guest for a while," he said with a courtly bow. "We will do what we can to make you comfortable."

"Who is it, Oliver?" A plump woman came into the hall. "Oh, my poor lady, you're chilled to the bone!" she exclaimed, bustling over to Guinevere. "Come to the fire. You must sup with us while the lieutenant has your chamber prepared."

Chamber! Surely she meant "cell." Guinevere was totally bewildered. It felt as if she was being welcomed to a particularly hospitable tavern instead of the Tower prison. She was not to know that since all their prisoners were noble, the lieutenant and his lady treated them as equals with all due courtesy and deference. Unless, of course, there were instructions to the contrary.

"I own I'd be glad of some fire, madam," she said, allowing herself to be drawn into a firelit parlor.

"You must take off that wet cloak. What a miserable night it is. Winter draws close, I fear." The lieutenant's lady rattled on as she helped Guinevere out of her cloak and urged her close to the fire.

"You have nothing with you, I see. No dry clothes." Despite her comfortable tones, her brown eyes were shrewd. She guessed correctly that the lady's imprisonment had been unexpected. It was often thus in these days when Privy Seal guided the king in the paths that suited himself.

"They will be brought," Guinevere said. "In the morning." She bent to the fire, warming her numbed hands at the blaze.

"I'll see what I can find for you . . . just until your own things arrive," the lady said. "You'll take a bite of supper now, won't you?"

"If it's not too much trouble, madam. You're very kind."

"Not a bit of it," the lady said cheerfully, vigorously ringing a copper bell. A maidservant appeared in answer.

"Lisa, bring a bite of supper for our guest. A bowl of broth and a slice of that venison pasty and a mite of cheese."

The maid curtsied and withdrew. The lieutenant's lady excused herself for a moment and Guinevere was left alone at the fire. Some of her fear abated under this strangely friendly welcome, but it felt unreal and she was convinced that matters couldn't continue in this unthreatening fashion.

Outside the parlor door, the lady was talking earnestly to her husband. "The poor thing is frozen to the bone, Oliver. You must house her with a fire, at least for tonight," she said vehemently. "She has no clothes, no possessions. It must have been very sudden."

"Privy Seal is often precipitate," the lieutenant said. "But it seems from the order that Lady Mallory is here on the king's command."

His wife shivered slightly. "Another poor woman imprisoned on the king's orders," she murmured. "How has this one offended His Highness, I wonder? Did she refuse his bed, perhaps?"

"Hush your loose talk," her husband said in an undertone, glancing around to make sure they were not overheard.

"Well, 'tis to be hoped she doesn't face the same fate as the other he put in here," his lady said. "The poor Queen Anne."

"Was an adulteress; she betrayed the king's bed," her husband reminded her.

" 'Twas what they said," his wife agreed with a sniff.

"It's not for us to question," her husband told her firmly. "I will have this lady housed in the White Tower. The chamber there is quite commodious and I will have a fire kindled. There are no orders to the contrary."

"Then I am satisfied. She will sup here first, before she is taken away." His lady nodded and returned to the parlor where Guinevere waited.

The maid brought supper and Guinevere found to her surprise that she could eat. The broth warmed her, the pasty and cheese put heart into her, and the cup of wine cheered her spirit a little. She tried not to wonder how Hugh was explaining her absence to the girls. If she dwelled upon that she would weep and that would only make matters worse.

Her hostess regarded her with kindly concern as she ate. "Are you new come to London, madam?"

"As of yesterday," Guinevere answered, setting her spoon down in her empty bowl.

The lady waited, clearly hoping for enlightenment, but Guinevere didn't offer it. She finished the wine and said sincerely, "You are very kind, madam. I was in sore need."

"Aye, I could see that," the woman said. She turned as her husband entered the parlor.

"If you've supped, my lady, you'll be taken to your lodging now," he said.

"Yes, indeed. Your good lady has been most kind," Guinevere said, getting at once to her feet. She reached for her still-wet cloak.

"I'll fetch you a night robe, just to tide you over until your own things are brought." Her hostess hurried from the parlor, returning in a very few minutes with a woolen robe lined with fur. She handed it to Guinevere. " 'Twill keep the night chill away."

"My thanks." Guinevere draped the garment over her arm.

"If you're ready . . ." The Lieutenant of the Tower moved to the door. She followed him, her heart beating uncomfortably fast now that this strange interlude was over.

They crossed the court and went up a flight of stone stairs and through a door set into one of the round towers. A great oak door was set into the heavy stone opposite the entrance to the tower. Her companion had a key, a massive iron key. He turned it in the keyhole and pushed the door open. It swung inwards with a creak.

"If you would enter, Lady Mallory," he said politely, stepping aside.

Guinevere walked past him into her prison cell.

"I give you good night, my lady." The door closed and she heard the key turn in the massive lock.

She stood in the center of the small round chamber until her heart had stopped its wild racing. It was cold and dank despite a sullen fire in the small hearth. She touched the thick stone walls. They were icy to the touch. The floor beneath her feet was of the same thick uneven stone. A small square window was set into the wall high up above her head. There was no other outside light.

A tallow candle burned in a sconce above the door. That and the fire provided the only illumination. There was a narrow cot with a straw mattress, a pillow, and a thin blanket. There was a low stool, a lidless wooden pail, and a jug of cold water on the floor beside the fire. That was all the chamber contained.

She went to the fire. There was a scuttle of coals, so for as long as she stayed awake she could keep the fire burning. She shivered in her damp cloak and with a brisk movement flung it from her, wrapping herself instead in the borrowed furred night robe.

From somewhere beyond the stone walls of her prison cell came the lonely frustrated roaring of a lion in the royal menagerie. The miserable beast was as much a prisoner as herself, Guinevere thought. More so, perhaps, because he had no understanding of what had brought him to his cage.

She dragged the mattress off the narrow cot and set it before the fire, then lay down, covering herself with the blanket. Cold and damp were her two worst enemies. She was not going to let them kill her off with an ague. If the king and Privy Seal wanted her dead, they were going to have to fight for it.

16.

"But where is our mother, Lord Hugh?" Pen fixed him with a steady stare from intent hazel eyes. "She said she would be coming back last night."

"Yes, and she hasn't," Pippa chimed in. "Where is she? We want to see her." A tremulous note entered her voice.

Hugh lifted Pippa and held her in the crook of his arm. "The king wished to talk some more with your mother. She asked me to explain that to you and to say that she loves you and she'll be back very soon."

"If she thought that was going to happen, she would have said," Pen declared. "She would never have gone away without telling us."

"No, but this was rather unexpected," Hugh explained patiently. "She couldn't have known that matters would have taken this course. She wants you to stay here with Tilly, the magister, Crowder, and Greene until she's able to come back to you."

"But I want to *see* her!" Pippa shrilled, patting his face with impatient little taps. "*We* want to see her. Don't we, Pen?"

"Yes," said Pen flatly. "Where is she, sir?"

Hugh wondered how much these children knew of the Tower of London. It was possible they'd never heard of it and so to tell them the truth wouldn't alarm them any more than they already were. He glanced over Pen's head and saw his son's solemn countenance. Robin knew all there was to know about that dread prison. He couldn't be expected to conceal his impressions under the inevitable flood of questions from Pen and Pippa.

Hugh chose his words carefully. "Your mother is in one of the king's houses. It was her choice to stay there. She has work to do on this estate business and this morning I must arrange for her to have her books and other things she'll need."

"But she would have told us if she wanted to stay somewhere else," Pen stated. "And besides, she always works with Magister Howard. Will you take him to her?" Her voice took on an unwonted edge of hostility.

"And if the magister can go then so can we," Pippa added. "She'd much rather see us than the magister."

"Yes. Why can't we go to her?" Pen demanded. "If she's staying in this place because she wants to, then she'd say she wanted to see us."

This was turning out to be more difficult than Hugh had bargained for. Guinevere's children were not the kind to accept something simply because they were told it. Clearly they had not been taught an unquestioning acceptance of authority, which, knowing their mother as he did, should not have surprised him.

"For the moment I'm afraid you cannot go to her," Hugh stated firmly. "Your mother knows this, which is why she hasn't arranged for you to visit her."

"But *why* can't we?" Pen repeated.

"I imagine your mother will tell you herself as soon as she can," Hugh told her, setting Pippa on her feet again. "For the moment, you must accept what I say. Why don't you write a letter to her and I'll send it with her books and things."

"We'll ask her why we can't see her," Pen said. "Come, Pippa, let's write it upstairs."

Hugh blew his breath between his lips in a vigorous exhalation as they ran from the hall. He glanced at Robin.

"Is Lady Guinevere arrested, sir?" his son asked gravely. He knew without having been told that Lady Guinevere had not made this journey to London willingly, and he knew rather more about the workings of Privy Seal's world than did Pen and Pippa. It was a small step to guess why his father was being so evasive with the lady's daughters.

"In a manner of speaking," Hugh replied carefully. "Lady Guinevere will be obliged to defend herself on certain matters to the king's council in the Star Chamber in a few days. Until then she has chosen not to continue under my roof. The king himself designated her present lodging."

Robin looked at him in silence for a minute, then said hesitantly, "If you said you were no longer interested in the estate would that make a difference?"

"No," Hugh stated. "The matter is far more serious than that. Now, the morning advances and you have certain tasks to perform, I believe?" He raised a questioning eyebrow.

"Yes, sir." Robin turned, his lips tight set, and left the hall for his duties in the small steward's room where a ledger of household accounts needed balancing.

Hugh stood frowning in the middle of the hall. He felt that Robin in some way held him responsible for Guinevere's predicament. But it was not his fault that she now languished in the Tower, it was entirely the fault of her own obstinacy. And, of course, of her lack of understanding of King Henry's changeable temperament, the ruthlessness of whims that he indulged arbitrarily. Of course she could not be expected to understand that, never having frequented the court before.

Could he have prepared her better? If he hadn't been so anxious to keep her in his bed, could he have provided more objective preparation for what lay ahead of her?

God's blood! Every way he turned he seemed to be at fault.

"My lord . . . ?" The magister's soft voice broke into his reverie. "You sent for me, Lord Hugh."

"Yes, I wish you to deliver Lady Guinevere's books to her. You will take Tilly with you . . . she's packing up her mistress's necessities now. Jack Stedman will escort you. I doubt you will be permitted to remain with her for very long, but discover if you will what else she needs for her comfort."

"Where is my lady?"

"In the Tower."

The magister whitened and his pointed chin waggled. "The Tower," he breathed.

"The king made such disposition," Hugh said aridly. "If your lady had a better command of her tongue, she would not be so housed."

The magister plucked at the soft skin beneath his chin. He sucked in his cheeks and pursed his mouth. He looked up at Lord Hugh as he stood over him. " 'Tis a bad business," he stated bluntly. "There's no way my lady could be accused of murder. And I believe you know that, Lord Hugh."

"It is out of my hands," Hugh said.

Magister Howard shook his head. He seemed to hesitate, then spoke up with a clear and decisive courage. "It's been in your hands, Lord Hugh, from the first moment. We who serve Lady Guinevere know who she is and what she is. She's no witch and she's no murderer. You wish for her land . . . land that is not yours by right . . . then be honest and say so."

Hugh felt the color suffuse his countenance. First Robin and now the magister. "You overstep the mark, Magister," he said coldly. "I will not tolerate such insolence from a dependent of Lady Guinevere's. For the love you bear her, I will overlook it this time. But do not make such a mistake again. Not you or any other of Lady Guinevere's household." He fixed the magister with a hard and icy stare, then turned on his heel and strode to the door.

The magister drew closer into his furred gown. He stood by what he had said. With his lady in prison, he had nothing to lose by speaking the truth. He and Greene and Crowder and Tilly. They were nothing without their lady. And if, as Tilly said, there was more between Lady Guinevere and Lord Hugh than met the eye, then by the same token they had even less to lose by the truth.

Hugh stepped outside into the gray early morning, wrestling with his anger. He supposed that he should appreciate the loyalty of Guinevere's household. He expected it of his own after all. But it still rankled. If they'd been a little less loyal, a little more concerned for their own benefit, they wouldn't have caused him so much trouble since this business had started.

The rain had stopped and a fitful sun flirted with the clouds, but it was cool, the lingering warmth of summer finally banished.

There was one thing he could try. One way he might possibly influence the king in her favor.

Guinevere would be furious, would be bound to accuse him of manipulation, but whatever she might say, she could not willingly choose imprisonment in the Tower over the companionship of her children and the basic creature comforts of his home. Not now that she'd experienced the reality of prison. He could not bear to think of her in that desolate place. If she insisted upon rejecting his loving, so be it. But she *must* accept the comfort and security of his roof.

It was just after seven in the morning. If they took to the river without delay, they would reach Hampton Court by early afternoon. He turned back to the house and mounted the stairs with swift step. He knocked briefly on the girls' chamber door and then entered. "Tilly, dress the girls in their finest gowns. I need them ready within the half hour."

Pippa jumped up from the floor where she'd been overseeing her sister's letter-writing. Moonshine and Nutmeg tumbled from her lap. "Are we going to see Mama?"

"No, we go to see the king," he told her.

"Will the king take us to Mama?" Pen asked intently, nibbling the end of her quill. There was clearly no other consideration worth their attention in this matter of visiting England's sovereign.

"I don't know," Hugh said. "But it won't hurt to ask. Dress quickly now, we have no time to waste."

He left them and sent a servant to summon a barge at Blackfriars. A small, fleet craft if it could be found.

Robin received the news that he was to remain behind in Holborn in stolid silence. He had never seen the king. He didn't say that he wanted more than anything to accompany his father and the girls to Hampton Court, but he didn't need to say it. It was clearly to be read in his bright eyes and stoic mouth. Hugh offered no consolation. He would find some recompense for his son later, when he could turn his attention to something other than the present mess.

He changed his own dress for a ceremonial gown of green velvet over a gold doublet, and by the time he was satisfied with his appearance he was no longer angry with himself or anyone else. He had a plan that depended upon fate and good timing. If those two worked in his favor . . . if the king was where he hoped to find him . . . all then would depend upon Henry's mercurial temperament. And for that reason Hugh considered that his plan just might work.

He gathered up the girls and walked to the steps at Blackfriars. They peppered him with questions. What would the king say to them . . . what did he look like . . . when would he say they could see their mother . . . why were they going on this boat . . . how long would it take . . . was the palace very grand . . . why did the rowers sing as they rowed . . . what was this place on the bank called, and that . . .

Hugh answered steadily. Their barge was small and light, the six watermen powerfully built. They sped along the river with the help of the swift current to the accompaniment of Pippa's incessant chatter. Pen had subsided into a thoughtful silence broken only occasionally with a question or some reflection of her thoughts, all of which were once more with her mother. Hugh recognized that the time had come for a full revelation, to Pen at least. But it was not a burden he was prepared to take on unless or until it became clear that Guinevere could not do it herself. If his plan worked, she would be back under his roof maybe even as early as tonight.

The king stood foursquare in the center of the stable courtyard watching as his horses were paraded before him, the coursers and stallions that he rode himself in battle and in the jousting tournaments that he loved and at which he excelled. He nodded in high good humor as the magnificent beasts cavorted past, high-stepping, nostrils flaring, teeth bared. The best of them were of wild and vicious temperament, hard to manage by all but the most experienced horsemen.

The afternoon sun had now some warmth in it and it brightened the day, seemed to ease the pain of the king's ulcerated leg, giving him a sense of well-being. He leaned a hand heavily on the shoulder of the man standing beside him and trod to the white fence that separated the pasture from the yard. He watched the mares running with their foals, the little ones skipping, kicking up their heels.

The king chuckled and the elderly knight on whose shoulder he rested permitted himself a tiny smile. "Well, My Lord Rochester, you have the most excellent management of our horses," Henry said.

Lord Rochester bowed and beamed. "They are my delight, Highness."

"Aye, and ours too," the king said cheerfully. He turned slowly, like some great ship of state under a fading wind. "I'll ride to the hunt tomorrow. We'll follow the chase in Richmond. You'll be at our side, My Lord Rochester."

Lord Rochester bowed again.

Henry nodded in amiable dismissal and swayed away. He had no desire for company when he came to visit his horses, it was one time when he could be free of the petty distractions and irritations of his court. It gave him a malicious pleasure to think of his courtiers disconsolately pacing the antechambers and corridors of the palace while their king was for a short while out of reach of their grasping and their plotting.

He limped slowly out of the stable court onto the broad gravel path that led through the gardens that flanked the river and wished that he'd not left his stick in his chamber. He'd thought his leg so much improved he could do without the prop. It was a conceit for which he was now paying.

Ahead, at some distance down the path he spied three people coming towards him. Henry frowned, peering from beneath thick reddish brows. "Who comes here?" he muttered to himself, annoyed that his peace was about to be disturbed.

Then he recognized the man and grunted to himself. Hugh of Beaucaire. There was something about Lord Hugh that the king found refreshing. He lacked deviousness. Seemed to have little interest in lining his own nest.

And he had two little maids with him. That in itself was interesting enough to arouse the king's curiosity. He considered himself to be a man with an inordinate love of children. He would conveniently forget that his fury with his older daughter's intransigence frequently led him to treat her cruelly: locked away, deprived of even the most basic necessities of fire and adequate food.

There was a stone bench set into a little archway carved into the privet hedge and he sat down heavily. He stretched his massive legs out in front of him, folded his hands across the great overhang of his belly, and regarded the approaching trio with an air of mild and genial curiosity.

Hugh had a child in each hand. He had hoped that the king had not altered his practice when at Hampton Court of visiting the stables alone on fine afternoons. He had hoped that the timing would be such that they would waylay Henry as he was leaving a spectacle that never failed to put him in good humor.

So far, it seemed, so good.

Pippa was unnaturally silent as they approached the great mass of the king, all dressed in squares of crimson and black, his flat hat tilted at a rakish angle. A huge emerald glowed in the brim of his hat and around his neck hung a small gold dagger. Everything about him was huge, not excluding the padded codpiece of striped silk. Her eyes found it and somehow couldn't look away. She opened her mouth to say something and immediately Hugh squeezed her hot little hand in warning. Knowing Pippa as he did, it was not difficult to guess at what she was about to say.

He'd decided to give them no directions as to what to say, but to let their own innocence and natural wit speak for them. Now, he could only pray that his strategy had been the right one. They came up to the king and he dropped the girls' hands to snatch off his hat. He bowed low and the girls curtsied, bobbing up almost immediately, however, to regard their sovereign in wide-eyed awe.

"So, Lord Hugh, who have we here?" the king asked in an amiable bellow. "What pretty maids are these?"

"I am called Pippa, sir."

"It's Philippa," Pen corrected, with another bob of a curtsy. "That is my sister Philippa, sir. I am Penelope."

"So, little Penelope, of what family are you?"

"Our father was Lord Hadlow of Derbyshire," Pen replied, her voice strong.

A frown crossed the king's countenance. He rose from the bench, planting his feet firmly apart to aid his balance, his hands resting on his hips. "I have heard that name before." He glanced interrogatively at Hugh.

"Lady Mallory's second husband," Hugh said evenly.

"Yes, and we wish to go to our mother." Pippa spoke up urgently, recovering from her awe of this great sovereign. "We don't know where she is, but we *have* to see her. Please, sir." She fixed her eyes upon him and unconsciously touched his hand.

Henry looked down at her. He looked at her sister, met the intent pleading gaze of both pairs of hazel eyes. "You'll both be as comely as your mother, I'll wager," he said.

"We *have* to go to Mama," Pippa repeated. "You will not keep us from her, will you, sir?"

"She'll be so anxious for us," Pen said.

"You would have the children plead for their mother, my lord?" the king said slowly to Hugh. "You know that We are weak in the face of a child's pleading."

"I know that Your Highness has a generous temper," Hugh returned. "Lady Mallory knows nothing of the ways of this court. She spoke in haste. I would vouch for her present regret."

The king turned his padded shoulder to Hugh and stared back down the path towards the stables. His queen was due to present him with his third child in the next weeks. This child would be the son he craved and needed more than anything else. All the signs said so. The astrologers said so. The doctors swore to it. Jane, herself, was certain of it in her quiet way. Mercy and generosity befitted a king. And, mayhap, an act of kindness to these children would bring health to his newborn son.

"Lady Mallory will accept your roof?" He spoke without turning back to Hugh.

"Yes, Highness," Hugh said without hesitation.

"Then let it be hoped that she has learned to moderate her tongue and her temper," Henry said. He pulled a ring from his finger and turned slowly back. He handed the jewel to Hugh. "Here is my authority for the lady's release."

He bent down with some difficulty and chucked Pippa beneath the chin. He did the same to Pen. "God go with you, little maids. You will remember that you have seen the king today."

"Oh, yes," Pen said fervently. "Oh, yes, indeed, we will remember."

Henry beamed. He was an expert at detecting flattery and the sincerity in the child's voice delighted him. "Then go now." He straightened and gave Hugh a shrewd look. "You know your king, it would seem, Lord Hugh."

Hugh contented himself with another deep bow.

"Go." Henry waved them away.

Hugh backed off a few paces, drawing the girls with him, then turned and hurried them away back towards the water stairs.

"Did the king say we could go to see Mama?" Pippa asked, puzzled by what had happened. "I didn't hear him say so."

"He didn't," Pen told her. "But he said she was released. Is she in a jail, sir?" She looked up at him, her eyes gravely questioning.

"Temporarily so," Hugh told her.

"But why? Why would Mama be in a jail?" Pippa demanded, her voice rising with alarm.

"Your mother is going to explain that to you herself," Hugh stated, feeling like a coward. "We must make haste back to London. The sooner we get there the sooner you will see your mother. Good, the boat is still at the steps." He swung them both onto the barge they had left a bare half hour before. Had they been any longer the boatmen would have been forced to yield their place to new arrivals and their embarkation would have been much delayed. As it was, they were once more in midstream with the turned current in their favor within a few minutes.

The girls were quiet on the way back to the city. They were both hungry, not having eaten since an early breakfast, but the day's events had so overwhelmed them that they were barely aware of their grumbling stomachs.

Hugh, aware of his own, cursed himself for being in such haste that morning that he had ignored such practicalities. He watched the sun's measured progress and bit his tongue on the urge to press the watermen to greater speed.

It was close to six o'clock when they bumped the landing stage at Blackfriars. Hugh sprang ashore and lifted the girls beside him. "Wait here," he instructed the watermen. "I'll need you again in five minutes." He took the girls' hands and hurried them almost at a run back to his own house.

He left them at the door then turned and ran back to the barge. "The Lion Gate at the Tower," he instructed as he jumped aboard.

The watermen took up their oars and pulled east down the river beneath the bustle of London Bridge to the Tower dock.

The Lieutenant of the Tower regarded the king's ring when it was laid upon the table in front of him. He picked it up, examined the royal insignia. "So, Lord Hugh, I am to deliver the prisoner, Lady Mallory, into your charge."

"That is the king's will."

"She had visitors this morning."

"Aye, her tiring woman and Magister Howard. I sent them with some necessities for her."

"I gave them leave to remain with her for an hour." The lieutenant sounded as if he was seeking approval for his clemency.

"I'm sure Lady Mallory was grateful."

"Aye. My lady wife took a fancy to her last even. She supped at our table. I had a fire lit in her chamber."

Hugh merely nodded, hiding his impatience.

The lieutenant rose to his feet. "Come, my lord, I'll take you to the prisoner. I trust you'll find she has not been ill-housed."

They crossed the Tower green where the ravens were gathering for the night along the ramparts and in the deep shadows of the high walls. They climbed the steps to the tower where Guinevere had her cell.

She was sitting by the still sullenly smouldering fire, her cloak draped around her shoulders, an open book on her lap. But she hadn't read a word in several hours. The visit from Tilly and the magister had cheered her but now, as the shadows of night closed in upon her prison, all optimism left her. She could see no point at all in still trying to marshal a legal defense. No one would listen. They might pay lip service but in the end they would take from her what they wanted.

She turned her head lethargically at the sound of the key in the lock, expecting to see one of the uncommunicative guards with a supper tray.

"Hugh?" She rose from the stool, automatically closing the book over her finger to keep her page. "What brings you here?"

The lieutenant hovered in the doorway and Hugh said quietly, "Leave us, if you please."

The man bowed and withdrew, closing the door behind him. He did not turn the key.

"Do you bring me news of the girls?" Guinevere asked, laying down her book upon the stool. Her face was drawn and anxious. "Tilly and the magister brought me all else that I need, for which I thank you. How . . . how are they?"

"Impatient to see you. Their questions have gone beyond my ability to answer." He stood by the door making no attempt to approach her. His eyes raked her face, took in every line of strain, read there every moment of the fear that had haunted her since he'd left her in the guardhouse at Hampton Court. His heart leaped towards her but he held himself still. He could feel the wall she'd thrown up between them, it was almost as solid as the door at his back.

"They cannot come here," she said, gesturing emphatically to her grim surroundings.

"But you may go to them," he said. "I have the king's orders for your release, as long as you're willing to accept my hospitality."

"How did you manage that?" Her eyes were suddenly narrowed, her posture as graceful and erect as ever.

Hugh shrugged. She'd find that out eventually but he was in no hurry to make the disclosure. "Henry is changeable. He can be manipulated with the right tools. I had them."

Guinevere did not press for further information. "But to leave here I must accept you as my jailer?"

"In essence."

She turned away, back to the fire. She felt so vulnerable, so aware of his body behind her, of the piercing light in his wonderful eyes that seemed to see into her very soul. She yearned for his arms, for his mouth upon hers, for the strength his loving would give her. And yet she was so afraid that in the end it was not strength but weakness that she would draw from him. This man was going to stand as witness against her and he would weaken her with every touch he laid upon her body.

She turned back to him, making her voice hard and bitter. "And must I expect to have my body violated by my jailer in exchange for his hospitality?"

The color drained from his face. His nose was suddenly pinched, a blue shade around his mouth. He raised a hand in an involuntary gesture, then it fell immediately to his side. His fingers curled into his palms as if only thus could he keep them from her.

Guinevere took a shuddering breath. She looked away, saying in a low voice, "Forgive me. I don't know why I said such a thing." She had wanted to hurt him, to drive him from her, but now she felt only self-disgust at the words that still rang in her ears.

Hugh said nothing for a minute. He was too angry to find instant forgiveness. He turned back to the door. "The bells will ring for curfew in a very few minutes. You have until then to make your decision. If you choose not to come with me, then I will have your children brought to you here. They may share with you the king's hospitality. I can't hide the truth from them any longer myself. I suggest you decide what you wish to tell them." He opened the door. "I'll return for your answer when the bells ring."

"Hugh?"

"Well?" He didn't turn back to her but remained with his hand on the door latch.

"I will come with you." What choice did she have? He had known that she could not subject her children to the Tower. Just as she could not allow them to suffer her absence without explanation.

"Then let us waste no more time," he said, his voice still cold. "I'll send someone for your things when we get home."

Guinevere clasped her cloak at her throat. She glanced around the small room. *Would they bring her back here after her trial? After she'd been found guilty? Would she await her execution here?*

Then vigorously she dismissed the black thoughts. Her earlier depression receded, her natural optimism flooding back. While she had her freedom, anything was possible. She was going back to the girls. She'd need all her energies finding a way to explain the truth to them.

She glanced up at Hugh as she walked past him through the door. His expression was still grim. "Forgive me," she said again. "It was a terrible thing to say."

"Yes, it was," he agreed. "I wish I knew what I'd done to deserve it." He took her arm and directed her down the stairs to the green as the bells for curfew rang out.

London Bridge was quiet now as they were rowed beneath it. At curfew the bridge was closed to traffic between the north and south banks of the river. The city itself, though, was still very much alive, lights and noise drifting across the river from the taverns along its banks. The brothels that lined the South Bank were brilliantly lit and Guinevere could see the women hanging around the doors, calling raucously to the men who scrutinized them as they walked by.

"The Bankside brothels do a roaring trade," Hugh observed, following her gaze.

"Only on the South Bank?"

"Mostly."

They lapsed into silence. Guinevere wondered when if ever he would forgive her. But she had wanted to put a distance between them so maybe she shouldn't try to heal the breach.

They left the barge at Blackfriars and in the same silence walked to Holborn. Guinevere's step quickened as they entered the grounds of Hugh's house. The door was flung wide and she was engulfed in her children's welcome.

"Mama . . . Mama . . . we missed you so!" Pippa shouted into her ear as she bent to embrace her. "Why were you in a jail? We talked to the king and he said we could see you . . . didn't he, Pen?"

Pen, clutching her mother's free hand tightly, nodded, her emotions in such a turmoil of anxiety and relief that she couldn't speak.

"*You* spoke to the king?" Guinevere looked at them in bewilderment. She glanced up at Hugh for explanation.

He gave a tiny shrug as if to say, *Well, what would you have had me do?*

Guinevere knew that whatever he had done, it had been the only possible way to achieve her release. And as she held her children to her, she could only be grateful.

17.

Hugh came out of his house, absently stepping over Nutmeg who was playing intently with a fallen leaf on the step. The kitten's sister batted at a worm in a puddle on the driveway. The creatures were so pampered they hadn't had to learn the difference between leaves, worms, and mice, Hugh reflected, but without too much rancor.

He strode down the drive towards the orchard where he knew Guinevere and the magister were walking. As always they would be intently discussing the finest points of legal argument. In the three days since he'd brought her from the Tower, Hugh had never been alone with Guinevere. There was always someone with her; if not the girls, or the magister, it would be some member of her household. She retired to her chamber immediately after they had supped and remained closeted there until daybreak, when she would appear, polite but withdrawn, to continue reading with her children or working on her defense. She had surrounded herself with an impenetrable wall, protecting herself from the enemy.

It was driving him to distraction, not helped by his own confusion. After his afternoon in Matlock, he knew enough about her marriage to Timothy Hadlow and the circumstances surrounding his death to have a firm opinion; not so with Stephen Mallory's death. But he did know that a trial before the king's council would never get at the truth. He knew that his evidence, inconclusive though it was, would be all the grasping Privy Seal would need to condemn her.

He couldn't blame her for retreating from him and yet he could feel whenever he was within a few feet of her how much she needed his support and friendship, how much she craved the loving that brought them both so much joy. But she would not yield. In her eyes, he and her own longings were the enemy, inextricable.

He heard them talking before he saw them as he turned under the trees. Magister Howard was expounding a point of law with meticulous detail.

Hugh called out before he came up with them, unwilling that she should even consider that he had been listening to their conversation. "Lady Guinevere?"

"Lord Hugh." She greeted him with a cool smile as he stepped in front of them. The smile was cool but as always her eyes burned when they fell upon him.

Hugh wondered how long she could keep it up. He wondered how long he could keep his hands and his mouth from hers. At the moment he knew that if Magister Howard had not been bobbing beside her, he would have taken her in love, there on the damp, sweet-smelling grass beneath the gnarled branches of the apple trees, and she would have cried her passion and her need against his mouth as their bodies joined in that one long sweep of union. And he saw in her eyes that she knew it too. She moved infinitesimally closer to the magister, as if instinctively seeking protection.

Guinevere looked away. The power in his gaze was too much to bear. It was brighter and hotter than the sun; would, like the sun's rays, scorch her own eyes if she stared into them.

Magister Howard coughed behind his hand. Hugh greeted him. "I give you good morning, Magister." He turned to Guinevere, said neutrally, "My lady, I have this last hour received notice from Privy Seal that you are commanded to appear before the king's council in the Star Chamber on the morrow."

Her eyes darted to his. The color rushed into her cheeks and then drained as quickly. She put out a hand and instinctively he took it, his fingers tightening around hers.

"Tomorrow?"

"Aye."

"I see." She slipped her hand from his. Her color returned to normal, her voice when she spoke was steady. "Well, 'tis better to face the devil than anticipate him, I believe. May I have the magister's counsel in the Star Chamber?"

Hugh shook his head. "You must appear alone."

Magister Howard put a hand on her arm, his own face drawn and tight. She laid her hand over his. "I am well prepared, Magister. I could not have had better preparation."

"I don't think we've left a stone unturned," he muttered. "I can think of nothing, madam, that we've neglected."

"Neither can I," she said. "So let's talk no more of this for today. I'll let my mind lie fallow."

"Aye, madam. 'Tis always good to rest the mind before a challenge." But the magister didn't look any happier.

Guinevere was aware of a great calm. Her mind was a clear, cool space. There was no fear now, only relief. At last she was to go face-to-face with the demons that were Privy Seal and King Henry of England. She *would* win. She would admit no possibility of failure.

"You will be there, Lord Hugh?" she asked neutrally. "You will bear witness."

"I am so commanded."

"Of course." She turned to follow the magister who had moved away through the trees.

Hugh put out an arm, resting his flat palm on the trunk of an apple tree, blocking her path. He spoke with some urgency. "A moment, Guinevere. There's something we have to discuss. It's not easy but it must be addressed."

She stopped; his arm rested against her breast. Her nipples hardened. She said steadily, "Must it be here? Surely we can talk in the house."

"No, we need to talk about this away from any other ears." After a second he let his arm fall so that she was free to leave if she wished. He would not give her the opportunity to accuse him again of coercion.

Guinevere stayed where she was. She crossed her arms over her breast and looked out across the orchard where the neat alleys between the trees stretched towards the house. Whatever he had to say that was so private had to be personal. She didn't want to hear it, but felt that she must.

Hugh felt for words. He had rehearsed this speech so many times in the last several days but now, when faced with the reality, his carefully chosen words flew to the four winds.

"Guinevere, I think it would be wise for you to draw up some document that will make clear your wishes for the girls."

She drew a deep breath. "You think I will fail to prove my innocence? I assure you I do not intend to fail."

He said with difficulty, "Some things you must take into account."

She was silent. She knew he was right, but admitting it weakened her. Finally she said in a flat voice, "I don't know what provision I'll be permitted to make. Do you?"

He shook his head. "No, but I believe that if you make some provision, if you state your wishes, then there's some chance that I might be able to fight for them."

"And you would fight for them." It was a statement, not a question, and he took it as such.

"I would wish to make provision for their education, for dowries." She steepled her fingers against her mouth, smelling the faint musky scent of her soft doeskin gloves, forcing herself to say out loud what had tormented her innermost thoughts since Hugh of Beaucaire had ridden into her courtyard at Mallory Hall. "Will this be allowed, do you think?"

"I don't know. You can but try." He hesitated, clapping his hands together as if there was a chill in the air, but the September day was mild. "I believe that if you put your daughters under my guardianship, that will not be contested."

Guinevere looked down at the ground. She noticed how a blade of grass sparkled in a ray of sunshine that caught the drop of dew at its tip. She noticed the silvery gray trail of a slug across a fallen leaf. She felt the faint warmth of the autumnal sun on the back of her neck, penetrating the silken folds of her pale hood.

"You would care for them," she said softly, her eyes still on the ground. "But you would have little means to provide for them. I know how important it is for you to gain my lands to provide for Robin.

How can you supply the needs of my daughters when they're left destitute?"

He spoke steadily, evenly, as if he was a neutral counselor giving her advice. "I believe that if you designate some reasonable part of your estates to provide for your children you'll not find the king hostile. And Privy Seal must follow his king's instructions."

Guinevere raised her head but she didn't look at him. "I'll consult with the magister. We'll draw up a document that's legally sound. But it will need a notary's seal."

"I will have it notarized for you before your trial. Give it to me in the morning."

She nodded. "My thanks. I had hoped not to worry about this until afterwards, but you were right to remind me that the outcome is probably inevitable. Optimism is foolish, isn't it?" She gave him a taut and bitter smile, then glided away through the trees.

It was inevitable, Hugh thought. It was right that she should acknowledge it. She had to make such decisions now, before the chance to do so was lost. He would not stand her friend if he didn't point it out to her. So why did forcing the brutal truth upon her make him feel like her betrayer?

That night, Guinevere sat late with Magister Howard. He wrote at her dictation, his expression dark as the grave. He asked no questions, merely checked on legal points as they came up and occasionally offered a suggestion as to wording.

"And in conclusion," Guinevere said, staring into the fire in the hall, "I leave to my faithful servants who have been with me since earliest childhood, the small manor of Cauldon in Derbyshire to dispose of as they see fit."

"Madam, there is no need . . ." The magister held his quill above the parchment.

She smiled. "Yes, Magister, there is every need. I've no idea whether my wishes will be honored, but Lord Hugh has said he'll do his best to ensure that they are." She rose from the settle. "Let us go to bed now. It grows late."

The magister carefully sanded his papers and handed them to her. "My lady is too generous."

"Not so, my friend." She folded the sanded sheets carefully and slipped them into the pocket of her gown. "I do what I can to repay kindnesses that could never adequately be repaid." She touched his hand and then went to the stairs.

Tilly was awake, sitting beside the fire mending a tear in one of Pippa's gowns. "I gave the lassies a little belladonna, chuck," she whispered apologetically. "Poor Pen is worn to a frazzle with worry an' Pippa's full o' tears."

Guinevere had not told the girls about the murder charges she faced, but they knew now that matters were very serious. They understood their mother might be thrown into a jail again although no one had mentioned the possibility of her death. Guinevere could see little point in that. The prospect of losing her to prison was more than they could deal with.

She laid the parchments on the dresser then undressed with Tilly's help. She climbed into bed beside her children. They were curled tightly together, breathing heavily. Tilly snuffed the candle and settled back onto the truckle bed. Guinevere lay in bed, feeling her children's soft bodies beside her, unmoving as they slept the heavy sleep of the drugged. She prayed that they would not wake before she left for Westminster in the morning. If the worst happened, she would be permitted to make her farewells later. A hard lump of tears blocked her throat and she swallowed fiercely. She would not allow herself to think of defeat. Not yet. Not until she had to.

The fire threw flickering shadows on the plain lime-washed walls. She thought of Hugh, asleep now, surely? And despite her determined optimism, she thought of how after tomorrow it could all be over. After tomorrow she would never love again. And the reflection was unbearable.

As if sleepwalking, she slipped to the floor, reached for her night robe, picked up the parchments. Vaguely she thought they would give her an excuse for what she was doing. She could leave them with him and return to bed. She *could* do that.

She was in the passage, was outside his door, was within his chamber. It was lit only by the banked fire.

"So you have come." He spoke from the deep shadows of the bed.

"Yes." She placed the parchments on the mantel.

Hugh turned back the bedcover in a gesture of invitation. She dropped her night robe and slid in beside him. He drew the covers over her and held her.

He held her quietly for a long time until the stiffness and the cold left her and her body relaxed against his. There was no urgency to his hold, nothing to prevent her from easing away from him, out of the bed, away from temptation. But she stayed in his embrace, her head in the hollow of his shoulder, her legs twined with his.

She thought she slept. A deep and dreamless trance where there were no fears, only peace, where her mind was spindrift, light as air, swept upon the wind.

And at last his hold changed as he gathered her yet closer to him, rolling onto his back so that now she lay above him, every curve and hollow of her body molded to his length. Dreamily she smiled down at him, adapting herself to this unexpected position. His mouth curved in response and he ran his fingers through the silken silver river of her hair, drawing it over her shoulders to enclose them both in a shimmering fragrant tent. His square hard hands cupped her face, drawing her mouth down to his.

This was her kiss. Hers to initiate, hers to drive. Her lips rested for an instant passive against his as she reveled in the simple sensation of their touching mouths. Then her tongue penetrated his mouth deeply, tasting wine and salt as she explored the insides of his cheeks, the back of his throat, slid over his teeth. She nibbled his bottom lip, then drew her tongue over his lips, touched the corners of his mouth, licked around the firm contours of his jaw, feeling the prickle of stubble against her tongue.

She moved to his ear, her tongue darting within the tight shell, flicking in the whorls and contours, stroking as her teeth nibbled the sensitive lobe. She could feel his heart beating faster against her breast where her nipples, erect and hard, were teased by the wiry softness of the gray curls on his chest. The ridged muscles of his thighs pressed upwards, powerful against her own softness, and the slight roundness of her belly fitted into the concavity of the one below.

His hands smoothed down her back, lingering over her waist before caressing the flare of her hips. The languid, seductive stroking chased away the last trancelike threads of her dream state. Excitement seethed, she pressed her body down to his, encouraging him to tighten his hold. Her loins were heavy, her sex ached and pulsed. He moved a knee to part her thighs and with a slow twist of his hips thrust upwards into her eagerly welcoming body.

Delight touched every corner of her, body and soul. She wanted to take him into the very core of her self, to encompass and hold him, to become a part of him as she made him a part of her. There was no thought now, no fear, no logic, no past and no future. Only this present, only the white-hot excitement of pure sensation.

He drove upwards with a soft cry of joy and there was one miraculous moment when she hung on her own precipice holding the throbbing power of his completion deep within her, feeling the pulse of his flesh high up against the walls of her sheath that contained him; a moment that sent ripples of indescribable glory streaming through her. And then she fell, tears streaking her cheeks, hearing from far away strange little female sounds coming from deep in her throat.

She lay beached upon him, the wild beating of her heart matching his. Her lips were pressed into the hollow of his throat, sipping the salt sweat gathered there as if it were fairy nectar. Their sweat-slick bodies slithered against each other as still joined they waited in exhaustion for the desperate beating of their hearts to subside.

His hands flattened against her back and he rolled her gently onto the bed beside him, moving with her, prolonging the moment of disengagement as if he could not bear to lose her. She clung to him as he slipped away from her, then let her arms fall to her sides.

"How can it be?" she whispered, fluttering her fingertips against his side as he flopped onto his back.

"I don't know." His hand rested on her belly. "There was much pleasure . . . much pleasure, deep and abiding pleasure . . . with Sarah, but never quite like this."

"No," she murmured. "Never quite like this. There are no words."

They lay together as the sweat dried on their bodies, then Hugh reached down and drew the covers over them.

"I should go," Guinevere protested feebly.

"No, sleep. I'll be awake long before the house stirs." He pushed a hand beneath her and rolled her into his embrace.

She slept, soothed by his breath in her hair, by the steady thump of his heart beneath her ear, by the solid warmth and strength of the arms that held her.

Beside her, Hugh kept vigil until the sky beyond the window took on a gray hue. They were to be at Westminster by eight that morning. He slipped his arm from beneath her, gently so as not to waken her, then slid from the bed. He stood looking down at the sleeping woman. She was so peaceful with her thin blue-veined eyelids concealing the passionate intelligence of her eyes; the soft glow of sleep upon her cheeks, her hair tumbling over the white shoulder, the rounded forearm.

Had she killed Stephen Mallory?

Did it matter?

He went to the fire, bending to stir up the embers. As he straightened his eye fell on the folded parchments on the mantel. He opened them, read them. They needed a notary's seal. For safety's sake they had to be notarized before her trial. They needed to be signed and sealed before judgment was rendered so that they could be brought into the courtroom to be discussed as an extension of that judgment.

He dressed rapidly and left the chamber. It would take him half an hour to rouse the attorney, who lived over the printer's shop two streets away, and get his stamp. He would be back in time to waken her.

He paused again by the bed. Looked at the sleeping woman.

Had she killed Stephen Mallory?

Did it matter?

18.

The Star Chamber in the palace of Westminster. Aptly named, Guinevere reflected, unable for a moment to tear her dazzled gaze from the ceiling where a mass of brilliant gilded stars winked down upon the chamber and its occupants.

"Pray be seated, Lady Mallory." At Privy Seal's harsh voice she turned her gaze steadily to the horseshoe-shaped table at one end of the chamber.

The king sat in the center, his massive carved armchair raised on a dais. He was clad in black, his padded sleeves slashed with purple and gold. A great double dog rose was embroidered in gold across his broad chest. His meaty hands rested on the arms of the chair, the rings on his fingers rivaling in their dazzling brightness the golden stars on the ceiling.

Guinevere curtsied deeply, her black skirts falling gracefully around her, her head in its dark gray hood submissively lowered.

Privy Seal sat to the king's right. His black gown was edged in whitest ermine and one plump hand encased in a jeweled glove unconsciously stroked the corded bag that hung from his girdle. It contained the Privy Seal, the badge of his office.

Bishop Gardiner, in his scarlet robes, his angular face pinched, his eyes sharply piercing and full of suspicion, sat at the king's left hand.

The other lords Guinevere didn't recognize as she rose from her curtsy. There were twelve of them, six to each side of the horseshoe. They regarded her with a curiosity that had little of friendliness in it.

Guinevere took the seat that Privy Seal indicated. An armless chair set just outside the well of the horseshoe. On two sides of the chamber rose several tiers of benches for witnesses and spectators. She was aware of murmurs, shiftings, the rustle of silks and velvets. Hugh of Beaucaire was among the men on the first tier, ready to stand and give witness when called upon. He was just behind her, out of her line of sight. She could see only the majestic figure of the king and the men of his council.

She folded her hands in her lap and waited quietly.

"You are here to defend yourself against the charges that you were responsible for the death of one at least of your four husbands. How do you answer, madam?"

"I am innocent of any such charge, my lord."

"And how do you answer the charge that you bewitched four men, took them into your bed with the lures of witchcraft, and compelled them with the aid of the devil's arts to enrich you with all their worldly goods. How do you answer that, madam?" Bishop Gardiner leaned forward over the table, drumming his fingers on the polished mahogany, his blue, shaven chin jutting aggressively.

She thought of her four husbands, two of whom had been either fools or brutes. Stephen had been both. The very idea that she might have bewitched them was laughable. Mayhap she had bewitched Timothy, but she had been bewitched in her turn. And there had been none of witchcraft in that lusting passion that had brought them together.

"How do you answer, madam?" the bishop demanded in bullying tones.

She wanted to pour scorn on this prating prelate with his greedy fanatical eyes. But caution held her back. He wanted a victim and it would take nothing for her to serve his purpose. For all its absurdity, witchcraft was the most dangerous charge against her because it was the hardest to refute.

She returned calmly, "I have no knowledge of witchcraft, my lord bishop. No one has ever accused me of such before. My husbands came willingly to my bed." She met his fierce glare steadily, but she was clasping her hands tightly lest their shaking betray her.

"I would suggest to you, madam, that you carefully plotted your marriages." Privy Seal's voice flicked at her like a snake's tongue. "I would suggest that you chose men whose death would enrich you; men who, quite unaccountably, were willing to sign whatever contracts you drew up."

"Aye," the bishop chimed in. "No right-thinking man, no man not under the influence of witchcraft, would behave so foolishly as to give a woman such control over him."

"My husbands understood that I am learned in law and that I have no small talent for administering estates, my lords."

"Do those talents also include manufacturing documents to bolster your claims?" Privy Seal inquired smoothly. "I put it to you, madam, that the appearance of the premarriage contract between Roger Needham and his first wife was . . . convenient, shall we say. That it just appeared . . . came to hand . . . at the very moment when it seemed Lord Hugh's claim could not be disputed. I can't help wondering why you didn't produce it before, my lady. I understand you had many months of correspondence with Lord Hugh and you never mentioned the existence of such a significant document." His hard, unpleasant gaze raked her face.

Guinevere was for a moment thrown off course. Why had he not accused her of this at their first interview? But of course the accusation was designed to confuse her, make her stumble in her defense, here in front of all these lords. *But it would not.*

She gave him a faintly incredulous smile. "I beg your pardon, my lord. You are not suggesting I *manufactured* this document? It has a notary's seal."

Bishop Gardiner spoke, his voice carrying a zealot's edge. "Madam, we all have enough respect for your brains and cunning to know that if a notary's seal would be of use to you, you would find a way to acquire one."

"Not so, my lord bishop," she said flatly. "I know my law, but I do not resort to trickery. You can have no possible justification for making such an accusation."

There was a breath of silence in the chamber, a strange sense of waiting. Guinevere continued, her voice rising a notch. "While such talents as I possess are perhaps rare, there is nothing inherent in womanhood that says a woman is by her very nature incapable of them." She was careful not to mention the Lady Mary this time.

"Only my second husband, Lord Hadlow, preferred to keep the day-to-day management of his own estates in his own hands."

"His *own* estates?" Privy Seal pounced. "*Only* his own estates. When you contracted these marriages, you ensured, did you not, that your husbands had no part in the wealth you had inherited from their predecessors?"

"That is customary, my lord, when a widower remarries. His new wife is not endowed with anything more than a jointure, which is often no more than her dowry."

"But you, madam, were a widow, *not* a widower."

"That is self-evident, my lord."

The king shifted a little in his chair, there were slight rustles from the spectators behind her.

Hugh closed his eyes briefly. How the hell far did she think she could go in this company? She was on trial for her life. He'd told her over and over to keep a bridle on her tongue, but he might as well have saved his breath to cool his porridge.

"I would remind you, madam, that you are in the presence of His Highness the king and the most august lords of the realm," Privy Seal observed, moistening his thin lips, his hard eyes narrowed.

Guinevere chose her words more carefully. "I meant no insult, Lord Cromwell. But I don't see that my sex is relevant. I have done only what men do as a matter of course."

"Men do not murder their wives in order to enrich themselves," snapped the bishop.

"There is no evidence that I have done so," Guinevere pointed out. "No witnesses and no evidence to justify bringing such charges." She wanted to look over her shoulder, to find Hugh among the eyes she could feel upon her back, but she resisted the temptation.

"There are circumstances that lend themselves to such an interpretation," Privy Seal stated.

"I would venture to suggest, My Lord Cromwell, that you are as familiar as I am with the pitfalls of circumstantial evidence," Guinevere said. She could argue this legal issue with the best lawyer in the land . . . until Hugh produced his evidence of the lies that had been told him. The weight that that would add to the circumstantial evidence would damage her arguments beyond repair.

Privy Seal leaned forward across the table, his hands resting one atop the other. "You have had four husbands. Each one has died in less than transparent circumstances. Each one has left you a considerably richer widow than the last. I suggest, madam, that you plotted each marriage, and each death, in order to leave yourself in possession of wealth beyond the dreams of avarice, and not coincidentally the greater part of the county of Derbyshire." He sat back, as if nothing else remained to be said.

Guinevere's gaze swept the table. The king regarded her impassively; the twelve lords, so far silent, had similar expressions. It seemed that only the bishop and Privy Seal were to conduct this trial.

As if in confirmation, the bishop leaned forward in his turn. "And I suggest, madam, that you used the arts of witchcraft to compel these men into marriage. Whether they met their deaths through witchcraft I'm not prepared to say, but only witchcraft could have compelled them into accepting such terms of marriage as you insisted upon."

"I refute your suggestions, my lord." Guinevere stood up and faced them. She had nothing to lose now. Once Hugh was called upon to give his evidence then it would be over. But while she had the floor, while their eyes, now both startled and fascinated, were fixed upon her, she would say her piece.

"A woman, my lords, has only her face, her figure, her charms, if you will, as currency. She must attract men if she's to have the basic necessities, food, a roof over her head, a fire in the hearth. She must use what nature has given her to ensure her own survival. And you would call this witchcraft."

She gave a short mirthless laugh. "If a woman has more than her share of wit and learning, she must use those too for survival. Is sorcery the only explanation you can find for competitive talents in a woman?

"There is no sorcery here, my lords. I use what female charms and natural wit I possess to ensure my own future and that of my daughters. A woman who fails to attract a man to support her is a pitiable creature, blamed for her lack of charms, considered unworthy of support. You would not deny this, my lords." Her gaze swept them, and now there was no concealing the contempt in the purple depths of her eyes.

"This view of woman degrades our humanity by judging us only on our physical merits. I stand guilty of questioning this practice, these assumptions, and I stand guilty of attempting to ensure that I and my daughters are not so degraded. But that, Your Highness, my lords, is all of which I'm guilty. I consider myself to be any man's equal." She sat down again, folding her hands once more in her lap.

The king stroked his reddish gold beard. The bishop pointed a finger at her, declaring triumphantly, "Heresy. It is written that a woman must subjugate herself to her husband, who is her lord and master as God is his. You would set yourself up against the writings of the Church."

"No, my lord bishop. I preach no heresy. I voiced only an opinion. I merely said that I consider myself any man's equal. I accept that others may disagree." She paused, then couldn't help herself from continuing, "And in *some* areas, my lord, I consider myself the superior of *some* men."

The king spoke at last, his voice booming through the chamber. "Body o' God, madam, but you sail very close to the wind."

Guinevere rose again and curtsied. "I do not force my opinions on anyone, Your Highness. I merely hold them to myself. And the word of the Church is open to many interpretations, I believe." She met Henry's momentarily astounded gaze. She had challenged him personally. A man who interpreted the rulings of the Church any which way he pleased.

"Body o' God!" he exclaimed. He folded his arms across his barrel chest and regarded her now with a hint of amusement.

Hugh breathed again. For some reason, the king was in generous humor, willing to appreciate courage and honesty. Of course such appreciation could well be short-lived. A flare-up of his ulcer, an inconvenient itch, and His Highness could turn into the cruel and petty autocrat that was his other self.

"I think we've heard enough of your inflammatory views, madam." Privy Seal coughed dryly. "You deny the charges brought against you?"

"I do, my lord." She took her seat again.

"Very well, then let us look at the evidence. Lord Hugh of Beaucaire, we would hear your findings."

Guinevere felt Hugh stand up behind her. Again she resisted the temptation to turn her head. The skin on her nape prickled, her scalp contracted, as she waited for the words that would damn her.

Hugh faced Guinevere's accusers. Her passionate words still sounded in his head. Why should she not consider herself any man's equal when she manifestly was? Why should she not use the gifts God gave her to secure her future? A future that as she had said rested entirely in the hands of men. He had never before questioned this ordering of society, but Guinevere had sowed the seeds of doubt. Had she done so in the minds of any of her accusers? He looked at the hard countenance of Privy Seal, at the fanatical eyes of the bishop, and knew that there at least she had not.

Had she murdered Stephen Mallory?

Did it matter?

He began to speak. In measured tones, he described his journey, his arrival at Mallory Hall, the scope of his investigations. "As you know, my lords, I was disputing Lady Mallory's ownership of some portion of her land. It seems however that my kinsman, Roger Needham, was indeed entitled to leave the land to his widow. I do not dispute the authenticity of the premarriage contract."

"Ah." Privy Seal shrugged. "Well, that is up to you, Lord Hugh."

"Indeed," Hugh responded.

"My sympathies," Privy Seal murmured.

Hugh contented himself with a wry smile. "Lady Guinevere was in childbed when Roger Needham fell from his horse during a stag hunt. It's hard to implicate her in that death."

"Witchcraft," muttered the bishop, hissing irritably between his teeth.

"I could find no one in the countryside who would entertain any implication of witchcraft," Hugh said definitely. "My men conducted extensive inquiries in the villages and among her tenants. There was not the whisper of a rumor, and indeed the suggestion met outrage."

"That's no proof of innocence."

"Maybe not, but neither is it proof of guilt," Hugh said gently. "Lady Mallory's third husband died of the sweating sickness that swept the country that year. Again I could find no evidence to discredit that account. There was barely a family in the countryside who didn't lose some members to the sickness." He shrugged. "I can see no reason to suspect foul play."

"A conveniently timed death mayhap," the bishop suggested eagerly. He cast Guinevere a brooding glance.

Again Hugh shrugged. "You *could* believe that, my lord bishop. But I doubt justice or faith would be served."

The bishop stroked the bluish skin of his shaven chin and adjusted his priest's cap over his ears. "And what of the second husband? You have not mentioned him."

"Brought down by an unmarked arrow. His wife was at his side. Many men were abroad in the forest, their lord having made them free of the game for that day. It is more than likely that an unlucky arrow went wide of its mark," Hugh said calmly. "No man would acknowledge it for fear of the consequences. But it is certain sure that Lady Mallory did not loose the arrow that killed her husband."

Cromwell frowned. "She could have arranged it."

"Indeed. But there's no evidence."

"But there's motive. Circumstances lend themselves to such a conclusion."

"From all that I could gather, Lord Hadlow and his wife were a devoted couple. They had two children. Lady Mallory was already wealthy in her own right and Lord Hadlow, of all her husbands, was the least affluent . . . although such matters are always relative," Hugh added somewhat aridly, thinking of the riches of coal and iron to be mined on the land Hadlow had left his widow.

He continued. "Hadlow was known to be generous with what he had, almost to a fault, and spent freely to ensure the comfort and well-being of his tenants. His wife according to all reports supported his expenditures and the very generous settlements he made on his death to his tenants. Settlements that certainly reduced her own holdings. In short, my lords, his death brought her considerable administrative burdens and less material wealth than one might have imagined. She continues her late husband's philanthropy and generosity to the tenants. I see no financial motive there."

Guinevere listened in near disbelief. *So that was what he'd discovered at Matlock. Why hadn't he told her he absolved her of that death, instead of leaving her to fret and wonder what surprises he was going to spring?*

But then she reminded herself that she had kept Needham's premarriage contract to herself. They had been playing a game of cat and mouse, each holding cards to their chests.

In the face of Hugh's report it would be hard for this court to fail to absolve her of these three deaths, but Stephen's . . . ? Ah, there lay the snakepit.

She closed her eyes for a minute, reliving that evening. She could hear his heavy lumbering step, his thick drunken voice berating her. She saw him raise his fist, lunge for her. Lips, teeth, eyes, cheekbones, he didn't care what he hit. She put out her foot . . .

"Lady Mallory?"

She opened her eyes, aware that she was swaying slightly on her hard chair. Privy Seal had spoken sharply to her. "Forgive me," she murmured.

"Bring wine for the lady," the king demanded. "She's uncommon pale. I'd not have her swoon under these questions, Thomas."

Thomas Cromwell heard the faint rebuke and his mouth thinned. The king, it seemed, had taken one of his arbitrary fancies to Lady Mallory. One minute he had her thrown into the Tower, and the next was listening to her insolence with every sign of amusement, and now he was defending her from her questioners. As if, indeed, these proceedings were not as much for Henry's material benefit as his Privy Seal's. Only the bishop could be absolved from a venal motive in pursuing the lady. Gardiner wanted a witch.

A gentleman usher hurried from the chamber and returned within minutes with a cup of wine. He gave it to Guinevere who would have declined except that she thought she'd probably risked the king's displeasure enough for one day. To turn aside his kindness would be true insult. She sipped a little and handed the cup back to the usher.

"Ah, that's better. There's a touch of color in your cheeks, my lady," the king announced with satisfaction. "You may continue, Thomas."

Cromwell bowed to his king and turned again to Hugh, who in the interval had taken his seat again. Hugh couldn't see her face but he had felt it in his own body when the weakness had washed through her. He could do nothing for her . . . not yet. But he ached to hold her, support her with his own strength.

Had she killed Stephen Mallory?

It didn't matter.

"Lord Hugh. What can you tell us of Lord Mallory's death?"

Guinevere breathed slowly and evenly, holding the panic at bay.

"Rather more than of the others, Lord Cromwell."

"Ah, good." Privy Seal settled back in his chair. "Pray continue."

"Lord Mallory was often deep in drink." Hugh chose his words carefully. Most of these lords knew what it was to be so incapacitated and wouldn't consider it a failing. "He was a very large man. When he fell, it was sometimes impossible to get him back on his feet."

"He was drunk on the evening of his death?"

"Aye. He had guests for dinner. My lieutenant spoke with them and they all swear that he was as drunk as they'd ever seen him. His wife went to her chamber early in the evening. As I understand it, she found drunkenness offensive and didn't scruple to tell her husband so."

There was a murmur of disapproval. Guinevere looked up at the gilded ceiling.

"Lord Stephen's guests also felt that Lady Mallory showed a lack of respect for her husband . . . but they vouch for his drunkenness, and for his anger at his wife."

"A man does not care to be criticized in front of his friends," one of the lords stated.

"No, indeed not," Hugh agreed. "One might consider that when it comes to motive for injury, Lord Mallory had it rather than his wife. A large man, my lords. By all accounts, a man very much taller and heavier than his wife. A man given to violence."

He paused to allow this to settle in.

"So what are you telling us happened that night?" the bishop demanded testily. "Lord Mallory was entitled to punish his wife for her insolence. Did he do so?"

"Lady Mallory was not in her bedchamber when he went to find her at the end of the evening," Hugh said. "She was with her steward and tiring woman in the steward's pantry going over household accounts. It seems that Lord Mallory, overdrunk and in a fearful rage, somehow fell from the open window of his wife's chamber. The sill is low. I can find no other explanation."

Guinevere tried to make sense of what he was saying. He was describing it exactly as it had happened with one vital exception. One exception and the one little lie that would exonerate her. No mention of deceptions, of the lies of her household. Nothing.

"So, Lord Hugh, you believe Lady Mallory to be innocent of all wrongdoing?" Privy Seal asked into the attentive hush.

"Lady Mallory was not guilty of causing the deaths of any of her husbands," Hugh said steadily.

Abruptly Privy Seal leaned forward across the table, one finger pointing accusingly at Guinevere. "Your husband, Stephen Mallory, was friend and supporter of the traitor Robert Aske," he stated, articulating each word slowly and deliberately.

The king sat up, his air of amusement vanished. "What's this?"

"The lady's husband supported the Pilgrimage of Grace, Highness," Privy Seal said smoothly. " 'Tis reasonable to assume that his wife was also involved in that treason. Aske's rotting carcass hangs in chains in York, as befits such a traitor. Stephen Mallory is dead. But his wife, a lady who one must assume took her husband's beliefs and followed the course he set, sits before us."

"Your pardon, my lord, but I fail to understand why you would make such an assumption about Lady Guinevere," Hugh said, his smile unwavering. "As we've already established, the lady has a mind of her own. Her independent nature is what brought her before you today. I would wager that she would be the last wife to take on beliefs that were not her own."

The king frowned and turned his heavy head towards Guinevere. "Was your husband a supporter of the traitor Aske, madam?"

Guinevere was struggling with this new threat, which seemed to have come out of nowhere. She shook her head. "He knew Aske, Highness. But dropped all association with him as soon as the Pilgrimage of Grace started." Her lip curled slightly. "Stephen Mallory was not known for his loyalty or for the strength of his convictions, my lords."

"And you, madam? What are your views on Aske and his Pilgrimage?" Henry's gaze seemed to pierce her skull.

Now she must be careful. If ever there was a moment for deception and diplomacy this was it.

"Ill-judged, Highness," Guinevere said swiftly. "One must respect sincerely held convictions, I believe, but Mr. Aske struck me as more interested in fomenting rebellion and enjoying the power of leadership than in following his heart."

She sent a silent prayer for forgiveness to the wretched man who had died such a hideous death for his beliefs. But if she was to save herself from a like fate, she had no choice but to dissemble.

The king nodded slowly. "I have no further interest in Aske and his rebellions. The price has been paid." He glanced at Cromwell, who was pursing his mouth in clear disappointment, then turned his gaze onto Hugh.

"So, Lord Hugh, you do not believe the lady murdered any of her husbands?"

"I do not, Highness. And I am prepared to marry her myself to prove my conviction."

A collective gasp ran around the Star Chamber. The bishop sat up, pulling at his cap; Privy Seal looked first astounded and then furious. It took several seconds for his expression to assume its customary arrogant impassivity. The king leaned forward in his chair, his little eyes bright in the doughy cheeks.

"Well, well, Hugh of Beaucaire. That is confidence indeed. You have no fear of poison, of sorcery, of the knife in the night." He chuckled deep in his chest.

Hugh regarded Guinevere's still figure, her straight back, the erect set of her head. He thought of her as she had been last night. So afraid, and yet so full of courage. He declared quietly, "I have no such fears, Highness."

"Well, well. So, my lady . . ." The king turned to Guinevere. "What say you to Lord Hugh's proposal?"

19.

"Witchcraft! Sorcery!" declared the bishop, pointing his finger accusingly at Guinevere. "She has woven her evil spells around Hugh of Beaucaire."

There was an instant of silence, then Hugh began to laugh, a deep rumble of amusement. He stood with his feet braced, his hands resting on the bar in front of his seat. And he laughed, his brilliant blue eyes alight with merriment as he regarded the bishop. It took a minute, then there came slight chuckles and half smiles from the men who knew Hugh. The idea that this practical, squarely built soldier who exuded power, both mental and physical . . . the very idea that Hugh of Beaucaire could succumb to a woman's sorcery was clearly absurd. The grim solemnity of the chamber dissipated.

Privy Seal's thin mouth seemed to disappear and he stroked his chin with restless fingers. The king's gaze flicked between the bishop and Privy Seal with more than a hint of malice at their discomfiture. It was very rare to see either of these men outmaneuvered in their plots.

"My lord bishop, I can assure you that I am far from bewitched by Lady Mallory," Hugh declared. "I have spent close on two months in her company and I am not blind to her faults. She's both arrogant and stubborn in her opinions and in the way she conducts her affairs. But those faults do not make her either a witch or a murderer. I have no intention of allowing her to dictate the terms of any contract we might enter into. But I do believe in her innocence and her virtue. And I doubt any man in this chamber would disagree that she is a very beautiful woman. One any man would be proud to claim as his wife."

"And when one adds her riches to her beauty, you have an irresistible combination," the king rumbled. "I see nothing of witchcraft in that. We can well understand your desire to wed the lady, Lord Hugh, if you're certain you won't join your predecessors sooner rather than later." He raised an eyebrow and Hugh merely bowed in response.

The king stroked his beard again. There was a tense silence in the chamber as they awaited his judgment. Finally he spoke almost ruminatively, almost with a question behind the statement. "So it seems we must find the lady innocent of all charges?"

An imperceptible murmur ran around the chamber, almost like a collective sigh. Hugh was aware that his mouth was very dry, his neck stiff as he held himself rigid and unmoving. *He had won. Or had he?*

"Lady Guinevere, how do you answer Lord Hugh's proposal?" Henry repeated, his gaze swinging back to her, as she sat, white-faced and motionless on her chair.

Guinevere was in shock. Her emotions whirled in a dizzying turmoil. Her relief at this reprieve was so intense that she could neither think nor speak coherently. She struggled to understand what Hugh had said. *Why* had he saved her? He had lied for her. This duty-bound man of such rigid principle, such a pronounced sense of honor, had lied to save her. And she knew in her heart that he was not convinced of her innocence. Even when they made such wonderful love, she knew he still doubted her.

Her thoughts tumbled wildly and she was unaware that she was staring blankly at the king. Hugh had saved her because he wanted her wealth. He had said as much. He had said that he would not permit her to write any contract they entered into. He would dictate the terms himself. He would marry her and save her from death, but at the expense of her independence.

But what choice did she have? Only Hugh could save her. Her own eloquence, her legal arguments would avail her nothing. But Hugh of Beaucaire was so highly regarded, his honesty and probity so absolute that no one would dare to question his declaration.

He would marry her and save her from death but at the expense of her independence.

"Madam, you appear to have lost your tongue," the king said, and now there was a touch of impatience in his voice, the amusement gone from his eye.

What choice did she have?

Guinevere forced her thoughts into some order, her tongue into motion. She rose slowly. "Your Highness, I am overwhelmed by Lord Hugh's offer. Please forgive me if my silence seemed ungrateful. It was quite the opposite. I am overwhelmed with gratitude."

"Ah, that is prettily said." The king beamed. When he was inclined to be generous and merciful he found the world a very pleasant place and he took delight in using his power to make others happy. He was drawn to the lady, and he remembered her daughters, such pretty little things and so sweetly spoken. And he would like to see Lord Hugh gain some material reward, particularly when it didn't have to come out of the privy purse. Yes, it was very pleasant to use his power to good purpose.

"So, my lady, you accept this offer of marriage?"

Hugh held his breath. Despite her murmurings about gratitude, he was by no means certain that she would take the way out he had offered her. Sometimes he thought she had to be the most stubborn woman who ever lived. But surely her intelligence, her sense of self-preservation, her fear for her children, would make her accept him.

"I do, Highness," Guinevere said clearly and steadily and Hugh breathed again.

Henry patted his hands together and rose heavily from his chair. He paused for a second to see if his ulcerated leg would start to throb and when he felt no pain declared smilingly, "We shall see you wed in two days' time in the chapel at Hampton. The queen will be pleased to attend." He beamed. A wedding would cheer Jane. He worried that her advanced pregnancy was taking its toll on her spirits.

"Two days will be sufficient for the contracts to be drawn up." He nodded at the dour Privy Seal. "Thomas, you will make sure that all's as it should be on that score." And he strode from the Star Chamber, the short gown that hung from his massive shoulders swinging richly at each weighty step.

The lords in the chamber had risen with their king and stood bare-headed until an usher closed the door behind him.

Privy Seal regarded Guinevere who still stood white-faced at her chair. "It seems, madam, that you have found favor with the king," he stated. "Your life is spared." His lips moved soundlessly as he looked down at the papers on the table before him and only the bishop heard the soft "For now."

Hugh moved out of the tiered benches and into the center of the chamber. Formally he bowed to the motionless Guinevere. "Madam, your business here is done. If you would come with me now."

It was a command couched in pleasantry. Guinevere heard it as it was intended to be heard. She inclined her head in faint acknowledgment and walked ahead of him out of the chamber without looking once at her accusers, who remained on their feet.

Privy Seal glanced at Bishop Gardiner as the lords in the chamber started to follow the vindicated woman.

"She is guilty," the bishop said through his teeth. "I can smell a witch from afar. She has bewitched Hugh of Beaucaire as surely as she bewitched her husbands."

"That I doubt, my lord bishop," Cromwell said thoughtfully. "She is a clever woman, and a beautiful one. But she's no witch. A tricky lawyer, yes. Maybe a murderer." He shrugged. "Who's to say and what does it matter in the end? I will still have what I seek from her."

The bishop looked sharply at him. "How will you do that, Thomas, now that the king has given her his blessing?"

Privy Seal smiled a thin smile and answered with one of his favorite expressions. "There's more than one way to skin a cat, Bishop Gardiner," he said.

Guinevere remained silent as she walked with Hugh through the courts and corridors of Westminster Palace and down to the water steps. The weak late September sun was now high in the sky. It had been but a hint on the horizon when she'd awoken that morning to find herself alone in Hugh's bed, the memories of their loving embedded in her skin, present in the delightful languor of her limbs.

The girls had still slept the belladonna sleep when Hugh and

Guinevere had left for Westminster. She had kissed their sleeping faces, keeping her silent agony to herself. Now her step quickened involuntarily with the need to see them, to hold them, to reassure them that there was no longer anything to fear, that all was once again well. If marriage to Hugh and the loss of her independence was the price, then she would pay it and conceal her anger and resentment at his trickery. She knew that Hugh would not deprive her children of their dowries even if it pleased him to make their mother dependent upon his good will and charity.

Hugh gave her his hand to step into the wherry that responded to his summons at the water steps. Her gloved hand merely brushed his as she embarked and sat upon the thwart. He sat opposite her, as silent as she, idly tapping the back of one hand into the palm of the other.

The two wherry men took up their oars and pulled strongly for Blackfriars. Guinevere raised her face to the slight warmth of the sun. She inhaled deeply of the mélange of smells that rose from the river and came off the embankments on either side. Gutter smells of rotting meat and vegetables, of human waste, of green river slime, of fish and thick black mud. And occasionally a whiff of fresh baking would waft amid the others as a hawker walked the riverbank with his trays of pies and loaves. She could detect a hint of late summer roses from one of the small gardens that came down to the river. The colors everywhere were brighter, clearer than she'd ever remembered. The city's cacophony was music to her ears. The smells both rank and sweet were so precious she could not stop taking deep breaths, drawing the air far into her lungs. She was alive, and she was free.

Hugh watched her. He could make a fair guess at her thoughts. Soon, when the first flush of relief had faded, she would want to know why he had lied for her. He wasn't certain of the answer. He hadn't known he was going to vindicate her until he spoke the words. He had been stirred by her own defense, certainly, but that would not have been enough to make him do something so out of character as to perjure himself.

He loved her. He lusted after her. He felt a deep and abiding passion for her. But he was not convinced of her innocence. And yet he had lied to save her.

There was the money, of course. Had his motive been purely venal? He didn't like to think so. He wanted what he had claimed for Robin, but he would have received that anyway. It had always been understood between himself and Privy Seal that those estates were his in exchange for delivering Guinevere Mallory. But he was going to insist upon much more in the marriage settlements. He was going to insist upon the customary arrangements whereby a woman brought her wealth to her husband.

He had no intention of making Guinevere's life miserable, but he certainly did not intend to bow his head meekly to whatever legal financial arrangements she considered appropriate. He was no hapless male caught in the toils of a clever woman. Guinevere must understand that he would be a husband quite unlike her others.

Her wealth would ensure that Robin could take his place in a world that would give him advancement, bring him wealth in his own right. Hugh loved her but she would not ride roughshod over him. He would gain more from this arrangement than the joys of a passionate and loving partnership. It was his right, both legal and moral, to do so.

The wherry tied up at Blackfriars steps and Guinevere stepped ashore unaided, as Hugh paid the oarsmen. She stood looking around the thronged steps, once again conscious in every fiber of being alive. She heard Pippa's high voice in her head, Pen's more gentle, less piercing tones, and without waiting for Hugh set off with a swift stride along the familiar lane between the cramped hovels that led to Hugh's house.

Hugh hastened after her. He understood her urgency. He caught up with her before she reached the gates to his house.

He laid a hand on her arm. "Guinevere?"

She stopped, startled at the sound of his voice after the long silence. "We will talk at length when we can be private," she said. "I must go to my daughters."

Hugh let his hand drop. He had wanted to establish just a smidgen of private contact with her before they were engulfed in the children's needs. Just to garner a sense of how she felt about him now. But his needs were not important, not compared with her children's. He understood that. He nodded quietly but tucked her hand into his arm so that they walked up the drive united.

He opened the door himself, then stepped back to allow her to precede him into the square hall. Guinevere stepped in, her eyes adjusting to the dimness after the brighter light outside.

"Mama . . . Mama!" Pippa slid from the settle by the fire where she'd been curled with her kitten. The mewling ball of fur flew unheeded from her lap as the child hurtled across the floor to her mother. "Pen . . . Pen . . . Mama's here. She's not in a jail! She's not." Her last words were muffled as she buried her face in her mother's skirts.

Wordlessly, Guinevere bent and lifted her. She held her tight, pressing her face against the child's warm cheek, running her hand over the back of her head, feeling the childlike shape of her skull, breathing in the sweet vanilla scent of her.

"It's all right, sweeting," she whispered. "It's all right now."

Pen, her face tear streaked, her eyes swollen, almost fell down the stairs in her haste to get to her mother. She clutched Guinevere around the waist and Guinevere knelt down, lowering Pippa to the floor so that she could embrace them both.

"It's all right now," she repeated softly, tears pricking behind her own eyes, a lump in her throat as she held their dear familiar bodies and thought of how close she had come to being unable to do this ever again. Never to see them grow, to hear them laugh, to wipe their tears.

She must not think like that. She must not break down now. Not at the end, when she had been so strong before.

But joy and relief after such terror were too much.

"Why are you crying, Mama? Don't cry." Pen stroked her mother's eyes, trying to wipe away the tears that now fell without restraint. "Are you sick, Mama?"

"You said it was all right now," Pippa said, nuzzling her mother's cheek, trying to bury herself in her mother, tears thick now in her own voice. "Please don't cry."

"I'm crying because I'm happy," Guinevere said, reaching around Pippa to wipe her eyes with the back of her gloved hand. "I need a kerchief."

"Here." Hugh bent down and handed her his own.

"My thanks." She took it and wiped her eyes properly before gently disengaging from the children and standing upright once more. "I have not cried," she said softly. "Not a tear before."

"No, I know," he returned as softly, his hand for a second brushing her damp cheek.

She didn't turn from the fleeting caress, but neither did she return it with hand or eye, although she knew his sympathetic understanding was genuine. There was still too much to be resolved between them to rush gratefully into his arms. She saw now that Tilly, the magister, Greene, and Master Crowder had joined them and stood a little apart, their expressions tense and questioning.

She went to them, holding out her hands. "My friends," she said softly, clasping each one's hand between both of hers.

" 'Tis truly over, chuck?" Tilly asked, dabbing at her own eyes with the edge of her coif.

"There are some complications, but we're safe," she replied. "And you will all stay with me and the girls, unless you wish otherwise."

"That's a piece of nonsense," Greene declared gruffly. "Where you go, my lady, we go."

"My thanks," she responded. "I need you as much now as I've ever done." She smiled at them and turned back to the children as Crowder and Greene left the hall. The magister and Tilly remained where they were, hesitant in the shadows of the staircase.

Pen and Pippa regarded their mother in solemn puzzlement. "You're happy because everything's all right now," Pen said firmly. "That's why you were crying."

"Yes, sweetheart, that's why."

"I'm very happy that matters turned out for the best, madam." Robin spoke with a stiff gravity that concealed his emotions. He had been standing in the shadow of the settle watching the reunion. He was aware of enormous relief that his father had somehow managed to divert the devious course of justice in Lady Guinevere's favor. He had no doubt but that his father had arranged for Lady Guinevere's acquittal.

"Why, thank you, Robin." Guinevere turned to the boy, smiling warmly as she gave him her hand. She had a shrewd idea that Robin had known more about the gravity of her situation than he had let on to Pen. She held his hand for a little longer than necessary, imparting a more than ordinary warmth. Hugh could kiss Pippa with utter naturalness, but Robin, even from his about-to-be stepmother, would definitely squirm at such a display.

Robin's fingers twitched and she released his hand immediately. Still smiling at him, she brushed a drooping lock of hair off his forehead in a gesture that could only be interpreted as maternal. She waited for Hugh to say something.

He said nothing.

Guinevere spoke. "I am to marry," she said to her daughters. *'Tis the price of freedom.* But that she didn't say. She bent and kissed their astounded faces.

"*Again!*" demanded Pippa in ill-concealed dismay. "The last one was so *horrid*! Why must you marry, Mama? We don't want another father! Do we, Pen?"

But Pen was silent, looking at her mother.

"Stepfathers," declared Pippa, "are nasty and rough. They shout and throw things. We don't want one, Mama. We want to go home and be like it was."

"Would you accept *me* as a stepfather, Pippa?" Hugh asked with a quirked eyebrow.

"*You!*" exclaimed Pippa. "You, Lord Hugh?"

"Aye," he affirmed calmly. "Your mother has agreed to become my wife. And I am not in the habit of shouting and throwing things."

Pen's eyes darted to her mother, became fixed on her face with an almost painful intensity as if she had some inkling of the devious channels that snaked beneath this startling decision.

Guinevere smiled at her and gave her a little nod of reassurance.

"Maybe not, sir, but you don't like cats," Pippa pointed out. "What will we do when Moonshine and Nutmeg have kittens if you're going to live with us?"

"I suppose that increase is inevitable," Hugh said with a mock sigh. "Well, when that happens you'll do pretty much what you have been doing." His tone was light and easy. "Keep them out from under my feet and I see no reason why we can't coexist perfectly happily."

Pippa absorbed this. She looked at her sister and saw that Pen, while she appeared still puzzled, was looking much less anxious and unhappy. That was enough for Pippa to decide that perhaps this strange turn of events was not necessarily a bad thing.

"I expect it will be all right then," she said judiciously. "Even if you don't like cats. Will we go back to Mallory Hall?" She plucked at her mother's skirts. "Or will we stay here? Pen and me, we want to go home. Don't we, Pen?" She turned to her sister for corroboration.

"That hasn't been decided," Guinevere said before Pen could respond to her sister. For the first time Guinevere glanced up at Hugh with a hint of challenge in her eyes. He acknowledged it with a tiny gesture of his head. They would draw battle lines soon enough.

Robin had said nothing. He was looking at Pen. If she was to be his stepsister, they couldn't walk hand in hand along the riverbank, or pick flowers together, or . . .

He glanced up at his father and saw his sympathetic smile. "Sisters make the best friends, Robin," Hugh said gently.

Pen looked momentarily startled, then she blushed, catching his meaning. She hadn't thought about consequences for herself and Robin in their parents' marriage. She glanced shyly at Robin, unsure what she felt about this new turn of events, wondering what he would think. He didn't meet her eye and she looked away again.

Pippa frowned over this, then her face cleared as she said, "Oh, I see. If Pen and Boy Robin are brother and sister then they can't like each other the way they do." She frowned again. "That's not very fair."

"We don't mind," Robin said gruffly.

"No," agreed Pen, slipping her hand into her mother's. "We don't mind."

"Oh." Pippa was about to ask how one minute you could say you loved someone and the next say you didn't, but something told her it wouldn't be wise to ask awkward questions at this juncture.

"You will enjoy having a brother," Guinevere said, caressing Pen's cheek. "I always wanted one of my own."

Pen looked a little uncertain but managed a game smile.

"We have cause for celebration," Hugh stated. "A more than ordinarily good dinner is in order, I believe. Robin, will you go and arrange matters with Master Milton?"

"Pen and Pippa will go with you," said Guinevere, putting a hand on each child's shoulder. "I believe that Master Crowder should have some contribution to make to this . . ." She hesitated, then continued,

"To this *joint* celebration, Lord Hugh?" She raised an eyebrow. "If we are to blend our households we must find some way to share domestic responsibilities."

Hugh frowned. Guinevere, of course, would have her own household as always. Two stewards under one roof could prove problematic. "There's time enough to work out such details," he said pacifically. "Milton and Crowder seem to have managed well enough so far."

"Indeed, but Master Crowder has accepted his position as guest under your roof," she pointed out. "That's about to change."

"As I said, we will discuss such details later. Robin, if you please . . ."

Robin gave a jerky bow and turned towards the kitchen regions. Guinevere gave the girls a little push to follow him and they went half hesitantly, half willingly.

Tilly came forward. "So, 'tis to be another wedding, chuck," she observed, regarding Lord Hugh with an expression neither favorable nor otherwise.

Magister Howard stepped forward. "We'll be drawing up contracts then, madam?"

Guinevere heard the question in his voice and guessed that her tutor and mentor had a shrewd idea of what had transpired. "Yes," she stated. "Lord Hugh will have his own lawyer, I'm certain. We will sit down together."

She faced Hugh, met his gaze steadily. Saw the flash of warm amusement in the brilliant eyes, understood that he would not answer her challenge with his own. He had no need to do so. He had the upper hand and he knew she knew it.

"We will sit down together," she repeated.

"Aye," he agreed. "I'll send for Master Newberry forthwith. Will tomorrow forenoon suit you, madam?"

"Certainly." She inclined her head. "The time is yours to set, Lord Hugh. We remain beneath your roof."

He laughed as he'd laughed in the Star Chamber and her heart turned over. She loved the sound of his laughter. It wasn't mocking, not in the least. It was purely appreciative as if she'd made a joke that tickled him. A private joke that would mean nothing to anyone else. She gave a tiny half shrug.

"If you'll excuse me now, Lord Hugh, I would go to my chamber. It's been a somewhat trying morning one way and another."

"Of course." He bowed. "We'll dine at two o'clock. A little late, I know, but if we're to sit to something rather more elaborate than usual, we should allow the kitchen time to prepare."

Guinevere nodded agreeably, then turned from him. "Tilly, Magister, perhaps you would accompany me."

"Oh, one other thing." Hugh arrested her as she reached the stair. She turned, her hand on the newel post.

"I would appreciate it if you and Magister Howard could draw up a complete list of your holdings before our meeting tomorrow. I have some idea of their extent, but I'm sure there's much of which I'm not aware." He smiled blandly as if his request had no significance.

"The estates I own are a matter of public record," she said distantly.

"Ah, but I would have to journey back to Derbyshire to avail myself of such records," he returned with the same bland smile. "A tedious journey. I'm certain you could save me the trouble. The king is anxious for the wedding ceremony to take place in two days' time, and we must have the marriage contracts signed and sealed by then. I doubt the king would tolerate a delay. He is a man of changeable humor."

There was no mistaking the threat. Guinevere knew he spoke only the truth, but he was also reminding her of how tenuous her reprieve was until the marriage had been celebrated. As if she needed such reminder. She contented herself with a curt nod and resumed her ascent of the stairs, Tilly and the magister in her wake.

"So 'tis to be another wedding," Tilly said again as they entered Guinevere's chamber. She shook her head. " 'Tis to be hoped this one will turn out better than the others. But," she added with cheerful bluntness, "since you're no stranger to Lord Hugh's bed, you know what you're doing, I'll be bound."

The magister fiddled awkwardly with the ribbons of his cap at this indiscreet statement. It was one thing for Tilly to share such confidences in private, quite another for her to speak thus to their lady in his presence.

" 'Tis a very sudden decision, this, my lady," he said with a dry cough.

"Aye," agreed Guinevere, drawing off her gloves. "A decision that circumstances forced upon me, as I expect you can imagine. Lord Hugh is going to extract a heavy price for saving me from the executioner." She gave a short laugh. "Can one blame him? I would probably do the same if the shoe was on the other foot."

The magister sucked in his cheeks. " 'Tis for that reason that he wishes to review your holdings?"

Guinevere nodded. "But what you and I can do this afternoon, perhaps, is to see how much if anything we can put beyond his reach. Land that is entailed for instance, or mine only during my lifetime and therefore not at my disposal."

"And Lady Pen and Lady Pippa's own holdings, left them by Lord Hadlow," the magister said, warming to the theme. "We could mayhap extend those to include some of the land around Ilkeston. It's not specifically mentioned in Lord Hadlow's will, but we could make a case for it, I believe, since the lands abut."

He stroked his chin even as he continued to suck in his cheeks. "Lord Hugh would not interfere with your daughters' inheritances?" He looked at her interrogatively.

Guinevere shook her head. "Lord Hugh would do nothing to harm my daughters," she said definitely.

And he would not harm her either, except for her pride.

He had come after her initially to claim some of her land. Now he had the chance to claim much more than the land he had wanted for Robin. He would simply see such claims as payment for services rendered she supposed. She would have to swallow her pride. In her present position pride was not a luxury she could afford. But it would hurt. To be obliged to give up what she had worked so hard first to gain and then to maintain and improve. Simply to hand it over to someone who'd done nothing for it. Who simply claimed it as a husband's due.

Oh, yes, it would hurt. But not as much as the headsman's axe. A grim smile touched her mouth.

20.

Master Newberry was long and thin. His brown furred gown hung from his shoulders as if on a coat hanger. His black flapped hat was securely buttoned beneath his pointed chin and one pale eye wandered at will while the other remained disconcertingly steady. He looked as if he had not eaten a square meal in many a month.

He bowed low as Guinevere entered the hall the following morning, accompanied by the magister.

"My lady, may I offer my congratulations."

"Why, certainly you may, Master . . ." she hesitated, "Master Newberry, I believe."

"Just so, my lady."

"Allow me to present Magister Howard. He's long been my advisor."

The two men acknowledged each other with brief nods that did nothing to conceal their mutual suspicion.

Hugh entered the hall from the back regions of the house. He'd been riding and he carried the fresh morning air on his skin. He was bareheaded and his cropped iron-gray hair was slightly ruffled by the wind.

He pulled off his gloves and tossed them onto a bench beside the kitchen door as he greeted the three occupants of the hall pleasantly. "I give you good morning . . . Lady Guinevere, Magister, Master Newberry." He cast an appraising glance at Guinevere. All night he had been hoping that she would come to him as she had done before, but he had slept alone . . . alone except for his dreams.

After tomorrow though . . . ah, after tomorrow, she would share his bed as his wife.

She was looking cool and composed in a gown of pale gray figured silk; the fall of her dark blue hood was pinned up, revealing the slender white length of her neck around which nestled a collar of magnificent pearls. So tall and willowy, with her porcelain complexion, she looked as if nothing could ever disturb her composure, cause her to make a misstep, say something out of place. If he hadn't known better, he would have said ice water ran in her veins. There was no hint of warm red blood flowing beneath that pale skin.

His fingers twitched to loosen her hood, take down her hair, run his fingers through the silvery silken tresses as they flowed down her back. The longing was so intense he thought he must be able to project it into her own mind. But Guinevere gave no hint of such a trespass. She merely gave him a cool enigmatic half smile.

He was not to know that she had lain awake through most of the night in a fever of longing, forcing herself to stay in her own bed, knowing as always that while she still had to fight him she could not afford to be weakened by passion. And she had decided that she was going to fight him over the marriage settlements. If he intended to rob her, he would not find her a lamb to the slaughter.

"Let's sit at the table." Hugh gestured to the long dining table. He walked over and took a seat at the head. Guinevere and the magister sat to his right, Master Newberry to his left.

"You have compiled a list of your holdings?" Hugh inquired of Guinevere.

She gestured to the magister who laid a closely written parchment on the table. Hugh picked it up and looked down it. In fact it held no surprises for him. Privy Seal had his own records of the widow's wealth and the estates on which it was based. Hugh had familiarized himself with it before making his first approach to Lady Mallory. Now he was interested to see if they had doctored the list in any way, attempted to shelter any of her holdings from him.

"This land ceded to the girls on their father's death?" he murmured, glancing towards Guinevere. "I don't recall all this land around Ilkeston being a part of it."

"Don't you?" she said blandly. And was once again silent.

He couldn't help admiring the brazen nerve of the woman. He noted that the lead mines at Brassington appeared to be held by Guinevere only in her lifetime. They were rich mines and he certainly hadn't seen any such proviso on Privy Seal's records. He had no way of proving the truth of her statement without access to the public records in Derbyshire. If it was true then the property could not form part of the marriage settlements since it did not actually belong to her. This, of course, had been his original argument in his claim on Roger Needham's land. If it was untrue and he believed or accepted the lie, she could dispose of the land without his knowledge or interference.

He glanced up at her again as he tapped the edge of his quill against the offending item. It would be typical of Guinevere, he thought, to turn his own arguments against him. She showed not a sign of discomfort, merely regarded him with an air of serene indifference. He looked at the magister. Magister Howard was staring into space, sucking in his cheeks.

What a clever pair they were. They'd been collaborating for so long over Guinevere's affairs it was no wonder they should be so cool.

"Here is what I propose," he said, suddenly brisk. "Robin will receive outright the lands between Great Longstone and Wardlow that had been in our own family."

Guinevere had expected nothing less so she merely nodded. Master Newberry began to write. Magister Howard made a small note.

"Your daughters will continue to hold the property ceded to them by their father to furnish their dowries, including the land around Ilkeston that did not appear in the original documents." He shrugged; in the sum of things, that little deviation was hardly important. "Then, with the exception of Mallory Hall and the mines at Brassington, the remainder of your lands will be ceded to me, your husband, as is customary."

He continued swiftly, ignoring Guinevere's sharp intake of breath. "On your death, your daughters will receive half of those holdings. On my death . . ." His eyes flicked over her stunned countenance and he continued with deliberate emphasis, "Should I predecease you, on *my* death, my son will receive the other half. Should there be children of our marriage, then a just proportion of all the holdings will be made over accordingly at the time of their births."

Guinevere had told herself to expect the worst, but in the back of her mind had been the hope that while Hugh would take something from her for his own payment, his feelings for her would place a rein on his demands. He knew how vital her independence was to her.

In her more sanguine moments she had painted a rosy picture, seeing them living together and sharing what she had in comfortable amity. Maybe he would share the estate work and administration with her. She could become accustomed to such a partnership.

But he had let her down, fulfilled her most gloomy predictions. He would take every last vestige of independence from her. And she found she could not bear it. All platitudes about swallowing her pride flew to the four winds. She could not endure such daylight robbery.

"Everything!" she exclaimed, her face whiter than ever, her purple eyes blazing. "You are calmly suggesting that you would rob me of all my lands?"

A flash of anger crossed his eyes. "Hardly robbery, madam. I am to be your husband. A settlement such as this is entirely legal and customary. I realize you've arranged matters differently in past unions, but I am not going to yield *my* rights just because other men have done so. You will go short of nothing, I assure you, and your daughters are more than well provided for. I take nothing from them and I leave you as the sole possessor of Mallory Hall. In the circumstances, I'm being very reasonable, I believe."

"You have done nothing to merit such a settlement," she declared. "The estates and holdings are richer now than they were when I came into them because I have worked on them. I've administered them, spent much money on improvements. And now you think you can just take them from me."

"It is a customary marriage settlement, my lady." Master Newberry put in his twopennorth.

"I know what is customary and what is not," Guinevere said curtly. She turned to Hugh. "It's not seemly to brawl like this in public. I insist we discuss this privately." She stood up from the table.

"There is nothing to discuss," Hugh said in level tones. "These terms are nonnegotiable."

"I do not have to agree to this marriage," she stated, her mouth taut.

"There's some truth in that." Hugh rose from the table. "So it seems we do have something to discuss. It is after all a woman's prerogative to change her mind. The morning's pleasant. Do you wish to walk in the orchard?"

"A companionable stroll is not what I have in mind," she retorted.

"My chamber then." He strode ahead of her to the stairs.

"I should wait here, Lord Hugh?" inquired Master Newberry.

"Yes. In our absence, you and Magister Howard may go through the settlement point by point. The magister needs to be satisfied of its legality before Lady Mallory signs it."

Guinevere closed her lips tightly and brushed past him as he stood aside to let her precede him up the stairs. She had so wanted to maintain her calm, to hold onto what dignity and pride she possessed, to accede with gracious generosity to his demands, but he had cut the ground from beneath her feet.

Hugh leaned over her shoulder to lift the latch on his chamber door. He placed a hand in the small of her back, easing her into the room. She sprang forward away from his touch and went to stand beside the window.

"This was why you lied to save me," she accused bitterly. "So that you could become a wealthy man. I had thought better of you. I had not thought you so greedy and grasping. Of course I expected you to want some payment, but that you would rob me of everything I possess! I had not believed you capable of that!"

Hugh frowned suddenly. Was he robbing her? Of course he wasn't. Her life would be the same as it always had been. She would lose nothing. She was overdramatizing.

Lose nothing but her independence.

Oh, but that was nonsense. Her independence was a mere perception. She would have a husband, a lover. In those ways only would her life change. And when she was prepared to put aside her pride, she would see that. She would see that the changes would only be for the better. That she was gaining not losing.

He said in level tones, "Guinevere, you make too much of this. I have no idea why your previous husbands allowed you to dictate the terms that you did, but I am not of their ilk. I am not in thrall to you and I will not be managed by you. We will marry under the customary terms. Your children will have half of your estates. I and my son the other half. And Mallory Hall will be yours to do with as you please."

Guinevere crossed her arms over her breast and stared at him in silence. She *could* say she would not marry him under such conditions. She *could* say that, if she were inclined to commit suicide.

She felt so helpless, so vulnerable. Until Hugh of Beaucaire had ridden into her courtyard, she had known little of such weakness. But ever since that day such frailty had been her near constant companion. And now the sense of powerlessness, of desperation, was overwhelming.

Hugh took another tack, his voice moderate and reasonable. "Just think for a minute, Guinevere. If I allowed you to dictate the terms of this contract, as you have done in the past, Bishop Gardiner's charges of witchcraft would have some resonance. I can promise you that these settlements will be scrutinized by Privy Seal if not by the king himself. If they detect anything amiss, anything out of the ordinary, there's no telling what construction they'll choose to put upon it."

"You're telling me that that's the real reason for this rape?" she demanded derisively. "It's not *just* your greed?"

Hugh kept a tight rein on his temper. "It is a fact, as you would see for yourself if you would just think about it. And don't accuse me of greed again. My patience won't stand it."

Guinevere said nothing, merely continued to stare at him. He had a point, she had to admit . . . but only to herself.

After a minute he continued, "It strikes me as entirely reasonable that I should benefit in some material fashion from this marriage. I had not intended to wed again . . . after Sarah."

He paused before confiding with difficulty, "I swore I would protect myself from the hurt of another such loss." He turned away from her intent and angry gaze, his expression somber.

"Should I die prematurely, I doubt you'll suffer much heartbreak," Guinevere said coldly. "A woman you married purely for material gain can hold little place in your soul."

He spun back to her and she saw with some satisfaction that she'd finally ruptured his composure as surely as he'd ruptured hers. "Don't be foolish!" he said harshly. "You know full well that I love you. Money alone wouldn't compel me to perjure myself in the Star Chamber."

They stood in silence, staring at each other, wary, assessing, angry, neither willing to back down, but neither willing to make an irrevocable move.

"But you intend to become rich at my expense," she said finally.

His response was blunt. "Hardly at your expense. You will live as well as I. I would ensure Robin's future first, then I fail to see why I should eke out my life in my present less-than-comfortable fashion when the law, my dear Guinevere, entitles me to live in the manner to which *you,* my wife, are accustomed."

"And when it comes to dividing the land among our children, just how do you intend to apportion it?" she asked bitterly. "Some properties, as I'm sure you're aware, are of considerably greater value than others."

"We'll examine each property and divide them on merit as evenly as possible," he replied readily. "I assume your accounts will reflect the value of each."

"Of course," she said with undisguised scorn at such a question.

"And I assume you'll not attempt to distort the value of those assets in any way?" He regarded her through narrowed eyes.

"If you're not astute enough to detect any tampering with the figures, my lord, you're not astute enough to manage a fortune as considerable as the one you're taking from me," she retorted. "You will, I imagine, manage my estates yourself?"

"Unless it would please *you* to continue doing that."

"Oh, I see. That's a neat arrangement. The money goes to you, the labor to me. Quite a partnership that. I congratulate you, Lord Hugh."

He laughed suddenly. The speed and sharpness of Guinevere's wit could always be relied upon even in extremis.

"What a hornet you are!" He reached for her and despite her resistance drew her into his embrace. "It is as it must be, Guinevere, if we're to pull these coals out of the fire. Regardless of any benefit to me, you must see that this settlement is politically expedient. If we're to perform this play convincingly, then the scenes must pass muster. Privy Seal will not let go easily."

Guinevere knew she had to concede. Hugh was honest at least. And he said he loved her. Perhaps he did. Did she love him? Was it love that created this strange connection between them? She felt passion, lust, certainly. Even now in her anger and disappointment, she desired him. The heady scent of his skin and hair, the power of the body against her own, the strength in the arms that held her all sent her senses whirling, set the pulse deep in her belly to beating, her loins to fill with a languorous warmth.

She knew him to be tender, loving, humorous. She knew him to be harsh, judgmental, rigid in his sense of duty and honor.

He had lied to save her.

"It is as it must be," she repeated softly, accepting defeat.

He cupped her face in both hands as he kissed her. It was a kiss of affirmation, of possession, of promise. And she thought that perhaps in defeat there was also victory. She had no need to fight him anymore, therefore no further need to resist him. In their loving they were both victors.

As he raised his head and they drew back from each other she said, "You lied for me. Is that because you believe I didn't kill Stephen Mallory?"

He regarded her in silence for a minute before asking, "Did you?"

Had she? A little frown crossed her brow. Had she *intended* to trip him? As always it was a question she could not answer. But Hugh required an answer.

"No," she said.

Hugh didn't believe her. He had seen her frown, sensed her hesitation. But he had cast the die.

"The issue is moot now," he said with a shrug of his square shoulders. "It matters little whether I believe in your innocence or not. It matters only that others believe that I do."

He watched her face for some indication that his lack of conviction discomfited her. If she was truly innocent then surely she would be angry, would try to convince him. But her expression gave nothing away and she remained silent.

He moved back to the door. "Are we agreed? Can we finish with this business now?"

"It seems I have little choice," she responded. "I would prefer to get it over with quickly."

"I also." He held the door for her.

Downstairs, Guinevere signed the papers without further speech. The magister was clearly distressed, his head bobbed, and he looked more like a carp than ever. But in the teeth of his lady's silence he made no comment and the business was concluded grimly with only the sound of the quill scratching on parchment.

"I will take this directly to Lord Privy Seal, Lord Hugh." Master Newberry sanded the parchment before folding it. He melted wax and dropped a blob on the fold. He held it for Hugh to press his signet ring into the soft wax.

"The marriage is to take place tomorrow forenoon at Hampton Court," Hugh said. "The king's instructions came this morning. The queen is most anxious to attend."

"Such an honor," the lawyer muttered, one eye shooting into the corner of the hall, the other remaining on the sealed and folded parchment in his hand.

"Quite so," agreed Hugh.

"We're coming to the wedding, aren't we, Mama?"

They all turned at the sound of Pippa's voice. After the grim silence it was as refreshing as rain after a drought.

"Where did you spring from?" Hugh inquired.

"I was following Moonshine. She ran in here. I know you said we should stay outside, Mama, but I had to catch her." Pippa clutched the silver kitten and regarded her mother somewhat anxiously. "I didn't hear anything," she said. "Only just what Lord Hugh said about the wedding tomorrow."

Guinevere wasn't sure she believed her daughter. Pippa heard much that she should not. But it seemed easier to let it go. "Where's Pen?"

"She's with Robin in the stables. Robin's cleaning tack. They won't talk to me. They've got secrets." The child pulled a disconsolate face.

"I don't think they've got secrets, sweetheart." Guinevere drew the child against her knees. "It's just that they have to work some things out together."

Pippa nodded and forgot about her sister and Robin, reverting to a more important topic. "We are coming to the wedding, aren't we?"

Guinevere glanced at Hugh who shook his head. "The king's command didn't include children. You and I are the only ones bidden to this particular event."

"I'm sorry, sweeting." Guinevere stroked Pippa's cheek. "But we'll not be gone long."

"And we'll celebrate when we get back in the afternoon," Hugh said. "A big wedding feast."

Pippa's face split into a delighted grin. "Oh, yes. And me and Pen, we can decorate the hall, just like we do for Christmas and Twelfth Night. And we can have marchpane on the cake."

Guinevere had wanted the ceremony to be as brief and businesslike as possible, as befitted the spirit of their contract. A grand wedding feast didn't figure into her plans at all, but now in the face of Pippa's delight she didn't have the heart to refuse.

"A *small* wedding feast," she demurred.

"Not a bit of it," Hugh said cheerfully. "This is most definitely an occasion for the fatted calf."

"A calf?" Pippa said with a puzzled frown. "At Mama's wedding feast to Lord Mallory we had peacock and venison and carp and all sorts of sweetmeats. But we didn't have a calf."

"I think your mother might prefer it if we do things a little differently this time," Hugh told her.

"But there'll be music and dancing," Pippa said. "There's always music and dancing at a wedding."

"Go and talk to Pen about it," Guinevere said, gently putting the child from her.

Pippa ran off and the room seemed strangely empty. Master Newberry coughed and gathered up his papers. "I'll take this to Privy Seal then, my lord."

Hugh nodded. "If there's an answer, bring it to me straightway."

"Aye, sir." The lawyer bowed punctiliously to Guinevere, nodded at the magister, and hastened away.

"Music and dancing," Hugh mused. "I must seek out musicians."

"There's no need for that," Guinevere said firmly. "There is no need for music; there is no need for peacocks or fatted calves. There's no reason why the day should be anything special. We'll let the children decorate the hall if they wish, but there's no need for anything else."

"On the contrary," Hugh said, his eyes gleaming with a certain mischievous malice. "There's every need. I have only had one wedding in my life. I can understand that you might find them rather . . . rather mundane shall we say? . . . but they're still quite a novelty for me."

Magister Howard was abruptly taken with a violent fit of coughing. With a gesture of excuse, he hurried away, burying his face in a large and none-too-clean kerchief.

"Your sense of humor strikes me as somewhat misplaced," Guinevere declared to the now openly grinning Hugh. "You've won your victory, must you gloat, too?"

"For some reason, I don't feel victorious," he said, smiling at her now, his eyes warm. "I feel pleasure, eager anticipation, certainty that my life from here on will never be boring. But, no, I don't feel victorious."

His gaze pulled her in. The invitation was irresistible. She stepped back, one hand lifted slightly as if to ward him off.

"Come to me," he said, and his expression now was utterly serious, utterly compelling. "Come to me, Guinevere."

"No," she said, her voice barely more than a whisper. "No. You cannot have everything your own way."

He frowned, the light fading in his eye. "I don't want this just for me. You know that."

She did. Their loving had no place in the conflicted world they shared. There was no dissension, no confrontation, when their bodies and minds were joined in love. But the stubborn streak that kept her strong kept her from him now. She turned to leave the hall.

"God's bones! You are the most obstinate woman!" Hugh declared to her back, wanting to shake some acceptance into her.

She said over her shoulder as she prepared to go up the stairs, "I daresay you'll learn to live with it, my lord."

"I daresay I shall," Hugh muttered.

Guinevere dressed in black for her wedding. The girls sat on the bed and chattered as she dressed. Their artless prattle flowed over her, soothing her. It was for this that she was about to be wed at the king's bidding in the chapel at Hampton Court. It was for them that she had lost her independence. If she dwelled upon the injustice of a situation she had done nothing to deserve, she would never find peace. She must think only of what she had gained. Their futures were secure.

Hugh knocked upon her door. His turquoise gown was slashed with black and trimmed with ermine. His doublet, fashionably wadded, was of black velvet, his hose turquoise, molding the muscles of his calves and thighs. He wore a velvet cap with the brim turned up at the side and fastened with a sapphire broach.

"Oh, you're so smart!" Pippa exclaimed.

"Yes, indeed," Pen agreed.

"My thanks, little maids." He bowed solemnly, then turned to Guinevere. He raised an eyebrow. "Perhaps I too should have dressed for a funeral."

"I am a widow," she responded.

"For the moment," he agreed. "The king's barge awaits us."

"The king sent his barge for us?" Guinevere was startled out of her distant manner.

"Well, it's his musicians' barge, but they were instructed to stop at Blackfriars for us," Hugh told her. "It's still a mark of some consideration."

"I'm overwhelmed."

Hugh chuckled. "Should the king decide to honor us with his presence at the ceremony, don't forget to tell him how overwhelmed you are."

"I'll endeavor to remember."

"May we come and see the king's barge?" Pippa jumped off the bed.

"I see no reason why not. Robin can accompany us and escort you home. Are you ready, Guinevere?"

She drew on soft kid gloves embroidered with seed pearls. Tilly laid a cloak of black velvet over her shoulders. It was thick and warm and the black was as deep and rich as the darkest night.

"I am ready." She went to the door before Hugh could offer her his arm.

Hugh spoke to Tilly. "While we're gone will you have Lady Guinevere's belongings moved to my chamber? You will know how best to arrange matters. You may make whatever changes to my chamber that you think necessary for your mistress's comfort."

Tilly nodded. "Aye, my lord."

"There's no need for changes, Tilly," Guinevere said from the door. Why did she still find it so difficult to accept the permanence of this future?

"I'll see, chuck," Tilly said. "You just leave it to me."

It was hardly the first time she'd had such arrangements to deal with, she reflected, once she was alone. But for all Lady Guinevere's apparent reluctance for this match, and the magister's vigorous disapproval of the settlements, Tilly was optimistic. Her lady had made one love match before, and there were elements in this one that reminded the tiring woman of Guinevere's marriage to Timothy Hadlow.

Just so long as this one didn't end in a premature death.

2 1.

The queen was a soft-faced fair woman of twenty-eight summers. She sat in her closet adjoining the Chapel Royal at Hampton, her hands busy with the purse she was netting.

She smiled warmly as Guinevere was presented. "Lady Mallory, such a happy occasion. My Lord, the king, knows how much I enjoy weddings."

"Your Highness is very kind to honor our wedding with your presence." Guinevere curtsied low. "Particularly at such a time." Her eyes skimmed the nine-month bulge beneath the queen's barely laced stomacher.

The queen caught the look and lightly brushed a hand over her belly, her smile growing complacent. "You have children, I believe."

"I have two daughters, Madam."

The queen nodded and stated, "I will present My Lord, the king, with a son within the week."

"Your people's thoughts will be with you, Madam," Guinevere said.

Jane smiled, the vague and distant smile of a woman whose mind was turned inward upon the life she carried. "My son will gladden his father's heart," she said.

"Indeed, My Lady." Guinevere had carried three children to term. Her son had been stillborn. Her daughters had lived. She had suffered two miscarriages, both early in pregnancy, and she counted herself fortunate for that. She had grieved long and hard for her son although she had not held his living body in her arms. Now, as she looked at the gravid queen she could only wish her the safe delivery of the son that would ensure her the king's continued love and protection.

"I wish you health and joy, Madam," she said softly.

The queen's smile became focused. "As I wish you, Lady Guinevere." She set aside her netting and rose from her chair, her women hastening to help her, to straighten her skirts, to place a shawl over her shoulders.

"My chaplain will conduct the service in the chapel. I will attend above."

Guinevere curtsied low and waited for the queen and her ladies to leave the apartment for the queen's room in the Royal Pew that looked down upon the body of the chapel.

Hugh had not been summoned to the queen's closet and awaited Guinevere in the chapel. There was no one there but the queen's chaplain. There was a stir from the rear of the chapel and he turned to see Privy Seal in his furred gown enter.

"Lord Hugh, I would not fail to attend your nuptials," Thomas Cromwell said, his expression impassive, his eyes hard and arrogant, as he walked up the narrow aisle to where Hugh stood. "You have snared the widow and her fortune very well, I believe." A thin smile flickered over his lips. "Settlements worthy of the most . . . most avaricious gentleman. I congratulate you. I could not have written them better myself." He touched Hugh's arm.

Hugh resisted the urge to step back in revulsion from the man who seemed to exude an evil avarice of his own. Instead he smiled, bowed in acknowledgment of the apparent compliment, and said, "I don't see my lord bishop. Will he not grace the proceedings?"

"Gardiner wants a witch," Thomas said airily. "You failed to give him one. So he has no further interest."

"And you, My Lord Cromwell? Have you still an interest in the widow?" Hugh glanced idly upwards as if he had little interest in Privy Seal's answer. Instead, he seemed to be admiring the great vaulted ceiling newly installed by the king; the beautiful moldings, the carved and gilded pendants, the brilliant turquoise studded with golden stars.

Privy Seal smiled coldly. "For as long as the lady remains unwidowed after this ceremony, Lord Hugh, I have no reason for interest."

Hugh merely raised an eyebrow, his gaze still fixed upon the ceiling. His eye caught a movement behind one of the bay windows that looked down upon the body of the chapel. It was the king's private room in the Royal Pew where he sat during services.

Privy Seal followed Hugh's gaze and said softly, "Ah, it seems the king has decided after all to be present. I shall go and join him." He turned to make his way above just as Guinevere entered from the queen's closet.

"My Lady Guinevere." Privy Seal bowed. "May I offer my congratulations."

"Thank you, my lord." She offered a hint of a curtsy but her eyes were cold and challenging as they rested on his round arrogant face.

An unpleasant smile flickered on his mouth. Privy Seal was accustomed to inspiring fear, not defiance, in the king's subjects. He gave her a tiny nod as if acknowledging the challenge and continued on his way.

Guinevere stepped up beside Hugh and stood quiet and still, her hands in her habitual posture clasped against her black skirts. The queen's chaplain said the words that united them; they made the ritual responses. They knelt for the Mass; they rose.

Guinevere was no longer a widow.

She stood beside her husband, for a moment too stunned by the speed at which her life had changed to move or speak. She became aware of the glorious light flooding through the stained glass of the great double window at the east end of the chapel. It caught Hugh's profile, touched the lobe of his ear with rose color. The lobe had a tiny crease at the base. Her tongue moved inside her mouth. Her lips moved. She thought of her tongue flicking that soft pendant skin. She thought of how it tasted, of how soft and delicate it was, like a baby's skin. She thought of her teeth grazing over it, nibbling it. She thought of how sensitive his ears were. When she kissed them, explored them, Hugh would wriggle, would murmur, would make little protesting sounds that were not protests at all.

He turned to look at her and saw that her skin was delicately flushed, her lips slightly parted. The sun through the stained glass lay across her cheek, accentuated the dark shadow of her eyelashes, the curve of her brow. The line of her pale hair visible below the dark hood and the white coif took on a pink tinge, like fire opals.

She looked up and her eyes were almost black as they met his.

"Madam wife," he murmured, bowing over her hand. He flicked a glance upwards, and the light in his eyes was pure mischief.

"My lord," she responded as softly, tilting her head to one side with a glance as wicked as his own.

"I doubt that, but we shall see," he whispered and she laughed, a soft, delighted, totally unexpected chime in the hushed chapel.

The chaplain looked vaguely pained as if such laughter denied the solemnity and significance of the words he had just spoken over their heads.

A young woman appeared beside them. "Lord Hugh . . . Lady Guinevere . . . My congratulations. Our Lady, the queen, wishes to speak with you." She gestured towards the door at the rear of the chapel that led to the queen's closet. "Would you follow me?"

They followed her, aware of the electric charge that crackled between them. Hugh's hand brushed Guinevere's and her stomach plunged as a tingle of anticipation raced through her, lifting the fine hairs on her arms and on the nape of her neck.

She thought: the fighting is over. It's time now for love's victory. Then she schooled her features, attempted to compel her unruly body into submission, and curtsied deeply as Hugh, bareheaded, made a low bow.

The queen was not alone. The king stood beside her chair, one hand resting on its back, the other playing with the gold dagger he wore around his neck. He looked very pleased with himself. Of Privy Seal there was no sign.

"Ah, here are the newlyweds," he declared. "A very pretty ceremony . . . very pretty indeed. But I would have had you bring your little maids, madam. They should have attended you."

Guinevere held her curtsy and made no reference to the lack of invitation to her children. "I was afeard that they might have become overexcited, Highness."

"Charming little maids," he said. "You should have brought them." His beam faded and he frowned at her.

Hugh knew that once the king latched on to something that he decided affronted him his mood would change in an instant and he was very hard to distract.

The queen, however, came to the rescue. She looked up serenely from her netting. "My dear Lord, you are all consideration to have arranged this ceremony. You know how much I enjoy a wedding."

The king looked down at her and his face cleared. "Yes . . . yes . . . so you do. It pleased you, Madam?"

Relieved that that fearsome attention was diverted from her, Guinevere rose gracefully from her curtsy.

"Most excellently." Jane smiled at Henry, then she signaled to a lady. "Lady Margaret, would you bring the king's gift?" She turned her smile upon Guinevere and Hugh. "His Highness wished to mark this happy occasion." She took two packages from her lady and under the king's now complacent eye gave them ceremoniously to the newlyweds.

The king's gift was a pair of jeweled gloves for Hugh and for Guinevere a scarf of gold tissue embroidered in amethysts with Henry's own insignia, the double dog rose. They thanked the monarch and his queen, offered their prayers for the queen's safe confinement, and received their dismissal from the now amiable king. Within a very few minutes they had reached the peace and anonymity of the base court.

"It would appear," Guinevere murmured, "that we are married, Lord Hugh."

"Aye," he agreed, looking down at her. "So it would."

"The children have a wedding feast prepared for us," she said, looking out towards the river.

"Aye," he agreed. "A tedious time it will take before we can be private."

"Most tedious." She watched the progress of a barge along the river.

"We could, perhaps, postpone our return for an hour or so?" Hugh's eyes followed hers.

"Perhaps? If we could be sure that we returned in time to enjoy their feast without worrying them with a delay."

Hugh looked up at the sun. It was far from its zenith. "I see no reason why that couldn't be done. As it happens I did make some arrangements just in case we should feel unwilling to hurry home."

"Such foresight," she murmured. She turned her face to his. "Then let us consummate this marriage, Hugh of Beaucaire, before either of us changes his mind."

Privy Seal paced his apartments in the palace. He paused now and again to dip bread into a dish of salt, to take a sip of wine. His spy stood silent in his black cloak against the stone wall, waiting until he was called upon to speak.

Eventually Privy Seal spoke. "Hugh of Beaucaire . . ."

"Aye, my lord."

"You will ensure an accident . . . not an obvious accident. A mishap perhaps . . . or slow poison perhaps. You will find someone who can accomplish this."

"Aye, my lord." The man shrugged closer into his cloak and moved towards the door assuming he'd received his orders. They were the kind of orders he was accustomed to receiving.

Privy Seal held up a hand. "And the son," he said.

The spy stopped.

"See to the son. Quick or slow, that matters not."

"Aye, my lord." The man slipped from the chamber.

"There's more than one way to skin a cat," muttered Privy Seal to himself as he sipped from his goblet.

Guinevere lay on the soft mattress in the deep shadows of the bed curtains in a small chamber under the eaves of a half-timbered cottage in the village of Hampton. The sheets smelled of fresh air and the iron, brass, and copper gleamed in the fireplace where coals burned redly; the simple furniture glowed with beeswax.

She stretched languidly, enjoying the slight throb between her legs, the sense of her body having been used to the full. The air was cool on her overheated flesh. That had been a mad scramble of a loving. She smiled to herself, ran her hands over her body in sensual memory. There had been a wildness to match that first time in his tent, a great outpouring of passion, an uninhibited tearing, biting, scratching, a shameless devouring. She could still taste him on her tongue, the scent of his sex was still upon her, her thighs were wet and sticky with their mingled juices.

And she felt more truly alive than she could ever remember feeling.

She heard the door open and close softly. Hugh stepped into the shadows of the bed curtains. He wore his shirt, only roughly buttoned, hanging over his hose that were ungartered. He had no shoes on his feet. He looked like a man who had risen in haste from his lover's bed. Which, of course, was exactly the case.

"Sustenance," he said smiling. He set a flagon of wine on the floor and sat on the edge of the bed. His hand caressed her belly and for a long moment he just looked at her, closely, intimately, as if he would allow her body to have no secrets from him.

She stirred a little beneath the intensity of his gaze and his hand moved between her thighs to cup the moist mound in his warm palm. He gazed down at what he held, as if seeing her sex for the first time, his fingers delicately opening the lips, twisting the damp, tightly wound curls around a fingertip. Then he bent his head and kissed her, inhaling deeply of the rich lingering fragrance of their passion.

Guinevere shuddered and curled her fingers into his hair, pulling his head up. He kissed her mouth and she could taste herself, breathe in her own intimate scent. He laughed softly against her lips, dipping his tongue into the corner of her mouth, before raising his head.

"Wine?"

"Mmm." She nodded on the pillow, watching as he took the stopper from the neck of the flagon. Before she realized his intention he had poured wine into the deep indentation of her navel. She wriggled at the cold trickle and he laughed again before bending to lap up the wine with a delicately sipping tongue. He let a few drops fall onto her belly and licked them off with a quick swoop of his tongue.

"When you offered me wine I hadn't realized this was what you meant," she protested, squirming.

Hugh straightened, his eyes shining like blue diamonds. He took a deep draught of wine and set the flagon back on the floor. Leaning over he took her face between his hands and, holding the wine in his mouth, slowly brought his lips against hers, pressing them open to fill the warm sweet cavern of her mouth with the wine from his own.

Guinevere closed her eyes, concentrating on the delightful enticing sensation; the coolness of the wine mingled with the warmth of his probing tongue, the taste of wine and Hugh melded deliciously.

When he finally took his mouth from hers, let his hands fall from her face, she remained motionless on the bed, her face still upturned, lips slightly parted, her eyes still closed.

"More?" he asked.

Guinevere nodded dreamily still without opening her eyes. Hugh chuckled. He took another draught of wine and kissed her again.

"That was a very novel way to drink," Guinevere murmured as he drew back at last. "I fear it could become a habit."

"It could indeed." He brushed aside the damp hair that clung to her brow. "So wonderfully wanton you look."

"So wonderfully wanton I feel," she responded. "And what they must have thought belowstairs when you appeared half naked, I can't imagine."

"They are not paid to speculate on what goes on in this chamber," he said, tilting the flagon to his lips again.

"How many women have you brought here?" she inquired casually.

His eyes glinted. "Would you believe none before you?"

"If you say so," she returned amiably. "But I'd ask how you knew of such a love nest."

"I have friends who possess many kinds of useful information."

"Ah." She nodded and held out her hand for the flagon. He gave it to her and rose from the bed, beginning to button his shirt properly.

"We must leave," she said, correctly interpreting his movements.

"Aye, if we're to reach home before they send out search parties."

She drank from the flagon and reluctantly dragged herself from the bed. "I can barely move."

He smiled with a touch of smugness and observed, "I have more scratches and bruises than I've ever acquired on a battlefield."

Guinevere stretched and examined herself. A large bruise was purpling on her thigh, a smaller one on her arm. "I would never have believed loving could be such a wonderfully savage business." She poured hot water from the ewer into the basin on the dresser and dipped a cloth.

Hugh watched her covertly as she wrung out the cloth and pressed it to her throat, washing her body slowly, languidly, lifting her breasts, sponging between her thighs, lifting each foot in turn, balancing easily on one leg.

If she was aware of his scrutiny she gave no sign. He loved how comfortable she was in her skin. How the little imperfections didn't trouble her. She had no vanity it seemed. She was as she was. Her long hair flowed over her shoulders, fell across her breasts as she bent forward. The fluid curve of her body made his heart race and he could think only that he could watch her forever. She was his. And he was certain she had never enjoyed such wild heights of passion before, even with Timothy Hadlow.

For all their love for each other, he and Sarah had not reached such heights either. Their couplings had been pleasant, courteous, gentle. But Sarah had not been a woman of fire. She had been gentle as a forest stream. Not like Guinevere. Guinevere was a volcano, a turbulent crashing waterfall, a midsummer storm, forked lightning and thunderclaps, and when he was with her, he found those same qualities in himself.

They left the cottage without seeing a soul. Guinevere knew there were people around, she could hear sounds from the kitchen at the rear of the small building, but she had seen no one on their arrival and there was no one to bid them farewell. It was a most discreet love nest, one more suited to clandestine loving than the consummation of a marriage that had just been performed in the presence of the king and queen in the Chapel Royal at Hampton Court. The reflection made her smile.

They said little on the journey back to Blackfriars. There was no musicians' barge on the return, but the queen had put at their disposal one of the royal barges used to carry lesser court officials on their errands. It was a small craft, but it had a cabin to keep out the wind that got up as the afternoon faded, whipping up the gray water, bringing a light drizzle with it.

Guinevere held her hands to the brazier's warmth and allowed herself to feel the joyous relief from the despairing tension that had been so intense she had almost forgotten what it was like to live without it. Nothing could hurt her or her daughters now. She had lost her independence, but she had Hugh's love. She had no doubt of that. And if she cleared away the residue of resentment, of the sense that he had been responsible for all this that had happened to her, she knew that she loved him in return. It was said that time would heal all wounds. And she had no need of her independence if she and Hugh lived in love and amity and mutual respect.

She would make this marriage work.

"Such deep and serious thoughts," he said, reaching to touch her face.

She only nodded and he didn't press her.

It was almost dark when the barge bumped the steps of Blackfriars. The drizzle had turned to rain and Guinevere drew up the hood of her cloak, waiting while Hugh gave the oarsmen their douceurs. He gave generously as befitted a man who had been married that day.

"Come quickly now," he said, putting an arm around her, hurrying her through the wet lanes that led to the gates of his house. Men huddled in doorways staring morosely out at the rain as the two passed. They didn't pay any attention when one man slipped from shelter and came after them. His fingers curled expertly over the knife concealed in his sleeve.

They had reached the end of the dark narrow lane when Hugh suddenly spun on his heel. Some soldier's instinct for danger had alerted him. He had a sword in his hand even as he turned, shoving Guinevere aside so that she fell against the wall of one of the houses.

The dark-clad figure sprang at him, the knife a dull flash in the dark rainy evening. Hugh's sword slashed, caught the man's wrist. The man screamed as his hand fell uselessly to his side, the knife falling into the mud. Blood poured from a gash so deep it had almost severed his hand from his arm.

Guinevere stared, her mouth open but no sound emerging. She was too shocked to speak or even cry out.

Hugh stood over the man as he lay howling, bleeding in the mud. The city was full of such footpads on the lookout for easy prey. The lane was dark and narrow. Such an attack was far from unusual. He bent and picked up the knife and wiped it on the man's cloak, then he tucked it up his own sleeve.

"Bastard," he said savagely as he straightened. "I hope he bleeds to death."

Guinevere stepped away from the wall, aware that her hands were shaking. "Where did he come from?"

Hugh shrugged. "They're everywhere, outlaws, felons, lurking in the lanes. A man has as much chance of getting his throat cut for a groat in the streets of London as he does in the slums of Paris."

"He was going to rob us?"

"I can think of no other reason for such an attack," Hugh responded, glancing sideways at her. "Can you?"

"No." But her head buzzed with only one thought. She had been about to lose her fifth husband. Hours after the wedding, he had faced death in her company. *What kind of curse was it that dogged her?* She remembered Hugh's words on their first meeting. *"Men die in your company."*

She looked down at the man whose howls had become moans. He lay curled in the mud under the rain. It was hard to imagine he could be a threat. "Shouldn't we . . . ?"

"No!" Hugh said shortly. "If he has friends they'll take care of him. If he has enemies they will do him the same service in their own way. Come. It's not safe to linger."

Still she hesitated. "It seems so harsh."

"God's bones, Guinevere! This is London town. 'Tis not some quiet hamlet in the northern wilds!" But even as he said it he thought that quiet Derbyshire hamlets also held death in their hearts.

"Come!" He took her arm and there was no gainsaying him. Guinevere allowed him to hurry her out of the dark confines of the lane.

Once in the open he asked more gently, "Are you very shaken?"

Her thoughts had shaken her more than the event, Guinevere realized, but she could not share with Hugh her horror at the prospect of losing yet another husband to a violent accident. Instead she reassured him hastily, "A little, but it was so quick . . . you were so quick . . . there was barely time to react."

However, when they reached the driveway, safely behind his gates, she paused and took a deep breath. "Let me just compose myself a minute before we go into the house. I don't want the children to think something's wrong."

They could hear music coming from the house now and voices raised in laughter and song.

"I think they've started without us," Hugh observed, holding her against him under a dripping tree, one hand rhythmically stroking her back. "I gave Robin permission to begin the revels at mid-afternoon. He seems to have taken me at my word."

"Who's invited?"

"No one alarming, no one important. Just the household, some of my friends, some old campaigners," he said. "You didn't produce a guest list of your own." He gave her a quizzical smile, and she could see that he was completely unperturbed by the murderous attack. How could he be so cool, so calm, when he had just hacked off a man's hand?

It gave her the strength to master her own shock and horror. "How should I have done? Besides, I saw little reason then for celebration."

"And now?" The quizzical smile remained.

"And now . . . perhaps," she returned.

"Perhaps?" He shook his head in mock reproof. "I suppose I must be satisfied with that for the moment." He glanced back at the house where the windows threw candlelight onto the path. "Then let us go in if you're ready."

"I'm ready." She straightened her shoulders and smiled at him, her face still very pale in the dim light beneath the tree.

"Then come, madam wife."

22.

Agreat deal of effort had gone into the preparations for the wedding feast. The hall was decorated with swags of greenery, interspersed with branches of holly sporting their bright berries against glossy leaves. Chrysanthemums and daisies massed in great copper jugs glowed golden and orange. The long table was spread with a white cloth and lit with plentiful wax candles.

It occurred to Hugh as he stood in the doorway taking in the scene that Master Crowder must have had the ordering. His own steward at this juncture had no access to the funds necessary to produce so much splendor. He glanced at Guinevere. Had she given her steward instructions? She looked as astonished as he, and, he thought, more than a little chagrined. Someone had taken matters into their own hands, he decided. Guinevere had not been anxious to make much of this wedding.

The explanation appeared with the children, who rushed upon them the instant they opened the door. All three were dressed in their finest. They attempted a solemn welcome that disintegrated into an excited babble with Pippa explaining how she and Pen and Tilly and Master Crowder had decided on the details of the feast.

"We had to have wax candles, Mama," Pen said.

"Yes, but Master Milton only had tallow in the stores," Pippa declared. "Robin said to him that it would be all right to lay out the cloth and send out for wax candles."

"Of course it was," Robin said, but with a touch of bluster. He looked a little anxiously at his father. "Master Milton thought it would be a suitable occasion to kill the bullock we were saving for Christmas, sir. I thought so too."

"And Greene went across the river and shot a deer and ducks and pheasants in the fields," Pen put in. "We have an enormous game pie that Tilly showed the cooks how to make. As well as the bullock."

"I trust nobody's toes were trodden upon," Guinevere remarked.

"Oh, no," Pen assured her earnestly. "Everyone's been very happy. We've had such an exciting day!"

"And see how beautiful it all is!" Pippa swept her arm in a wide circle and Guinevere smiled.

"It's very beautiful, my loves. All of you must have worked so hard."

" 'Tis a marriage after all," declared Robin, his voice just a trifle thick.

"Indeed it is," agreed Hugh, regarding his son with a shrewdly assessing gaze. Robin was flushed, excited and excitable. Hugh glanced at the table. The jugs of ale and flagons of wine had not yet been broached but he could hear raucous laughter coming from the back regions of the house. He guessed that the men of his troop and other members of his household had started the festivities a little early. He had instructed Robin that they should broach two hogsheads of strong October ale at the beginning of the celebration. Robin, it seemed, had joined the men's premature revels with some enthusiasm.

"Where's Jack Stedman?" He looked around the hall with a frown. Jack would have kept a watchful eye on the boy. He also had an urgent task for his lieutenant that would take him away from the feast for a while.

"He went hunting with Greene," Pippa explained before Robin could reply. Very little occurred without Pippa's knowledge. "They've been drinking together in the butchery ever since they got back. I went to talk to them but they told me to go away. So I did."

"Fetch him for me, Robin," Hugh instructed. "There's something I need him to do."

Robin hurried off, his step to Hugh's eye just a little unsteady. Robin was used to ale and small beer. On the journey to Derbyshire he had joined his father and the men in the taverns and drunk with them, but always, under his father's eye, in moderation. The October ale was particularly strong. The boy knew that perfectly well, Hugh thought, and he was not in general foolish. His emotions must be in some turmoil over his father's sudden marriage, and the acquisition of two sisters. An acquisition that would have taken some getting used to at the best of times without the added complication with Pen.

"We should greet the household and your guests," Guinevere said, seeing the eager welcoming circle forming in front of them. She drew off her gloves and handed them to Pippa. She gave Pen her cloak. "Take these to my chamber, loves."

"Lord Hugh's chamber you mean," Pippa said importantly. "We've put flowers in there too."

"That's lovely." Guinevere waved them away.

She and Hugh stepped forward to receive the congratulations of Hugh's friends and the household. Tilly and the magister embraced her tearfully; Crowder seemed even more dignified than usual and Guinevere understood that the ordering of this feast had produced some tension between himself and Master Milton, whose own congratulations were delivered with a distant respect. But those were problems for another day.

They drank a toast with the assembled guests and moved to the fireplace to hold an informal court before the feasting itself began.

Jack Stedman hurried into the hall. "I ask pardon, my lord. I should've been here," he mumbled, his face rather red as he bowed. "May I offer my congratulations, my lady."

"Thank you, Jack."

"Well, 'tis no great matter," Hugh said, reaching into his sleeve for the knife he'd taken from his assailant. He handed it to Jack. "We were set upon in the lane just before the house. Go and see if the man's still there. I wounded him sorely. If he is, see if you can discover what he was after."

"I thought you said he was a simple footpad." Guinevere looked at him in surprise.

Hugh shrugged. "I believe him to be so, but I'd like to be sure . . . Take the knife, Jack, see if anyone recognizes it."

"Aye, my lord." Jack tucked the knife into his own sleeve.

"My apologies for depriving you of the feast," Hugh said with a smile.

Jack shook his head in disclaimer and went off.

"But if it wasn't a robbery, who would want to kill you?" Guinevere asked, her voice muted. A shadow fell over her as she relived the horror of the moments of that attack . . . the terrifying dread of some curse that dogged her.

"I have no idea," Hugh returned. He gazed into the contents of his wine cup as if he would read the answer there. Then he seemed visibly to shake off his thoughts and looked up, his frown vanished.

Robin weaved his way through the crowded hall, Pen and Pippa beside him. "I sent Jack to you, sir," he said, sounding out his words with great care.

"Yes, so I saw," Hugh returned. "Shall we begin the feast?"

"I'll tell the herald to play the summons." Pippa ran off, her velvet skirts flying around her.

"I wanted to do that," Robin said. " 'Tis my place to do that."

"You'll have to get up very early in the morning to be ahead of that little maid," Hugh observed. "I'm sure Pen learned that a long time ago."

"Oh, yes, sir, almost as soon as Pippa was born," Pen said. She glanced at Robin. "I also learned that mostly what she wants to do isn't worth fighting over."

Robin flushed and looked as if he'd received a rebuke of some kind. "There are *some* things."

"Well, maybe," Pen agreed thoughtfully. "But when you get used to the idea of her as a sister you'll find it easier not to mind her most of the time."

"Wise words," commented Hugh.

The trumpet's call sounded from the small minstrel's gallery and they moved to the table.

Pen was aware that Robin had been drinking most of the afternoon with his father's men. He was almost a man and entitled to do so but she couldn't help feeling anxious about him. Besides, like her mother, she had seen too much of the evil effects of drink on a man. She tugged on her mother's sleeve as they took their places at the table and Guinevere immediately bent her head to listen to her daughter's whisper.

"Robin's had too much to drink, Mama. What should I do?"

"I imagine Lord Hugh is aware of it," her mother said. "He'll take care of his son."

Pen was a little reassured but still determined to exercise her own influence if she could. Pointedly she refused wine herself, hoping he would take the hint. But Robin was oblivious, joining in the men's raucous conversations, shouting across the table, laughing immoderately.

Guinevere waited for Hugh to intervene as Robin filled and refilled his drinking cup to the brim but he said nothing. She glanced sideways at him, saw the frown in his eye, a certain tension in his jaw. As Robin's voice grew louder, his words more slurred, Guinevere finally said in an undertone, "Should you not say something to him, Hugh?"

Hugh shook his head. "He's on the road to manhood and has to learn to make his own mistakes on the way. At least he's making this one in the safety of home. The only consequence will be a sore head on the morrow that he'll not be permitted to indulge." His tone was curt and Guinevere knew that he was finding it very difficult to sit and watch his son make his mistake.

Robin reached again for the ale jug, his movement jerky and uncoordinated. His sleeve caught a bowl of gravy and sent it spinning to the floor, splashing Pen's gown.

Pen could bear it no longer. "Look what you've done, Robin! How could you be so clumsy?" She spoke in a fierce undertone.

Robin looked at her in surprise and confusion. He'd never heard the gentle Pen use such a ferocious and impatient tone. " 'Tis nothing," he mumbled, bending to dab at her skirts with his napkin.

"Yes, it is!" she snapped, pushing his hand away. "You're drunk!" There were tears in her voice. "I *hate* it when men get drunk. Why would you do it?"

Robin stared at her. "I am not!" he denied loudly. "And you have no right to . . . to *nag* at me like some shrew. A man's entitled to his ale, Miss Prim."

"Oh, you mustn't quarrel," Pippa cried in dismay. "Not today. Not at a wedding feast."

"That's true enough, little maid," one of the men boomed cheerfully. "Master Robin's not drinking fair. I say the lad pays the forfeit."

A chorus of agreement ran around the table, and men rose to pounce upon Robin who at first didn't realize what was in store. They lifted him bodily from the bench to carry him to the manacle on the wall. And then he understood. He struggled, suddenly terrified, all bravado gone.

"No!" Pen cried, looking in anguish at her mother. This was now her fault. She had drawn attention to Robin, had forced the quarrel upon him.

"Stop them, for God's sake, Hugh!" Guinevere said urgently. "You can't let them do this."

Hugh was looking as anguished as Pen but he said grimly, "If he wants to drink like a man then he must pay the price like a man."

"That's nonsense!" Guinevere told him. "You can't let them do this to him in front of Pen. Not here, not now. Don't you understand? He'll never recover from the humiliation."

Hugh looked at her then he looked to where Robin still struggled against his captors. He said, "You think the humiliation of being rescued by his father and carted off to bed will be less than paying that forfeit?"

"I am telling you it will be," she responded. "In front of Pen, today. Let him be a child, just for today."

Hugh pulled at his chin. Was she right? Women had such different views of these things. He'd never had to consider a woman's view in his dealings with Robin.

Abruptly he rose to his feet. "Let the lad be," he called, striding across to the wall where the men had finally managed to haul Robin.

They looked reluctant to give up their prey. They were flushed with drink and excitement, their good nature now mixed with malice.

"I said leave him be." Hugh's voice was suddenly dangerously soft, his eyes hard and cold. He had seen Robin's face and his son's desperate fear turned his heart.

The men moved aside and Hugh with one movement dipped his shoulder and tossed the boy over. He straightened, saying with some ferocity as he bore the still figure from the hall, "Don't you dare puke down my back, my son."

Pen heaved a sigh of relief. Pippa, who for once had been totally silent during the short drama, said soberly, "I'm so glad Lord Hugh wouldn't let them fasten him. It would have been *horrid*!"

"I think it's time you two went upstairs as well," Guinevere said. There was a rough edge to the noisy jollity now and she knew from experience how swiftly the situation could deteriorate. In her own home, she would have left the table herself, but she couldn't do that as yet. Not at least until Hugh returned.

"It's early," Pippa protested. "For a wedding feast, it's very early. And I was going to have some more cake!"

"You'll be able to have more tomorrow," her mother promised. "There'll be plenty left."

"Come along." Pen tugged at her sister's sleeve. "We don't want to stay here any longer."

Pippa hesitated then got up. "If Robin hadn't been drunk we could have stayed," she observed bluntly. "*And* had cake."

"I don't *wish* to stay here another minute," her sister said. "If you're not coming, I'll go on my own."

"I'm coming!" Pippa cried. "I was only saying . . ." She trailed after her sister.

"You want I should go with 'em, my lady?" Tilly appeared at Guinevere's elbow. She was a little flushed and had clearly been enjoying herself in a group of the more staid servants.

Guinevere shook her head. "No, there's no need. I'll look in on them when I go up."

"But you'll be wantin' me to 'elp you to bed," Tilly said.

Again Guinevere shook her head. "No, that won't be necessary. You have no tasks for tonight, Tilly. Just amuse yourself."

Tilly looked as if she might protest this, then a burst of laughter came from the group she'd been sitting with. "Well, if y'are sure, my lady . . ." she murmured and went back to the enticements of gossip and mild flirtation with the head stableman.

Hugh returned to the hall a few minutes later. He took his seat again beside Guinevere.

"How is he?"

"Well, let's just say I managed to get his head to the bowl in the nick of time." Hugh reached for his own wine cup. "You sent the girls away?"

"It seemed best. Matters can grow out of hand very suddenly and they've seen enough of such things."

Hugh was silent for a minute before observing, "A bachelor's household is no doubt rougher than one where a woman holds the domestic reins. My men are inclined to play hard when the opportunity arises. If it offended you, I'm sorry for it."

Guinevere shook her head. "I took no offense. They're entitled to their celebration. The only sufferer will be Robin in the morning, poor lad."

Hugh frowned. "I can't think what possessed him to be so foolish."

"Can't you?"

"Well, perhaps I can," he said ruefully. "But I should imagine tonight's little display will cure Pen of any lingering affection."

"Pen's far too levelheaded to hold it against him," Guinevere said. "But I have a feeling that they're already falling into an easy way with each other that has more of friendship than anything else to it. Living in such close quarters breeds familiarity, and love flourishes on the unknown, on a sense of mystery about its object. Don't you think?" She regarded him with a glimmer of mischief in her eye.

"I have little time for mysteries," Hugh returned. "I like things to be straightforward. I like to understand things. That may sound prosaic . . . boring even. But it's how I am."

"Yes, I know," she said, teasing him. "I am wed to a plain man who has no time for frills and fancies. A plainspoken man who likes only the unvarnished truth."

"And is there something wrong in that?" He would not respond to her teasing manner. His expression was grave, his gaze intense as it rested on her countenance.

"No," Guinevere said. "Nothing at all. But women, you should know, tend to be a little more devious than men. They approach things in a rather more roundabout fashion."

Hugh wondered what she was trying to tell him. This was no idle conversation, he was sure of it. So what point was she making?

"You sound as if you're warning me of something," he said.

"I merely point out that when men think they've arranged matters to their satisfaction, women have a way of upsetting such arrangements," she responded lightly. "And men, in general, are completely taken by surprise. Complacency, my lord, is dangerous when it comes to women."

"There's no fear that anything you do will take me by surprise, Guinevere," he said quietly. "Complacency is not a fault of mine, I promise you."

For a moment their eyes held, then Guinevere's soft laugh broke the tension. "We're well matched, my lord. I foresee some interesting times ahead."

Hugh's eyes narrowed. "Well matched, indeed, my lady. Both between the sheets and out of them."

"On which subject," Guinevere said, "I wish you to understand that there'll be no bride-bedding at this feast."

"It's a little late for that," Hugh responded with a quick grin. "This bride has already been bedded. Well and truly, I would have said."

"Well and truly," Guinevere agreed, rising from her chair. "I'm going to slip away now while they're all too deep in drink to notice and decide to play more games."

"I'll come as soon as my guests have left." He reached for her hand. "Be ready for me."

"As you command, my lord." She gave him an ironic smile and glided from the hall.

Hugh smiled to himself and wondered how long he could wait before joining her. There was delicious torment in the delay.

"My lord . . ." Jack Stedman appeared at his shoulder.

"Sit you down, Jack. Help yourself to meat and drink." Hugh gestured to Guinevere's vacant chair and the still-laden table. The cloth was no longer pristine, the wax candles burning down, but there was still food aplenty on the great serving platters.

"My thanks, sir." Jack took the seat and pulled a platter of roast venison towards him. He ate ravenously, spearing the meat with his dagger, sopping up juices with a hunk of barley bread. He drank deeply from the ale jug and cut a hefty chunk of game pie.

Hugh waited patiently until the man's first hunger had been appeased.

He sipped his own wine, leaning back in his chair, eyes half closed. But anyone who thought he was relaxed would have been mistaken.

"Well?" he prompted finally when Jack began to show signs of satiation.

" 'Tis passin' strange, sir." Jack wiped his mouth on his sleeve. "The man was still there, lyin' in the dirt, bleedin'. No one 'ad come near 'im. Ye'd think some folks would've taken a look-see. Robbed 'im of summat."

Hugh nodded. "Was he still alive?"

"Jest about. Folks were jest standin' around watchin' 'im bleed to death." Jack shook his head. "Never seen the like. They wouldn't go near 'im. 'Twas almost as if 'e 'ad the plague."

"Did he say anything?"

"He was in deadly fear, m'lord. An' not just of dyin'. Clammed up, wouldn't talk even when I offered to take 'im to a leech. Kept mutterin' about 'is orders."

"Orders?" Hugh mused, stroking his chin. "Orders from whom?"

Jack shook his head. "Wouldn't say nuthin' else, sir."

"What did you do with him?"

Jack looked surprised. "Why, I left 'im there, sir. Wasn't nuthin' else to do with 'im. You didn't say to bring 'im in. Should I go an' fetch 'im?"

Hugh considered. He had little interest in saving the man's life; it would hardly be a public service. Once an assassin, always an assassin. "No," he said. "What about the knife? Did you learn anything from that?"

Jack put it on the table. "I asked if anyone recognized it, if anyone knew who 'e was, but if they did know, they wasn't sayin'. One old biddy screeched about devils but they shut 'er up fast."

"Devils?"

"Oh, she was 'alf out of 'er senses, sir." Jack drank again from the ale jug.

Hugh picked up the knife and examined it carefully. There was nothing out of the ordinary about it that he could see. Nothing that would give him a clue as to his assailant's identity. But the man had been acting on orders. Someone wanted Hugh of Beaucaire dead.

Guinevere stopped in the kitchen on her way upstairs. She grimaced at the chaos, the litter of dirty pots, the half-drunk and dozing potboys and scullery maids. In her own kitchens at Mallory Hall there was always order however large the banquet. Master Crowder saw to that. But, of course, he had no authority here. She filled a tankard with hot water from the kettle on the range and selected herbs from the racks in the pantry where they were dried. She pounded them in the mortar with the pestle and mixed them into the hot water.

Carrying the tankard in one hand, an oil lamp in the other, she went silently into Robin's chamber, next door to the girls'. She set the tankard on a small table in the sparsely furnished chamber and approached the cot, shielding with her hand the light from the lamp as she looked down at the boy lying waxen-faced on his back. His eyes fluttered open as he became aware of her presence and he groaned wretchedly.

"Are you feeling very sick, Robin?"

Another groan was her answer. She set the lamp on the table and took up the tankard. "Drink this, love. It tastes vile but I promise it will settle your stomach." She knelt beside the cot, slipped a hand behind his head, and lifted him just enough to take the contents of the cup she held to his lips.

Robin drank, coughed, spluttered, wailed in utter misery, then fell back onto the pillows, closing his eyes.

"It will help you sleep," she said, brushing the damp hair from his forehead.

He made no answer and she took the lamp and left the little chamber that reminded her of his father's in its spartan air.

But Hugh's chamber now held some surprises. There were flowers, as Pippa had said, and wax candles on the mantel. Guinevere had brought with her to London the linens, pillows, cushions, the china and glass from Mallory Hall that had been destined for the manor at Cauldon and Hugh's bed had been made up with her own sheets and coverlets. Her little silver orange tree where she hung her rings stood on the dresser with her jewel box, her own silver candlesticks beside them. The ewer and basin on the washstand were of the finest Delft porcelain, and cushions now graced the deep window seat.

Guinevere surveyed the room in frowning silence. How would Hugh react to having his own chamber so invaded? He had told Tilly to make what changes she considered necessary, but he could not have envisaged anything quite this comprehensive.

She sat down at the dresser and began to uncoif. The door opened and Hugh came in. He stood in silence on the threshold for what seemed a very long time. She turned on her stool to look at him, the long pins from her loosened hood still in her hand.

"God's bones!" he muttered. "My chamber's been turned into a boudoir."

"It was not my doing."

He took off his velvet cap and scratched his head. "I suppose I couldn't really expect you to give up the luxuries you're used to. I hadn't realized you'd brought so much with you."

"They were in the cart that Crowder drove. They were going to furnish the manor at Cauldon."

"I see," he said dryly. "You couldn't do without such things even when attempting a desperate escape?"

"I saw no reason to deprive myself of *everything,*" she said tautly. "And I don't believe my personal possessions are included in your marriage settlement. Or did I miss that clause?" She gestured to her jewels, her ring tree, the silver candlesticks. "Do you now own these things as well? Even the clothes on my back, perhaps?" She placed the long pins on the dresser and lifted the hood from her head, turning her attention to the pins in her white coif.

"I have no wish to quarrel with you tonight," he said, coming over to her, tossing his hat onto the bed. "Your personal possessions are your own, and you know it. I was just taken by surprise. This is my chamber, after all."

"Then is there another that I could claim for my own?" She turned back to him, the coif now in her hands, its crisp linen folds falling over her black velvet lap. "I would gladly remove my personal possessions to somewhere I could call my own." She let the coif slip to the floor at her feet.

"Oh, no," he said softly, placing his hands on her shoulders. "There will be no separate beds in this marriage, wife of mine. If I must sleep in a silken boudoir, then so be it. My chamber is yours. And you may do whatever you wish with it."

"Such consideration, my lord. I thank you." But despite the ironic tone her earlier antagonism had gone. She knew it would take a long while for her resentment over the marriage settlements to fade, and there would be times when her anger would surface as it just had, but Hugh had to understand that.

She began to take off her rings, hanging them on the little silver tree.

Hugh watched her, a tiny frown in his eye. They had not exchanged rings at the ceremony. Guinevere had not suggested it and neither had he. He guessed that the symbolic gesture had struck Guinevere as out of keeping with the practical nature of their bargain. For himself, he had not the resources to buy a piece of jewelry that could bear comparison with what hung on the tree and nestled in the jewel box. And pride would not let him offer her something inferior.

He could buy what he pleased now, of course. But again his pride balked at using Guinevere's own wealth to buy her a gift.

But there *was* one thing he could give her. He began to unpin her hair.

23.

Hugh came into the hall early the next morning when Guinevere and the girls were breaking their fast in the company of the magister. He bent to kiss Guinevere full on the mouth, an easy proprietorial salutation that caused Magister Howard to bury his head in his ale tankard. Public displays of intimacy had played no part in the Lady Guinevere's previous marriages.

Hugh greeted the girls cheerfully and said, "Where's Robin this fine morning?"

"I haven't seen him," Guinevere replied. "But I should imagine he's still abed."

"Oh, no," Hugh said definitely, shaking his head. He'd been about to sit down at the table but now he turned to the stairs.

Guinevere said nothing as he strode away. She'd interfered last night in his dealings with his son but was determined to use what influence she had sparingly. She would pick the issues carefully. Nevertheless her heart went out to the lad.

"I expect Robin's feeling ill," Pippa observed knowledgeably. "He probably needs to sleep it off."

Her mother made no response, merely continued with her breakfast. Pen looked dismayed and pushed a rasher of bacon around her plate without appetite. She wasn't sure how to greet Robin when he did appear. She didn't want to remind him of his behavior at the feast but neither could she act as if they hadn't quarreled.

"You must start your lessons again properly today," Guinevere said. "If it's convenient for Magister Howard?" She glanced interrogatively at the magister.

"Oh, yes, indeed, my lady," the magister agreed, spreading butter with a liberal hand on a manchet of wheaten bread. "We'll start with some French reading straight after breakfast." He beamed at the prospect, blithely oblivious of his pupils' gloomy aspect.

Hugh and Robin came down the stairs. Hugh looked rather grim; his son looked at death's door. Robin's face had a greenish tinge to its waxen pallor and his eyes were half closed.

"Have some breakfast, Robin," Hugh instructed briskly. "You need food."

"I couldn't," the lad whispered. "I couldn't eat anything."

"I'll make you a drink," Guinevere said with a sympathetic smile. "Something to ease the pain in your head." She rose from the table as Hugh sat Robin down. "Don't force him to eat, Hugh. He'll only throw it up."

"He can't do a day's work on an empty belly," Hugh pointed out, but he made no further attempt to persuade Robin to eat, and the lad sat miserably at the table, his head resting on his elbow-propped palm while his father helped himself liberally to coddled eggs and bacon.

Pen regarded Robin in anxious sympathy, and Pippa said earnestly, "Mama will get you something to make you feel better. She always gives us special drinks to make us feel better when we're sick, doesn't she, Pen?" She patted Robin's hand as she spoke.

Robin attempted a wan smile and Hugh observed, "I doubt either of you have suffered from what ails Robin."

"I expect you have though, sir. Haven't you?" Pippa regarded him with a certain challenge in her hazel eyes that reminded Hugh forcibly of her mother. He glanced at Pen and saw that she too was looking at him with disapproval. His apparent lack of sympathy for his son was not finding favor with his stepdaughters.

"That is no affair of yours, Pippa," he stated repressively. "If you've finished your breakfast I suggest you find something to do that *is*."

Pippa was saved from a response by Guinevere's return with a steaming cup that she placed at Robin's elbow. "This isn't as vile as the drink I gave you last night," she said, brushing the lank hair from his forehead. "But drink it while it's hot. It's more palatable that way."

"You physicked him last night?" Hugh looked surprised.

"I gave him something to ease the nausea and help him sleep."

"Oh, I've had that," Pippa said, leaning over to examine the contents of the cup. "I had it when I had the fever and my head was bad. It tastes quite nice if you put honey in it. Shall I put some in for you?" She reached for the honey pot.

Robin shook his head feebly and took a tentative sip from the cup.

"If you and Pen have finished eating, you should go and get ready to start your lessons," Guinevere said. "They'll be ready for you in their chamber in half an hour, Magister."

"I'll go at once and search out the books we'll be using," the magister said happily, rising from the table. "Ah, it'll be good to get back into a normal routine, my lady. Will you and I be reading this afternoon, as usual?"

"If it can be so arranged," Guinevere replied.

"The lad could use some schooling," Hugh said thoughtfully as the magister hurried off after the girls. "He's lettered and has some ability with accounts and figures but no knowledge of the classical tongues. Or French, for that matter."

He glanced at Robin who was gazing blankly into the cup, deaf to his father's words. "I hadn't thought it necessary for a soldier, but now that he'll have no need to earn his bread in that manner he could use some knowledge of the gentler arts. What d'you think, Robin? Robin?"

Robin looked up, wincing. "I beg your pardon, sir?"

"I was suggesting you might usefully spend some time with your sisters under the magister's tutoring. You can't take your place at court as an unschooled bumpkin."

"But I wish to be a soldier," Robin said, finally stung out of his miserable absorption in his bodily ills. "I've always wished to be a soldier . . . like you, sir."

"I think you'll find that changed circumstances don't always change people, Hugh," Guinevere pointed out with a sweet smile as she rose from the table. "If Robin's determined to be a soldier, I doubt you'll make a courtier out of him simply because he can afford to be. Now, if you'll both excuse me, I'm going to try to sow some seeds of peace between Masters Milton and Crowder. Matters are somewhat awry in the kitchen."

Hugh stared after her, frowning with annoyance. She was right, of course. But she didn't have to sound so pleased about it. He supposed she was merely getting a little revenge and he began to wonder how long she would feel the need to do so. If she threw the marriage settlements in his face at every opportunity, he was going to start regretting them, even though he had not the slightest reason to do so. Anyone but Guinevere would consider them to be perfectly usual, perfectly reasonable.

He glanced over at Robin. The lad did look very unwell despite whatever Guinevere had put in his drink. "When you've finished your morning tasks you may return to bed, Robin," he said.

Robin lifted his head from his hand with some difficulty. "Thank you, sir," he mumbled.

Guinevere stood in the kitchen surveying the general chaos. Not much had been done so far this morning to clear up the debris from the feast and the place looked pretty much as it had last night when she'd made Robin's physic. Slovenly potboys and slatternly scullery maids moved slowly, heavy-eyed, presumably feeling like Robin after the previous night's indulgence. Flies buzzed over a pile of well-picked bones and a couple of dogs prowled nose to the floor on the lookout for dropped or discarded scraps.

The door stood open to the kitchen court letting in some fresh air to dispel the odors of stale food and cooking. Master Milton and Master Crowder stood at the door talking with a gaunt man who was not familiar to Guinevere. There was something about the way the two stewards were standing that reminded her of dogs at bay. Their backs seemed to bristle with hostility.

She went over to them, stepping over debris, holding her blue silk skirts high. It was not her place to have the ordering of the kitchen, it was the steward's. She guessed that Crowder was deeply offended at the condition of this kitchen and had had difficulty keeping his opinion to himself. Such criticism would certainly have put Master Milton's back up.

"Good morning, gentlemen."

They both turned at her cool greeting and bowed. "Good morning, my lady."

The man they'd been talking with clasped his hat to his chest and bowed almost to his knees. "My lady," he murmured reverently. He straightened and offered her an obsequious smile that showed blackened stumps. His eyes were close-set in his thin angular face and his nose looked as if it had been broken on several occasions.

"Who is this?" she asked of the two stewards.

The man spoke up for himself. "Name's Tyler, m'lady. I'm after work. Thought as 'ow you might 'ave summat fer me. I can turn me 'and to most anythin'. Kitchen work, stable work, garden work." He peered around the two men and looked into the kitchen. "Looks like you could do wi' some 'elp in there."

"That's certainly true," Guinevere agreed, glancing at Master Milton. She stepped back a little, indicating that the steward should accompany her. Out of earshot, she said quietly but firmly, "I don't wish to interfere, Milton, but none of your people seem to have the first idea what to do about this mess."

The steward looked discomfited. "We aren't accustomed to such feasting, madam."

"No, I understand that. But someone needs to encourage the servants to show a little more energy. Get the dogs out of here, for a start, and protect the food from the flies."

She paused, then said as if it had only just occurred to her, "Of course, the household has become much bigger and probably will increase even more. It's a deal of work for one man to manage. I wonder if it might make sense for Master Crowder to take charge of the kitchens and the stores, leaving you the ordering of the rest of the household? I've been so impressed at how well it's run. The chambers are always clean, the linen kept fresh and mended, the fires always bright. And Lord Hugh will likely be entertaining more than he has been doing . . . there'll be a need of guest chambers and the like."

The steward was no fool. He knew he had been given an instruction couched though it was in pleasant compliment. "If Lord Hugh is pleased with such a disposition, madam, then of course I will do as you say," he responded with a stiff bow.

"I think you will find Lord Hugh will be pleased," she said gently. "But if you wish to go and ask him, then feel free to do so."

"That won't be necessary, madam," he said hastily.

"Good. Then I will explain the situation to Master Crowder and I trust that you and he will be able to work together in harmony." She smiled warmly at him and turned back to the door where Crowder still stood with the man called Tyler.

"Crowder, it's been decided that you and Master Milton should divide the work of the household between you," she said. "I put the kitchens and the stores entirely into your hands." She gestured to the mess behind her. "You'll have your work cut out."

"Oh, aye, madam," he said with a certain grim satisfaction. "And I'll take this man on for a start."

"You won't regret it, sir." Tyler twisted his cap in his hands. "I've a wife and six children, m'lady. If I can't find work I'll 'ave to find me bread on the streets. I used to work the wherries on the river, but I burned me 'ands an' I can't pull the oars no more." He held out his hands, revealing hideously scarred palms. "They're all right fer most things," he said. "But pullin' oars is summat different."

"Yes, I can imagine," Guinevere agreed. "Very well. You'll work under Master Crowder." She nodded and made her way back through the kitchen.

Tyler looked after her, his eyes hooded, then with a nod at Master Crowder he entered the kitchen, rolling up his sleeves.

He found instant favor with the servants. Any man willing to shoulder more than his share of the work was welcome. He seemed to be everywhere at once and his casual questions drew no comment.

Robin staggered into the kitchen to fetch a sack of grain from the pantry for the dovecotes. He stood in the middle of the kitchen blinking blearily trying to remember what he had come for. His head pounded and every joint in his body ached.

"Who's that then?" Tyler asked a scullery maid as he helped her hang the now clean copper pots on their hooks on the ceiling.

"Eh, 'tis the young master," the girl said, looking over her shoulder.

"Master Robin. He looks right poorly. I wonder what's up with 'im."
She handed Tyler the last pot with a distinctly come-hither smile.
"Thankee, Tyler."

Tyler acknowledged the inviting smile with a grin and a pat on her
plump rear that made her giggle, then he turned to the lad still standing
in the middle of the floor oblivious of the mop swishing at his feet in
the hands of a lackadaisical scullion.

"Can I 'elp you wi' summat, young sir?"

At the strange voice, Robin started. He gazed blankly at Tyler. "I
came in for something but I can't remember what it was. Oh, yes, now
I remember. Grain. I need grain for the dovecotes." He stumbled towards the pantry, his one thought now that once his tasks were completed he could put his aching body to bed.

Tyler followed him. " 'Ere, let me carry that fer ye, Master Robin."
He hoisted the sack onto his shoulders and strode from the kitchen,
Robin at his heels.

"Just leave it over there, thank you." Robin indicated the two tall
dovecotes standing in the center of the herb garden. "What did you say
your name was?"

" 'Tis Tyler, sir. You sure you don't want me to pour it fer ye?"

"Quite sure, thank you, Tyler." Robin slit the sack with his knife. "I
know just how much to give them."

"Right y'are then, young sir." Tyler strode away. He didn't return to
the kitchen but made his way around the house to a side door. He
slipped inside and stood still in the small dark hallway from which a
narrow staircase rose to the upper floors. He could hear nothing. He
ran soundlessly up the stairs and lifted the latch on the door at the top.
It opened onto a broader landing, a passage leading off it. He could see
three doors along the corridor.

His casual questions in the kitchen as to the general layout of the
house had borne fruit. Behind one of those doors he would find the
boy's chamber.

He stepped onto the landing, paused, listening. Then he tiptoed
down the passage, listening at each door. He could hear voices, a child-
ish treble, coming from behind the third door. Nothing at all from behind the others.

Tyler opened the first door a mere crack, just wide enough to peep in. It was a large chamber with a large bed but it had the air of being unoccupied. A guest chamber he assumed. He closed the door and turned his attention to the one next door.

It was a small, sparsely furnished chamber with a narrow cot. He slipped inside and closed the door behind him. This was the boy's room. A lad's sword hung in its sheath on the wall; the cloak behind the door would not fit a man. He opened drawers in the dresser and found gloves, hose, small clothes. All a perfect fit for the boy.

He worked quickly. He exchanged the candles in the two pewter sticks for the ones he carried in the satchel he had not taken from his back since he'd arrived at the house. He filled the oil lamp from a small vial he took from a pocket of the satchel, then taking a screw of parchment from the same pocket he began to sprinkle its contents inside the boy's gloves, in his hose, among his shirts. Finally he pulled the coverlet back and sprinkled the fine white powder on the top of the sheet and the pillow where it would be close to a sleeper's face.

He replaced the coverlet and glanced around. Everything looked perfectly normal, no indication that the chamber was now lethal. A footstep sounded in the corridor outside and Tyler dived behind the door, pressing himself against the wall. His hand closed over his dagger.

The door opened. "Robin?" A man stepped inside but he still held the door open. He looked around the deserted chamber, then backed out, closing the door behind him.

Tyler breathed again. He guessed from the man's attire, the commanding posture, that he had just seen Hugh of Beaucaire. His second quarry. Tyler had a trick or two up his sleeve for Lord Hugh. And *he* wouldn't make the mistake of underestimating his victim.

His lip curled slightly as he thought of the previous night's botched attempt to do away with Lord Hugh. The would-be assassin hadn't known what he was doing. Fortunate for him, really, that he'd died in the attempt. Privy Seal had unpleasant methods of responding to failures.

Tyler waited a few minutes, then slipped from the room, made his way down the back stairs, and headed for the stables. A man could make himself very useful there.

Hugh left Robin's chamber and went in search of his son. He was beginning to think that he'd been too harsh, forcing the boy out of his bed when he was so clearly in pain. But he was pleased too that Robin hadn't given in to his misery and returned to bed early despite his father's orders. Hugh had thought he'd heard a sound coming from Robin's bedchamber but he was glad to discover that he'd been mistaken. The boy knew perfectly well that his father would relent if he really couldn't keep going. It was pride not fear that would keep Robin on his feet through his wretchedness.

Hugh was smiling with satisfaction at this reflection as he reached the hall. Guinevere was standing by the fire, a parchment in her hand. She looked up and held the parchment out to him. " 'Tis addressed to you. But unless I'm mistaken, the seal is Privy Seal's."

He took it, said calmly, "No, you're not mistaken," and slit the seal with his thumbnail. He unfolded the sheet and pursed his lips in a soundless whistle. "It seems we are bidden this evening to revels that Lord Privy Seal gives in honor of the king and queen. Revels to celebrate the imminent birth of the queen's child."

"I would think the queen would prefer to revel with her ladies at such a time," Guinevere observed caustically. "When a woman is about to be brought to bed, the last thing she needs is a crowd of *reveling* men around her."

Hugh raised an eyebrow. "It pleases the king to have his queen honored."

"But not rested, it would seem." She shrugged. "Must we go?"

"One does not lightly turn down Privy Seal's invitations."

"I would turn this one down with much gravity," she replied. "Many excuses, much begging for forgiveness, much acknowledgment of the honor done us."

Hugh laughed. He reached out and touched the soft parting of her hair below the white lining of her hood. "I would spend this night alone with my wife."

"Will such an excuse serve?"

He shook his head. "No. We must go."

"I don't like the feeling that we remain at Privy Seal's beck and call," she said slowly. "Can we leave London? Go back to Derbyshire?"

Again he shook his head. "Winter is close upon us. We can't travel now, not such a great distance, until the spring. Besides, I am the king's servant. I need his permission to leave London."

"I hadn't realized your life was so circumscribed." She turned away towards the fire, holding out her hands to its warmth as she added, "And mine now, too."

"I serve the king," he repeated.

"But you do not serve Privy Seal." She remained with her back to him, her body curved gracefully towards the fire.

"Not directly," he agreed. "But insofar as Privy Seal is the king's chief servant, it's inevitable that I am at his beck and call, as you put it."

"I suppose so." She raised her slender shoulders in a tiny shrug. "But I do not like such an arrangement. It makes me uneasy."

Hugh said nothing. He could think of nothing that would reassure her since he agreed with her. He didn't care to be dangling on Privy Seal's string but for as long as Thomas Cromwell found favor with the king there was nothing he could do about it. Of course, the king's favor was withdrawn as often and as randomly as it was granted. Cromwell could make one mistake and Henry would have his head. In such a case, Hugh would not want to be known as one of Privy Seal's creatures since servants went down with the master at Henry's court, so it behooved him to tread a very fine line.

"Your pardon, sir."

He turned at Robin's voice behind him. "Ah, there you are." He gave the boy a shrewdly assessing scrutiny. "Feeling any better?"

"Not really," Robin replied, rubbing his bloodshot eyes with the heels of his palms. "I've finished the stable work. Is there anything else I should do?"

"No, get you to bed." Hugh patted his shoulder. "And I trust that you've learned something of the merits of moderation."

Robin carefully nodded his painfully throbbing head.

"Would you like me to make you another physic, Robin?" Guinevere asked.

"What I had this morning made my head ache less," he said. "But it's bad again now."

"I'll bring it up for you."

Robin trailed away with a murmur of thanks and Guinevere went into the kitchen. Matters had improved considerably. Meat was turning on the spit for dinner, pans bubbled on the range, the floor and tabletops were scrubbed clean.

She prepared the physic and took it upstairs to Robin who was curled up in bed, the sheet pulled up to his chin. "What about dinner?" She gave him the cup when he had sat up.

"I don't think I could eat anything, madam. I seem to be hungry but if I think of food I want to puke again."

"Then don't think of it." Guinevere went to the door. "A couple of hours' sleep will see you right as rain."

She went into the next door chamber where her daughters were closeted with the magister and their books. They looked up hopefully at her entrance. "Is it dinnertime, Mama? Can we stop now?" Pippa asked.

"Not yet. I would have you read for me."

"They've forgotten much since we left Mallory Hall, madam," Magister Howard said with a sorrowful headshake. "We have had to begin anew with the French tenses."

Guinevere perched on the windowsill and listened to her daughters stumble through the French text. Their indifference to the joys of learning still surprised her. Her own thirst for knowledge was never slaked.

She stayed with them until the horn sounded the summons for dinner and they went down to the hall together.

"Are we to eat at these revels of Privy Seal's?" she inquired, taking her place at the table.

"Cromwell is renowned for the lavishness of his banquets," Hugh returned. "I can promise you a most vulgar display of wealth."

"Then I will eat sparingly now." Guinevere sighed. The prospect of the coming ordeal weighed heavily. "Where is it that we must go?"

"To Privy Seal's house in Austin Friars. It will be best if we ride there."

"Well, that's some compensation. It seems an eternity since I last rode Isolde." She took a sip of wine and shook her head when Hugh offered her the platter of mutton.

"Where's Robin?" Pen asked anxiously.

"In bed," Hugh told her. "Sleeping himself to a full recovery, I trust."

Pen looked relieved. Pippa said through a mouthful of meat, "I hate being ill. I hate to go to bed in the daytime. Shall we take him the kittens, Pen? To keep him company."

"I should just leave him to sleep," Guinevere advised. She nibbled a little cheese. "What time must we go, Hugh?"

"A little after three o'clock."

Guinevere grimaced. She noticed that Hugh was frowning down the table. "Is something the matter?"

"There's a face I don't recognize." Hugh gestured with the point of his knife. "A stranger at my table."

"Oh, his name's Tyler. I hired him this morning to help out Crowder. Crowder is going to take charge of the kitchens and the stores while Master Milton takes charge of the rest of the household. Matters will run much more smoothly now."

"I see," Hugh said dryly. "I hadn't noticed they weren't smooth. What does this Tyler have to recommend him?"

"A willingness to turn his hand to anything," she responded. "He has a family to keep. Crowder seemed to think he would be a good man to have around, and in general I trust my steward's judgment on such matters." She looked at Hugh, clear eyed, challenging. "Do you have a problem with that, my lord?"

He shook his head. "I don't, but I suspect Milton might. He's not accustomed to having any hand but his own on the domestic reins."

"He'll become accustomed," Guinevere declared. "I have no intention of living in an ill-run household and there are certain areas where Master Milton is less than effective. You have a wife now, my lord. And I am an able administrator."

"Oh, I don't doubt it," he said, his eyes glinting at her. "That was after all one of the more persuasive reasons for this marriage."

"Quite," Guinevere said, and took up her wine cup again.

24.

Jack Stedman and three of Hugh's men accompanied them to Privy Seal's house at Austin Friars. The road was lined with pikemen in Cromwell's livery, keeping back the crowds who had gathered to cheer as the king and queen passed by and who gawked openmouthed at the procession of guests in iron-wheeled carriages and on horseback, picking their way through the mud and refuse of the streets.

Cromwell had torn down the dissolved monastery of Austin Friars to build his mansion; the small cottages around it had been part of the friary's outbuildings and Privy Seal had had no compunction in moving them if they interfered with his architectural plans. He had erected a high stone wall a half mile long that enclosed his garden and had swallowed the plots of some twenty modest cottage gardens.

Guinevere gazed up at the weather vanes mounted on the steep pitched roofs. Shaped like men-at-arms they gleamed golden in the early dusk, their lances tipped with gilded banners that almost seemed to flutter in the rising wind.

"A mansion indeed," she murmured with a little shiver, a strange sense of menace gripping her as they entered through the wicket gate into the inner court. All was bustle and shouting as grooms ran to take horses, to open carriage doors, and gentlemen ushers hastened to escort the guests into the great hall that stretched as long as the house itself beneath a magnificent gilded ceiling.

They were shown to places at one of the long tables that were ranged down each side of the hall. Men sat at one side of the table, the women facing them. Guinevere gazed around her, fascinated despite the chill, the sense of menace, that she couldn't shake.

A tucket of trumpets heralded the arrival of the king and his queen. The guests rose to their feet as the rich arras at the rear of the dais was drawn aside and Their Highnesses entered, their ladies and gentlemen behind them. The king and queen took their places alone at the table on the high dais. Their retinue stood in a semicircle behind them. Presumably they were to go hungry in the royal service, Guinevere reflected.

To her relief Privy Seal was not seated at their table. But she could see him clearly at the head of the table just below the dais where guests of true importance were seated. His eyes were everywhere, ceaselessly roaming the great hall. There was a moment when he caught her eye and held her gaze. Unblinking, expressionless, he locked eyes with her until she turned her head away.

She looked across at Hugh, immediately comforted by his solid, square presence. He was talking to his neighbor but as if sensing her gaze looked up. Slowly he winked and she couldn't help smiling.

No one seemed interested in talking to her and she guessed that these occasions were times when influence was peddled, when it mattered enormously who talked to whom and about what. Allegiances were formed, noted, for good or ill. And she was a stranger, a nobody. On the whole, she was not sorry to sit ignored amid the din as voices rose, competed with the clatter of dishes and cutlery. The plates were gold, the glass Venetian crystal. Trumpets sounded at the beginning of each meat course. And there were many. Cranes, peacocks, swans, boar. Nothing as humble as venison. Servers ran with platters and carafes of fine rhenish filling goblets without cease.

Guinevere drank little and ate less. She was wondering why it had pleased Privy Seal to invite them to this ostentatious display of his wealth. The queen looked physically uncomfortable and her boredom was apparent even through the polite smile fixed upon her face. The king leaned forward, his heavy head nodding as he watched the spectacle below him, chewing vigorously all the while on whatever he seized from the serving platters as they passed in front of him.

An entertainment had started in the main body of the hall. A fountain sprang up like magic from the floor, swans sailed gracefully on a tiny lake, while wood nymphs danced around them chased by a trio of satyrs. The king applauded this heartily. Guinevere's head began to ache with the noise. She couldn't imagine where the fountain had come from and had absolutely no interest in the wood nymphs' struggle with the satyrs.

She glanced across at Hugh and he raised an inquiring eyebrow, gesturing with his head towards the arras to his right. Correctly interpreting the gesture as an invitation for a reprieve, she nodded and rose from her stool. Hugh rose too and moved around the table to take her arm.

"There's a gallery just above the hall where we can walk a little. It's cooler perhaps, quieter certainly."

"My head rivals Robin's," she said. "What a disgust—"

"Hush!" He pinched her arm hard and urgently. "There are ears everywhere."

She bit her lip. "Forgive me. We do not have such ears in Derbyshire."

"They are a fact of life here," he murmured grimly, holding back the arras for her. She slipped past him and found herself at the foot of a curving staircase. Neither of them noticed the man at the opposite end of the hall who had witnessed their disappearance and now ducked behind another arras.

Guinevere climbed, one hand on the gilded banister, the other holding up her skirts. The staircase wound upwards and opened onto a wide gallery that looked down upon the hall.

Guinevere sighed with relief. Just the sense of space around her brought some peace. "Let us walk a little then."

Hugh tucked a hand beneath her elbow with the same proprietorial ease she had noticed about his kiss at the breakfast table. She found that she rather liked it. They began to walk along the gallery, Guinevere looking down over another gilded rail into the body of the hall where it seemed the satyrs were getting the better of the nymphs. She noticed that the queen and her ladies had left but the king remained, apparently still entertained.

"Well, well, my lord. You've come in search of a little privacy, I see."

She looked up to see a man coming towards them from the far end of the gallery, his gait swaying, his massively padded doublet over a considerable belly of his own giving him an absurd figure, his striped codpiece jutting aggressively. His eyes were small and hard and although he both sounded and acted drunk, she would have laid any odds he was as sober as herself.

"That's a pretty piece you have there, my friend. For a little tumble with such a wench, I'd leave the king's feast myself." He leered at Guinevere as he came close.

She felt Hugh stiffen beside her, felt the movement as his hand went to his sword hilt. But he said calmly, "Go back to your goblet, man. You'll find better entertainment below."

The man came yet closer. He pushed his face into Guinevere's. "A kiss, my pretty. Your . . . your *protector* . . . he won't mind. You're willing to share, aren't you, friend?"

She heard Hugh's swift intake of breath, felt his hand tighten on her elbow. But again he said calmly, easily, "You'll find no sport here."

The man made a move to his sword, half pulled it from its sheath, his eyes sharp, knowing, resting on Hugh's face. "Come now, my friend, you'll not begrudge a man a slice of this pretty pie. I've heard many others have had a nibble."

Guinevere couldn't believe Hugh would stand there and listen to such insults. And yet he stood there. His hand had dropped from his sword and he merely regarded the man steadily. She could feel his anger in the body so close to her, but none of it showed in his face.

"You will excuse us," he said softly. "We would continue our walk." He put a hand on the man's shoulder and spun him, seemingly without effort, out of his path and against the rail. Still holding Guinevere's elbow he propelled her past him.

They heard the scrape of a sword being drawn from its sheath. Hugh did not turn, his breathing did not change. He continued to walk them both along the gallery. They reached another curving staircase at the end. The staircase their friend had taken to the gallery.

Guinevere looked back. The gallery was deserted. She looked up at Hugh and saw how white he was, how tense, his jaw clenched, his eyes ablaze. "What was that?" she asked softly. "He wanted to force a quarrel upon you, didn't he?"

"So I believe." Hugh turned his gaze upon her. There was an arrested, questioning look in his eye. "Do you know the penalty for drawing a sword under the roof where the king sits?"

She shook her head.

He continued to look at her for a minute, then said, "The loss of an eye is considered lenient. A head severe but quite usual."

Guinevere shuddered. "Why? Why would he try to force you to do that then?"

"I have no idea."

She drew a deep breath. "I do not like this place, Hugh. May we leave now?"

"Not before the king." He gestured that she should precede him down the curving staircase. She felt his eyes on her back at every step.

"Did you know the man?" she asked as they reached the bottom of the stairs.

"No. I have no recollection of ever having seen him before." His gaze, questioning and unreadable, rested for a moment on her face. Then he eased her through the arras and back to their places at the table where there was no opportunity for further speech.

The king followed his wife through the arras at the rear of the dais shortly thereafter and they were free to leave. Privy Seal moved around the hall to greet them as they made their way to the door.

"Hugh . . . my lady of Beaucaire." He smiled his thin, cold smile. "I trust you enjoyed my little entertainment."

"A revelation for me, Lord Cromwell," Guinevere said. "We have not such wonders in Derbyshire."

"No, I don't imagine you do." He pinched his nose as he regarded her steadily. "But we shall show you more of our wonders. I dare swear you will be amazed."

Guinevere offered a small curtsy. "I am already amazed, my lord." She hesitated, then added, "And most grateful for your consideration."

He raised a finger. "Gratitude, madam, is a wise virtue." He glanced at Hugh. "You enjoyed yourself, I trust, Hugh?"

"Certainly," Hugh agreed readily. "We were honored with the invitation, my lord. We pray for the queen's safe delivery."

"Ah, yes. A son will bring peace and harmony." Cromwell nodded. "The king will be content." His hard eyes rested speculatively on Hugh. "You have a son. You know the joys."

"I do." Hugh took Guinevere's arm. "Our horses await."

"Safe journeying." Privy Seal turned from them as if they no longer interested him and strolled away through the crowd of his departing guests.

Jack Stedman and his men awaited them in the inner court, holding their horses. Guinevere used the mounting block and arranged her skirts decorously across the saddle. The air was chill, clearing her head.

Hugh swung astride his black charger but for a moment made no move to walk the horse to the wicket gate. The crowd eddied around them but he seemed not to notice. A deep frown was between his thick brows, his mouth and jaw were taut. He turned to look at her as she sat her milk-white horse beside him and again there was an unreadable question in his gaze.

"Let us go," she said. "I cannot bear this place another minute."

He nodded, then turned in his saddle to Jack Stedman. "Jack, somewhere in this throng is a man wearing a green-and-yellow-striped doublet, a black gown trimmed with marten, I believe, green hose, a yellow hat. A man of around forty with a clipped beard and a considerable belly. See if you can find him. I have a certain interest in who his friends are."

Jack looked doubtful. "I'll do what I can, m'lord. But 'tis like the needle in the haystack."

"I understand that. But you may be lucky and I have a score to settle with him."

Jack dismounted and disappeared into the crowd still pouring out of Privy Seal's door.

"He'll never find him," Guinevere said as they rode out into the street, carried on the tide of their fellow guests.

Hugh shrugged. "Perhaps not." He said nothing more until they reached home.

The hall was well lit, the fire stoked despite the late hour. Guinevere tossed her cloak over the back of the settle and yawned deeply. "I'm exhausted."

"Go to bed. I'm going to wait up for Jack." Hugh poured wine from the carafe left ready for him on the table.

Guinevere hesitated. "Do you think he meant to kill you?"

"He meant to make trouble," Hugh said shortly. "For some reason someone seems interested in disrupting the hitherto smooth course of my life."

Again she hesitated. "Why?" she asked softly.

"If I knew that, I might know where to look for whomever it is," he responded. "Get you to bed, Guinevere. I'm in no mood to be good company tonight."

She left him then, concealing her hurt at this abrupt dismissal. Upstairs, she quietly entered the girls' chamber. They were sleeping peacefully, Tilly snoring gently on the truckle bed. Guinevere bent over her children, breathing in their sweet scent, smiling unconsciously at the rosy flush of sleep on their cheeks. Moonshine and Nutmeg blinked indolently at her as they snuggled into the warm space between the children's bodies.

Guinevere smoothed the coverlet, brushed their soft cheeks with her lips, and tiptoed from the chamber. Outside Robin's room she paused. A faint gleam from the oil lamp showed beneath his door. She could hear him coughing, a dry rattle in his throat.

She slipped inside, leaving the door ajar. Despite the lamplight, he seemed to be asleep, although he was restless, murmuring under his breath. Guinevere touched his cheek and found it hot and dry. He coughed again. She frowned down at him. This couldn't be the consequence of overindulgence.

"What are you doing?"

She spun around, her hand at her throat, at the voice from the door. She hadn't heard Hugh's approach and the sudden sound in the hush of the sleeping house startled her. He stood in the doorway and the frown was still in his eyes.

"I always check on my children before I go to bed," she whispered. Robin coughed again and muttered, flinging his arms above his head.

Hugh approached his son's cot. He touched the boy's flushed cheek. "He's hot."

"Yes, he has a fever," she returned, still whispering. "I could prepare a dose of hyssop and echinacea which would help to cool him."

"No!" Hugh said with sudden force. He dropped his voice immediately, saying more moderately, "Sleep is his best medicine. Leave him now." He took her arm and urged her towards the door.

"Turn out the lamp," Guinevere said. "I don't know who left it lit. The light might disturb him."

Hugh turned down the lamp and the room was in darkness. They went out into the corridor and Hugh closed the door gently behind them.

"Is Jack returned?"

Hugh shook his head and went to the stairs. "Don't stay awake for me."

"No, I won't." She turned to the corridor leading to their own chamber.

Hugh stood where he was, waiting until she had disappeared into the bedchamber, then he returned to Robin's bedside. He rubbed his mouth as he looked at the feverish boy. Robin had always been healthy, rarely overtaken with childhood ailments. What could have brought this on? He hadn't been anywhere in the last few days where there was fever. Indeed, he'd been closer to home than usual.

Closer to home . . . closer to . . .

Oh, it was ridiculous to permit such a thought. But he couldn't lose it.

"So he wouldn't rise?" Privy Seal sat back in a carved chair beside the fire, his fingers restlessly drumming on the arm, one foot tapping on the tiled floor before the hearth.

"No, my lord. I drew on him myself but he didn't turn a hair." The man in the green-and-yellow-striped doublet shifted uncomfortably as he stood at his master's elbow.

"He's a man of cool temperament," Privy Seal murmured, "but I had thought he might be pricked." He gaze flicked over his servant and the man felt his gut loosen with terror at the cold menace in the hard eyes.

"I seem to be surrounded by dolts," Cromwell murmured. "You

accost Lord Hugh dressed as you are, like some gigantic, hideously colored bumblebee. You think he won't attempt to find you? You think he wouldn't recognize you instantly?" He took up his wine goblet and regarded the man contemptuously.

"He had better not find you," he said after a minute while the man trembled before him. "I would not grieve to see you spitted on Lord Hugh's sword, mind you. But I have no faith in your ability to keep a still tongue in your head beforehand."

"I would say nothing, my lord. Not even on the rack," the man whimpered.

"Get you gone from here at first light. One of my ships is leaving for France on tomorrow's evening tide from Greenwich. Be sure you're on it. And get out of those ridiculous clothes before you take a step from this house."

The man bowed so that his forehead almost touched his knees, and scuttled from the terrifying presence although Cromwell had already turned from him to contemplate the fire.

It seemed his faith must now rest on the endeavors of his good servant Tyler, Cromwell reflected. Privy Seal liked to attack a problem from as many different points as possible. If one approach failed, then there were others in place. Thus far his minions had squandered two attempts. He would wait and see how Tyler fared before thinking afresh.

Then there were the daughters to consider. He stretched his plump legs across the tiled forehearth and stroked his round chin. With their mother's execution after the deaths of Lord Hugh and his son, the will would become null and void, all the property forfeit. But with a decent dowry apiece, the daughters could be used to make alliances useful to Cromwell. He could divert some of their mother's holdings to their dowries. Their lineage was good enough to attract the highest bidders in the land. Men anxious for advancement, anxious to keep Privy Seal's favor.

All in all, it was a pretty scheme.

For as long as Thomas Cromwell kept the king's favor.

Privy Seal heaved himself up from his chair. If Queen Jane presented the king with yet another daughter there was no knowing what turns Henry's temper would take.

But that was a problem for a new morning. He called for his gentlemen to help him to bed.

❧

Hugh stayed up, feeding the fire, until Jack returned in the early hours of the morning. So far he had only failure to report. None of the servants he'd spoken to knew of a man matching the stranger's description. He'd watched at the gate until the porter had closed the wicket on the last guests and had seen no one resembling Hugh's provocateur.

"I've left Will Malfrey to watch at the gate throughout the night. Just in case anyone slips out before dawn. If we've no joy then, I'll make some more inquiries in the mornin', m'lord."

"I'm sure he must have slipped out unnoticed in the flood of guests. I can see no reason why he would stay in Austin Friars overnight." Hugh rose and stretched wearily. "We'll leave it there, Jack. My thanks, anyway. I'm sorry for keeping you up so late."

" 'Tis my pleasure to serve you, sir." Jack touched his forelock and left the hall. He hesitated at the back door. If Lord Hugh considered the matter closed, then there was no reason for Will Malfrey to watch throughout the night at Privy Seal's gate. But it would do him no harm either, Jack thought with a grim smile. The man had some penalty coming to him for a night last week spent in a Bankside brothel when he was supposed to be on duty. Will knew this night's duty was a forfeit for that truancy. He didn't need to know that it was an unnecessary duty. Jack went to his bed.

Hugh stood in the hall for a minute after Jack's departure, finding himself strangely reluctant to join Guinevere in his chamber. He could not bring himself to give expression to the suspicion that needled him despite every effort to banish it. It was like a burrowing worm eating at his peace of mind. But it was ridiculous. Guinevere knew no one in London. How could she possibly in the short time she'd been in the city have managed to seek out such men?

But she had Greene, Crowder even, to do such work for her. Hugh knew full well how resourceful they were. How utterly loyal to their lady. They had covered up any possibly incriminating details about Stephen Mallory's death. They had plotted her escape to Cauldon. He didn't think they had much love for their lady's new husband. The marriage settlements would have outraged them. Magister Howard had made no secret of his indignation.

No, it was too absurd.

But she had warned him. Warned him not to be complacent, not to think that he had won in the battle over the marriage settlements.

No, it was too absurd.

But she had amassed her wealth through her previous husbands. She had shown no scruples there.

Dear God! This way lay madness!

He strode up the stairs and into Robin's room. He lit one of the candles on the table and came to the cot. Robin was coughing violently, his skin seemingly hotter than before. He opened his eyes as Hugh knelt worriedly beside the bed.

"Thirsty," he mumbled. "I'm so thirsty."

Hugh filled a cup with water from the jug on the washstand and held it to Robin's parched lips. The lad drank eagerly, then coughed, his body convulsing as he struggled to breathe.

"My head," he groaned. " 'Tis worse than this morning. Does a hangover last so long?"

"This is no hangover, lad," Hugh said gently. He wiped Robin's face with a damp cloth. "You have a fever. I'll send for the leech in the morning."

"But Lady Guinevere has medicine." Robin fell back on the pillows, his eyes closing. "I hate to be bled, sir. I'd rather take Lady Guinevere's physic."

"Lady Guinevere is not a physician," Hugh said. He pulled the covers up tightly, ignoring his son's feeble efforts at resistance. "You need to sweat it out, Robin. Keep the covers up."

Robin gave up and curled on his side. Hugh stood over him, holding the candle high. Then he blew out the candle and left, making his way to his own chamber.

Guinevere was not asleep but some instinct told her to pretend that she was. Hugh had made it clear he had no desire to talk, no wish to discuss with her what had happened. No wish even to discuss Robin's fever. She lay breathing rhythmically, listening to her husband's now familiar step as he moved about the chamber in the dim light of the low-turned lamp that she'd left for him. Then the lamp was doused. The feather mattress dipped beneath his weight as he climbed in beside her.

She lay still, wondering if he would touch her, move close to her, but he remained still at the far edge of the bed. She could feel the tension in his body across the space that divided them, could hear the slightly ragged edge to his breathing. Now she wanted to speak, to break the tension, but she found herself tongue-tied. He had thrown up some barrier between them every bit as high and as thick as the one she had thrown up on the journey from Derbyshire after the night in his tent, when she had resisted him in desperation, knowing that only thus could she be strong enough to fight him.

But this had come out of nowhere. They had been in near perfect amity before Privy Seal's revels. Why was he holding himself from her, forcing this distance between them? What need did he have to fight her?

For some reason, she was deeply afraid to ask him.

25.

Will Malfrey shivered in the predawn chill, pulling his head into the hood of his cloak like a snail withdrawing into its shell. He cursed Jack Stedman for landing him with this vigil. Jack would be warm in his bed, gloating that he'd found the perfect penalty for Will's supposed crime. It hadn't been a crime at all. Will had found someone else to stand in for him that night. He had just neglected to mention the change to Stedman.

He stamped his feet and thrust his gloved hands deeper into the pockets of his cloak. His breath was white in the gray darkness. Of course he should have known better. Jack Stedman's master, Hugh of Beaucaire, was a hard man to cross. A military man with exceedingly high expectations when it came to the loyalty and sense of duty of those under his command. Jack as his lieutenant upheld the standards with what Will considered to be uncalled-for enthusiasm.

The creaking of the wicket gate aroused him from his disgruntled reverie. He stepped backward into the angle of the wall where he would not be seen. The wicket opened and a large, burly man stepped out into the lane. He turned to say something to the porter at the gate, clapping his arms across his chest.

Will peered at him. The man turned his head and the watcher could see a clipped beard on a fleshy face. He was shrouded in a cloak of a rather startling yellow. Will had been told to be on the lookout for a colorful man. A fleshy man with a considerable belly, and a clipped beard.

The man set off briskly towards the river and Will Malfrey followed at a safe distance. At the river, the man stepped into a waiting barge where he stood in the light of the swinging cresset in the stern, his expression that of a very unhappy man.

Almost as unhappy as Will himself had been a few minutes earlier, Will thought with an inner chuckle as he put two fingers to his lips and sent a piercing whistle towards the group of skiffs waiting for passengers a little farther along the embankment. He sprang lightly into the boat that beat the competition and told the two oarsmen to follow the barge. With action came enthusiasm. His vigil had produced results and results were always rewarded in Lord Hugh's service, just as faults were invariably penalized.

Robin was worse the next morning. Hugh stood at his bedside beside the leech, hiding his terror at the sight of his barely conscious son. The boy's breathing was thin and fast, the cough wracked him almost constantly, his eyes were half closed and his skin burned hot and dry.

It was a gloomy day and the candles and lamp had been lit to throw more light for the leech's grim work. Robin barely protested as the vile creatures were pressed to his arms and into his groin.

" 'Tis a severe fever, my lord," the leech muttered, removing new bloodsuckers from the bottle, ready to replace the ones already sucking when they'd had their fill. He was a short, fat little man with a long beard and malodorous breath. His clothes had seen better days and his boots were cracked. Medicine was not a lucrative profession unless a man had the luck to serve the household of a great nobleman.

"I can see it's severe," Hugh snapped, revolted by the fat slugs on his son's body. "What else can you give him?"

"Well, I've a potion here that might help," the leech muttered uncertainly, diving into his sack. "But if 'tis the sweating sickness . . . or God forbid, the plague . . ."

"Dear God, he's not sweating!" Hugh declared savagely. " 'Twould be better if he were! And there's no plague hereabouts. There can't be. The boy's barely left the house for the last week."

"And everyone's well in the house?" The leech scratched his head and frowned.

"As far as I know."

"What are you giving him?" Guinevere's quiet voice spoke from the door. She looked as worried as Hugh as she stepped to the bed and asked the leech, "Hyssop and echinacea might help, don't you think?"

He shrugged. "I doubt it, madam. When a fever's as bad as this there's nothing to be done but bleed the patient and pray." He replaced the fattened leeches with new ones.

"You shouldn't be in here," Hugh said to Guinevere. "You don't wish to catch this yourself. You'll spread it to the girls."

"As will you," she pointed out. "I would like to nurse him. Tilly too. She's a skilled nurse. Skilled with simples."

Hugh shook his head. "No, I don't want anyone to do anything for him but myself."

"But why?" she asked. "Why would you refuse to let me do what I can?"

Hugh shook his head again but didn't answer her. He bent over Robin, lifting his eyelids. The whites of the boy's eyes were streaked with yellow.

Guinevere watched him for a moment, then she turned and glided from the chamber.

The girls were gathered at the door. "What's the matter with Robin, Mama?" Pen asked, grabbing her mother's hand.

"Is it still the wine?" asked Pippa from her other side.

"No, love. Robin has a fever. The leech is bleeding him now."

"Can we see him?" Pen asked.

"No, in case you catch whatever he has."

"We could sniff the pomanders," suggested Pippa. "They keep away fevers, don't they?"

"Not always. Go to your lessons now. Maybe later today, when Robin's feeling better, you can visit him."

The girls trailed off to their books and Guinevere made her way downstairs. She understood Hugh's agonized fear for his child. But she didn't understand why he wouldn't let her nurse the boy.

Hugh escorted the leech from the house then came to the fire in the hall. Guinevere set aside her embroidery frame and leaned her head against the high back of the settle to look up at him as he stood with one foot on the fender, his frowning eyes fixed on some point in the middle distance.

"I am not a great believer in bleeding," she said quietly. "In most cases it merely weakens the patient further."

"You are no physician," he returned. "A lawyer, an able administrator, I grant you, but you lay no claims to being a physician too. Or am I mistaken?"

Guinevere tried to ignore the barbed tone. She shook her head. "No, I make no such claim. But as a wife and a mother, I've had some considerable experience of nursing."

"Experience, certainly, but how much success?" He turned his gaze upon her, a brilliant piercing stare. "How many of your husbands did you nurse back to health, Guinevere?"

She closed her eyes briefly. "I understand your concern for Robin, Hugh, but it doesn't give you the right to attack me in such fashion."

He shrugged. "I merely asked a question. Not an unreasonable one. I presume you had a hand in nursing those of your husbands who survived, however briefly, the accidents and ailments that eventually killed them."

Would this suspicion lie forever between them? She turned up her palms in a small gesture of resignation and rose to her feet. "I have matters to discuss with Master Crowder."

Hugh watched her leave the hall with her fluid grace, her head erect, her back so straight. He hadn't intended to say what he'd said but the words had spoken themselves. Fear and suspicion were maggots in his head now, eating away at reason. With a muttered exclamation, he strode back to the stairs.

As he turned into the corridor to Robin's chamber, he came face-to-face with the man called Tyler. "What business d'you have up here?" he demanded irritably of the servant. Kitchen staff didn't in general frequent the family's private quarters.

"Master Crowder, m'lord. 'E sent me to refill any oil lamps that needed it," the man said, his eyes lowered, his entire posture that of a submissive servant. He held up a leather flagon of lamp oil in evidence. "I was jest checkin' in the bedchambers, sir."

Hugh frowned. "I understood Master Milton was to have charge of all matters outside the kitchen."

"Master Crowder's steward of the stores, sir," the man responded, still keeping his eyes lowered. " 'E wanted to know 'ow much oil 'ad been burned last even."

"Oh." Hugh could find no fault with this explanation although he didn't like the idea of strange servants roaming the upper floor of his house. He made a mental note to bring the subject up with Crowder himself and dismissed the man with a curt nod before hurrying into Robin's chamber.

The oil lamp, presumably refilled, was turned low and in its soft light the boy lay still, barely breathing it seemed to Hugh. Guinevere had been right. The attentions of the leech seemed to have had no effect at all, apart from weakening him even further.

Hugh slammed the fist of one hand into the palm of the other, struggling with his terror. He had the absolute sense that his son was dying before his eyes. Robin coughed weakly, his eyelids fluttered, and for a second he stared up at Hugh without awareness. His lips were dry and cracked, his skin lifeless.

The conviction and the compulsion came out of nowhere. He had to get the boy out of this house. There was a malevolence, an evil in the very air. Hugh was not a man given to such fancies. He had no time for curses, for the evil eye, for talk of witchcraft. But he acted now under the spur of something that had no root in rational thought. Some*one*, some*thing*, was killing his son and he had to get him as far from this house as he could.

He bent over Robin, wrapping him securely in the blankets and covers, then he picked him up. The boy was terrifyingly light, as if he'd lost all substance. Hugh almost ran with him out of the chamber and down the stairs.

Guinevere had returned to her place on the settle. She jumped up as Hugh rushed to the front door. "Hugh, what are you doing? Where are you taking Robin?" She stepped towards him, her hand outstretched.

"I'm taking him away," he said, turning at the door, the boy held tight in his arms. "This is not a healthy place for him to be."

Guinevere paled as she met his gaze. There was a wildness to his eyes that she had never seen before. And there was something else . . . something unbelievable. There was accusation. Her hand dropped to her side. "What do you mean?"

He couldn't say the words, couldn't speak his suspicions. He had no grounds, only this deep certainty that some evil was at work on his son. And Guinevere had a motive for that evil. "I'm not sure what I mean," he said and left the house.

Guinevere stood still in the hall, her hand at her throat. It wasn't possible that he held her to blame for Robin's illness. *It wasn't possible.* He might still harbor doubts about her innocence in Stephen's death, but never, not in the wildest flights of nightmare, could he imagine she would harm Robin. She was a mother. He could not believe such a thing of her.

And yet she knew that when he'd looked at her with such wild eyes that that was what he believed.

She felt sick and faint. She passed a hand over her brow, feeling it clammy. How could she live with a man who could for one instant believe her capable of such a monstrous thing? How could she share his bed, bear his child?

Slowly she passed a hand over her stomacher. Slowly she sat down again, resting her head once more on the high back of the settle. She had always known well before the signs were clear when she had conceived. The knowledge that she now carried Hugh's child had been on the periphery of her awareness for several days. She hadn't examined the knowledge, had let it lie until she could be absolutely certain. Certain enough, at least, to make the news public. It would be another week before she could do that. Until then the secret that had given her so much joy belonged only to her.

Perhaps Hugh had not thought that monstrous thing. She could have mistaken his meaning. He was terrified for Robin, desperate. He hadn't known what he was saying, what he might have been implying. Of course that was it. When Robin was out of danger they would talk again.

Unconsciously she pressed her fingers to her mouth. Robin *must* get better. It was unthinkable that he wouldn't. But where was Hugh taking the boy? It was madness to rush out into the cold with him, sick as he was. But she could not have stopped him. She felt his eyes on her again. Accusing. Condemning.

Hugh laid a small heap of silver coins on the table in the low-ceilinged, dimly lit house place of the small cottage on Ludgate Hill. "There's coin, Martha, for the leech, the apothecary, for whatever Robin needs." He twisted his large square hands together as he looked across the room to the straw pallet where his son lay and asked painfully, "Will he die?"

The old woman who was bending over the pallet straightened stiffly, one hand at her back. "I cannot say, m'lord. He looks bad. But if, as you say, there was an evil influence in the 'ouse, then, God willing, ye've moved him in time."

She crossed herself. "Poor mite. Such a roarin', healthy babe 'e was when I delivered 'im. An' his sainted mother, God rest 'er soul. Never a sound out of 'er. Two days she labored, an' never made a sound. Such a sweet soul she was." She crossed herself again.

Hugh swallowed. The lump in his chest, now in his throat, was painful. He was close to tears, closer than he'd been since Sarah's death, and he clung to what fortitude he could muster. Martha was his only hope. Only Robin knew her, knew that Hugh paid her a tiny pension, all he could afford, in recognition of her service as Sarah's maid and the midwife who had brought Robin into the world. No one else knew of this humble cottage. No one would find Robin here.

Robin coughed, feebly but for an eternity it seemed to his father. The sweat of fear dampened Hugh's brow. Martha stirred something in a cup and bent once more over the pallet. She raised the boy and put the cup to his lips.

"Get you 'ome, m'lord. There's little ye can do 'ere. Come back this evenin' an' we'll see."

"I can't leave him."

"I work best alone."

Hugh hesitated, then approached the pallet. He bent and kissed Robin's burning brow, smoothed the lank hair. He ached with a desperate helplessness that he had never known. And in the far reaches of his mind came the recognition that Guinevere must have felt this same hideous powerlessness to help her own children during the last dreadful months as she struggled in a net that he had cast for her.

What did it mean to her, knowing that he now knew exactly how that felt?

"Get you 'ome," Martha repeated softly. "Come back this evenin'. We'll know better then."

Hugh still hesitated, then with a helpless little gesture he opened the door and left the single-roomed cottage. He mounted his horse tethered at the gate and turned the charger down the hill leaving the church of St. Paul's behind him.

The horse skittered uncertainly and uncharacteristically on the rutted lane. Hugh drew the rein tighter and felt his saddle slip slightly. He reined in the horse and dismounted. The girth had worked itself loose and it had unsettled the horse. Hugh tightened the strap, running a finger between it and the animal's belly to satisfy himself that it was once more snug. He frowned, feeling a small nick on one side of the leather. Someone in the stables was not keeping a close eye on the tack.

That was Robin's task, of course. The care of his father's equipment in particular fell to the son's hand. Hugh's nostrils flared as he struggled with the upsurge of fearful despair. He remounted, his mouth set in a grim line, and turned his horse towards Holborn once more.

He had no wish to go home, no wish to see Guinevere, no wish to sit beside her at the dinner table, break bread with her, drink with her. He didn't think he would be able to keep his suspicion to himself. But somehow he must. He had to watch her. If she was plotting Robin's death, she would also be plotting his own.

He rode into the stable yard and Tyler came running from the stables to take his horse. " 'Ow's the lad, m'lord?" he asked with concern as Hugh dismounted. "I've one jest the same age at 'ome."

Tyler had saddled Hugh's horse earlier and had held Robin while his father had mounted. The man's sympathy had been open and genuine as he'd handed the sick child up to Lord Hugh.

"He's in good hands, thank you," Hugh replied, regarding the man thoughtfully. Tyler, it seemed, was certainly a man of all work as Guinevere had said. Kitchens, stables, domestic quarters. He was everywhere, rapidly making himself indispensable.

"Check that girth, will you?" Hugh said. "It slipped while I was riding home. The leather seems to have a slight nick at one side."

"Aye, m'lord. I'll check it as soon as I've unsaddled 'im."

Hugh nodded and strode back to the house.

Tyler watched him for a minute, his eyes narrowed. He'd lost the boy. Unless Lord Hugh had removed him from the bedchamber too late. It was possible, probable even. But he'd have to make sure. For the moment he'd concentrate his efforts on the father.

Jack Stedman accosted Hugh as he entered the house through the back door. "A word, m'lord?"

"What is it, Jack?" Hugh drew off his gloves.

"Well, it's jest that Will Malfrey's disappeared, sir. I left 'im at Privy Seal's wicket all night an' sent fer 'im to come 'ome just after dawn. But 'e wasn't there."

Hugh frowned. "You left him there all night even though I decided there was no point in watching?"

" 'Twas a matter of discipline, m'lord."

"Ah." Hugh would not question Jack's dealings with the men. "Could he have left of his own accord?"

Jack shook his head. "Unlikely. He's a good man, jest a bit awkward like once in a while. But he'd never leave 'is post, I'd lay any odds."

"Could he have met with an accident?"

"Mebbe, but, I don't know, sir." Jack shook his head again. " 'E's 'andy with a sword an' with 'is fists. 'Twould take a good few to get the better of 'im, I would 'ave said. But we've been searchin' the alleys around."

"So where d'you think he is?" Hugh guessed that Jack had his own opinion.

"That I can't rightly say, sir. But if 'e 'appened on our man, sir, like as not, 'e'd go after 'im."

Hugh slapped his gloves into the palm of one hand. "If that's the case he'll be back."

"Aye, sir."

"Then let's wait and see."

"Aye, sir."

Hugh gave him a nod and strode off to the hall. Jack's explanation struck him as odd. Privy Seal's guests were unlikely to roam the streets before dawn.

"Where's Robin, sir? Is he going to get better?" Pippa rushed upon Hugh as he entered the hall. "Where did you take him?"

Hugh had to force the smile that normally came so naturally around the child. "He's going to get better," he said firmly.

"Where is he, Lord Hugh?" Pen's softer voice joined her sister's clamor.

Hugh glanced across the girl's head to where Guinevere was standing beside the dinner table, her eyes on him, questioning and anxious.

He forced another smile. "He's with an old friend," he said. "Someone skilled at nursing. Let's dine. It grows late and I've business to attend to this afternoon."

They sat down, the household filing in to take their own places. The atmosphere was subdued, Robin's absence keenly felt. Covertly Hugh watched Guinevere. He told himself that to suspect her of trying to poison him at his own dinner table was absurd. He was allowing his fearful fancies to get the better of him. There was no way that at a crowded table she could contaminate food or drink of which he alone would partake. But he was wary nevertheless, choosing only the dishes she herself selected.

Guinevere had no appetite. The man beside her was once more the harsh, judgmental, suspicious man she'd first met. There was no humor, no warmth, none of the passion for her that usually ran so close to the surface. Even in anger, that passionate desire had been obvious. But now it was doused, in its place something she could only describe as revulsion. And it was unendurable. It was unbelievable and unendurable and slowly her dismay faded to be replaced with pure anger.

"We must talk," she said abruptly. "After dinner."

"If you wish," he responded distantly. "I can spare a few minutes."

She said nothing more to him, confining her conversation to the girls and the magister, who did his best to fill the silences with intense scholarly discussion. Hugh said nothing to anyone, but his preoccupation was easily explained as worry over Robin.

As soon as the meal was over, Guinevere rose from the table. "Magister Howard, would it please you to take the girls out for a walk this afternoon? It's a pleasant afternoon and there's much they should learn about the city and its history."

"They need an escort," Hugh said sharply. "An old man and two small girls wandering alone around the city! Don't be absurd . . . Jack?" He beckoned to Jack Stedman who was about to leave the table.

"Aye, sir." Jack came over immediately.

"Arrange for three men to accompany Magister Howard and Lady Guinevere's daughters this afternoon. They wish to go for a walk."

Jack nodded and strode off. Pippa regarded Hugh with wide eyes. "You're cross," she stated. "Why are you cross, Lord Hugh?"

"He's not cross," Pen told her. "Lord Hugh's worried about Robin."

"Yes, Pen," Hugh said in slightly softened tones. "I'm not cross with anyone, Pippa." He smiled at the child and chucked her beneath the chin. "Enjoy your walk."

Pen hesitated, her sensitive gaze doubtful, questioning, as if she saw the effort it cost him to smile, to sound like himself once more. She glanced at her mother who said softly, "Go and fetch your cloaks. Don't keep the magister waiting."

Pen grasped her sister's sleeve and pulled her away to the stairs.

Hugh turned to Guinevere. "You wished to talk with me, madam." His voice was expressionless, his eyes unreadable.

"Let us go abovestairs," she said tautly. "This business is best conducted in privacy." She turned to follow her daughters up the stairs, her anger visible in every line of her erect body.

She entered their bedchamber leaving the door open behind her so that he could follow her in. He entered and closed the door firmly.

"Well?"

"What do you mean, *well*?" she demanded, spinning to face him. She stood in the window embrasure, her back to the light, her hands as always clasped quietly against her skirts. The light behind her bouncing off her white silk hood created a golden halo. "What is going on here, Hugh?"

He rubbed his face with his hands, hard and fast, trying to decide how to respond. He couldn't voice his suspicions. Not without proof. He couldn't begin to find the words to accuse this woman. Despite his conviction, he couldn't speak the words. "I'm concerned for Robin. That's all."

"Oh, yes, I understand that," she said, her voice suddenly very soft but the anger still there, still dangerous. "But why am I to be attacked, Hugh? Why do you look at me in such fashion?"

"What fashion?" He tried to sound normal, reasonable.

"You know. What is it that you suspect?" When he said nothing, she repeated, "What is it that you suspect, my lord? Oh, come now, surely you have the courage to confront me!" She gave a short bitter laugh. "Say it, Hugh. *Say it.*"

"Say what? There is nothing to say." He turned from her, pushing a slipping log back into the fireplace with the toe of his boot. "My son is at death's door. What else is there to say?"

"That you suspect me of having some hand in his illness," she threw at him. "I killed my husbands, or one of them, at least. Of that you're convinced. So why wouldn't I continue the pattern? If I want my lands back, I have to get rid of Robin and then you. Or you first. It matters little." Her voice dripped contempt. "I cannot live with a man who could believe such a thing of me."

"I do not believe it," he stated. "You're talking arrant nonsense, Guinevere. I am at my wit's end about Robin. Of course I'm not behaving in my usual fashion. Now, if we've finished with this nonsense, I am going back to my son." He stalked to the door.

"If you don't believe it, why won't you let me nurse him? Why would you remove him from this house?"

He stood with his hand on the latch. "I don't know. I'm not myself. I'm not capable of rational thought at present. I would have hoped for some understanding from you." He opened the door and left.

Guinevere sat down on the window seat. He had denied his suspicions, but what else had she expected? He wouldn't admit to something so monstrous, not without proof. Was he trying to throw her off guard while he found such proof?

Hugh entered the stable yard shouting for his horse. Tyler brought the charger at a run. "Ye want I should accompany ye, m'lord? 'Old the 'orse fer ye. Walk 'im while ye goes about yer business."

Hugh hesitated, absently checking the animal's girth. It seemed snug, the leather intact. He didn't really like to leave his horse unattended in the lane for any length of time and he didn't want to have to hurry over his visit this afternoon. Someone to keep an eye on his horse while he was with Martha and Robin would be useful. He was reluctant to reveal Robin's whereabouts, even to a servant, but he could leave Tyler and the horses outside the Bull Tavern, a few lanes away from the cottage.

"Don't you have other tasks to perform?" He swung into the saddle.

"No, I'm off fer a couple of hours, m'lord. I'd be 'appy to 'elp out." Tyler touched his forelock with an ingratiating smile.

"Very well." Hugh controlled his prancing charger. "Fetch a horse then."

Tyler reappeared within minutes, leading a dun pony. He mounted somewhat awkwardly and they rode out of the yard, Tyler's pony keeping a discreet distance behind the charger.

Hugh rode fast, his anxiety making his heart race. What would he find? Had Robin worsened in the last few hours? He found he couldn't think about his conversation, if that was what it could be called, with Guinevere. He didn't know if his denial had convinced her, he suspected not, but until he had proof he couldn't confront her. Once Robin was out of the woods he would match plots with plots. But until then, he could think of nothing but his son.

Outside the Bull he dismounted and waited for Tyler to catch up with him. "I don't know how long I'll be. Take ale if you wish, but walk him every hour. I'll find you here."

"Aye, m'lord." Tyler took the charger's reins and tethered him with his own horse to the hitching post beside the ale bench. Lord Hugh set off with his long loping stride and once he had disappeared around the corner, Tyler followed at a run. He stalked his quarry, ducking into doorways, waiting at corners, until Hugh turned up the narrow pathway of a small cottage.

Then Tyler returned to the horses and the ale bench.

Hugh entered Martha's cottage, ducking beneath the low lintel, blinking as his eyes adjusted to the dim light. "How is he?" His voice rasped, harsh with fear.

" 'Oldin' steady, m'lord," Martha said from the low stool beside the cot. "If 'e gets no worse, we can start to 'ope."

Hugh felt a rush of relief. He strode to the pallet, bending over Robin. The boy was still hot, his eyes closed, his pulse rapid, but there was something about him that gave hope. He seemed less in pain, no longer struggling for breath. "How's the cough?"

"A bit better. Whatever the lad was breathin' he isn't breathin' it anymore. Not in 'ere."

"What do you mean?" Hugh straightened, staring at the old woman.

She shrugged. "I'd say the boy was breathin' summat unhealthful," she said. "I'd say ye did well to get 'im out o' the 'ouse."

"Poison?"

She shrugged again. " 'Tis not fer me to say, sir."

"No," he agreed, turning his gaze back to his son. "No. Not for you to say."

26.

Tyler walked the horses every hour as instructed. He guessed that the boy was in the cottage. If so it would make his task all the speedier. If matters went according to plan, he'd dispose of both of his quarry by soon after sunset. On his last walk with the horses, he stopped them in a narrow dark lane formed by the high brick walls of two large properties. The sun rarely penetrated this muddy and rank space and Lord Hugh's horse whistled through his nostrils and pawed the wet ground uneasily.

"Steady now," Tyler murmured, laying a hand on the animal's neck in brief reassurance. He leaned under the horse's belly and slid a finger beneath the girth, lifting it away from the hard round swell of flesh, feeling for the perfect spot at which a swift, deft slice would cut the girth two thirds through. He would need to do it without looking since he couldn't cut the strap until Lord Hugh was mounted. If it was weakened it would slip sideways as soon as the man pulled himself up.

His original plan had been to weaken the girth over a period of days until it finally gave way, preferably when he was nowhere in the vicinity. Once Lord Hugh was unhorsed there would be Tyler's own hired hands to finish the task off, but no suspicion would rest upon the indispensable servant. Unfortunately Lord Hugh had discovered the original cut. Tyler had a dislike of sudden action, mistakes were made in haste. But in this instance, he had no time for devious approaches.

He straightened. Again he stroked the animal's neck for a minute or two before he took from his pocket a tiny stone, its edges wickedly sharpened. Patting the charger's flank he bent and lifted his left rear hoof. He pushed the stone beneath the iron shoe where it would dig into the soft pad of flesh, then he set the hoof back on the mud.

"Come on, then, laddie," he exhorted cheerily, taking the reins. "Let's see 'ow this feels." He led both horses out of the narrow alley and back into the wider thoroughfare.

He tethered them once again at the Bull and then retraced his steps to the lane where he'd seen Lord Hugh enter the cottage. He stood at the corner of the lane in the shadow of a doorway and scrutinized the small building. Just a ground floor, no dormers in the front, low-pitched thatched roof. A tiny front garden given over to herbs, a few vegetables, an apple tree. Narrow front door, two shuttered windows on either side. Smoke curling from a single chimney. The wall of the cottage next door on the right abutted this one, but a narrow path led around the side between it and its left-hand neighbor. There would be something at the back. Chickens probably. A rooster. Noisy birds.

No, an approach would be best made directly through the front door. He would create a diversion that would cause the occupant to open the door. He would be positioned behind it. Tyler fingered the garrote he carried in his pocket. A silent killer. It would take care quietly of whoever came to the door. No one would be aware of what was happening. He would push the lifeless body inside and deal with the boy. Even if he was recovering, the lad would be weak, bedridden. It would be over in a heartbeat with no sound and no one the wiser. He would make his escape through the rear. Again it was all a little precipitate for Tyler's taste, but the job now needed to reach a swift conclusion.

He smiled and picked a leaf from the next-door privet hedge, crumbling it between his fingers, inhaling its scent.

The cottage door opened and Lord Hugh appeared. He turned to speak to someone inside before coming down the path.

Tyler ran back to the Bull. He sat down on the ale bench, stretching his legs with every appearance of taking his ease, and looked at Lord

Hugh's horse dispassionately. The stone would start to irritate under his rider's weight within five minutes. Five minutes would take them to the bottom of Ludgate Hill. At that time of day there would be crowds from the dispersing street markets, raucous tavern-goers, boatmen from the river. The city gates would be closing for curfew. A bolting horse in a dark alley . . .

Lord Hugh came around the corner. He raised an acknowledging hand to Tyler. His posture, his whole demeanor, lacked the heaviness of before, Tyler thought. The boy must be on the mend.

He rose from the ale bench and hurried to untie the horses as Hugh reached them. "All well, m'lord?"

But the glance Tyler received in response, distant, deeply troubled, made nonsense of his earlier assumption. "All well, m'lord?" he repeated with careful hesitation.

Hugh's gaze focused. "Yes," he said brusquely. "Come, it grows late." He swung onto the charger with one easy movement.

"A moment, sir." Tyler bent to the stirrup, his knife concealed in the palm of his hand. "The leather's twisted."

Hugh lifted his foot from the stirrup while Tyler adjusted it. He paid no attention to the man, barely noticed his actions. He needed to get home. And yet home was the last place he wanted to be.

They rode down Ludgate Hill. Hugh was deep in thought. Robin was getting better. He knew instinctively that his son would now live. Out of the poisonous atmosphere of the house at Holborn, Robin was recovering. But now Hugh faced the unthinkable. His marriage was over. Until Guinevere was out of his house, Hugh could not think of bringing Robin home. He still had no definitive proof of her hand in his son's poisoning, but he didn't need it. No one else had a motive for destroying Robin. History and the circumstances were too heavily weighted against her. He had to be rid of her. But how?

He could denounce her to Privy Seal. Cromwell would delight in having her once more in his power. He would have her executed, but he would also ensure that the marriage settlements were void. Privy Seal's plan all along had been that Guinevere should forfeit her estates to the crown. Hugh would receive some reward that would benefit Robin but would leave Hugh himself little better off than before.

Even as the thought of a woman who could plot the death of an innocent child filled him with revulsion; even though he felt what could only be called loathing for the woman who was now his wife, Hugh did not want her death. It would do him no good and he could not endure to have her motherless children on his conscience. He would take care of his wife himself. He would ensure that she could harm no one again. He would banish her. Send her back to Derbyshire. She could do him and his son no harm from there. He would keep her in virtual imprisonment with a guard of his own men.

What possible alternative was there?

His horse stumbled and he pulled him up with more roughness than the animal was accustomed to. The cobbles were slimy with refuse. The horse whinnied and tossed his head. Hugh stared in front of him, unaware of the folk swarming around them.

"We'll lose the crowd if we go thisaway, m'lord."

Tyler's insistent voice pierced Hugh's thoughts. "What?" His eyes followed the direction of Tyler's whip, pointing into a lane to their left. "Oh, yes. These damnable crowds." He turned his horse towards the narrow entrance to the alley.

Tyler's pony followed. Hugh's charger stumbled again, whinnied, lifting his hurt hoof. Tyler brought his crop down over the animal's crupper. The charger reared, the cut girth gave way, and the saddle slipped sideways. Hugh plunged to the ground, one foot still caught in the stirrup. The charger pranced on three legs, his hooves inches from his rider's head.

Hugh twisted, dragged his imprisoned foot free, pulling the saddle down with him, just as the hurt and outraged animal brought his front hooves crashing to the muddy ground of the alley, trampling Hugh's outstretched hand.

Hugh gave a cry of pain. In the same moment Tyler leaped from his horse, his knife in one hand, his whip in the other. He slashed at the horse again and the high-strung animal reared and crashed around the narrow alley in anger and confusion.

Hugh knew he had to get to his feet, away from the plunging hooves. His hand was useless; it was his knife hand. He rolled sideways, curled his body, and sprang to his feet almost in the same movement. Tyler leaped for him, his knife poised to cut deep into Hugh's chest. Hugh kicked out, caught the man in the groin. Tyler yelled in pain but kept coming. The knife came down. Hugh twisted and it slashed across his forearm.

Hugh couldn't free his sword from the scabbard on his left side. His right hand was useless and the sword was too heavy and cumbersome to drag out and up with his left hand. He ducked as Tyler came at him again and with a silent prayer dived beneath the charger's belly. One hoof caught him a glancing blow on his shoulder but then he was out the other side and the wildly thrashing animal lay between him and Tyler.

He hurled himself up onto the animal's bare back. Then he turned him in the narrow alley and set him to ride at Tyler. The man went down with a scream beneath the frantic horse's hooves. The charger trampled him, nostrils wide and flaring, foam flecking his mouth, his teeth bared. Hugh let him have his head.

When Tyler's screams had ceased Hugh pulled the horse around. The animal still reared, maddened by the stone in his hoof, but Hugh drove him down the alley, leaving the broken body behind in the mud. They emerged into a square, a community well in its midst. Skinny, dirty children with wooden pails were gathered around the well. They stared with blank indifference at the man on his foam-flecked sweating horse.

Hugh drew rein and leaned over the animal's neck speaking softly to him, gentling him with a stroking hand, and eventually the charger quietened down enough for Hugh to risk dismounting. Still talking to the animal he lifted the hoof and found the stone. He rested the hoof on his upraised knee, supporting it gingerly with his trampled hand, and pried the stone loose from the reddened, swollen pad of flesh with the point of his dagger, then he took the reins in his good hand and walked the limping horse out of the square.

Tyler. Now it was all clear. Guinevere had hired Tyler. Guinevere and Crowder. Tyler had been roaming the upper floor of the house. Robin had been inhaling poison. Tyler had been filling oil lamps. Tyler had had charge of Hugh's horse.

A deep rage swelled within Hugh. He pushed back the torn sleeves of his gown and the doublet beneath to examine the knife cut. It was long but seemed superficial, the blood congealing along its length. But the knife could have been poisoned. It would be a trick right up Tyler's alley. His right hand hurt fiercely and setting his teeth he explored the damage with his good hand. The skin was purpling and swollen but he didn't think any bones were broken although the pain as he prodded drained the color from his cheeks and brought a sweat to his brow. His shoulder throbbed where the horse's hoof had caught it.

His anger grew until it blocked all thought. He had loved her. She had bewitched him. Cast her lures, spun her web, caught him. And then she had set out to destroy him as she had destroyed every other man she had snared in the silken strands of her spinning.

He walked home in a fog of fury and cold despair. He left the horse in the stable with orders for the injured hoof to be poulticed, and strode into the house.

Guinevere was in the kitchen talking with Crowder as Hugh entered from the stables. She looked up quickly and then paled as she saw his face. "What has happened? Is it Robin?"

"Come with me," he said, barely moving his lips. He took her wrist and she saw the cut on his arm. Her gaze traveled to his mangled hand, which he held supported in the opening of his doublet.

"Good God, Hugh! What has happened?" she whispered in horror, filled with a dreadful foreboding.

"Come with me," he repeated in the same voice, his fingers tightening painfully around her wrist.

She said nothing further but went with him out of the kitchen, up the back staircase, into the quiet of their bedchamber. He dropped her wrist as if it was something distasteful and stepped away from her, moving to the far side of the room.

"Is it Robin?" she asked again, her voice sounding clogged.

"Until I removed him from this house, Robin was being poisoned," he said clearly. "By your creature."

She shook her head. "No . . . no, what are you saying? What creature?"

"Tyler!" he spat at her. "Tyler. The man *you* hired, the murderer you brought into my household! The man who just narrowly missed killing me."

"Tyler?" Guinevere shook her head again, her eyes wide with fearful confusion. "I don't know what you're talking about, Hugh."

He took a step towards her and she flinched at the savage rage in his eyes. "Save your breath, madam! I know you. At last I truly know you. Robin will live and so, by God, will I." He spun from her, took up a candle and went to the fire. He thrust the candle into the flames and the wick caught with a yellow flare. He took the flagon from the side table, pulled the stopper out with his teeth, and poured into the cut on his arm.

"Here. Burn the cut!" He shoved the lighted candle at her. "For all I know your creature's knife point was poisoned. Burn it." He pushed his soaked arm into her face.

"Hugh, stop it!" she cried. "You don't know what you're saying."

"On God's blood, I do. I *know* you for what you are. *Burn it clean!*"

Slowly Guinevere took the candle. He was in the grip of some madness; he had to be humored. "Let me wash it first," she said.

"No, damn you! Cauterize it. *Now!*"

"Very well. Put your arm on the table."

He did so and she held the candle flame to the cut, running the flame the length of the wound. The liquor ignited. The hairs on his arm burned, his flesh burned, the smell filled the room. His face grew whiter, his jaw was locked, his mouth so thin it was barely visible, but his arm stayed steady. Guinevere didn't look at him, didn't flinch from the task. Grimly she continued until the blue flame of the alcohol had died down around the blackened cut.

"There," she said. "Does that satisfy you?"

His nostrils flared, a vein throbbed in his temple, the skin around his mouth was white. He seized a linen napkin from the washstand and wrapped it around his burned arm, clumsily using his teeth and his mangled hand to tie it.

Guinevere made no attempt to help him. She found she didn't dare try to approach him. "What happened to your hand?" she asked, trying to keep her fear from her voice, trying to sound calm, composed, reassuring, as if she was not terrified of this mad stranger.

Hugh shot her a look of utter contempt and did not reply.

She swallowed, took a breath. "Let me put some salve on it and then bind it for you."

"I don't want you anywhere near me!" he declared. "Never again."

She looked at him bleakly. It was madness for him to believe what he did. She spoke slowly, clearly, setting out the facts so that there should be no possibility of error. "You think I tried to poison Robin? You think I set Tyler to kill you?" Surely he would see the absurdity of it now. When it was put so plainly he must see that it could not possibly be true. Surely he would see that his own desperate fear for his son had overset his reason.

He looked at her again with utter contempt. "Three attempts have been made on my life since I was fool enough to marry you."

Despair washed through her. How could she convince him? What possible words were there? Her voice shook. "But I love you, Hugh."

He raised both hands, pushing against the air as if to keep her from him. "You lie! But God help me, I loved *you*! Now, get out of my life! I never want to lay eyes upon you again. I want you out of this house and on the road back to Derbyshire by dawn tomorrow."

And there it was. In the face of that brutal conviction, the savage certainty in his eyes, she had to accept that he had never truly believed in her innocence. He had allowed love, lust, whatever he chose to call it, to block out his conviction of her guilt in Stephen's death.

She tried once more although she knew it would do no good. She spoke as calmly as she could. "You said it was too late in the year to make such a journey, Hugh." She stood with her hand at her throat. Her world had spun out of control; the man she loved had become a vicious, blind stranger. She had always known he had a rigid, harsh side to him, but until now she could never have believed him capable of this.

"You will go with all speed. Your daughters will ride pillion with my men so they will not need to rest so much. Without rest days, there's no reason why you should not reach your destination by the beginning of December, before the first snowfall. This time there'll be no carts laden with luxuries to hold you up. If your servants go with you, they'll ride at the pace set by my men who'll escort you and then remain at Mallory Hall to guard you."

"As jailers?" she whispered, the full horror dawning.

"If you wish to call them that," he said coldly. "You'll not leave Mallory Hall without my permission."

"My children?" Her hand touched her belly in an unconscious gesture. "Are they too to be prisoners?"

"If they go with you, they will share the conditions under which you will live. If you wish to spare them that, or the dangers and discomforts of the journey, they may remain with me. I do not hold them responsible for their mother's evil."

Guinevere turned away from him so that he would not see the despair and horror in her eyes. There was nothing she could do or say to change anything. He had convicted her and condemned her. And now she thought that even if she could convince him of her innocence she could no longer live with a man who could believe her capable of such monstrous deeds.

"My children come with me," she stated, adding sotto voce, "*All* my children."

She stood with her back to him, as erect and graceful as ever, her head held high, her shoulders straight, her hands clasped quietly in front of her. *Such grace, such elegance, such beauty. A shell,* he thought. An exquisite shell concealing such brazen greed, such a barren soul.

He commanded harshly, "You will be ready to leave at first light. When I return to the house in the morning, you will not be here." He left the chamber, closing the door behind him with a definitive click.

Guinevere remained standing in the middle of the chamber, her hand still unconsciously resting on her belly. She had felt despair in the last months since Hugh of Beaucaire had ridden into her life, but now she understood that she had not known what true despair was. Now she was a black void, for the moment incapable of feeling, of action. She was bereft, hopeless, and helpless.

She didn't know how long she stood there, unaware of the lengthening shadows. Finally she heard her children's bright, inquiring voices outside the chamber. They were calling her, knocking on the door, and she came back to hard reality. Once again her children's needs made her strong. She must protect them as she had always done.

She opened the door to them.

"We've been knocking for ages, Mama," Pippa said. "Didn't you hear us?"

"No, I'm sorry, sweeting, I was deep in thought," she said, lightly pulling the child's braid. "We have to move out of the house rather suddenly. Will you run and ask Crowder and Tilly to come to me?"

"But why must we move out, Mama?" demanded Pippa. "I thought we were to stay here for Christmas and Twelfth Night."

"Is it because of Robin?" Pen asked, her hazel eyes sharply questioning.

"Partly," her mother said, improvising. "Lord Hugh and I decided that it would be best for us to move. We don't want you to catch Robin's illness. We think it's better that we should leave this house in case there's something unhealthful in the air."

"Like the plague?" Pippa's hazel eyes widened.

"I doubt that," said Guinevere gravely. "Robin is on the mend, but until we know what caused his illness, it's safer to stay somewhere else."

"I'll go and tell Crowder," Pippa said excitedly. "I know he'll be glad. I heard him telling Greene that he thought working with Master Milton was a pesky business. And Greene said he thought it must be. Pen can fetch Tilly." She ran to the door.

"Is everything going to be all right, Mama?" asked her more perceptive sister with a worried frown. "Is Robin truly getting better?"

"Yes, he is, and yes, everything's going to be all right."

"But is Lord Hugh coming with us?" Pen pressed.

"No," her mother said. "He'll stay with Robin."

"But you're his wife. Shouldn't you stay with him?"

"These are unusual circumstances," Guinevere said, forcing a smile. "Now, run and ask Tilly to come to me. We must talk about what we're going to take with us. We have to pack lightly because we must make all speed to leave."

Pen hesitated, frowning at her mother as if she had some question. "Go and fetch Tilly, Pen," Guinevere repeated calmly.

Pen's frown didn't lift but she left on her errand and Guinevere went to the dresser where lay her jewel box, her ring tree. She was thinking with cold clarity now. She was not going to go meekly into a life of exile and imprisonment. She would leave Hugh. But she would not subject herself or her daughters to the miseries of the kind of journey he had decreed. They would never understand the reasons for it.

She would need money to maintain herself. She no longer had access to the income from her estates, but he couldn't prevent her from taking her jewels. They constituted a small fortune. Crowder would take charge of selling them, or pawning them. In addition she had some ready money left over from what she'd brought with her on the journey to

London. Her jaw tightened. She would be far from penniless and Hugh of Beaucaire would learn that while he could destroy her soul, her happiness, he couldn't take her independence from her.

"What's all this then, chuck?" Tilly spoke from the door as she bustled in. "Pen says we're to leave 'ere."

Crowder came in on her heels looking very grave. Pippa pranced behind him.

"Yes, within the hour. If it can be arranged." Guinevere turned from the dresser, a sapphire necklace running through her fingers. She saw Pippa and said more brusquely than she'd intended, "Pippa, I didn't ask you to come back with Crowder. Go to your chamber and decide what you wish to take with you."

"I only wanted to know where we're going."

"You'll know when I'm ready to tell you." It was not a tone to invite argument and Pippa went off looking hurt.

Guinevere tried to smile but her lip trembled and tears stood out in her eyes.

"Ah, chuck. What is it? What's 'appened?" Tilly flew to her, embracing her. "Tell Tilly, now." She patted her back as she had done when Guinevere was a child. Crowder stood to one side, anger flaring in his eyes as Guinevere unburdened herself to the people who had always stood her friends, served her without question, stood by her, defended her.

"Well, I never heard such lunatic nonsense!" Tilly cried. "I'll soon put him right. Just you wait and see, chuck."

Guinevere dashed the tears from her eyes, smiling despite herself. "No, Tilly, that's not the way I want to deal with this. We will leave here, but of our own accord."

She turned to Crowder, who was pale with anger. "Crowder, I think we must stay in London for the moment until I decide exactly how to deal with the situation. Can you think of lodgings anywhere that would be suitable? Rooms in a tavern, or private house?"

"You'd not stay in a tavern, chuck!" Tilly exclaimed, flinging up her hands in horror. "Not with the lassies. The Lord only knows what they'd see. That Pippa would be up to all sorts."

"I don't believe that will be necessary, Mistress Tilly," Crowder put in. "The cook has a sister who runs a lodging house in Moorfields. 'Tis out of the city a bit, but nice and quiet. A very respectable kind of person, he assures me. He was telling me she's just lost her lodgers and is at her wit's end to make ends meet."

"Will it house all of us?"

"I believe so, m'lady. Should I go straightway and see about arranging matters?"

"Yes, if you would. I wish us to be out of here within two hours at the latest. We'll take only the barest necessities. Clothes and bed linen for the most part. Once I've decided what we'll do permanently, then we'll see about setting up our household again." She thought of her books and then resolutely put them from her mind. There was no time now to crate them.

She handed Crowder a leather pouch. "We'll take the lodgings for a month to start with, Crowder. I can't see any farther at the moment."

"Aye, madam." He took the pouch, coins clinking as he slipped it into his pocket. "I'll be back within the hour." He hurried away, outrage in every dignified line of his lean frame.

"Ay! Ay! Ay!" Tilly exclaimed. "What a thing! My poor babe." She flung her arms around Guinevere. "For two pins, I'd cut 'is black heart out. To believe such a thing of my nurseling!"

For a minute Guinevere allowed herself to be comforted with Tilly's soft endearments. She could not carry alone this confusing paradox of despair and fury that made her long to be rid of all memory of Hugh even as her heart yearned for his love, his smile, the tenderness of his touch, the savage passion of his lust.

How could she live without him?

But she could not live with him. So she would as always be responsible for herself and for those who depended upon her. She would not hide from him. She would make no attempt to conceal her whereabouts as if she was somehow afraid of him. As her husband, he could object to her independence, but he would have to use main force to wrest it from her, and that, Guinevere knew, Hugh would never do. Or at least she thought she knew. Before today, she would have been certain of it. But now she'd seen a side of him that threw all preconceptions into doubt. Well, she would cross that bridge when she came to it.

"There, there, Tilly," she said. "That's enough weeping now. We have much to do and I don't want the girls to guess too much, not until they have to."

"You'll not keep this long from Pen," Tilly said, going to the armoire. She began to take out gowns. "But 'tis a shameful thing. And you carryin' into the bargain."

"So you know," Guinevere said. It didn't surprise her. It was the sort of thing Tilly would know.

"Aye, o' course I know," Tilly said with a hint of scorn. "What d'ye take me for?"

Guinevere didn't answer the rhetorical question. She began to sort through her jewels.

27.

Jack Stedman set his ale pot down on the stained planking of the table in the Dog and Duck and wiped froth from his moustache with the back of his hand, his eyes never leaving Will Malfrey's countenance as he listened to the other man's tale.

It had taken Will an hour since his return to find Jack, who was whiling away the tail end of the evening in the nearby tavern. Now Will told his story slowly and in detail. His quarry had been deposited by the barge on the water steps at Greenwich at around mid-morning. The barge had still been at the steps when Will's skiff had arrived some half an hour later.

" 'Twas one of Privy Seal's barges, sir," Will explained. "The oarsmen knew it well. Lord Cromwell keeps it at the steps for 'is own convenience."

"So our friend was a guest of Lord Cromwell," Jack mused. "An important one if 'e gets to use Privy Seal's own barge." Now he pinched his lower lip between finger and thumb.

"Well, I don't know about that, sir," Will said thoughtfully. "I spoke wi' the bargemen. Right scornful they were of 'im. 'E 'adn't given 'em a sweetener, mind you, an' that put 'em in a bad 'umor. But I got the impression 'e was more of a servant like. On orders from 'is master."

So, no guest but a servant. That was something Lord Hugh would find interesting. Jack glanced up at the smoke-blackened timbers above. "What took ye so long to get back 'ere? 'Tis past ten now an' ye say our man was dropped off at Greenwich mid-mornin'."

"Aye, but 'e didn't leave until this evenin'," Will explained. "I thought I'd do best to see what 'e was up to. 'Ang around a bit, see what else I could pick up."

"You always was an obstinate bugger, Will," Jack observed without heat. "Takin' matters into yer own 'ands. Writin' yer own orders."

"No point leavin' a job 'alf done," Will pointed out. "Anyway, I found our man in a tavern drinkin' deep. I 'ad a pot or two of ale with 'im, but powerful closemouthed 'e was."

"Privy Seal's man. More than 'is life's worth to blab," Jack declared.

"Aye, I thought so. 'E seemed scared silly, lookin' over 'is shoulder, sweatin' like a pig, jumpin' at the least sound. An' no one came any-where near 'im. Folks looked at 'im as if 'e was some kind o' river rat. Got so I felt they was lookin' at me in the same way so I left 'im to 'is drink and 'ung around outside, waitin'. Our man come out about mid-afternoon an' goes to the docks. 'E goes aboard a ship an' that's the last I seen of 'im. The ship sailed around five on the evenin' tide."

"Where to?"

"France." Will spat on the floor. "Neat little craft, fast too. One of Privy Seal's runners, they said. Goes back an' forth with 'is spies, is what I 'eard. No one wanted to talk much even though I bought a good few pots of ale."

"No one in their right mind tells Privy Seal's secrets."

"So ye'll pass it on to Lord Hugh?"

"Oh, aye. Ye did a good job, Will. 'E'll 'ave summat to say to ye, I'll be bound."

Will looked satisfied. "I'll be off to me bed, then. Bit short o' sleep I am, one way an' another," he added pointedly.

"Reckon ye can take the day off tomorrow, if'n ye fancies a visit to the 'ouse over the river." Jack grinned and laid a finger to the side of his nose.

"Mebbe I will an' mebbe I won't," Will returned with a similar grin. "I bid ye good night, sir."

"'Night, Will."

Jack sat over his tankard a while longer. Something was up in Lord

Hugh's household and Jack for once was not in his master's confidence. First Master Robin had fallen ill and Lord Hugh had rushed him from the house. The next thing, Lord Hugh, looking like something the cat had dragged in, had ordered Jack to have an escort ready and provisioned at dawn to go into Derbyshire with his lady and the little girls. There'd been no explanation either for the master's injuries or for his orders, and Lord Hugh had gone off again immediately, all bruised and battered as he was, leaving an injured horse in the stables.

Jack had chosen the escort, given his instructions, and left the bustle and chaos of the stable yard for the peace and his thoughts in the Dog and Duck, where Will had found him. And Tyler appeared to be missing now as well. Not that Jack thought much of him. Too slimy by half. Still it was a puzzle to add to all the others.

He tossed a coin on the table and stood up, adjusting the set of his sword at his hip. Lord Hugh had told him where to send a message as soon as Lady Guinevere and her escort had left but Jack reckoned he'd not be sorry to be disturbed earlier for an account of Will's day.

Jack rode through the streets to Ludgate Hill, keeping to the center of the road, his sword in his hand. At the top of the hill he came to a cluster of cottages. Lord Hugh's second-string horse was tethered to an apple tree in the small front garden of one of the cottages. Despite the late hour, lamplight showed faintly through a crack in the shutters and smoke curled from the chimney.

Jack hobbled his horse in the garden and knocked on the door with the hilt of his sword.

The bolts scraped back and the door was opened. Lord Hugh stood in the light, his sword in his hand as if he was expecting trouble.

"Jack? What the devil's amiss?"

"Summat I thought ye'd like to know straightway, sir." Jack thought he had never seen Lord Hugh look so dreadful, not even after a day on a battlefield. Heavy bags pouched beneath his black-shadowed eyes, his mouth was drawn with pain, his complexion sallow and parchmentlike.

" 'Ow's Master Robin?" Jack asked making no attempt to conceal his anxiety.

"Better, I thank you." Hugh stood back and held the door wider. "Come you in."

Jack entered the cottage. Robin was lying on a pallet in the corner, on another before the fire slept an old woman covered by a thin blanket.

Hugh sat down on the stool beside his son's pallet and gestured to Jack that he should take its pair. He returned to tending his son, bathing the sweat from the boy's brow with lavender water. "The fever's broken," he said. "He'll live, thank God."

"Thank God," echoed Jack. He looked around the small room. Despite this happy news, the atmosphere was more suited to a charnel house, he thought. Lord Hugh seemed to have shrunk, the brilliant hue of his eyes dulled. His arm and one hand were bandaged and he moved with obvious pain. But it was more than physical pain. It was a pain that seemed to come from deep within him.

"Will Malfrey came back, sir."

"Oh? What had he been up to?" Hugh sounded as if the information was of little interest.

"Seems like the man you was interested in, sir, could be one of Privy Seal's servants."

Hugh didn't seem to react for a minute, then slowly he raised his head and looked at Jack. His hand stilled on Robin's brow. "What makes Will think that?"

Jack gave him an account of Will's day. "Powerful scared 'e was," Jack said. "Will said 'e was as jumpy as a rabbit headin' fer the pot. An' folk kept away from 'im. Will didn't like the way they looked at 'im too when 'e was drinkin' with the fellow, so 'e up an' left 'im, jest watched 'im until he went on the ship."

"He's certain it was one of Privy Seal's ships?" Hugh turned back to Robin who moaned softly and tried to brush away the cloth from his brow.

"Certain as 'e could be, sir."

Hugh busied himself with Robin, lifting him to put a cup of water to his lips, wiping his mouth, smoothing the sheet.

Jack stood uncertainly, wondering if Lord Hugh had really heard him. He didn't seem to be reacting at all.

But Hugh had heard. Had heard and understood the implications. But were they significant? His mind twisted, examining, looking for flaws. Privy Seal's servants acted under the orders of only one man. The man who had accosted him at the revels hadn't seemed like a servant. But then Thomas Cromwell had servants in every walk of life. The fact that it was Privy Seal's ship didn't necessarily mean anything. Cromwell's friends, acquaintances, a guest at his revels, could have been given the freedom of one of his vessels. He could be generous when it suited him.

Was it possible that he had been wrong? That Guinevere had had nothing to do with Robin's poisoning, with the attempts upon his own life? Tyler had been her man. She and Crowder had brought him into the house.

Hope fluttered in his brain, set his heart racing. But he told himself he mustn't give in to it. It couldn't be possible that he had been wrong. So much evidence, so much history, such compelling motive was against her. He had to think clearly, not rush to believe something that he would give a year of his life if it were true.

He remembered the man who had attacked him in the lane on his wedding day. A man who talked of orders. Who was left to bleed to death in the alley because no one would go near him. If he had been one of Privy Seal's men, one of his agents who prowled and snooped for his master around that part of London, it was possible that folk would have known him and if so they wouldn't have offered a finger of help. Flail Crummock, as Cromwell was known to the general populace, was loathed as much as he was feared.

He closed his eyes, rubbed his face hard.

Jack could see a change in Lord Hugh. He seemed suddenly to sit straighter, the color in his eyes deepened, his skin seemed to fill out, to lose its waxy texture.

"They told me this afternoon that that man Tyler's gone missing, sir," Jack said into the intense silence.

"I know," Hugh said slowly, opening his eyes. "You'll find him trampled to death in a lane at the bottom of Ludgate Hill." Hugh stared at the wall. It was possible Tyler's body was still where he'd fallen. It was possible Tyler's body might hold some clue. He looked down at Robin. The boy was asleep again, his breathing peaceful and even. Hugh rose to his feet with sudden energy. "Let's see if Tyler's body can tell us anything, Jack."

"Aye, sir," Jack said, sounding as confused as he felt. "But 'ow d'ye know where 'e is?"

Hugh indicated his bandaged wounds and said shortly, "He very nearly did away with me this morning."

He went to the pallet before the fire and gently shook Martha awake. "Martha, I have business to attend to. I must leave you. Robin's asleep. I'll come back for him in the morning."

Martha sat up, immediately awake. She regarded Jack with mild curiosity and gave him a brief nod. He bowed his head in polite response.

Martha thrust aside the blanket and got to her feet somewhat stiffly. She went to Robin and examined him briefly before nodding. "Aye, he's out of the woods now, poor lad. But before he's to go 'ome, ye'd best 'ave sulphur burned in his chamber, an' get rid of 'is clothes, anythin' that's to touch 'im. I don't know what poison caused the damage, but it might linger still. A pestilence that's for sure."

Hugh nodded. "I'll fetch him later and he'll sleep in a different chamber." He flung his cloak around his shoulders. "Come, Jack."

They rode to the bottom of Ludgate Hill in silence. Jack made no attempt to ask for enlightenment. He had a feeling it wouldn't be forthcoming.

Hugh reined in his horse and looked around. He had been so abstracted that morning he had been properly aware only of the crowds and noticed little else of his surroundings. He'd simply followed Tyler's suggested way out of the throng.

There were several lanes stretching dark and dank from the bottom of the hill. "This way." Hugh gestured with his whip towards one leading off to the left that looked familiar. Tyler's body might not still be there, but who in this city would trouble to rid a lane of a dead body?

Unless, of course, he *was* one of Privy Seal's agents and his master had sent out search parties for his spy? Again his heart leaped, again he forced himself to be realistic. Even if the body was still there, it could well have been plundered and if there had been anything to tie the man to Privy Seal it would no longer be there. And without conclusive evidence could he risk believing in Guinevere's innocence?

They both drew their swords and entered the lane gingerly. It was dark and apparently deserted. A few yards in, Hugh discerned a darker shape on the ground. He pointed with his sword and then dismounted. He didn't dare to hope. And yet he was filled with it.

Jack dismounted and felt in his saddlebag for flint and tinder. As carefully as before they approached the shape. Tyler lay, his face in the mud. Jack struck a light and knelt with Hugh beside the body. It didn't look as if it had been disturbed but it was so badly trampled it was hard to tell.

"Go through his pockets," Hugh instructed, turning the man over. Gritting his teeth, he slipped his hand inside the man's bloody shirt, feeling for inner pockets, while Jack examined the outer garments.

Hugh's fingers closed over something hard beneath the lining of the doublet. "See here," he murmured, drawing a soft leather pouch from a cunningly sewn pocket. His fingers shook slightly as he loosened the strings and tipped the contents into the palm of his hand.

Jack brought the light closer to shine upon a miniature seal, the kind used by travelers . . . the kind used by spies. Hugh examined it in the light.

"Privy Seal's," he said softly, his voice flat, hiding the rush of emotion. "Tyler would have used it to identify missives that he sent to his master, and to mislead those Cromwell wished misled." He replaced the seal in the pouch, drew the strings tight, and tucked it back into the pocket in the doublet. For a minute he sat back on his heels and let the incredible joy sweep through him.

Jack rearranged the clothes, turning the body back into the mud. Instinctively they both looked around. Were they being watched? No one must know that they had identified Tyler as one of Privy Seal's men. Cromwell had his spies in every corner of the city, and that kind of knowledge brought the arrest in the night, or the knife in the back.

Jack looked curiously at Lord Hugh, squatting in the mud beside the body. He seemed mesmerized, immobile, staring down.

"Sir?" Jack said tentatively. "We should get out of here."

"Yes . . . yes, of course." Hugh stood up. What little starlight there was on this overcast night couldn't penetrate the alley. The air around him smelled of death.

But at home lay his wife. His warm, loving wife. His guiltless wife. He was so full of joy he almost shouted aloud. He couldn't wait to hold her. To pour out his sorrow for doubting her, to kiss the grief from her eyes, to repair the damage he had done. He could put this right. She loved him. She had said so. She would welcome him, would be as eager and ready as he to start anew, with no shadows between them.

"Let us go home, Jack." He turned back to his horse.

They rode in silence, Hugh urging his horse to greater speed. In the stableyard Hugh, despite his injuries, almost jumped from his horse in his haste. "My thanks for your help this night, Jack." He handed him his reins and made his way to the house.

The house downstairs was dark. No lamps or candles wasting when everyone within was abed. Hugh lit a candle from the banked fire in the hall and trod softly upstairs.

No light showed beneath the door of their bedchamber. He laid a hand on the latch.

He stepped quietly into the chamber. The fire was almost out, just a faint glow of embers in the hearth. And immediately he knew that something was dreadfully wrong. There was no one in the room. He didn't have to look to know that. All spirit, all sense of Guinevere was leached from the room they had shared. Everything that belonged to her had gone, the chamber was as sparsely furnished, as lacking in feminine softness, as it had been before their wedding.

He stepped farther in, went to the bed, knowing that it would be empty. The rich coverlets, the soft pillows were gone. The white sheets gleamed in the darkness, mocking him.

He spun to the night table, struck flint on tinder and lit a candle. She would have left him a note. She would not have walked out of his life without a word. He searched, frantically, turning over the bolster, peering in the empty armoire, lifting the jug and ewer. There was nothing. It was as if she had never entered the chamber.

He left, half running to the chamber the girls shared with Tilly. The door was ajar. The chamber was as empty as his own. The fire extinguished. No kittens mewled at him.

He stood, hands crossed over his chest, shivering deep inside with the knowledge of what he had lost.

His relationship with Guinevere had started with death. Death had laced their love with suspicion . . . death's own peculiar venom. Suspicion. A serpent that fed upon its own tail.

He saw her now, so still, so quiet, the golden light behind her, as she'd listened to his vicious accusations. Once again he heard her say: "I love you, Hugh."

He had thrust her from him, judged her a liar, a murderer. He had believed that a woman who had given up everything for the sake of her daughters was capable of hurting his son.

He lay down on the bed where her children had slept and stared up into the darkness.

28.

Moorfields, you say?" Hugh raised his head from his folded arms where they rested on the mantelshelf above the dull glow of the banked fire and turned to look at Master Milton. A flicker of life entered his hollow-eyed regard.

"Aye, m'lord." The steward thrust his hands into the loose sleeves of his gown and clasped his elbows. It was barely dawn and chilly in the hall, the fire not yet stirred into its daytime blaze. He had been dragged from his bed by an urgent summons to wait upon his master. Despite this, he had the complacent air of one delivering momentous information.

"Just afore I went to my bed I heard Master Crowder asking the cook for details of the lodging house his sister ran in Moorfields. I didn't think anything of it at the time, sir. Master Crowder didn't say anything about leaving the house. If he had, of course I'd not have gone to my bed," Milton added a mite defensively, as if he could in the absence of his lord somehow have prevented the Lady Guinevere and her entourage from doing whatever pleased them.

He paused, then said, "But I asked in the stables and apparently they all left just afore eleven. They took their horses. Magister Howard, the little maids, Mistress Tilly, Master Crowder, even the huntsman, Greene. All gone. Lady Pippa said to the grooms that they had to go because the air in the house was unhealthful and they didn't want to get sick like Master Robin."

Milton regarded his lordship with a certain shrewdness. "It seemed a trifle sudden I thought. I understood they were to leave anyway this morning for Derbyshire," he said with a faint question in his voice.

Hugh made no response. It mattered little to him what his household thought of these sudden events. Guinevere had obviously given the girls an excuse but he doubted his own servants would believe it. They would guess the humiliating truth. The Lady Guinevere had left her husband. And they would assume that he would bring her back, as any self-respecting husband would.

Why had Guinevere made no attempt either to conceal her whereabouts or to leave in secret? Hope flickered. Was she waiting for him to come for her, having made her grand gesture? But he didn't think so. Such games were not Guinevere's style. She didn't make empty gestures. He guessed that she knew he would not force her to return to him and so had seen no reason to conceal her whereabouts.

"Get me the directions to this lodging," he demanded impatiently. "And have my horse saddled again."

"Aye, m'lord. I'll fetch the cook. He's just starting the fires in the kitchen." Milton hurried off, his black gown rustling around him.

Hugh paced the hall. Once she knew the truth about Privy Seal, once she understood his remorse, his overwhelming grief at how he'd hurt her, then surely she would come back to him.

Milton came back with the cook who wiped floury hands on his apron as he gave Lord Hugh directions to his sister's lodging house. " 'Tis in a respectable part of the village, m'lord. Plenty of fields an' woods around. Good clean air fer the lassies. 'Tis to be hoped they don't catch what ails Master Robin."

"I'm certain they won't," Hugh said curtly. He strode from the hall, out into the graying dawn. It was beginning to rain and the air was raw and damp.

A shivering boy held Hugh's horse on the driveway. The horse looked as miserable as his groom at having to brave the elements again so soon. Hugh mounted, nudged the animal into a canter down the drive, and turned east. He rode over the narrow bridge across the Holborn River and along Cheapside. The city gates were now opened for the day and he passed through Bishopsgate into the green fields beyond the city walls.

Moorfields was a small hamlet just beyond the city walls. Under the cold gray light of very early morning, the collection of cottages and taverns gathered along a single cart-rutted lane looked warm and hospitable with smoke curling from their chimneys and lights showing in the chinks of the shutters. There was the smell of frying bacon and baking bread on the air.

Hugh's destination turned out to be a house on the outskirts of the village, more substantial than many others, with lime-washed, half-timbered walls and a well-maintained thatch. The door from the street was closed, the windows shuttered.

He dismounted, tethered his horse, and knocked on the door, controlling the urge to bang it with his sword hilt in his anxiety and urgency. There was no response to the knock.

He tried again and this time heard muffled voices within, the sound of a door opening and closing. He knocked again.

There came the sound of bolts being drawn, the door was opened a crack. Master Crowder surveyed Lord Hugh without surprise and with distinct hostility.

"My lord?"

"Tell Lady Guinevere I'm here," Hugh said, putting a hand on the latch.

"My lady knows you're here, sir," Crowder said. "She is unable to receive you, I'm afraid." He made to close the door.

Hugh held on to the latch, his knuckles whitening. "I need to speak to her, Crowder. Don't stand in my way."

"I obey my lady, sir. She does not wish to receive you." Crowder's voice was smooth, his eyes frigid.

Hugh let his hand fall from the latch. He kept his own voice cool, controlled his anger at the man's insolence, reminded himself that Guinevere's people were loyal only to her. "Then I'd like you to give her a message."

"Certainly, my lord."

Hugh hesitated. He couldn't say to Crowder what he needed to say to Guinevere. "Do you have parchment, a quill?" he demanded impatiently.

"If I might be so bold, sir, there's a decent tavern just down the road." Crowder gestured to the right. "They'll provide you with such things."

Hugh turned on his heel and left the door. He seethed with humiliation at such treatment at the hands of a mere servant, and yet he knew he couldn't blame the man. Crowder would know what Lord Hugh had believed about his beloved mistress. He would know how Hugh had hurt her. And given half a chance, Crowder and the rest of Guinevere's entourage would see his head on a pike for it.

He found the tavern and entered, ducking his head under the low lintel. It was wash day and the smell of soap and boiling linen from the washhouse in the back filled the low-ceilinged taproom.

A round-faced woman appeared with arms reddened to the elbows, her coif limp with the damp heat of the washhouse. She looked suspiciously at Hugh and he realized that he hadn't washed, shaved, or changed his clothes since the fight with Tyler. The bandages on his hand and arm were now filthy and he could smell the reek of the city streets mingling with his own sweat and blood. A great weariness washed over him.

"Bring me parchment, quill, and ink," he instructed. "And a pot of mulled ale."

The authoritative tone compensated for his disheveled appearance. The woman bobbed a curtsy and left the taproom, returning in a very few minutes with writing materials and a tankard. She set the materials on a table and took the tankard to the fire, placing it on a trivet over the flame. She heated a poker and thrust it into the contents of the tankard, which hissed and steamed.

"Will that be all, sir?" She placed the tankard at his elbow.

"Yes, I thank you." Hugh waved her away and addressed his composition. What to say? How to begin? He must explain about Privy Seal, abjectly apologize for his own utter blind stupidity, beg her to return. He must say how he couldn't bear to lose her. Tell her how he couldn't bear to think of the enormity of his accusation.

He knew what to say. If he could see her, hold her, he could convince her. But these words on parchment. These black symbols. They had no feeling, none of his warm blood in them. He was a blunt man, had no skill at pouring out his emotions on a piece of parchment. He had written the truth but there was none of the depth of his feelings there.

But it was all he could do. When she'd read the letter she'd have to see him. And then he could convince her in the only way he knew.

He read the unsatisfactory words again, then sanded the sheet and folded it. He didn't attempt to seal it. None of her servants would read it.

He finished his mulled ale and was a little cheered by its warmth in his belly. He left a copper on the table and went back to his horse.

When he knocked this time the door was immediately opened as if Crowder had been waiting for him. The steward took the folded letter with an impassive expression, bowed, and very firmly closed the door.

Hugh stepped back, looking up at the house. The shutters were closed against the rain and the raw chill, but then he saw that the one directly over the door was cracked a tiny bit and he could see a shadow behind it. He waited, stamping his feet, clapping his gloved hands. He waited for the door to open and Crowder to bid him enter.

But nothing happened. The door remained closed. The shadow remained motionless behind the shutter. He waited for close to thirty minutes. At last he remounted and turned his horse back to the city gates.

Guinevere stood behind the shutter on the upper floor and watched him leave. She had stood there and watched him as he'd waited for her to admit him. She ached for him. He looked so ghastly, so defeated. A man who had gone without sleep for so long he was dead on his feet. He had not slept since the night Robin had fallen ill. And she knew he had not slept this last night. Robin had fallen ill two nights ago. Was it only two nights ago that this horror had started?

She reread his letter. She had no difficulty reading the emotion beneath the blunt words. She knew Hugh. She felt a deep and abiding rage at Privy Seal, but Hugh had fallen into Cromwell's trap and Guinevere could not forget that. He had believed her capable of murdering Robin . . . of murdering himself. She had told him that she loved him and he had ignored that, choosing to believe a horror of her instead.

How could she ever forget that? And if she couldn't forget she couldn't live with him as if nothing had happened. It would always lie between them.

Once again, she could only regain her strength for her daughters by denying Hugh. If she allowed him to come to her, she would yield to him. She could not yield to a man who had done such things. She had to be strong. She had to make plans, decide where to live and how they should live. Guinevere knew herself. She knew that her stubbornness was both a besetting sin and a lifesaver. But at this moment she needed the lifesaver.

"Mama . . . Mama?"

"What is it, Pippa?" She heard the weariness in her voice. Holding the letter against her skirts, she turned to the child.

"That was Lord Hugh."

"Yes, I know."

"Why didn't he come in?" Pippa stroked Moonshine, who was wriggling in her arms.

Guinevere knew that she would have to tell her children as much of the truth as she could bear to. They didn't have to know about Hugh's accusations, but they had to know that they would no longer be living under their stepfather's roof. And they would need a reason. But she couldn't think of anything. Her brain seemed to have shriveled, become numb.

"Are you ill, Mama?" Pen came anxiously towards her mother, her hand outstretched. "You look ill."

"Now, don't pester your mother this morning." Tilly took her head out of the armoire where she'd been hanging clothes. "She's very tired. It's been a very tiring time for her. You run along downstairs and get your breakfasts. Mistress Woolley has everything ready."

The girls looked at their mother and she smiled. "I'm feeling a little tired, my loves. I didn't get much sleep last night. I'll rest a little this morning."

"Must we have lessons?" Pippa asked.

Guinevere shook her head. "No, not today. You may do whatever you wish so long as you don't trouble Mistress Woolley."

"I shall ask Greene to take me hunting," Pippa announced. "He promised he would the very next time he went. Are you coming, Pen?"

Pen still looked at her mother. "Are you ill, Mama?"

"No, sweeting, but I am tired. I shall rest this morning. Don't worry now." She bent to kiss the child and lightly caressed her cheek.

Pen didn't look too reassured but she left the chamber.

"Morning sickness, chuck?" asked Tilly matter-of-factly.

Guinevere shook her head. "No, I have had none so far. But I'm awearied, Tilly."

"I'm not surprised, all these goings-on. You go back to bed and I'll bring you a sack posset," Tilly said, turning back the covers on the bed. "Come now, chuck. You'll do no good for yourself or the babe exhausting yourself."

"No." Guinevere allowed her maid to unlace her. A weary spirit was one thing, but she couldn't afford a weary body into the bargain.

Hugh rode back through the incessant drizzle. What could he do if she wouldn't hear him? He had to go back. He had to keep knocking until she admitted him. He could make it right, if he could only hold her, tell her how he felt. He knew he could. She was fair-minded. She was just so damned stubborn! If she would only listen, she would understand.

He left the horse in the stables and entered his house through the back as was his custom. He was aware of inquisitive looks as he walked through the kitchen. He ignored them. In the hall, the fire was blazing, lamps had been lit, but he could take no comfort from the warmth. He stood absently running a hand over his chin, feeling the stubble rough against his fingers.

With an oath he strode vigorously upstairs to his bedchamber. Its bleak emptiness hit him as he entered and the surge of energy drained away as he heard his voice in his head, accusing, condemning, pushing her from him. How could he possibly hope to get her back?

He rang the large handbell loudly and insistently, grimacing at his own smell, at the dried blood on his sleeve. He stripped to his skin, demanding hot water of the servant who answered his summons. He could think of only one thing to do. He was going to woo his wife. He had never courted a woman before. His marriage to Sarah had been arranged by her parents. His marriage to Guinevere had certainly come about without the gentle art of courtship.

Now, if he was to have his wife back, he must court her, woo her, convince her of his love.

He shaved awkwardly with his uninjured left hand and cursed as he nicked the skin beneath his chin. He scrubbed himself with soap and hot water, and in different circumstances he would have laughed at himself for making such a fuss over his appearance. Ordinarily it never concerned him, ordinarily he paid no attention to the kind of impression he was making on people. But not this morning. He would go to her looking his best. His appearance was not going to sway her one way or the other, but surely it would demonstrate how hard he was trying to convince her to hear him.

He dressed with elaborate care and examined his reflection in the mirror of beaten copper. His image was distorted, wavery, but he could still see how tired and drawn he looked. Maybe food would help. He couldn't remember when he'd last eaten.

He returned to the hall where Milton was waiting for him. "Fetch me bread and meat and ale, if you please," Hugh asked as he came down the last stair.

"At once, my lord." The steward bowed again and hurried off. Hugh poked the fire, holding his hands to the blaze. She'd said she loved him. Even at the end when he was saying such dreadful things to her, she had said she loved him.

He clung to that as he ate, standing up, tearing bread from the warm loaf, using his dagger to slice into the round of beef, drinking straight from the ale jug. Every muscle strained to rush to her but he forced himself to eat and drink. When she saw him, he must be reasonable, measured in his appeal for forgiveness. He'd shown her a violent side of himself that he hadn't known he possessed except in the bloody hurly-burly of battle. He must do everything he could to erase that memory. A thought occurred to him.

"Milton?"

"My lord?" The steward was standing to one side as his master ate.

"Did Lady Guinevere take her books?"

"I don't believe so, my lord. They remain in the magister's chamber."

"Crate them at once. Have them loaded onto a cart. Cover them against the rain."

Milton looked astounded but there was something in his master's manner that told him it would be unwise to question the order. He went hastily on his errand.

Hugh finished his breakfast and paced the hall waiting to be told the books were crated and ready to go. It was a gift. The only gift he could give her that would say that he understood she had the right to leave him. That acceptance would tell her more eloquently than anything he could say how much he realized what a dreadful thing he had done. If she accepted his remorse, then she would listen to him. He had to believe that she would.

Guinevere was asleep, in an exhausted, dreamless coma, when the door knocker sounded again. She didn't hear it. Didn't hear Tilly creep softly into the room. Was unaware of the woman standing by the bed, watching her.

Tilly pursed her lips and left the chamber as softly as she'd entered it. The steward waited on the landing outside.

"She's fast asleep, Master Crowder. I'll not wake her. It would be criminal."

Crowder nodded. "I'll tell Lord Hugh then."

"Aye, but don't tell 'im she's asleep. Tell 'im she'll not see 'im," Tilly said flatly. "She'll 'ave to say fer 'erself whether she'll see 'im or not. I'll not 'ave 'im thinkin' 'e's got the better of 'er when she's not said it 'erself."

Crowder nodded again and went back downstairs to deliver his message. Two servant lads were bringing the books in from the cart, piling them in the small parlor where Magister Howard was counting them in, fussing over each spine, castigating the boys for careless handling.

Crowder opened the door. Lord Hugh stood in the street, one hand resting on the hilt of his sword, the other in a fist against his hip. Everything about his stance proclaimed impatience and anxiety.

"Your pardon, my lord, but my lady cannot see you," Crowder said. He took a hasty step back as Lord Hugh stepped forward, his face now black as thunder.

"Cannot?" Hugh demanded. "Why not?"

"She said to tell you, my lord, that she cannot see you," Crowder said steadfastly.

Hugh turned away without another word. He didn't look back but went straight to his horse. For two pins, he would have thrust the steward out of the way and marched into the house, but it would do his cause no good. He was about to mount when a high voice called him.

"Lord Hugh? Lord Hugh?" Pippa came racing around the side of the cottage, her hood flying off, her hair damp with rain. She hurled herself on him with her usual uninhibited welcome and he picked her up, held her and kissed her.

She patted his face with her hand as she often did while the words tumbled forth. "Have you come to stay? Why aren't we staying with you anymore? How's Robin? Is he home yet? When can we see him? Mama's asleep. She's very very tired. She said she has to rest all morning and Tilly won't let us disturb her until dinnertime. Will you stay for dinner? Pen . . . Pen . . ." She called over her shoulder. "Lord Hugh's come to see us."

Pen came more slowly towards them. "Good morning, Lord Hugh." She regarded him gravely.

"Good morning, Pen." He let Pippa slide through his hold to the ground and calmly bent to kiss his elder stepdaughter. "Your mother's asleep, I understand."

"Yes, sir. She's very tired. We didn't get here until late," Pen said solemnly. "Did you wish to see her?"

"No, I won't disturb her when she's sleeping," Hugh said. "When she wakes, tell her I came and that I'll come back this afternoon. I brought her books."

"Oh, she'll be so pleased." Pen's earnest expression lightened and a smile glowed in her hazel eyes. "She didn't say anything last night, but I know she was upset to leave them behind."

"Why did she?" He waited curiously to see how the child would answer.

Pen frowned. "I don't know," she said, meeting his gaze directly. "We were in a hurry. I don't know why we were in such a hurry. Do you know why, Lord Hugh?"

"Only your mother can tell you that," he replied gently. "When she wakes, give her my love and tell her I'll come later this afternoon."

Pen nodded. "I'll tell her."

"Good girl." He kissed her again quickly, did the same to her sister, and went for his horse.

"Lord Hugh looks tired like Mama," Pippa observed to her sister, blinking raindrops from her eyelashes as they stood watching their stepfather's departure. "Why are they tired, Pen?"

Pen didn't reply at once. She frowned down into the puddle forming at her feet.

"Why, Pen?" Pippa tugged at her cloak.

Pen raised her head and looked at her sister with something like pity in her eyes. "You're such a baby, Pippa."

"I am not!" Pippa cried. "I just asked a question."

"They're tired because something bad has happened," Pen explained distantly.

"Bad? What bad thing?" Pippa looked dismayed.

"I don't know," Pen said. "But whatever it is it's making them both unhappy and I don't know what we can do about it. I wish Robin was here," she added fiercely, more to herself than to Pippa.

Abruptly she declared, "I'm going inside, it's too wet out here." She turned and ran back to the house.

Pippa hesitated for a second, then gathered up her sodden skirts and ran after her. "Wait for me, Pen!"

Hugh barely noticed the rain as he rode back to Holborn. Guinevere was asleep. He had to believe she was asleep and her servants had lied to him. Pippa and Pen would not make up such a tale. Unless, of course, she was taking some much needed privacy by pretending to her daughters that she was sleeping.

But he wouldn't think like that. He would be optimistic.

Guinevere woke just before midday. She lay feeling drugged with sleep gazing up at the embroidered tester above her. The shutters were now closed again and the chamber was dim and gray, only the flickering fire in the grate giving any light. Rain beat on the roof and against the shutters.

She thought of the child she was carrying. Hugh's child. Her hand rested on her belly. She had awoken thinking of the child as if somewhere in her dreamless sleep her mind had been focused on the life growing within her.

Hugh's child. As much his as hers. A child who had the right to its father. A father who had a right to his child. A father who would cherish and nurture his child. Who would love his child with the same unconditional love he bestowed upon Robin. Upon his stepdaughters.

The door opened softly. Her daughters crept into the chamber and approached the bed on tiptoe. Guinevere turned her head on the pillows and smiled at them in the dim light.

"Are you awake, Mama?" Pen leaned closer.

"Just about. Light the candles, love."

"I'll do it!" Pippa snatched up the tinderbox before her sister could take it. "I'll light the candles."

Pen sighed and hitched herself up on the bed beside her mother. "Lord Hugh brought your books."

"I was going to tell Mama that," Pippa cried. "I was going to tell her Lord Hugh was here."

"It doesn't matter who tells me," her mother said dampeningly.

"Oh." Pippa came and sat on the other side of the bed. "He said he was going to come back this afternoon. He sent his love to you. Pen and me, we want to know what bad thing has happened."

Guinevere sat up against the pillows. Hugh had brought her books. She understood immediately what he was saying. He was prepared to give her up because he accepted that he had no right to expect her to return.

"We want to know, Mama." Pippa tugged at the loose sleeve of her mother's night robe. "Is something bad happening again? You won't go to a jail, will you?"

"No," Guinevere said firmly. "Indeed I won't." She was carrying his child. Father and child had a right to each other. He knew what he had done to her. Understood the enormity of it. Was that enough for forgiveness? Was it enough for her to let down her guard? Accept his love again? *Depend upon his love again?* There lay the crux.

"Is it because Robin's sick?" Pen asked tentatively.

"It has something to do with it, sweeting. But I don't wish to talk about it until Lord Hugh and I have had a chance to think about things . . . to talk about things."

"He's coming back later," Pen said.

"Yes," her mother agreed gravely. "And we shall talk then. Now, let me get me up. It must be close to dinnertime."

"There's jugged hare that Greene shot this morning and a fish pudding, Mistress Woolley said," Pippa informed her, sliding off the bed. "And apple tart." She seemed to think the matter of Lord Hugh and her mother already resolved.

"Which gown will you wear, Mama?" Pen was burrowing in the armoire.

"Oh, it doesn't matter, Pen. The gray silk will do very well."

"I don't think you should wear that," Pen stated. "I think you should wear this one." She drew out a gown of turquoise flowered silk that opened over a black taffeta underskirt. It had a deep lace collar low on the shoulders and full, lace-edged sleeves.

"Why that one?" Guinevere inquired. It was a gown she wore on the most formal occasions.

Pen didn't answer and it was her sister who piped the accurate response. "Because Lord Hugh looked very smart when he came this morning. He was wearing that emerald doublet with the gold-striped hose and gown. So you should look as smart when you see him."

"I see," Guinevere said dryly. "Nevertheless, I will wear the gray silk. It's quite smart enough for a lodging house in Moorfields."

Pen looked disappointed but offered no further argument.

Hugh waited until evening before returning. He spent the afternoon in the print shops of Cheapside and eventually he found what he was looking for. A beautifully illustrated volume of Tully's epistles bound in the softest Italian leather, the paper thin as finest silk, the letters illuminated in gold. Mother-of-pearl edged the corners of the cover. It was a lovely thing, quite apart from its content, and he knew it would please Guinevere from both perspectives.

He had the book wrapped in oiled leather and tucked it beneath his cloak as he set out in the dusk once again for Moorfields. The rain had stopped but it was still chill and dank.

Light shone from behind the shutters of the lodging house, smoke curled from its several chimneys, and he fancied that this time the house welcomed him. That it knew he would not this time be turned from its door.

He tethered his horse and knocked firmly.

Crowder opened the door within a very few minutes. "My lord." He bowed and stepped aside, holding the door open.

Hugh entered the lamplit hallway. A flight of stairs rose at the rear. A door to the right opened a crack and he caught a glimpse of Pippa's eager face. Suddenly she was pulled back inside and the door closed sharply.

Despite his anxiety he couldn't help a slight smile.

Crowder took his damp cloak and said, "You will find my lady's chamber behind the double doors at the head of the stairs, my lord."

Hugh nodded his thanks and strode up the stairs, his blood fast in his veins, his heart sounding in his ears. Only once before, when he had feared for Robin's life, had he been so tense, so overwhelmingly anxious. But then as now there were no words for what he had at stake.

He stood for a second outside the double doors. Light shone beneath them. A reassuring golden glow.

He didn't knock. She knew he was there. Softly he raised the latch and pushed the doors open.

Guinevere was sitting in front of the fire, her slippered feet on the fender. She rose as Hugh stepped inside and closed the doors at his back. Her hands moved against each other, a bare brush of her fingers against her skirts.

"Guinevere." He came farther into the chamber. It was imbued with her presence. Her scent, her breath in the soft, warm air. He loved her now as he had never loved her before. No . . . he loved her with the all-encompassing power that until he was about to lose her he'd never admitted to himself.

And now, in the face of the wrong he'd done her, he must find the words to convince her of that love.

Guinevere didn't move, didn't speak. It was for him to begin. But her heart was jumping as it always did when he was near her. He had wronged her, but she loved him.

"Guinevere," he said softly. He watched the firelight glancing across her cheek; he gazed into her deep purple eyes and saw the turmoil of her emotions reflected therein.

He laid his wrapped gift on a small table beside the door. He would not risk her thinking he believed he could buy forgiveness. Later he would give it to her. Later, when . . .

He crossed the room swiftly, took her hands in his. They were cold. "I do not know how to ask for your forgiveness," he said, holding her hands to his lips, his breath warm on her fingers. "That I should think such a thing of you."

Into her silence, he said painfully, the words dragged from him, "I don't expect your forgiveness. How could I?"

Guinevere looked at him. She read in his eyes the agony of remorse, the desperate need as he waited for her response.

"I had thought Robin my child too," she said finally, unable to keep the accusation or the hurt from her quiet voice.

"I know it." He let her hands drop from his. "I have always known it. I have no excuse for what I did, for what I said."

He took a deep shuddering breath and ran his hands through his hair. "I can't believe I could have been so blind. I know Privy Seal. I know how he works. Such a simple plan he had. So simple, I should have seen it at once. And yet . . ."

"And yet you held on to a suspicion . . . no, a belief . . . that made Privy Seal's machinations possible." She spoke softly as she sat down again on the low chair before the fire.

He looked away for a minute, then turned his gaze back to her. "*Did you kill Stephen Mallory?*"

Guinevere turned her hands palm up on her lap. "I don't think so. I wanted him dead. I made no secret of that. He brutalized me and would eventually have done the same to my daughters. He came at me. The window was open. I put out my foot. He tripped and fell."

She looked up at him. "Did I intend to cause his death?" She shrugged. "I don't know. I will never know." She rose again from her chair. "Did I kill Stephen Mallory? I can give you no straight answer, Hugh."

"But why didn't you tell me this before?"

Her smile was sad. "Because I didn't trust you to understand the ambiguity. You're a plain-spoken man, as you take pride in telling me.

You have no time for half-truths, for the less-than-straightforward."
She looked down at her hands. "You believed me guilty. If I'd told you
the truth, I would have confirmed that belief."

"Must I carry this guilt alone?" he asked. "When we have loved,
there's been trust. Could you not then have told me the truth?"

"Perhaps," she agreed. "But always there was so much at stake. My
life . . . my children's future. Always that was at stake. And you saved
me . . . saved them. Perjured yourself. But look what you gained as a
result. How could I be sure of you?"

"I love you," he stated, taking her hands once more, feeling them
now warm in his hold. "I've made grievous errors. I ask your forgiveness." His eyes held hers but he made no attempt to draw her closer as
he waited for her answer.

"The times make it difficult to trust," Guinevere said. "This place . . .
this city . . ." She loosed a hand and flung it wide in an all-encompassing
gesture of repulsion. "This is a murderous den of deceit."

"Do you forgive me?"

"I love you," she said simply.

"Do you forgive me?"

She inclined her head in a helpless little gesture. "How can I not? I
too failed to trust." She went into his arms then, burying her face
against his throat, glorying in the feel of his arms tight around her.
Only love, it seemed, mattered. Hurt, despair were vanquished by its
balm. They would forgive, and soon they would forget.

He held her, breathed in her scent, still hardly daring to believe that
she had come back to him. After a minute, she took his hand, laying it
upon her belly. "Make the acquaintance of your child, my lord."

Hugh gazed down at her, amazement and disbelief in his eyes.
"You're with child?"

"Most assuredly," she said.

He kept his hand on her belly. "And you would not have told me?
You would have left me without telling me?"

"No," she said simply. "I could not do that."

"Is this why you have come back to me?" His gaze now was anguished with doubt.

"If I did not love you, did not know what it is to be loved by you, I would not have come back to you, not even for the child's sake," she said.

He drew her against him, his mouth meeting hers. "I love you. I love you so much it frightens me."

"Then let us face this frightening new world together," she said, smiling against his mouth. "Now love me, Lord Hugh, as you have never loved me before."

Epilogue

July 28th, 1540

The executioner held the head high for the roaring crowd. Hugh at the rear of the crowd turned his horse away from Tyburn Tree, Jack Stedman and his four men falling in behind, swords drawn. If they moved fast they would clear the crowd before it went wild in its rejoicing.

Privy Seal was dead.

Hugh and his companions were silent as they pushed through the rear of the crowd now pressing forward towards the block. Their horses stepped high, the heavy breastplates on the chargers' massive chests forcing a path. The herald blew a continuous note, demanding passage. There were shouted insults but for the most part the throng fell back and gave way to the armed party in its rich liveries, the man with his piercing blue eyes and distinguished bearing at its head.

"Home or Whitehall, m'lord?"

Hugh glanced over his shoulder at Jack's question. The king was today marrying Catherine Howard. A careful courtier would show himself at court. But today Hugh of Beaucaire had no mind to play the careful courtier. He had news for his wife, news that would bear much discussion.

He reached inside his doublet and felt for the parchment with the king's seal. It crackled beneath his fingertips. "Home, Jack."

"Aye, sir."

The small troop rode east to Holborn. They met crowds pouring west, hawkers, tumblers, musicians, men leading dancing bears. Today was a day of rejoicing. And not just because the king had taken his fifth queen. The hated reign of Thomas Cromwell, Lord Privy Seal, had ended at Tyburn Tree.

The crowd thinned as Hugh and his men came closer to the house. The party rode up the lane where Privy Seal's man had attacked Hugh on his wedding day. The herald blew his trumpet and the gatekeeper came running. The gates opened and they rode through into the quiet park.

The house at the end of the drive glowed under the sun. There was glass in all of the windows now, and they were ablaze under the mid-afternoon light. The lawns were tended, the shrubs pruned, flowers bloomed.

Hugh dismounted, gave Jack his reins. Jack rode off with the men to the stable yard. Hugh stood on the gravel sweep before his house and cocked his head, listening. A smile touched his mouth as he heard what he'd been expecting to hear. Pippa's high tones came from the shrubbery. Pippa, as usual, was instructing her small sister in some art or craft essential to a proper understanding of the way the world worked.

Hugh walked swiftly towards the voice. Where there were children, there would be Guinevere.

He took the narrow, well-swept, hedge-lined path into the shrubbery. It was a quiet place, heavy with the scent of roses from the trellised arbor in its midst. It would have been peaceful but for Pippa and her sister.

"Papa!" Anna struggled to her chubby legs and ran across the grass towards her father. He bent to lift her. Two years old. Round and bright as a button. Her eyes were a curious blend of blue and purple. Quite astounding, he thought, lifting her high to kiss her fragrant cheek.

"Did Crummock die, Lord Hugh?" Pippa, grown tall but still a hazel-eyed sprite with the basic belief that the world couldn't manage without her, brushed grass off her skirts and regarded him seriously.

"Aye, Pippa," he replied. "Where's your mother?"

"Here." Guinevere spoke from beneath the trellis of roses. "I was taking shelter from the sun. It grows hot in this pesky city." She was smiling as she stepped out of the shade.

Hugh gave his daughter to Pippa. "Take Anna, Pippa, and ask Pen to come here. Your mother and I have something to discuss with her."

"Not with me?" Pippa looked hurt.

"Not at this time."

Pippa, being Pippa, hesitated, but she knew her stepfather and there was something in his demeanor that silenced her instinctive protests. She glanced at her mother who was suddenly looking as grave as Lord Hugh.

"I'll fetch her then." Pippa hitched up the baby whose plump legs clutched at her sister's skinny hips, and left the arbor.

"What is it?" Guinevere asked quietly.

Hugh took the parchment from his doublet. "Two things. One of more import than the other. Let us sit in the shade."

He followed her into the cool shadows beneath the trellis and sat down beside her on the stone bench. He unfolded the parchment, smoothing it out against his thigh.

Guinevere waited and when he did not immediately unburden himself prompted into the silence, "So the long arm of Privy Seal is gone. Living under his shadow these last three years has not been easy. Hardly a day has passed when I haven't expected some new plot from him."

"The king's favor clipped Cromwell's claws," Hugh said. "Had we lost that favor, then you would have had cause to fear."

Guinevere laughed ruefully. "Keeping it was a laborious task. The girls did best at it, I believe."

"Aye. Henry has really taken a fancy to them. They're always so natural with him. They neither flatter him nor shrink from him."

He picked up the parchment again and said slowly, "Which brings me to this."

"It bears the king's seal," Guinevere said quietly, preparing herself for whatever was coming.

"Aye. The king has seen fit to confer the earldom of Kendal upon me."

Guinevere smiled. "That's hardly a matter for such gravity. It seems rather to be a matter for congratulation."

Hugh inclined his head. "Perhaps. But as we know, what Henry gives, he can take away as the whim moves him. I've accepted gracefully of course, and we'll see what happens next. But my real news concerns Pen."

"Yes?"

"Henry wishes her to take up residence in the Lady Mary's household. It's a considerable honor, now that Mary's made her submission and is restored to the king's favor, if not to legitimacy." He hesitated and when Guinevere made no response continued, "Pen's of the right age for such a move."

Still Guinevere said nothing. It was true that Pen at thirteen was at the age when the children of the nobility frequently took up residence in other households where they could make advantageous alliances. Robin, for the last three years, had been in the household of Henry Grey, the marquis of Dorset, whose wife was the king's niece. It was a good place for the new earl of Kendal's son and it would be a similar honor for the new earl's stepdaughter to enter the service of the king's daughter. The king would take a particular interest in Pen and would consider it his duty to promote a good marriage for her.

But it was not what Guinevere had wanted for her daughter. Pen was surely not ready to find her own way through the devious scheming, the plotting, the lies, the enticements and dangers of life at court. How would she avoid the pitfalls? How would she know who was true and who was false?

"Can we say no?"

Hugh pursed his lips. "At the risk of offending the king's majesty, yes."

"Not a risk worth taking," Guinevere murmured more to herself than to Hugh.

"No," he agreed. "But don't forget that for as long as we stay in London Pen will never be more than a few miles from us. She'll be free to come and visit as often as she likes. And she'll see much of Robin at court. He has some experience now in the ways of that life. He'll be able to help her clear a path for herself."

"If she doesn't wish to go, then I'll not press her," Guinevere stated, getting to her feet, her pale silk skirts settling around her. "And the king's favor may go to hell and back. We'll return to Mallory Hall."

"If that's what you want, then we will. But at least ask Pen . . . and without prejudice," he added with a half smile. "Let her make up her own mind."

"I always do!"

"You think you do. But Pen can read your mind and she always wants to please you."

Guinevere considered this and had to admit it was true. And she knew she couldn't stand in Pen's way just because she couldn't bear to lose her.

"You be the one to tell her then," she said. "When you've talked to her send her to me in my workroom."

She left him to await his stepdaughter under the trellis.

Half an hour later as she sat in her workroom, the door ajar, an open book in front of her, she heard her daughter's light step in the corridor outside.

"Come in, Pen."

Pen came in, quickly, gracefully, and stood in her gown of rose damask poised just inside the door, like a butterfly on a rose Guinevere thought, and then she saw the suppressed excitement in Pen's face and her heart beat fast with dismay. But she smiled and beckoned the girl in.

"Did Lord Hugh tell you?" Pen asked, coming up to the table where her mother sat.

Guinevere nodded. "And what do you think of the king's offer?"

Pen looked searchingly at Guinevere as if trying to read her mind and Guinevere remained quietly smiling, offering no hint of her thoughts.

"I think it would be very exciting," Pen said, her hazel eyes asparkle. She clasped her hands tightly. "I think it's time for me to do this, Mama, don't you?"

With a stab of loss Guinevere recognized that her daughter had made up her mind without any recourse to her mother's opinion. It was time to accept that Pen was all but grown-up.

"If you think it's time, sweeting, then it's time." Guinevere rose from her chair and came around the table. She put her arm around Pen and held her close. "I shall miss you, but you won't be far away."

"No, and Lord Hugh says I shall be able to come and visit often.

And Robin's in the marquis of Dorset's service and they are great friends of the Lady Mary's so I shall have my brother to guide me and stand my friend."

Guinevere kissed the top of Pen's head. Robin would take care of his stepsister. Their youthful infatuation had died a natural death but it had been replaced with a close and abiding friendship. Pen would never lack for comfort and support while Robin was near her.

"You should tell Pippa yourself," she said. "It will hit her hard."

Some of the light left Pen's eyes. "I shall miss her most terribly. Even all her chattering."

"Just think of all the questions she's going to ask you whenever you come to visit."

They both turned to the door at Hugh's easy tones. He stood foursquare, regarding them with smiling understanding that nonetheless held a hint of anxiety as his gaze rested upon Guinevere.

Pen's responding smile was a little misty. "She'll talk my ears off. But I expect I'll be glad of it."

"I'm sure you will be. You'd better find her now before she bursts with impatience." He came towards her and kissed her brow.

Pen nodded and lifted her face for her mother's kiss. "You really don't mind, Mama?"

"I *do* mind," Guinevere said. "But that's different from saying that I don't want you to do what's right for you. If I had my way I'd keep you as a child forever, but the world doesn't work like that." She caressed the delicate curve of Pen's cheek. "But we shall be here, Hugh and I. You'll not be alone. Remember that."

"I know that." Pen stood on tiptoe to embrace her mother. For a moment they clung to each other, then Guinevere gently drew back, but her hands remained resting on the girl's narrow shoulders.

Pen closed her own hands over her mother's then said firmly, "I'll go and talk to Pippa now." She closed the door behind her as she left.

"A new beginning." Guinevere turned towards Hugh. He held out his arms and she went into his embrace, her head nestled beneath his chin as he held her until he knew she was strong again.

"A new beginning for the earl and countess of Kendal." Hugh grinned down at her and the solemnity of the last minutes dissipated. "Should I perhaps give you the house and estates at Kendal as a belated marriage settlement? Since the original settlements *were* somewhat one-sided."

Guinevere's eyes gleamed. "You mean now that Cromwell is gone there's no need to pretend that you stole all my assets?"

"I would prefer *shared*," he murmured, lifting her chin on his forefinger.

"Well, since in reality that seems to be the case, I am content to leave matters well alone," she conceded. "That pot has been stirred sufficiently I believe."

"There is one that has not." His eyes narrowed as he licked a finger and traced her mouth with its tip.

She caught his meaning instantly. "Ah," she said. "Now that pot can never be stirred sufficiently." She sucked the finger deep into her mouth.

Hugh leaned over her shoulder and threw the bolt on the door.